I0586816

DECK OF SOULS 1

FATESEAL

BONNIE L. PRICE

Editing

K.T. Hanna & Ivy Sherrard

First Edition

ISBNs

E-Book: 978-0-9992067-8-2

Paperback: 978-0-9992067-6-8

Hardback: 978-0-9992067-7-5

Table of Contents

For my best friend, Nick, who has always encouraged me to live a better life and reach for my dreams.

Chapter One
Demo

Iris leaned against the wall, watching me with narrowed eyes.

My stomach lurched as I set my empty glass on the table. I picked up the visor and stared at it for a moment. Usually, I'd be giddy with excitement over a new game, but I just couldn't shake my unease. Meeting with Iris hadn't helped at all. In fact, it had made things worse.

I laid back on the sofa and lifted the visor, resolving to at least play the demo. It was entirely possible that I was just being stubborn because I had been enjoying Ebonwing's months of dominance in *Bengllor Online* so much.

1

"Three hours?" I asked to clarify.

She nodded. "I'll be back after you're finished with the demo."

"Thanks," I murmured as Iris left the room. The moment she was gone, I pressed the button on the side of the visor.

The world around me went dark and silent before greeting me with a spacescape. The words *Jeriskyr Online* hung over the closest planet to me, rays of sunlight filtering through the forged silver lettering. I made a motion with my hand and the scene faded to a fancy character selection screen, showing a near-perfect replica of myself leaning against the base of an old oak tree.

I examined the character summary and icon, finding no obvious way to select or change the character's class or review its abilities. Oh well, it was just a demo anyway. I could change it to something stabby or slashy later—assuming I passed their 'can you stomach killing shit?' test.

After staring at my clone for what could have been several minutes, I released a mental sigh and reached for the start 'button.'

It was too late to back out, after all.

I woke up in a crude barracks and took stock of my surroundings before moving to get off the bed. The room was small and didn't appear to contain anyone or anything aside from me, a single bed, and a chest of drawers. I clenched and unclenched my fist a few times before stretching tentatively.

When my spine popped in several places, I stopped. *That* was unnerving. Why the developers wanted to present such realistic scenarios and sensations was beyond me. Glancing down at my hands and clothes, I realized my surroundings weren't the only things that looked real.

Were the developers trying to show off?

The window nearby was ajar, allowing a temperate breeze to drift in from outside. It looked to be morning. The faint silhouette of a moon hung low and large on the distant horizon. A city stretched for miles around me, shifting to farmland toward the rolling hills in the direction of the moon. Below my room, armored soldiers had begun their morning drills.

I frowned, staring out the window at the nearby buildings. The architecture looked European, perhaps from the Mediterranean countries, but I couldn't quite get a handle on the time period. Inside, my room was incredibly plain.

Most fantasy genre games I had played focused on some kind of equivalent to the Dark Ages, but a quick look around showed hints of at least some forms of other technologies. If I had to hazard a guess, magitech came to mind.

After confirming that I was dressed, I strode out of my room and looked down the hallway beyond in both directions. Stairs heading up at one end, stairs going down at the other—and a very grumpy middle-aged man stalking toward me in chain mail. Lovely.

"Yer late, Otherworlder," the man snapped. "Get down to the yard!"

"Late for…what, exactly?" I crossed my arms.

"Are ya daft?" He leaned over me and squinted. "Ya got ta go through the same tests as anyone else, lassie. If ya don't go now, you'll be waitin' 'til tomorrow!"

"Fine, fine, I'm going," I shrugged, putting my hands in my pockets. I had to wonder how much of a penalty there was for attacking an NPC. I hadn't thought I'd find one I wanted to punch in the face so soon.

I mulled over the NPC's greeting as I made my way downstairs. 'Otherworlder.' Most games had the player storyline set up in such a way that they originated from the same world they were playing in. However, that one word implied that this was *not* the case in *Jeriskyr Online*.

Pursing my lips, I called up the game's UI as I lined up with the rest of the 'recruits.' Sixty percent NPCs, forty percent players, one hundred percent humans. Each player was the same as me, LV0. However, that was not the case for the NPCs. Some of them were as high as LV20, meaning that, at worst, they had one skill level in twenty separate skills.

I searched my surroundings, confirming that every recruit, soldier, and servant in my line of sight was human. None of the trainees appeared to have a total level above fifty. Even the prisoners lined up for execution were human. Supposedly, elves were also part of the Issradian faction, but I didn't see any.

"Outta the way!" one of the players yelled, pushing the NPCs aside. Despite his hurry to get to the front, he hesitated when he took the executioner's axe. The player raised the axe with some difficulty, his poor grip on the shaft making him teeter in place. When he swung down there wasn't enough force, and the blade sunk into the prisoner's back instead of slicing through his neck.

Blood sprayed from the prisoner's back, a scream of agony leaving him. The player's eyes widened in horror. He dropped the axe before doubling over, retching. Vomit spilled from his mouth as he ran through the throngs of soldiers and waiting players.

I cursed and stalked forward, hefting the fallen axe off the ground. Gripping it in both hands, I adjusted my stance briefly before swinging the blade down onto the prisoner's neck. There was a sickening squelch, a crunch, and the screaming stopped.

«Demo_01 has successfully completed the *'It Comes to a Head'* quest»

Are you fucking kidding me? I bit back a groan. *What is it with game developers and their need to make* terrible *jokes?!*

"Huh, well, would ya look at that," the executioner muttered as I held the axe out to him. "Guess you pass. The boss'll want to have a word with you about your options for serving the Issradian Empire."

The sensation of killing a person was indescribable, but I had been forced to do it once before in real life. A game had never been able to replicate that same feeling…until now. I kept my thoughts to myself and strode off in the direction the executioner had indicated.

"Guess you're nastier than ya look," the middle-aged man from before remarked, greeting me at the door of the large building. "Ya should really consider getting that name changed though, lassie."

"…I'm considering it," I answered dryly.

"Ya should do more than 'consider' it!" He released a hearty laugh and motioned for me to follow him. "We've not got much work for recruits 'round here but there's plenty to be done in the city proper. Never enough hands to cover all the problems and all that."

I glanced over the man's head and then at the other people working in the building. Again, majority NPCs. No quest icons or anything of the sort. The number of people on the *Jeriskyr Online* forums suggested that there were a lot of alpha testers and that most of them had rolled the Issradian faction. Where was everyone?

Instanced starting zone, maybe? Though companies hadn't resorted to that for a long time.

"We've got hunting jobs outside Darmos, guard jobs within it," the man continued, rifling through a stack of posters. "The brothels have been looking for bouncers due to all the riffraff—and demons've been tryin' ta break in, from what I hear."

Darmos…I guess that's what the city is called. Nothing about picking specializations? Just straight to jobs? I wondered, tilting my head as I considered the options he'd listed for me. "What kind of brothels are we talking about, exactly?"

"What kind?" the man echoed, baffled, before grinning. "We've got plenty of 'em here, so whichever suits yer fancy."

"Not quite what I meant..." I sighed, thinking on it. "Fine, fine. Are any of the ones with male 'workers' in need of bouncers?"

"Aye, most of 'em are." The man grinned more broadly and handed me at least fifteen posters. "Demons're intent on bringin' back their captured men an' women. Easier for 'em to target the places we hold the men, though. Their whores are under tighter guard."

That statement irritated me. It implied the workers weren't willing participants. Maybe I shouldn't have been surprised, given the apparent time period and what little I knew of the storyline. The humans and demons hated each other. If that was the situation in the Issradian Empire, then it seemed likely the reverse was the case in demon lands.

I kept my expression neutral and flipped through the posters. According to the game's interface, each of the brothels was run by players and specifically wanted players as guards. Not NPCs. Near as I could tell, the brothels had already reached the maximum number of NPC guards they could have.

"I'd recommend this one, personally," the man stated, tugging the edge of one of the posters. "Better part o' town and closer to the nearest guard station if ye find yerself needing backup.

Otherworlders have been causing problems 'round the brothels on top o' the demon mess. Other ones, ya'd be on yer own."

"Fine, I'll take that one then," I murmured, handing the rest of the posters back to him. He rummaged around in a nearby drawer before finally withdrawing a scroll and offering it to me. When I unrolled it, I found a map of the city and its immediate surroundings. "Thanks."

I left the building and quickly made my way to the nearest road. Once there, I confirmed that my UI did *not* have a map, or even a mini-map. I had to rely on the one the man had given me the same way I would have in real life. In fact, the UI could only be described as bare-bones.

It told me player and NPC names, their overall character levels, and let me access my own character information. However, there were no obvious innate stats for myself or for the clothing I wore. All it told me were my skill levels—most of which appeared to be locked due to not interacting with the appropriate trainer NPCs.

"You!" a voice exclaimed.

Looking up, I found a crowd of players rushing toward me.

"JOIN OUR GUILD!" they all started yelling over each other.

"...you *do* realize I'm playing a demo character, right?" I questioned, tilting my head. That didn't do anything, so I decided to push it a little further. "Did it ever occur to you that, perhaps, I'm part of the dev team?"

"Er..." One of the males paused and leaned down to look at

me. "I mean, I guess you could be, or you could've just named yourself something stupid because it's alpha."

"I don't have time for this," I snorted, brushing past them.

It wasn't entirely untrue—after all, the demo was limited, and I couldn't get a firm grasp on the passage of time. My UI didn't appear to have a real-world clock on it—or if it did, it was buried more deeply than I had time to scour. If I really wanted to get a handle on the game, I'd need to explore as much as I could, as fast as I could.

Maybe I should've flubbed the test intentionally. I hadn't thought they'd have a server-wide announcement for successes. Shrugging to myself, I glanced down at the map, confirmed the name of the brothel, and picked up my pace.

Making my way through Darmos, I spotted a wider variety of races handling menial tasks. There were elves, dwarves, and even a few centaurs. Relatively standard fantasy fare. However, there were also a handful of races I didn't know the names of, and my UI didn't tell me—only their names, which I doubted I'd be able to pronounce.

Players, however, were always human.

It wasn't until I neared the red-light district, adjacent to one of the nearby commerce areas, that I began to see the captive demons. They appeared to come in many varieties, but one thing was common to them all—collars and shackles, all of which had engravings and crystals inlaid in the metal bands. Under other circumstances, they might've been pretty.

At least, that's what I thought until I saw a demon nearby stop in place, convulsing. I thought he was throwing a fit at first, until he pulled at the band around his neck. His skin was quickly bruising, the magical charge creating branching figures from his veins.

The demon's owner was nearly half his height, but a swift strike across the poor bastard's lower back got him moving again. I had to fight off both my nausea and my desire to beat the shit out of the human responsible.

In the red-light district proper, male and female prostitutes, or 'escorts,' accompanied clients or ran other errands freely in the streets. The colorful cacophony of different attire and makeup was like nothing I'd ever seen in real life. It was completely different from the prostitutes I'd seen. Instead, they were more like courtesans from certain European and Asian time periods.

Well, this is close to where all the wealthy people live, by the look of it, I thought, before frowning to myself. *Well, NPCs, rather. Perhaps there's player housing around here too?*

"Looking for anything in particular, darling?" A male demon walked up to me, a sweet smile on his face and a smoldering kiseru—a Japanese-style pipe—in one hand. Like all the others I had seen, he wore a collar and cuffs. His, though, were much fancier than those of the demons who had been performing mundane work by the district's outskirts.

"Work, actually," I replied, holding up the poster.

"So, I will have the pleasure of seeing your lovely face more often!" he exclaimed, his mouth curving into an alluring smile. "Wonderful! I'm certain we'll get along famously—and the Madam will be pleased as well. You may call me Silas."

"Don't give 'im your real name, Otherworlder." A guard clamped a hand on my shoulder before I could speak up. "Demons can control those whose name they know. Unless you're lookin' to betray the empire—"

"Yeah, yeah, yeah, I get the point," I cut him off and shot him an irritated look. "Thanks for the warning. Now, if you don't mind, I have work to do."

"I will take you to see the Madam—I'm certain she will adore your fire," Silas spoke with a smile.

He offered me his arm, but it quickly became apparent that wouldn't work. Like most of the demons I'd seen, Silas was easily eight feet in height. I hesitated a moment, unnerved by the NPC's behavior, before allowing him to lead me away from the guard.

Every NPC I saw nearby was much higher-level than the players present. There were a few who possessed a cumulative level under a thousand, but many doubled that. Silas was a little over four thousand. Either he had eight skillsets maxed, a lot of levels between many, or NPCs adhered to a different leveling system than players did. I made a mental note to check into it when I got home.

"Silas? Where the hell have you been?" a tall elven woman

demanded the moment my demon 'escort' led me into a large, opulent building. Above her head I spotted an icon which, when I focused on it, expanded to show a guild name. So, this one was a player. Huh. "Since when did I say you could pick up clients off the— Ah! Demo?!"

"Demo?" Silas questioned, tilting his head. The 'Madam' of the establishment pointed to me and mouthed silently a few times, prompting the demon to look at me.

"Think of it like a nickname," I replied as Silas arched an eyebrow. "My parents and I would've had more problems than we already do if they had *actually* named me 'Demo.'" I turned my attention back to the startled woman. "You're the owner?"

"Yes, but what are you doing here?" she asked, baffled. I shoved her own poster in her face, but her expression only became more confused. "If you're capable of killing, guarding a place like this is *way* lower than your skillset…Oh! So, you're an *actual* demo…I see. Jeriskyr Studios is really going all-out, aren't they? Well, we *do* need more bouncers. However, if you're just playing a demo…"

"You're hesitant to pay me?" I shrugged. "I'll do it for free, or you can send payment the way of Ebonwing."

"E-E-E-Ebon—!" the Madam placed both her hands over her chest and took a step back. I found myself raising an eyebrow again, not sure what to make of her reaction. "That means you're—"

"Do you want help or not?" I crossed my arms.

"You Otherworlders say such strange things," Silas murmured.

He puffed his kiseru a few times before turning to look at the Madam. "We *do* need extra eyes to keep everyone safe. Her pretty face will lull our guests into a false sense of security. You did want to determine who we need to banish from your establishment, did you not?"

"Well…" Madam frowned before glancing at me. "Come with me. I'll brief you on how we run things and what I need you to do. We'll get you into a uniform, too. Silas, make sure the boys're getting ready."

"Are all your 'employees' NPCs?" I asked, once Madam had led me to a small room on the top floor.

"Sure are. NPCs here are a little eerie, aren't they?" Madam turned to look at me, frowning. "All my workers are demons whom the empire has captured. We serve nobles and royals—and anyone who can afford to pay the way they do. Most of our customers are men, but there's a few women too.

"Lately we've been having a problem with clients pushing boundaries. There're laws that're supposed to be upheld, even when dealing with slaves. Damaging the 'goods' is taken as an attack on the brothel and their sponsor. In our case, we're sponsored by the king's adviser. They're taking the problem seriously and want us to find out who is disrespecting them."

"Captured slaves, huh?" I murmured, before glancing over at Madam and her level—many times lower than that of the NPCs. "Do the NPCs run on a different leveling system, or…"

"You noticed Silas' levels, eh?" Madam grimaced, before turning to rifle through a dresser. "Their level is the sum of their skills, just like with us. That number isn't much use on its own, though—you should find a setting in your UI to show the icon for their currently-equipped skill trees.

"He may not look it, but Silas is an old demon. Sure, he's maxed out the skills needed for working in a brothel...but he's also damned high in his combat skills. Was a soldier in one of the demon king's armies before his capture. Prisoner of war."

"That seems like a lot of background for 'just an NPC,'" I remarked.

Madam turned to me and shrugged before holding her arms out, a pile of clothes appearing in them. "These should fit. People in these parts think that demons can enthrall you with their eyes, so any guards working in the brothels must wear a mask or dark glasses to hide them. Shouldn't be too uncomfortable."

"You don't have to wear something like that?" I arched an eyebrow.

"Brothel owner trait." She winked at me before heading for the door. "Hope you don't mind naked men, 'Demo'—you're going to be keeping an eye on them while they get ready. Can't have anyone trying to rescue them, you see."

The fact that they were NPCs seemed like it had desensitized the Madam to the storyline. Either that, or she was a bitch. I grimaced as I changed my clothes. For me, the more I heard, the more the Issradian Empire sounded like total twats.

The uniform looked sharp and was flexible, giving me full range of movement. Tugging at the material, I frowned slightly. It was luxurious to the touch. She hadn't been kidding when she'd said someone high up sponsored the brothel. I pulled the mask on over the top half of my face and frowned when I realized I couldn't see. Pulling it off, I examined it for a few seconds before finding a minuscule switch hidden in the trim.

After flipping it, the inside lit up with a screen that reminded me of augmented reality technology—except done with magitech. Interesting.

"Ah, there you are," Silas spoke cheerfully when he spotted me strolling down the hall. He looked me up and down, a satisfied look on his face. "It suits you. Perhaps you'll consider coming back to work here if you choose to stay in Jeriskyr?"

"Choose to stay?" I questioned him.

"You *are* an Otherworlder, after all." He crossed his arms and narrowed his eyes at me. "I've seen many of your kind come and go, both here and in my homeland. Some never return to Jeriskyr, likely choosing to remain wherever their home is. Others are seen often. Your conversation with the Madam implied that you haven't yet made your decision."

"Well, I can't claim that you're wrong," I replied, shrugging. "Those who left…I'd imagine they're likely people from my world. People who can't stomach the way the humans here treat the other races. Slavery has been illegal in my world for a long time. Many people fail to adapt to such different realities."

"And you?" Silas asked, his tone menacing.

I considered my reply for a moment before answering him. "My preference would be to instigate change, but I'm not so naive as to think that a single person is capable of changing an empire— let alone a world. Nor do I get the feeling I would survive long in the empire if I tried."

"When my king comes to rescue us, I'll have to make certain that you live," Silas said cheerfully. He put an arm around my shoulders and led me down the hallway. "Perhaps I'll even have you come work at my estate. We could always use more guardians."

"Layin' it on a bit thick, aren't you, Silas?" another male voice sighed heavily from behind a door. The demon in question slid it open and grinned at the dozen or more men inside—many of whom weren't clothed. None of them attempted to cover themselves.

"Aw, no reaction?" Silas pouted.

"I had forewarning—nor am I a child," I scoffed, shrugging off his arm. "If you need something, I'll be over here, you know, doing my job."

"What if I need your name, my lady?" Silas asked, giving me an extravagant bow and grasping my hand in his. "You don't believe the humans and their superstitions, do you? I can't very well protect you from our king's might if I don't know your name."

"…Cerys." I wasn't entirely sure why, but I felt compelled to give him an honest answer. He was right that I didn't believe in the human superstitions, but that wasn't the only reason. My instincts seemed to tell me that honesty was my best choice.

The fact that I'd answered him at all seemed to surprise his fellow prostitutes.

"I was right—you *are* different." Silas smiled and released my hand. He turned away from me to begin undressing, but paused to glance back at me. "What of your surname?"

"Unimportant—I intend to change it," I answered.

"Cerys, then." Silas nodded and turned to face away from me fully. "Cerys of Ebonwing, in fact. They've been making quite a name for themselves. I suppose it may be too late to change your mind…"

"Change my mind about…?" I tilted my head, intrigued. At the very least, this wasn't standard quest or relationship dialogue. Just how much effort had Jeriskyr Studios put into this game? I'd never seen an AI with such depth in a VRMMO before.

"Joining the empire," one of the other demons spoke up. "If you're 'different' like Silas thinks you are, then he's thinking you're too good to be a human. You Otherworlders get a choice in the matter, right? He's talking about that."

"It may not be too late, but it *is* difficult to get over two hundred people to agree on anything," I murmured, leaning back against the wall as I contemplated it. "I'm not a tyrant, you know.

Most of our decisions are left up to popular—"

"You're their leader?" Silas turned to look at me, a look of astonishment on his face. He seemed unaware—or unconcerned—that he was facing me while fully nude. "They've been spreading rumors about their 'fierce leader.' We thought perhaps you were just elusive."

"Elusive? No. Not in Jeriskyr yet? Yes." I studied him for a moment, attempting to determine just what was going through his mind—and not to look lower than his face. A task which was proving difficult. "Not to rush you, but aren't you all on a schedule?"

"You shouldn't let anyone else know you're part of Ebonwing," Silas stated, growing serious. "They've been making a name for themselves, as I said. As sympathizers. The crown is concerned that they're organizing to smuggle my kind out of the city and back to our homeland."

That certainly sounded like something they'd do. I shrugged, smiling, and said, "That's a dangerous game they're playing, if that's the case."

"She's right though, Silas, we're going to be late if you don't hurry." One of the other demons shot him a pointed look. "Cerys here can protect us from the leches, sure, but there's nothing she can do if you piss off the Madam, *again*."

A short while later, I found myself leaning back in the corner of an extravagant room while the prostitutes served food and drink to their guests. Several other men played instruments or danced to entertain the brothel's patrons. I remained silent and observed—both as part of my job, but also to look for anything strange.

Aside from myself, there was only one other player in the room, and she was the brothel owner. Every prostitute, noble, and the other two bouncers were NPCs. High-powered ones, too. I frowned. The flyers had said they wanted *players* to fill the role of bouncer. Were there really so few who could?

The way the guests treated the prostitutes made my skin crawl. Both their mannerisms and their speech made it clear that they thought of demons as little better than animals.

Silas and the others appeared unfazed by the treatment, but one of the younger males wasn't having such an easy time.

"Where'd you get this one, Madam?" One of the nobles strode up to me and peered at my half-masked face. "Surprised to see you hired a woman bodyguard. You don't think she'll breed your livestock dry?"

Punching him would've been a mistake, so I kept my expression passive and my breath shallow. The bastard reeked of booze and rotted teeth.

"We have a strict hands-off policy for our bouncers, my lord," Madam answered, shaking her head slightly. "Demo is just passing through on her way elsewhere. I offered her a room in exchange for a night's work."

"The 'hands off' policy doesn't apply to just me," I spoke,

glancing around the fat man to one of the other guests. "You, in the purple suit. Unless you're going to pay the Madam for further services, hands off."

"Or what?" the noble sneered.

"I'll lop off your hands and sew them to your forehead, for starters," I answered, taking a step toward him. "Where I come from, we cut the hands off of thieves."

At least, we had centuries ago. Details.

"You wouldn't *dare*—"

I spun into a kick and caught the man across the throat when he lunged at me, the force of my strike knocking him off his feet and to the floor. He grabbed my booted ankle as I applied pressure to his windpipe. The demons watched me with intrigue, the nobles moved away from me, and Madam simply giggled.

"Rules are rules, *my lord*," Madam spoke as she walked over to stand beside me. "Our sponsor expects everyone to behave themselves while in our establishment. If you can't, you will be removed. Demo, see to it that he makes his way out."

"Of course," I replied. Hauling the noble to his feet, I shoved him in the direction of the nearest hallway. "Come on, off you go."

After kicking the bastard out, I returned to the party room and took up my post again. It wasn't the most exciting job in the world, and watching greasy human nobles make out with handsome demons wasn't my idea of a fun time. However, the experience certainly provided me with some interesting insight into the workings of Jeriskyr.

The combat had felt real. My shin stung slightly from how hard I'd kicked the noble. Other games didn't have pain, yet my body felt similarly to whenever I fought or otherwise sparred in real life. Breathing also seemed to work the same as it did in the real world, and I'd been hungry for the past two in-game hours.

I quietly sorted through my UI settings while keeping an ear out for trouble. Soon enough, I found the setting Madam had mentioned and swapped it on so I could see the skill icons instead of accumulated levels. Madam appeared to have 'Proprietor,' 'Speechcraft,' and 'Procurer' set as her primary skills, making her overall class 'Brothel Keeper.'

Her employees, however, were inconsistent.

From my understanding of the game, each class was made up of three *specific* skill trees. Yet Silas' skills were 'Sex,' 'Charm,' and 'Conversationalist.' The prostitute nearest to him was 'Musician,' 'Sex,' and 'Submissive.' I spotted at least six other combinations, some of which didn't have the 'Sex' skill at all, yet they were all labeled as the same overall class.

The level of their individual skills was indicated by the color of their icon—wood, bronze, silver, gold, or platinum. Several of them appeared to have icons surpassing platinum, but I couldn't tell what material they were supposed to be. Each progressive icon was fancier than the last.

"Demo, escort Silas to the cellar while he fetches more wine,"

Madam called to me, breaking me out of my thoughts.

"Very well." I glanced over at her, attempting to mask my agitation, then looked up at the approaching demon. "After you."

"You don't like them," Silas commented once we were several halls away from the room.

"That obvious?" I tilted my head.

"To me, yes. To them, no." He smirked. "How much longer will you remain here?"

"I don't know," I replied. "Honestly, I thought my time would've been up by now. I'm pretty sure I've been here longer than three hours."

"You should come visit me if you and yours remain with the empire," Silas invited me, sliding his clothing off one shoulder. He shot me a sultry smile as he continued, "I'm certain I can make it worth your while."

"I can't tell if you're serious," I remarked, shaking my head. "If we stay with the empire my days will be spent hunting monsters and coordinating my guild's activities.

"Besides, you're implying a lot more than a friendly conversation—and I'm well aware this establishment is too rich for my blood."

"You aren't clueless like most of the Otherworlder women who come to Jeriskyr." Silas grinned, observing me. "I meant what I said about visiting me. I can be a powerful ally, should you need one."

I mulled over the meaningful look he'd shot me, before he turned to stride down the hallway again. "I'll keep that in mind."

"Good," he nodded. "Now then, about that wine…"

"You're going to have to return on your own, I think." I winced as a spike of pain shot through my temple, my vision growing blurry. "Ugh, that hurt. Must mean it's time to go…"

"Cerys?" Silas asked, quickly striding over to me, but his hand went through my shoulder. He withdrew and took a single step back, giving me space. "Keep in mind what I said. Regardless of which side you choose, there are those who can help you."

Chapter Two
NDA

I pulled off my headset and opened my eyes to see Iris Hughes smiling at me from nearby. She waited for me to put aside the headset and sit up before motioning to the table between us. On it sat a basket filled with various marketing materials, chocolates, and a boxed copy of both the game and the anime they'd made to promote it.

"If you enjoyed *Jeriskyr Online*, we want to offer you a VIP package," Iris said. "Of course, we would like your feedback as well."

"I'll compile my feedback for you tonight, then," I stated,

crossing one leg over the other.

"Compile?" Iris tilted her head slightly.

"It's a long list—we'll be here all night if I attempt to verbally deliver it all," I answered, watching her mouth tug into a frown. "I noticed inconsistencies, for one, but also some quality of life improvements that should be made."

"In that case," Iris began, shifting to pull a notepad toward herself, "this is my work address—not to be confused with the 'company representative' address that I contacted you with. Send me your feedback and I'll see to it that it's fixed immediately."

"Alright," I nodded, though I doubted her. Game companies never did *anything* immediately. "The game has potential…but I question your company's decision to make it so realistic. Aren't you pushing the boundaries of at least a dozen gaming laws?"

"Everything has been through a legal approval process, Ms. Collins," Iris replied with a brilliant smile. "We have limitations in place, both to negate illegal activity within the game as well as to keep the game's systems from breaking any laws. Negative sensations such as pain have a very short range to them and serve more as an indicator than anything else.

"If you're still concerned, the pamphlet that comes with the game details everything we've done to remain on the correct side of the law."

"Sure, I'll give it a thorough read," I said, rising to my feet. "I shouldn't take up any more of your time. I'm sure you're a busy woman."

"Of course," Iris smiled. "E-mail me if you need anything. Ah—before you go, I have the non-disclosure agreement here for you to sign."

"Right." I nodded, accepting the pen she offered me. The legalese appeared rather standard, but I read the entirety of the document anyway. In short, it was an agreement to not speak about or show anything from the game's testing state with people who weren't also testers. There were guidelines on what I *could* show, and to who, making it less restrictive than most NDAs I'd seen—but the overall intent was the same.

"Make sure you watch the anime we provided you with, not the one that Alice copied for you," Iris stated once I set the NDA down. When I gave her a questioning look, she shot me a smile that didn't reach her eyes and continued, "It is a much more accurate version than the copy she has. We recently finalized which scenes would be used."

"Right..." I kept my skepticism to myself and traded a few parting words with Iris.

As I made my way toward the elevator, carrying my massive basket of goodies, I grimaced. As soon as I got home, I planned to call Alice—one of my co-leaders within Ebonwing. By our powers combined, I figured we should be able to figure out the differences between her version and mine—and whether Iris was full of shit.

Chapter Three
Intelligence

I fingered the letter in my hand, a glimmer of magic by the corner of the illustration catching my eye. Silas had never been one to protect his work twice over. Intrigued, I undid his spell. The word 'Demo' and the illustration of the woman shimmered and shifted, revealing a new name: *Cerys*. The smile I felt come to my face was entirely voluntary.

"Your Majesty?" Elidyr called.

"Yes. Have our men keep watch for this woman," I ordered, handing the illustration to him. "And for any woman with that name. If she comes to Cejari-ir she will not be difficult to find, but we should make certain *we* find her before the Issradian spies do."

"Yes, Your Majesty!" Elidyr bowed deeply before running off to carry out my orders.

Cerys... I smiled, amused. *Your beauty is wasted on the humans. You will find our company far more pleasant.*

"You really think she's gonna switch sides, Idris?" Emrys stepped around the left side of my throne and glanced down at me. "I'll tell my men to look out for her too, but Elidyr is right. We shouldn't expect much."

"When was the last time an Otherworlder gave Silas their name?" I chuckled, shooting my friend an amused glance. "Here— read his report yourself. Poor girl does not know what she stumbled into. Nor does she appear aware that our kind is capable of telepathy. For her sake, I pray that she is a normal Otherworlder."

Chapter Four
Lore Dive

I looked between the two anime discs. The one Alice had given me was just a simple rip, while the one from the Jeriskyr Studio's CEO had official artwork on it and everything.

Nearby, I had spread all the posters and other swag out on my bed. I couldn't shake the feeling that there was something odd about that game. Something that went beyond their endeavors to make it seem so realistic. I gnawed on my lip as I put the two discs back in their respective cases.

Realistic graphics were something I could overlook. It was the interactions of the 'NPCs' that had unnerved me. After being out of the game for a few hours and giving the information time to sink in, my feelings of unease had grown worse. Still, I was waiting for Alice to get off work before I delved into either version of the anime.

"Mistress, are you turning in for the night?" Bruce, my household AI, questioned as I strode toward the bed.

"No, I won't be going to bed for a while," I muttered. The lights in my apartment shut off, plunging everything into darkness. My knee struck the foot of my bed, causing me to yowl. "Fucking hell! *Bruce!*"

"Fucking? Ah, do you wish for me to pull up porn for you before you retire, Mistress?" Bruce asked.

"*No!* Turn the lights back on!" I snapped. "I was heading over to the bed to examine the posters!"

"Very well, putting your porn search on hold."

The corner of my eye twitched as the lights came on, and I nursed my knee. Feeling a *little* better, I strode to my bedside and picked up two of the posters. The primary two factions had six posters representing them in the 'VIP Package' Iris had given me.

The lesser factions had no representation among the posters, though there were stickers with each faction's symbol on them. While the humans were united under the Issradian Empire, the other races were fragmented, according to the small lore book that accompanied the package.

Among the Issradian Empire posters there were:

Wullfric Hengist, Emperor.

Eadgar Odilo, Adviser.

Adric Alfhard, Captain of the Imperial Guard.

Dagfinnr Horsa, Forgemaster in charge of supplying the Imperial Army.

Sveinn Gebhard, one of the Generals in the Imperial Army.

Odalric Walchelin, a powerful merchant.

Together, those six men made up the most powerful people within the Issradian Empire.

Among the demon posters were:

Idris Bloodsong of Nabyr-zahn. **Race:** Incubus

Alwyn Silverscale of Siliarenth. **Race:** Draekin

Eifion Ebonmaw of Dynim-tor. **Race:** Kitsune

Folont Pyretusk of Hecald-zahn. **Race:** Ifrit

Gar Sablehusk of Verod-ust. **Race:** Lamia

Hywel Stormscythe of Enth-tor. **Race:** Djinn

Each of the six demon men bore the title of 'king' in their respective territories. They led separate kingdoms, but were hated equally by the Issradian Empire. In turn, the demons didn't have much love for the humans. What had caused the initial rift between them all wasn't clear.

I glanced in the direction of my computer, wondering if any of the alpha testers had created Rule 34 artwork of any of the demon kings yet, then shook my head. Looking up demon king porn would have to wait until later. I probably didn't have much time before Alice arrived, so my efforts would be better spent preparing snacks.

I set down the posters and busied myself in the kitchen, but my mind wouldn't leave Jeriskyr alone. There was no denying that what little I'd played intrigued me. Sure, I had my reservations, but that didn't mean it wasn't fun or interesting. Though after seeing what the demon kings looked like, I felt even more strongly about getting everyone in Ebonwing to roll demon instead of human.

For...reasons.

After some digging, Bruce and I had found the terms used to cover each of the five 'tiers' assigned to skill levels in *Jeriskyr Online*. Amateur was the tier everyone started at and was a simple icon with a wood texture. Novice was denoted by a slightly more intricate icon with a bronze finish. Apprentices were silver, Journeymen were gold, and Experts were platinum.

A sixth tier in the game, Master, appeared to be reserved for NPCs.

Most players in the game had taken to referring to levels by their tiers instead of numerical levels, but they still let noobies be confused by the numerical system. After all, if they'd had to deal with it when they started, why shouldn't others suffer the same fate? I rolled my eyes. Typical gamers.

"Mistress, Miss Alice has arrived," Bruce informed me. *"She is on the elevator now. Shall I open the door for her?"*

"Sure." I nodded, while continuing to prepare the snacks.

"Shall I resume your porn search?" Bruce inquired.

"...not now, Bruce," I growled, wishing I could stab the AI.

Shaking my head, I forced myself to refocus. There were thousands of potential class combinations, but only ninety-odd good ones. It didn't make sense that the devs didn't restrict what players could pair. Tailor and combat skills, for example, would have been silly. Did they *want* to give people the ability to make stupid choices?

"Cery!" Alice called cheerfully the moment she stepped through the door. "Oh! You got your own posters and stuff too, huh? The demon kings are *so* hot, right? I bet you're already plotting to make everyone reroll."

"...maybe." I puffed my cheeks out.

"Which anime do you wanna— Yay, food!" Alice threw her arms around me with enough force to almost topple me to the floor. "I'm starving! One of our new trainees didn't show up today so I didn't even get to take a lunch break!"

"Go sit somewhere and let me finish, then!" I huffed.

"*So*, how was your demo?" Alice asked. "I saw the forums are already blowing up about a new player capable of combat—I'm guessing that was you?"

"Yeah. I got swarmed with guild invites so fast. Ugh." I grimaced at the cutting board before plating our food. "I'm not really sure how to feel about the game. It's interesting for sure, but it seems a little…too real. If I didn't know any better, I'd ask if you were sure it isn't."

"You been watching too many isekai anime again?" Alice tilted her head.

"Ha. No." I sighed. "What do you want to drink? If we're watching both versions of the anime we're gonna be here for a while."

"Let's not get into the booze—we wanted to actually analyze both anime, right?" Alice brought a finger to her chin while she thought. "Let's go with soda or tea or something. Got anything for me to write on?"

"Yep. Put everything you need in the living room." I nodded to her. "Which anime did you want to start with?"

"Let's go with mine first—I brought the original disc with me." Alice rummaged around in her purse and held it up, grinning. "So, what'd you do while you were playing the demo?"

"Talked to a really hot demon, took up a bodyguard job at the brothel he worked at," I murmured, thinking. "Kicked a noble's ass for touching the merchandise without paying. That's about it."

"What skills did you take?"

"I wasn't prompted to take any, so, I just did fisty stuff."

"Fisty..." Alice smirked. "So, this brothel job—"

"Not that kind of fisty stuff."

"Oh yeah? You and that 'hot demon' didn't—"

"Alice, no. No, we did not," I groaned.

She squinted at me, clearly unconvinced, but dropped the subject. We made ourselves comfortable in the living room before dimming the lights. Alice spread out several notepads, pens in different colors, and even set her tablet up so she could take quick screenshots from the TV while we watched the two different anime.

"You really don't think Jeriskyr seems too realistic?" I asked.

"Its realism is part of why it's already so popular," she pointed out. "Plus, it's a great time-sink. Leveling up all the different skills and getting the gear and furniture to help improve them will take ages. It'll be even better once people figure out how to unlock the Master system.

"Then there's all the political stuff and battles between all the different clans and factions. The Issradian Empire wants to take over *everything*. Though if you're not human, they don't like you much. I've been running into all kinds of problems as an elf."

"Silas mentioned something about Ebonwing being known demon sympathizers," I remarked, pausing when she shot me a sly grin. "What?"

"Who's *Silas*, hmmm?"

"That demon I mentioned. Still kind of hard to believe he's

just an NPC," I replied, shrugging. "The way they seem aware of 'Otherworlders' freaks me out, to be honest."

"Uh huh…" She shot me a doubtful look. "Well, we have been doing stuff to help out the inhuman races. It's really hard to like the humans, but…playing demons was just so tough. Tails are way more unwieldy than I ever imagined."

"Well, if you guys have been drawing the attention of even brothel-working NPCs, you should be more careful. Otherwise you're going to have a problem on your hands before I've even gotten to make my character!" I crossed my arms. "Let's just focus on the anime for now."

It didn't take long for my dislike of the Issradian Empire to grow. Anyone under their rule who wasn't human was treated like trash and had access to only the lowest tiers of jobs. Many were indentured servants—especially the elves.

Somehow, the anime still managed to portray the humans as the good guys.

"Who is *that*?" I asked a few episodes in, pointing to the armored man on the screen. "And how can I get his armor?"

"Oh that? That's Idris Bloodsong—the king of Nabyr-zahn," Alice replied, handing me a sheet of paper with her handwriting on it. "He's one of the most powerful demon kings and is favored to unify them against the Issradian Empire. I knew you'd like him."

I opened my mouth to protest, but she unpaused the episode and let it continue. With a low 'humph,' I settled back in my seat to watch the scene play out. The musical theme that accompanied the arrival of 'Idris' made it painfully obvious that we were meant to think of him as the villain.

When he took off his helmet to glower at the human horde, I knew I'd found my favorite character. He was incredibly handsome, with sharp, masculine features. His wild, wavy hair was dark blue and hung down to the tops of his shoulders. Most striking were his brilliant crimson eyes and the effortless air of confidence with which he carried himself.

The way he addressed the humans made it clear he saw them as inferior beings. He somehow managed to combine a refined, aristocratic presence with that of a brutal warrior. A debonair villain who wouldn't hesitate to tear apart his enemies.

"Cerys, you're drooling." Alice poked my cheek.

"*I am not!*" I snapped, shying away from her.

"Seriously, what is it with you and the villains?" Alice rolled her eyes.

"I'm not convinced he's a villain—when do anime or stories have a real villain? Ever?" I puffed out my cheeks and glared at her. "The demons just want to be treated like people and get their land back, right? Does that really make them the bad guys?"

"You saw what he just did to those soldiers." Alice puffed her cheeks out right back at me.

"We've been watching the humans do the same things for the past two hours!" I argued, shaking my head. "To demons, to elves, to the dwarves—probably to other races we haven't seen in the anime yet, too. The Issradian Empire treats their inhuman citizens *and* slaves like total shit."

"The demons probably do too," Alice shrugged. "You're just biased because Idris is hot."

"No I'm not," I protested.

"Let's finish watching both versions of the anime before we decide who the real villains are," Alice offered dryly. "Though I'm not sure why you're so suspicious of the one Iris gave you."

"Her insistence that I watch her version instead of the one you copied for me just seemed plain weird," I replied, frowning. "She made it seem like I *had* to watch her version instead of yours."

"That is weird—though maybe they just want to show off the polished version?" Alice suggested.

"I guess we'll see." I sighed and motioned loosely to the TV. "Let's see where this goes."

The moment we started watching my version of the anime, Alice and I exchanged baffled looks. Watching the first few seconds was enough to prove that what we were about to see was drastically different from Alice's copy. It wasn't just a matter of being the 'final' version—it started with a prequel scene of the demon king, Idris, instead of the human emperor, Wullfric. Even the opening theme song and visuals were completely different.

"Okay... Sorry for doubting you." Alice glanced over at me, her expression one of pure confusion. "But...why would they make something so different? I mean, I guess it could end up being like an extra episode or something, but..."

"It's pretty obvious this is set up to be the opposite of the one you have." I leaned forward to grab my drink off the coffee table. "This is set up to show the demons as the good guys and the Issradian Empire as the bad guys. Like, straight down to the music and visuals too. That theme they're playing every time Idris or one of the other demon kings is on screen is like a 'hero' theme in single-player RPGs. The theme for the human elite is an even more ominous melody than Idris's in your version."

"It doesn't make sense." Alice shook her head hard. "The anime is being distributed before launch. Jeriskyr Studios doesn't have a reliable way to guess who will be playing what race, especially since so many people have been quitting the demon and beast factions due to tail physics. Not to mention this is going to be on TV! Which one are they gonna show?"

"You still writing down all the differences?" I pointed to her notebooks.

"I'm going to need more paper."

"Hold tight—I'll go get some from the other room."

I stood up and walked into the bedroom. Once there, I heaved a sigh and stretched. Hours of binge-watching anime on the couch was fun and all, but damn, was I stiff. After shaking out my limbs,

I set about looking for more notebooks. Finding out that my hunch had been right felt strange. Being suspicious was one thing, but validation was another.

I'd doubted my instincts because I couldn't think of a reason for Jeriskyr Studios to have two drastically different versions of the anime. Yet that had turned out to be exactly the case. They knew my guild had rolled the Issradian Empire, so why give me the demon-glorifying version of the anime? Sure, even without it, I had planned to convince the members of Ebonwing to reroll, but...

And even before finding out the demon kings were so hot. I grimaced when the thought crossed my mind. Maybe Alice was right—maybe I did have a problem. But hey, at least I could argue that they weren't *actually* villains now.

"Here you go." I offered Alice three more notebooks. "Want some caffeine? Looks like this one's gonna be longer than your version."

"Sure!" Alice grinned. "I should be done catching up on my notes by then."

By the time we'd finished with the demon version of the anime, we were both exhausted. The human version had been a mere twelve episodes, but the demon one had been double that. It'd been a long time since either of us had stayed up to binge something together—and it was a damn good thing Alice didn't have work the next day.

"Cerys, this is crazy!" Alice exclaimed, waving her notes in my face. I grimaced. Lack of sleep just seemed to make her more energetic. "None of the lore books or anything I've found in-game talk about the demons like this! This is incredible. You were right—they're totally *not* the villains."

I had to wonder if it had even occurred to her that both anime were styled as propaganda from each faction. "You going to compile all your notes after you sleep?"

"Sleep? *Sleep?* How can I sleep?!" Alice whacked my face with one of her notebooks. "There's no way I'm sleeping until I've got this all sorted! I'm so glad you invited me over to watch both versions with you. Mind if I use your guest room?"

"Go ahead—just let me sleep." I groaned and pulled a pillow over my head.

"Sure! Once you're up we can get breakfast and then brief everyone in Ebonwing about your demo." Alice shot up like a rocket and darted for the door. "I should have enough for us to tell them about the differences between the anime, too—oh! Let's have Bruce copy it and send it to all the guild members."

"Of course, Miss Alice," Bruce replied. *"Mistress Cerys, you should at least get into bed if you are going to sleep."*

"Oh Bruce, you're so charming!" Alice giggled.

"Effooooort," I whined, even as I rolled off the couch. "I'm going, I'm going..."

I rushed through getting ready, stripped off my clothes, and collapsed on the bed. Despite my exhaustion, my mind whirled with thoughts of Jeriskyr and the raging factions within it. I glanced toward the shelf beside my desk, examining the VR headset on it, then sighed. Tempting, but I was far too tired.

"Bruce, lights off…please…" I grumbled into my pillow.

"When would you like me to wake you, Mistress?"

"All-nighter…protocol…thanks…"

Chapter Five
Loading...

My fingers flew across the keyboard as I sent out messages to the Ebonwing officers with instructions for their dealings in Jeriskyr. Most of the guild had begun playing the game now and we had a better idea of how many of us could actually fight.

I sighed in agitation when I got lower on my list of guild mail. Alice had filled everyone in on the differences between the anime we'd watched and distributed copies to our members. However, everyone was divided on whether to reroll the other faction. They wanted me to roll a human or elven character in the Issradian Empire, thinking I'd change my mind if I played with them.

Humans were so boring, though. I leaned back in my chair and tapped my nails against my desk. Even so, I had the feeling that rolling a demon within the Issradian Empire would've been an even worse move. Being the 'inside man' could have been interesting, but Ebonwing was already under suspicion. Too many more missteps and we'd have to flee the empire anyway.

At least my spymaster, Mirela, had made some headway. She'd even finished finding ten more people to play the class combination I'd assigned for her branch of the guild. That, at least, was good news.

After I was done responding to all my mail, I stood and stretched before walking over to the nearest shelf. I plucked my VR visor from it and flopped down on the bed. Mail had taken all morning, but it was finally time to settle in and play some *Jeriskyr Online*. I remained apprehensive about the game's realism; however, I wasn't going to let that stop me. What kind of gamer would let that get in the way of anything?

I *had* resigned myself to making a human character first so that I could appease the guild and play with them for the day…but the option wasn't there. The emblem for the Issradian Empire wasn't just grayed out—it was completely missing. Only the Nabyr-zahn coat of arms hovered before me.

A faction lockout during *alpha testing*, of all things? I attempted to swipe the emblem in every direction possible, but it always snapped back into place. Well, with that, my guild couldn't really bitch me out. I literally had no other option, and I didn't intend to refresh the selection screen for the next however-many hours to get in. Sighing, I reached forward and prodded it.

«Please select your race»

I gawked at the list for so long that the system repeated its message. There were *dozens* of races available. The demonic races alone took up at least two dozen, then there were the beast races, humans, elves, and some races which appeared unique to *Jeriskyr Online*. Each one appeared to have its own relationship with Nabyr-zahn, some of which weren't at all friendly.

Mostly, I just wanted whatever I liked the appearance of, racial stats be damned.

«Please verify your selection: Succubus

«Confirmed. Would you like to load your physical appearance?»

I hesitated briefly before confirming again. It'd be a good starting point at any rate.

«Cerys Collins physical profile loaded. Do you wish to further customize?»

I growled and hit the button again so that I could actually begin customizing my character. I *really* wished I could punch the number of confirmation prompts.

I liked my facial features and physique well enough, but the default succubus model was way too tall. Well over seven feet in height, with the possibility to close in on nine feet. That needed to be shrunk down a bit. I also wanted to change my hair color, though I decided that my eyes could remain purple.

Finally, I decided on long, wavy, pearlescent white hair with purple streaks running through it—that was how I typically kept my hair dyed, anyway. Not one for mismatched colors, I made my horns and tail the same pearly white as well. I almost squee-ed when I found the option to make some of the tail scales a different material. Obviously, they had to be some kind of gemstone to match the purple streaks in my hair.

I looked through the menus for a while, but anything resembling makeup settings were noticeably missing. "Oi, how do I change my makeup?"

«Makeup can be purchased from boutiques or made with the appropriate skills»

"And where do I pick my skills?" I prompted, not having found those either. "Or starting armor?"

«Your first armor set will be gifted to you when you become a Novice in a specialization.

«You can acquire your specializations in the capital of Nabyr-zahn.

«You may select two plainclothes outfits in character creation»

"Can I save my appearance?"

«Saving... Are you ready to proceed?»

"*Yes.*" I resisted the urge to find and bitch-slap the AI.

Nauseating dizziness overwhelmed me for a second as my

consciousness was teleported inside of the character I'd created. After shaking the sensation off, I tested the feel of my body and the weight of my tail briefly before looking up at the rather small selection of clothes in front of me.

Well, calling them 'clothes' was a bit of a stretch.

Rolling my eyes, I picked the two sets most suited to traveling—a leather hunting set, plus a cloth set more suitable for a town. Both showed a questionable amount of cleavage, but that wasn't anything new to me. Or to succubi. You got used to it after so many games where chain mail or plate armor bikinis were your best in-slot set.

«Please enter your forename.

«Username 'Cerys' is available. Confirmed.

«Surnames are unavailable to demonic and beast races. You must earn yours.

«Are you ready to enter the world of *Jeriskyr Online*?»

"I've been ready for the past hour!"

«Loading the Nabyr-zahn starting zone: Veilwood Forest»

Chapter Six
Close Encounters of the Demon Kind

I was falling.

My eyes snapped open and my stomach dropped. Below me was mountainous terrain stained in scarlet. Glints of metal and wisps of magic shimmered throughout the dark rocks. Screams echoed across the valley. Snow fell from the sky, only to melt upon drifting to the fresh blood below.

This is not *a forest!* I quickly took stock of myself, confirming that I was indeed still in the game and appeared to have fallen out of the sky. My leather traveling clothes did little to shield me from the frigid air. My tail trailed behind me, tossed around by the wind.

If I didn't come up with something, fast, I'd become another bloodstain in the war-torn valley below.

I clenched and unclenched my fists a few times. There was a tickle in the back of my mind like with other VRMMOs, indicating some access to magic. Since we didn't get to pick our skills prior to interacting with trainers, I had to assume there were at least some generic abilities available to demonic player characters.

Black smoke exploded around me when I mentally 'yanked' at the sensation. Seconds later, I collided with the ground, sending foul-smelling mud and traces of shadow flying into the air. The impact knocked the air from my lungs, but at least I'd managed to keep from getting my guts smeared across the valley floor.

For now.

Blades crashed above my head as opposing forces fought around me. I scrambled to my knees and onto my feet, darting away from the slash of a halberd. Demons. Humans. Beastmen. Elves. Armor in dozens of different colors. I had no idea who was who, or whose side I was even supposed to be on. Everyone around me was in heavy armor and wielding large weapons. My clothing may as well have been lingerie, given the situation.

"Outta the way, woman!" a demon barked, stepping between me and one of the much-smaller human soldiers. He disarmed the man and gutted him before turning to look at me again. "Don't know how the hell you ended up here, but this is no place to be without proper—"

I tackled the demon around the waist and shoved him to the ground. An arrow pierced his shoulder, but the swing of the greataxe I'd spotted behind him missed us both. The surging tide of soldiers around us soon carried the greataxe-wielding human to his demise. The demon I'd tackled gave me a bewildered look as I scrambled to my feet and hefted a discarded sword off the ground.

"Not the place for chit-chat," I pointed out, tensing my jaw.

Okay. I needed to think this through. Most of the soldiers were male, and the demons and beastmen were way bigger than me. Many weren't wearing Nabyr-zahn colors.

I needed to find the easiest way out of the fighting.

A battle cry from overhead made the ground beneath me rumble and sway. I looked up and felt the blood drain from my face. Idris Bloodsong, King of Nabyr-zahn, was bearing down on me with a longsword in one hand and an enraged gleam in his crimson eyes.

«Idris Bloodsong, LV?????»

Fuck.

I leapt out of his way and landed in a crouch, keeping my grip firm on the sword I'd picked up. He rushed me as I swayed to my feet, giving me barely any time to parry his strike. Magic whirled around the length of his blade as he shifted and broke his weapon away from mine. The same motion flowed into a new attack aimed at my throat.

"The hell is your problem?!" I snapped, darting away again.

"You attacked one of my men, traitor!" he snarled, his voice gruff with rage. His response just pissed me off more.

"I didn't *attack* him, you imbecile!" I kicked his wrist, deflecting his sword to the side. "He'd have gotten an axe in his back if I hadn't—"

His foot connected with my stomach hard enough to send me flying backward into the backs of the nearby human soldiers. I scrambled to my feet and out of the enraged king's path again, now with the added issue of dodging the angry humans I'd crashed into. Magic flowed down Idris' sword and set the toppled humans alight on contact. Lovely.

Pissing off a demon king in my first few minutes of playing *Jeriskyr Online* was certainly *not* how I had envisioned things going. I doubted this was the actual starting scenario for new characters with this faction, either.

If it was a bug, it sure was a doozy.

Question-marked level, demon king, supposedly one of the strongest NPCs in the game, I thought quickly as I ran into the midst of the human soldiers. *Okay, so whatever his skills are they've got to be close to—if not past—the Master level. I shouldn't be able to hold my own against him. Is he holding back for some reason?*

How do I calm down a pissed-off demon king?

Several of the humans shot me baffled glances, taking in my leather clothing. Given that everyone else was in heavy plate or chain mail, I couldn't blame them. I didn't belong on a battlefield.

That, or maybe they didn't know why their enemy was chasing one of his 'kind' through their ranks.

Maybe a bit of both...

I skidded to a halt and leaned back from a human's strike. It took me a moment to register that their yells to 'take down the demon bitch' referred to me. Oopsies.

Alas, angry humans weren't enough to slow down the demon king.

Idris' sword arm lashed out around my shoulder as I turned to run past him. Behind me, I heard his blade connect with something. A human charged Idris with spear readied, aiming for the king's back. Gritting my teeth, I lunged forward and struck the shaft of the spear with my palm and knocked it harmlessly to the side, where its point buried itself in the mud. In my next motion, I shoved the blade of my sword up under the man's jaw and out the top of his head.

The bastard dropped like a bag of bricks, taking my sword with him.

"You're coming back to Cejari-ir for questioning, traitor," Idris spat as he pivoted to glare at me. He glanced at the man I'd killed before readying his weapon again. "I need you alive for that. Come quietly, or—"

I slugged the demon king in the jaw and ran away again, searching for another dropped weapon I could claim. Like hell I was going to let him take me somewhere for questioning! I slid to a stop, hefted a spear off the ground, and turned in time to dodge most of Idris' next attack. His sword grazed my cheek, leaving a line of stinging pain behind.

I could nurse it later.

I took off at a run, weaving my way through the ranks of human soldiers. Many yelled to kill or capture me. Cursing internally, I looked for somewhere else to run. Idris was sounding more and more pissed off—I couldn't bet on him going easy on me for much longer.

A human swung a claymore at me, missing my abdomen by mere inches. Growling, I called on the tickle of magic again and concentrated on taking the bastard down. Floating swords of darkness flew from over my shoulder, piercing the soldier in his throat. Good enough.

Glancing back, I realized that Idris was too close for comfort. He cut down the humans in his path with ease as he stalked after me, face twisted with rage and irritation. I fled toward the ranks of demons again. Humans obviously weren't going to help me. The demons, at least, appeared more numerous and had some women among them. Perhaps I could sneak through.

"Damned pest!" Idris roared, startling a squeak out of me. Magic lanced by, leaving the air sizzling in its wake. Either his aim sucked, or that had been a warning shot. I wasn't sure which was more dangerous.

I was planning to *roast* my guildmates for complaining about tails being unwieldy. Mine wasn't a problem. Clearly, they just needed to be dropped *into the middle of a fucking battle* to learn how to deal with them.

Wait—that was it. Tails. I took in the armored demons. Sure enough, their tails weren't fully encased in armor. A weak spot. Perfect.

I wove through the throngs of demon soldiers, doing my best to keep from running into someone else's attack. Idris' roared orders carried over even the clamor of battle, directing his men to apprehend me. I yanked on tails, dove between people's legs, and pulled several people's weapon belts loose. A good, hard yank on their tails seemed to do the trick for distracting them—though it also *really* pissed them off.

Now I had the demon king *and* what felt like half his army chasing me.

Great. Great going, Cerys.

An enormous hammer struck the ground in front of me, forcing me to slide to a stop. A demon cloaked in flames appeared beside it and lifted it like it weighed nothing, shooting me an intrigued look. His armor was fancier than the other demons' and I could've sworn I'd spotted him in the anime, but I couldn't recall his name. I didn't have the time to think about it, either.

I shot off to my left, diving into the nearest wall of soldiers in search of a way out. There had to be some fucking way for me to escape all the fighting. My lungs burned from running and dodging for so long, but I was determined to get away. I just had to keep pushing myself.

"No you don't!" Another demon lashed out. "Surround her!"

Before I could find another opening to slip through, the wall of demonic soldiers shifted to encircle me, their weapons held at the ready. I scowled and attempted to catch my breath. Not a great situation to be in, but not entirely dissimilar to some of the zergs I'd gotten trapped by in other VRMMOs. If I could buy time, I might find a way out.

"The traitor is mine." The voice from less than a foot behind me sent a chill down my spine. I whirled around, spear in hand, but Idris caught the shaft of the weapon just below the blade and gave me a condescending look. "She will be coming with me for questioning. Do not interfere."

"You got mud in your ears?" I snapped. "I'm not going with someone who won't listen to a damned word—"

Idris twisted his hand, snapping off the spearhead. He tossed it aside before lunging at me with his sword. "You are mildly interesting, at least."

Mildly? The corner of my eye twitched.

"Did the Issradian Empire send you to sow confusion?" Idris swung his sword lazily, giving me more than enough time to get the hell out of his way. "Or perhaps you are from one of the small—"

"Maybe you should fucking *listen* when someone tries to respond to you!" Frustrated, I launched myself at him and kicked him in the breastplate with the ridge of my foot. He arched an eyebrow at me as if to question if I'd really expected that to work. The answer was no, but that didn't keep me from getting madder.

"How vulgar," Idris sighed.

"And *you* are just playing with me!" I snapped, easily knocking his sword arm away when he slashed at me again. He shot me a cocky smirk that made my blood boil. "If you're going to fight me, then *fight* me, you son of a—"

"Enough of this," Idris spoke, his words possessing a melodic hum that caused the air to vibrate. "Come."

"I refuse—" My protest stopped short when a melody akin to a song left Idris' lips. My vision began to fade as I felt my knees buckle. *Great. I got my ass kicked by a bard.*

Chapter Seven
On Deaf Ears

When I came to, it was with my arms strapped behind me and my legs secured to those of a chair. The sound of dripping water and the smell of earth gave me the impression that I was underground. Around me were walls of hand-laid stone, and the floor was dirt with flat slabs laid haphazardly across it. Long stone channels along the walls, filled with flames, gave the room light. In front of me stood a very bored-looking demon king and two other demon men—one in fancy armor, the other in expensive clothes.

"Now then," Idris began, tilting his head to the side, "what possessed an unprotected woman to attack one of my men? In the midst of a battle, no less?"

"I didn't attack him!" I growled, straining against my bonds. "Like I tried to tell you before—"

"You pushed him into the path of an arrow."

"I pushed him *out* of the path of a greataxe!"

"And what proof have you?" Idris smirked. He strode forward and grabbed me by the chin with one hand, referencing a stack of papers with the other. "As I thought—you are Cerys. You Otherworlders do *so* enjoy body-hopping... Why Silas believed you would side with us is beyond me."

Okay, there's no way in hell this is a scripted or *random event.* I clenched my teeth and tried to pull my head out of Idris' hand, but his grip was painfully tight. *I should've listened to my instincts. This can't be just a game. No way. I've never passed out in a game before, regardless of what spells were used. Even a sleep spell or potion in other games don't render someone unconscious!*

"You still think this is a game?" Idris passed the stack of papers to the fancily-dressed man beside him before drawing a slender dagger from his belt. "For most, perhaps. Whether it holds true for you is simple enough to find out."

He raised the blade and pulled my chin higher.

When his intention to slit my throat became clear, I mentally screamed, *Log out!*

Chapter Eight
Demanding Deities

I bolted upright in bed and threw my VR visor across the room. That had not been a game. That had been real. There was no way in hell it had been anything else. I reached up to the cheek that had been injured in *Jeriskyr Online*, and sure enough, it stung. Goopy blood came away on my fingertips. I swung my legs over the side of the bed, but didn't get more than three steps before the air in my room shimmered and three figures appeared by my door.

"What the hell?!" I yelped. I had no idea who they were, but their expressions were a mix of smug and impressed. "Get the fuck out of my room! Better yet, out of my apartment. Bruce!"

"I will begin tea for your guests, Mistress Cerys."

"That's not what I—"

"That will not be necessary, Bruce. Cerys will be returning with us."

Next thing I knew, my back slammed into a cold floor and I opened my eyes to find myself staring at the same spacescape that greeted players at the login screen for *Jeriskyr Online.*

I sat up slowly and looked down, grimacing at the twinkling stars below me. They, whoever the fuck they were, could have at least made the floor opaque. And less hard.

"You are much quicker than we expected, Cerys!" a female voice exclaimed with delight. I bolted to my feet and turned to glare at the three figures standing behind me. Two were male, but the female was most certainly a demonic version of Iris Hughes.

"You intended to *trap* me there?" I demanded.

"You're going to help Idris unite the demons," Iris continued like I hadn't said anything, a brilliant smile on her face. "We're choosing you to help the demons fight back against the Issradian Empire. I know you won't disappoint us."

"Fuck no, I'm not helping. Let me go back to my apartment!" I snarled, curling my hands into fists. When I tried to stalk forward, I found myself rooted in place.

"You can go home *if* you succeed in overthrowing the empire," the taller of the two males stated, narrowing his eyes at me. "If you do not choose to stay."

"Why the hell would I *want* to stay?!" I snapped. "And why the fuck are you using a *game* to—"

"The Gods of Earth owed us a new soul for the one we traded to them," Iris shrugged, still smiling. "We chose you. One of our comrades stopped Idris from slaying you and is explaining the situation to him. Poor boy couldn't tell you were helping from his angle."

Boy? 'Boy,' my ass. According to the anime and limited lore found in-game, Idris was meant to be centuries old. Certainly not a *boy*.

"Jeriskyr is a world of warring gods—us against the deities whom the Issradian Empire worships," Iris continued. "The Issradian Empire has grown too strong and too greedy. We need someone to liberate the demon and beast tribes—and to unite them in a common cause.

"You will need to work with Idris in order to bring our plan to fruition and usher in a new era of prosperity."

"Why should I *help* someone who tried to kill me and wouldn't listen to a word I had to say?" I ground my teeth together and stamped my foot. "That bastard—"

"She has a point," a new voice commented. I turned to see a smirking human in fancy clothing. Another one of the so-called gods, I figured. "The rules of our game state that champions must choose a side for themselves. You don't intend to break the rules now, do you?"

"Of course not," Iris scoffed. "We have prepared a body for her in the human lands as well. When the time comes, she can visit the empire. For now, she should return to her body in Nabyr-zahn. Preparations must be made."

"Fine. She will choose the glorious Issradian Empire regardless of where she stays." The smug human deity turned to look at me. "You are to choose the Issradian Empire or the Kingdom of Nabyr-zahn. Why you would choose to side with these barbarians is beyond me. Your guild is part of the Issradian Empire—I am confident you will choose us."

Before I could think up a sassy retort, everything spun, and my vision went dark. Seconds later, I felt a sensation like when I first began to wake up in the morning—except I was clearly in warm water, and someone was with me.

Startled, I snapped my eyes open and scrambled away from the intruding hands, managing to knee my own tail in the process. Cursing, I tucked my tail between my legs and clutched at it before looking to see who had invaded my privacy. A demonic woman in brightly colored clothes looked just as startled as I felt. After a moment, she smiled and gave me a shallow bow.

"I apologize for startling you—we didn't think you would wake for quite some time." The woman spoke in formal tones, raising her head to smile at me again. "You were filthy after your ordeal with His Majesty. I was asked to clean you up and then let you rest. However, now that you're awake, a servant can bring you food if you wish. His Majesty also wishes to meet with you."

"Why? So he can try to kill me again?" I huffed, giving the woman a suspicious look. "I can finish bathing myself."

"Do you know how to use our world's technology?" she countered, smiling.

"Er…" I glanced at the faucet and then pursed my lips. There weren't any obvious buttons, levers, or dials. "Perhaps not."

"Then allow me to assist you." She rose to her feet and moved to a nearby shelf, plucking a soft-looking cloth and a tray of glass bottles from it. "Most Otherworlders would not have been able to stand a place as grotesque as a battlefield."

"I didn't exactly get much time to process it with your king barreling after me," I pointed out, grimacing. "Why does he want to see me?"

"The gods claim you to be their champion—why *wouldn't* he want to see you?" She gave me a puzzled look before kneeling beside the bathtub. "Here, these cleaners are labeled. I will be in the next room preparing a change of clothes for you while you bathe."

I grimaced at the fancy bottles. The bottoms were wrapped in silver filigree and the glass was faceted like crystal. Brightly colored liquids with a faint shimmer swirled within them. Although the labels were clearly not in English, I had no trouble understanding the elegant script.

I opened one bottle and sniffed, relieved to find that it didn't smell quite as sweet as it looked. The floral scent was more on the musky side. There were three bottles for my hair, and two each for my tail and horns.

"Lady Cerys?" The woman knocked on the door frame briefly before walking in with an armful of towels. "Ah, permit me to turn the water on for you."

She placed her cargo aside and then knelt at one end of the bathtub. Moments later, water came from the faucet and she offered me a pail so that I could more easily rinse myself off. I grumbled my thanks and soon finished. For whatever reason, she seemed surprised that I was capable of bathing myself.

"Where are we, exactly?" I pulled one of the towels around myself, discovering it to be pleasantly warm to the touch.

"His Majesty's palace in Cejari-ir, my lady," the woman answered. "My name is Drysi. If you need anything, or need more information about your new body, please let me know. We should get you dressed. Should I send someone to fetch food for you?"

"I'm not hungry." I shook my head before toweling my hair as dry as possible. "Why are you being so formal with me?"

"You are the gods' chosen champion and His Majesty's guest," Drysi replied, leading me into an enormous bedroom. She noticed the expression on my face and smiled. "Better rooms will be prepared for you if you choose to assist Nabyr-zahn against the Issradian Empire. I hope these will suffice for now."

"Suffice?" I arched an eyebrow at her. "This is more lavish than anything I've ever seen in person. I'm not sure how anything could be 'better.'"

"Please, allow me to help you dress." Drysi motioned to a long gown of layered, dark purple fabric.

The open back had laces across it and a bow at the bottom of the V. By how low it extended, I could only assume that the top of my tail was meant to sit above the bow. I wasn't sure how to feel about that. One wrong move would expose my ass cheeks.

Or right move.

"I can dress—" I started to protest, but Drysi had already moved to place the gown at my feet so I could step into it. Apparently, the woman didn't think a bra or underwear was necessary. Granted, I wasn't sure how I'd manage underwear with a tail anyway. "…Thank you."

"You're welcome, my lady." She shot me another brilliant smile before offering me several simple silver ornaments to pin my hair up with. "This way, please."

Resigned, I followed Drysi through the extravagant palace. The architecture and decorations struck me as belonging to a blend of cultures—and were more advanced than a medieval civilization. Hell, it appeared that Cejari-ir was already ahead of the Issradian Empire in many ways.

Much of the stonework was gray, white, or black, be it marble, granite, or some other type of stone. However, there were splashes of color everywhere in the form of artwork, fresh flowers, rugs, tapestries, mosaics, and more. The variety of influences struck me as a mix of ancient European, Asian, and Arabian. Other things appeared wholly alien.

"Are some of these trophies? Or perhaps made by Otherworlders like myself?" I asked, my curiosity finally getting the better of me.

"Everything you see in Cejari-ir is purely of demonic design." Drysi shook her head. "Otherworlders have learned our crafts and our arts but were never permitted to infuse their home worlds into Jeriskyr. Any resemblance you see is purely coincidental—and the trophies of His Majesty's family are kept in a private collection."

When we entered a garden-filled courtyard, a familiar demon man blocked our path and crossed his arms. He examined me from head to toe, ignoring Drysi's uncomfortable look.

"What?" I crossed my arms right back at the man. He was most definitely the one who'd blocked my path with his hammer, but I still couldn't place his name. Wasn't convinced that I cared, either.

"*Emrys!*" Drysi pursed her lips.

"Why're you still here?" The hammer-wielding bastard narrowed his eyes at me.

"Supposedly I'm meant to meet with that damned minstrel you serve," I retorted.

"The gods already told you you're supposed to make a choice, haven't they?" Emrys didn't react at all to my attempt at a verbal jab. "You've got a guild on the other side. Probably human in your home world, too. You expect us to believe you're going to betray your guild or people?"

"I don't expect anything from you." I growled, grabbing what little cloth poked out over the top of his breastplate. He just laughed when I yanked him down closer to my height.

"Don't get ahead of yourself, pup." Emrys freed himself with ease, patted my head, and then turned his back to me. "I'm to make sure neither of you get plucked away by anyone on the way to His Majesty. Let's go."

Pup?! I fumed, stalking after them.

When we neared a pair of extravagant doors, Emrys threw them open without bothering to knock and strode into the room as if he owned the place. The guards both outside and inside saluted him before shifting to shoot me wary glances. I kept my eyes forward and my chin up as I walked into what must have been Idris' throne room.

Under other circumstances, I probably would have gawked. It was truly beautiful. Water flowed into the room from somewhere and cascaded down the wall behind the throne, under the floor, and into shallow pools on either side of the room. There was art everywhere and the stonework was incredible.

However, I refused to let that bastard think I was interested in anything.

Idris looked even *more* arrogant than before. He lounged in his throne with his cheek propped on his fist and his legs crossed. The small smirk on his face broadened when he spotted me behind Emrys. No longer clad in armor, the king wore clothing that seemed a little too casual for the throne room.

"Ah, you're awake!" Idris shot me a charming smile. "Good. We need to discuss your position in Jeriskyr."

He ordered everyone out, aside from Emrys and a few other male demons wearing courtly attire. I crossed my arms and tracked Idris cautiously as he rose to his feet. He closed the distance between us in a few long strides and looked down at me. His gaze seemed to soften as he examined me, his eyes twinkling. When I said nothing, his lips curved into an amused smirk.

"You do not intend to bow?" he questioned, glancing toward the bowing nobles as if to make a point.

"You're not my king." The corner of my eye twitched.

"Perhaps. Who *is* your king then?"

"We don't have kings in my world."

"Then how about I make you my queen?" Idris suggested. He grabbed my hand and brought it to his lips before I could shy away. "It would be such a waste to let you rejoin the human filth. Perhaps—"

"Your Majesty, you can't be serious!" the nobles exclaimed.

"Idris. Really?" Emrys crossed his arms and sighed.

"Are you out of your fucking mind?!" I demanded. "I'm already in this world against my will. Marrying a cocky minstrel who attempted to kill me sounds like an even worse idea."

"Watch your tongue!" one of the nobles snapped, while Emrys attempted to muffle a snort of laughter. "This harlot—"

"*Harlot?*" I yanked my hand out of Idris' and grabbed the noble by the front of his robes. "I should hang you from—"

"That's enough—both of you." Emrys laughed outright as he peeled me away from the noble. "Go on, Your Majesty."

"If you actually want me to help your side, this is a terrible way of going about it," I stated flatly, shooting Idris an annoyed glare.

"Marriage is our only hope for convincing you to join our kind." Idris made a dismissive motion with one hand as he returned to his throne. Once sitting again, his expression froze over and he examined me again. "We understand the likelihood of you joining us is slim. No one ever chooses us, regardless of the gods' intentions. I summoned you for a simple reason."

"And what is that?" I crossed my arms and glared back at him.

"When you rejoin the humans—"

"*If.*"

"...*When* you rejoin the humans," Idris gave me an unconvinced look, "you are not to divulge Silas' position or involvement to anyone. Do not betray his trust, or mine.

"Do this, and I will not have you executed when we take the Issradian Empire. I will do what I can to have you returned to your world, or give you asylum here if that fails. While I do not believe you will choose to side with us, we are aware that your guild, and likely you, are sympathetic to our cause."

"Why are you so sure that I won't choose to help your people?" I frowned at him. "Where does that confidence—or lack thereof—come from?"

"It is as I said. No one ever chooses us." Idris sighed, glancing away from me briefly. His jaw tensed as he paused to consider something. "I cannot say I understand why the gods chose a human to aid us."

"Humans are all there are in my world."

"And what is that world called?"

"Earth."

"…That is a stupid name."

"You're not wrong about that." I laughed, shaking my head, before adopting a more serious tone. "Demons are clearly superior to the humans of your world—so how did you end up subjugated by them?"

"The races all got along once," Emrys began when Idris said nothing. "We, that is, the demonic races, were too trusting. The humans wanted more and more.

"Eventually, our cooperation led to them attacking our cities in the dark of night. They burned villages, took our women and children, and killed thousands of our men in the confusion."

"While in a proper battle your people would have decimated the humans?" I asked, earning an odd look from them. "What?"

"You are strangely accepting of your kind's weakness." Idris narrowed his eyes at me.

"You have to accept your weaknesses before you can overcome them," I pointed out, raising an eyebrow at him. "I don't want to stagnate."

"Perhaps you are less barbaric than I gave you credit for," Idris murmured, shaking his head. "We trusted the humans. We lost lives and land for it. They keep our women and children as hostages to discourage us from outright warfare. Three quarters of the Issradian Empire is made of land previously owned by other races. Half belongs to the demonic kingdoms."

"And somehow your gods think that their 'champion' is supposed to right this mess?" I arched a doubtful eyebrow, earning a nod in reply. His grimace told me he was just as unconvinced as I was.

"The Great Unifier." Idris rolled his eyes before motioning to me.

He didn't appear interested in elaborating, and I sighed. If he hadn't been so damned stubborn and defensive, I wouldn't have minded listening to him talk more.

"Explain or don't. I don't particularly care," I stated, narrowing my eyes at the demon king. "I'll be blunt—with or without your explanation, there's no way in hell I can make an informed decision on such short notice.

"If bringing one side or the other to victory is my ticket back home, then that's what I'll have to do. My choice is going to hinge on which side appears to be the less shitty option."

"Such opinions are subjective." Idris shifted in his throne.

"Do your people burn, rape, or kidnap villages?"

"Absolutely not." He bared his fangs.

"Then you've already got a whole lot of points in your favor."

Idris fell silent and stroked his chin in thought before eventually returning his crimson gaze to me. "The gods have rules for their game, but that does not mean they can't bend them. A 'champion' hasn't chosen Nabyr-zahn's side in centuries—even if they themselves are demons or beastmen."

"You suspect foul play?" I frowned.

"Cejari-ir is always toured last." Idris motioned loosely around us with one hand. "By the time the champion arrives, their choice has already been made. They tour our city or our kingdom only to keep up appearances."

"Sometime between their first meeting with us and going to the humans, something happens to change their mind," Emrys added, as if for clarity. "Always."

"Something other than the minstrel?" I asked, jabbing my thumb in Idris' direction.

"I dislike betrayal," Idris stated.

"Well, if you'd listened, you would have known I wasn't 'betraying' you. Quite the opposite, really," I pointed out.

"Yet."

"Ugh." I pressed my fingers to my temples before looking at the infuriating man again. "How long do I have until these gods of yours send me on this ridiculous 'tour?'"

"A few days at best." Idris tilted his head slightly and gave me a look that sent chills down my spine. "I am still waiting for you to state if you will agree to keep Silas' secret safe. Understand that, if you divulge the information to the humans willingly, I will see you tortured to death."

"I have no interest in giving the humans information." I growled. "Threats of torture or otherwise, I never intended to tell anyone about Silas' position."

"Good. Then we're done here." Idris rested his cheek against his fist and looked away from me.

Emrys led me out of the throne room as I mentally cursed the king. I couldn't think of anyone I'd ever met who pissed me off so much, or with such ease. Hell, I was at a point where I'd probably get mad just listening to him breathe. It should've been a sin to let such a physically attractive man be so damned aggravating.

"It's nothing personal." Emrys glanced down at me. "We've watched dozens of champions come and go. You're lucky you got as much out of him as you did."

"Did it ever cross your minds that being more cooperative might increase your chances of a 'champion' choosing you?" I spat back, bristling.

"Of course—but if it doesn't, then our enemies will have more information to use against us," Emrys shrugged, shooting me a crooked smile. "We're grateful to you for saving one of our men.

Truly we are. But unless you formally choose us, no one here will trust you."

"Which is why she will be remaining in her world after all," a female voice commented. Iris appeared in front of us and sighed. "If only you had accepted his marriage proposal."

"Why in the hell would I?"

"Girl's got a point." Emrys motioned to me, his eyes on Iris. "Besides. You and I both know he only said it because there's no other way to convince her to stay."

"That is where you are wrong. She will choose Nabyr-zahn," Iris shrugged. "Emrys, take her body back to her rooms and see to it she is well-guarded. I am taking her soul back to her own world, for now. The other side is concerned that remaining in Cejari-ir will prematurely 'sway' her."

"They've never worried about that before, my lady." Emrys furrowed his brow.

"They are now." Iris shot him a smug look before motioning to me. "Come along, Cerys."

Chapter Nine
Faded Hope

"Emrys?" I frowned when he returned with Cerys unconscious in his arms. "Was a discussion with me too much for her to handle, perhaps?"

"Hardly," Emrys snorted, shaking his head before looking at me with seething rage in his eyes. "Corlyotir returned the girl's soul to her world. The human gods decided they don't want to risk us 'influencing' Cerys' decision."

"Influence...?" I trailed off and looked at the woman's peaceful face. Minutes prior, she had been guarded and glaring at us. With good reason, perhaps. Were I in her situation, I would have been disinclined to trust anyone. It was a shame she had not fallen for my proposal. However, if the gods were growing anxious… "They have never cared before. I wonder… Do they think their usual plans will not work with her?"

"Corlyotir wants her guarded." Emrys looked down at the woman in his arms and grimaced. "She seems to think Cerys is in danger. Maybe more than we'd normally expect."

"You will not hear me say no." I rose to my feet and strode toward him. "She is certainly an odd one, but I am not confident that it means she may choose us. Even so…she did save one of our men, and seemed genuine when she stated she would not betray Silas' position. For now, we shall be gracious hosts to her. However, do not grow attached. She will not be staying."

"Are you telling me that—or yourself?" Emrys questioned as I strode past him.

Perhaps both. I left the throne room behind and wandered through my palace with no specific destination in mind. My offer had been little more than a jest, yet her refusal stung. She had not hesitated in the slightest. However, I had to admit that the rage she had directed toward the nobles amused me—even if their behavior did not. *They should not be driving away new women. Not when we have so few left…*

I strode to the far side of one of the gardens and rested against the containing wall with my palms flat against the rail. The city sprawling below me was dying a little more each year. Too many lives had been lost to the Issradian Empire. Too few Otherworlders chose to side with or live with us.

She could be the last champion we received before Nabyr-zahn fell. I closed my eyes and sighed, collecting my thoughts.

I refused to allow myself to hope, but…she had given Silas her name willingly. He had to have some reason to trust her.

Chapter Ten
Summons

Dozens of sheets of paper were scattered about my desk and several days had passed since I'd returned to Earth. After sleeping off the initial shock, and perhaps a few dozen bottles of liquor, I'd settled in to do what I did best—gather information, arrange it, and plan around it. I knew there was no way in hell they'd just forget about me or their little game and leave me alone.

I intended to be prepared when I returned to Jeriskyr.

Idris may not have been forthcoming with information, but Emrys had given me enough to go on. With the limited story he'd told me, the two anime Jeriskyr Studios had given me, and the power of the Internet at my fingertips, I had been able to discover a lot more about the lore—or rather, history—of their world. I knew role-players and their fascination with storylines would come in handy at some point.

Emrys hadn't been kidding when he said the humans had become greedy. They truly wanted everything. Their goal was to dominate their own people, eradicate the other races, and take the world's resources for themselves. *Especially* the treasures and unique arts created by the gods. From what I'd found so far, it looked like the deities the humans worshiped were the reason for the whole mess.

I wasn't surprised. Even if the deities from Earth's history weren't real, the behavior was consistent with the records I'd found of Jeriskyr. Eternal beings were prone to growing bored. When they grew bored, they caused trouble for the mortal races. Trouble that lasted centuries or more. To them, a blink of an eye. To the mortals, lifetimes.

What I couldn't figure out was whether the demon gods were any different—and why, if they were. It made sense to me that the mortals would have different cultures and varying views on what constituted acceptable behavior, but I wasn't sure if the rules applied to deities within the same world.

I grimaced. It figured I'd escape a cult only to be thrown into a world with real deities. 'Home' wasn't really a place I wanted to think of, though I couldn't help but wonder about the look on my parents' faces if they were to meet *real* deities. I'd almost pay to see *that*.

I stood up and strode into the kitchen to refill my drink. My intuition told me that choosing to side with Nabyr-zahn was the 'right' choice. After all, siding with an empire hellbent on destroying or enslaving all the inhuman races seemed like a stupid idea.

A stupid choice that other champions had decided to make.

Just what were the human gods doing to convince them? I stared at my glass, swirling the liquid inside. I'd have thought that getting demons to betray their own kind would be difficult, even if they were from different worlds—assuming they knew of the Issradian Empire's goals, anyway.

What happened to the champion chosen for the other side if the Nabyr-zahn champion were to choose the humans?

Dozens more questions floated around my head. For everything new I learned about Jeriskyr, more questions appeared. There didn't seem to be a good reason behind the deity's game, leaving me to believe it was just that for them—a game. To them, it was probably the equivalent of when I picked what character to play in a MOBA.

It wasn't a comforting thought.

Furthermore, I felt more isolated than when I'd first come to this city. For the first time in years, I found myself in a situation that I couldn't realistically go to Alice or any of our other guild members about. They would just laugh it off and say that I'd been reading too much, or watching too much anime, or that I had a wild imagination.

That it was just a lucid dream.

I reached up and rubbed at my cheek with a grumble. The cut from Idris' sword had begun to heal, but it was still a damned good reminder that I hadn't been dreaming. That I wasn't imagining things. I was in one hell of a mess.

The stupid minstrel wasn't so bad, though. I downed the rest of my drink, refilled it again, and returned to my desk to work.

Thanks to all the information role-players and lore hounds had been finding via 'NPC' dialogue, I'd managed to look into Idris more since returning. Once I'd had a chance to calm down and think things through, I could understand why he'd gone so far as to suggest I marry him. He may have looked relaxed, but it hadn't taken much digging for me to discover that the demon kingdoms were in a poor state. Prior to me, over forty champions had been chosen—and refused to side with Nabyr-zahn.

And that wasn't counting the other five demon kingdoms or beastmen.

My search had uncovered that Idris Bloodsong was a full-blooded incubus with what was considered a grand lineage. He was favored by the gods to unite the demon kingdoms, and many of the other races loved him as well. Powerful, good-looking, skilled in battle—he was just about everything you'd expect an incubus ruler to be.

Yet he hadn't used his power to seduce me.

I didn't understand it. If they were truly so desperate for a champion to choose Nabyr-zahn, he could have easily used his power. Perhaps it wasn't 'allowed' by the gods' rules—but players hadn't found any references to the gods' game at all beyond mentions of champions.

Maybe incubi and succubi didn't have the same power they were rumored to have in Earth folklore. I shook my head and pulled over a piece of paper. Whatever his reasons, I was glad he hadn't taken that approach. I didn't like the idea of being stuck in Jeriskyr *permanently* as the gods' puppet.

"Mistress, you should get ready for bed." Bruce's statement made me frown and glance at the clock. It was early. *"You are due in Jeriskyr in fifteen minutes."*

"What?" I swiveled my chair to stare at the line of light that indicated Bruce's presence. "The fuck do you mean *fifteen minutes?*"

"Fourteen minutes." Bruce's light flickered with the syllables and I sighed. *"You will be touring the capital of the Issradian Empire, Darmos. Do not trust anyone."*

I paused by the door and glanced toward Bruce's light. To say it displeased me that the so-called gods had tinkered with my house AI was an understatement. Though I appreciated the warning about my upcoming visit—short notice though it may have been.

With even Bruce warning me to be careful, I was even less sure about what to expect. I slid off my slippers and robe as I made my way toward the bed. Trust wasn't something that came easily to me, yet Bruce had still given me the warning as though it were necessary. *That* made me uneasy. AI or not, he probably knew me better than anyone else. Better than Alice did, even. "Bruce, don't let anyone into the apartment."

"Of course, Mistress Cerys."

"If anyone does come in, contain them."

"I cannot contain gods."

"How about demons?"

"Humanoid species who are not deities can be subdued if seen as a threat."

"Then please subdue any non-deity persons who might enter or appear in the apartment, Bruce."

"Very well. Recalibrating.

"Ten minutes remaining. Would you like me to initiate sleep mode for the apartment?"

"Just for my room," I replied as I climbed into bed and pulled the sheets up over my shoulders. The lights dimmed before going out and the curtains slid shut on the far wall. I sighed, sinking into the mattress. Comfortable, but I knew it wouldn't last.

I was met by the sight of an opulent room of white and pale

green when I opened my eyes. My body felt achy, as if I'd been sleeping in the same position for a long time. When I shifted, my spine popped in multiple places. Wincing, I slowly sat up and rubbed at my eyes. Bright sunshine filtered in through the windows. I spotted glimpses of gardens and gilded stone architecture whenever shadows swayed over the glass.

"Y-y-y-y-you're awake!" The panicked stuttering came from closer than I would have liked, causing me to turn. A pale elf woman swallowed hard and dipped into a deep curtsy when my gaze fell on her. It didn't take me long to notice the skin around her wrists, throat, and ankles was raw from her metal bindings. "I will draw you a bath at once so you can prepare for the day, my lady."

Before I could protest, the woman fled into another room. She was frightened, and it took me a moment to realize her feelings were directed toward me. I pulled myself out of bed and cautiously stretched, listening as more joints popped. When I went over to a mirror, I frowned. My form here was basically the same as in Nabyr-zahn—but minus the demonic traits. My ears were still pointed, giving me the indication that my body here was some sort of elf.

An elven champion… Meant to destroy all other races. Right. I kept my doubts to myself and turned away from the mirror when I heard light footsteps nearby. The woman flinched and looked away from me when my gaze fell on her. I pursed my lips. "Did I do something in my sleep to make you so scared of me?"

"N-no," she replied, shaking her head hard before giving me a quizzical look. "You're the gods' champion. If...if you join the Issradian Empire..." she gulped and clutched her dress. "Then y-your duty will b-be to destroy everyone who isn't human. F-for you to betray your own race—"

"I'm human in my world—I don't know why I was given an elven body here," I replied, startling the woman. Her eyes ticked back and forth for a moment before she grew deathly pale.

"I-in that case..." She stared at me with wide eyes. "I-I'm so sorry."

She fled before I could question what she was on about. I sighed and made my way into the room she had come from, finding a steaming bath waiting for me. A long gown hung from a hook on a second door, which led into the bathroom. I opened it and peeked in, finding a mostly-empty wardrobe behind it. I resigned myself to taking a swift bath.

By the time I was drying off and getting ready to dress myself, the elf woman had returned. Her eyes were puffy, as if she'd been crying. My best guess was that she'd gone somewhere to hide while doing precisely that. She sniffled and then cleared her throat before curtsying to me.

"I apologize for running away, Mistress," she spoke quietly. "I... I am not allowed to tell you anything. Please do not ask. Lords Eadgar Odilo and Adric Alfhard will be escorting you today. These clothes were…their idea."

She glanced at the waiting gown with discomfort before returning her gaze to me.

"Their choice, huh?" I muttered, pulling the gown off the rack. It was translucent, low cut, and had an open back. It managed to make the dress I'd worn in Nabyr-zahn look conservative.

Without another word, I pulled on the dress and adjusted it in the mirror. I was lucky that I was so pale. If my nipples were any darker they would have shown through the translucence of the gown. I kept my expression passive, but internally I was seething.

Between their choice of dress for me and the obvious damage to the servant girl's skin, it was clear that elves were treated just as poorly as demons. I couldn't fathom why I had been given the body of an elf—and how I could be expected to eradicate 'my own people.'

"You don't need to apologize," I stated when she opened her mouth and dipped into another curtsy. "I'm not going to hold you accountable for their poor choices."

"Thank you…" She averted her gaze and dipped into a deeper curtsy. "This way please, Lady Cerys. It would be better for both of us if we did not keep them waiting."

I followed the terrified woman through my small suite of rooms and into the hallway outside. Two well-dressed wolves—I mean men—waited for us outside. Lord Eadgar Odilo was the emperor's adviser. He was old, fat, and looked at me as if he was already thinking of what manner of positions he could contort me into.

Adric, the captain of the Imperial Guard, appeared more pleasant. I wasn't yet sure if it was simply because he kept his expression neutral. He seemed young for someone with such an important role. He was brunette with lightly tanned skin, and his facial hair was little more than stubble in most places, aside from a thin but neatly-trimmed short beard. I noticed his ears appeared to be slightly pointed—though far less than an elf's—but had a feeling it would be better if I didn't inquire. His piercing green eyes were next to impossible for me to read.

No matter what I tried, thought, or willed, I couldn't seem to bring up anything resembling a UI. With that in mind, I figured it was best if I assumed their proficiencies were at least Master—and mine were nonexistent.

I glanced between the two men and then at the shivering elf girl. She had tucked herself slightly behind me and appeared more frightened of the fat one than the armored one. When I looked back to the two men, I finally decided to address them. "Lords Odilo and Alfhard, I assume?"

"Oooh, you've got a voice like a songbird!" Eadgar grinned, revealing yellowed teeth, some of which had been replaced with gold. Just looking at him made my skin crawl. "We have a busy day ahead of us, a busy day indeed."

"I will be protecting you and his lordship during your tour,"

Adric added. His expression wavered for only a moment before he turned his back to us. "We should get going, my lord, if you still wish to attend the party tonight."

"Of course, of course." Eadgar nodded before giving me a sleazy grin and motioning for me to join them. "Cerys, was it? I hear that you already had to deal with the barbarians of Nabyr-zahn, you poor dear. A city of barbarians is no place for a woman."

"Actually, the gods saw fit to drop me into the middle of a battle in some mountainous area," I remarked, earning a brief glance from Adric and a stunned stare from his blubbery companion. "During the struggle, I realized this world isn't some mere game like the people of my world believe."

"Ah yes, what sort of races inhabit your world?" Eadgar asked, rubbing his hands together. I got the distinct impression he was hoping for more slaves.

"Humans, my lord," I answered simply. "We have no other races on Earth."

"Ah, let me rephrase," Eadgar began, "what *animal* races do you have in your world? Demons? Elves?"

"The only animals we have in our world are, well, animals, my lord." I kept my voice level, but not enough, given the small upward twitch I noticed at the corner of Adric's mouth. "The only race we have in our world capable of speech, inventing, and so on is humans. Elves, demons, and other such beings are purely myth."

"Egads! The conquerors of your world's past must have been

truly talented to wipe out such filth!" Eadgar exclaimed, clearly uncaring of my apparent race or those of the servants around us. I expected the servants to shoot him scowls of disgust, but instead they cowered and did their best not to look in his direction.

"Perhaps. If such races ever existed on Earth, they disappeared thousands of years ago." I shrugged slightly. "No manner of scientist, anthropologist, or archaeologist has found proof of inhuman species existing in our world."

"Perhaps they were transported elsewhere," Adric suggested, glancing over his shoulder at me. "You are human in your world, then? This form…"

"Correct. I'm human where I'm from," I nodded. "The gods picked this body for me. Unlike with Nabyr-zahn, I was not given a choice here."

"Those demon gods are trying to make us look bad, no doubt!" Eadgar snorted as we walked into a courtyard. A carriage drawn by four horses awaited us. "Your status would be much different if you were allowed to be human, and they know it."

"Her status *could* be different, if you put in a word with His Excellence," Adric pointed out as he opened the door to the carriage.

"Take us around the city first," Eadgar ordered the driver, before hauling his enormous ass into the carriage. We hadn't even begun yet and I already felt sorry for the poor horses.

"After you." Adric gave me a barely noticeable bow and a

meaningful look.

I pulled myself into the carriage and sat across from the pudgy adviser with my shoulder beside one of the windows. Sharing such a tight space with the miserable man was not on my list of things I *ever* wanted to do, but I told myself I would tolerate it.

Idris' company was starting to look better by the minute.

"You will stay in the carriage—we can't have the citizens seeing me in public with one of the animal races, after all," Eadgar informed me, sneering. "Once you've seen our splendid capital, we will show you where you will be staying once you've chosen us."

I caught the look of discomfort that passed across Adric's face as he sat down beside the adviser. From what I understood, the guard captain had seen plenty of battles on the front lines before earning his current rank. If the adviser's plans could turn a battle-hardened soldier green, I sincerely doubted that I would want any part of it.

If they were that bad, then why did the adviser and the human gods seem so sure I would choose them? I stared out the window as the carriage began to move.

"Not one for talking much, are you?" Eadgar asked.

"I'm adjusting my expectations," I replied, giving the man a sideways look. "It's been hundreds of years since the people of my world stopped using architecture like this. Well over a century since we ceased using horse-drawn carriages, too. If I'm to judge your city on fair terms, I can't compare it to modern times in my world."

"*Ceased*... What in the hells do you use to pull your carriages?" Eadgar frowned.

"Our vehicles are no longer carriages and are fully mechanical," I replied after a moment's thought. They appeared to have some early forms of machinery in their possession—clocks and some other things—so I hoped they would understand. "Gears are useful for many things. The scientists of our world found ways to harness clockwork, coal, water, and steam power over the years. Eventually, they discovered how to produce and control electrical currents."

"Incredible!" Eadgar exclaimed. "Now I understand why the gods claimed you were most displeased about being summoned to Jeriskyr. Our empire must be like a fledgling's compared to yours."

It wasn't quite what I'd meant, but I decided to let him think that way.

I peered out the window, taking in the busy streets. Many of the buildings were built from stone and carved with elegant shapes and flourishes, reminiscent of Renaissance Italy. However, the further from the richer districts I looked, the cruder the buildings became. Most were built of stacked, rough-cut stone with thatched roofs. Some were being reconstructed with newer features, giving me the impression that the empire was in a transitionary period.

Darmos was most certainly the same city I had visited during my demo. However, I hadn't been to the sections of the city meant exclusively for the nobles. They appeared to have some manner of magical puppets running around, performing tasks and deliveries for their owners.

Slaves were even more abundant than what I had seen prior.

"You look displeased," Adric commented.

"Slavery is illegal in my world." I glanced at the two men, noting Eadgar's shock. I pursed my lips. "Does the Issradian Empire intend to enslave its own men and women once it eradicates the other races?"

"That's..." Eadgar frowned.

"Humans used to enslave other humans in my world," I commented, returning my gaze out the window. "It did not end well."

As the adviser's orders implied, the driver took us on a brief tour of the city. When we passed through one of the red light districts, I spotted Silas among the crowds. If I hadn't known any better, I would have sworn he noticed me in the window of the carriage. However, he turned away so quickly that I decided I must have been imagining things. Or he had better things to do with his time. Either/or.

A bad feeling welled up in my gut as we returned to the castle. Instead of stopping in the front courtyard, the driver took us around to the back, where it was darker and dirtier. When we came to a stop, Adric was the first to his feet. He shot me an apologetic look as he passed me and opened the door. I followed soon after, with Eadgar a little too close behind me.

"And this is?" I asked.

"The entrance to where you will stay once you choose us," Eadgar smirked.

It smelled like piss and shit. I suppressed a grimace and followed the two men. They were far too confident, and I really didn't like where things were going.

A guard opened a wooden door, which was flush with the floor near the stable. Eadgar went first, then me next, with Adric taking up the rear. We descended the stone steps and my hair stood on end within seconds. There were more smells than just urine and feces. Sex, vomit, and bad incense were even stronger.

However, it was the sounds that were truly horrifying.

"What is this place?" I demanded sharply, narrowing my eyes at Eadgar.

"The breeding pens!" Eadgar exclaimed merrily, spreading his arms wide. "Here, inhuman whores like yourself are bred to produce us the best soldiers. It's been several generations since our last '*champion*' stopped producing offspring. With you, we should be able to further refine the bloodline and have our perfect creations at last!"

"You expect me to *agree* to this?" I was stunned by more than just the sheer audacity of it all. All around us were women, some pregnant and others not, being bred like animals by human soldiers and nobles alike. Some of the women struggled and screamed, others were entirely broken. They all had scars and fresh wounds from their bindings. Signs of both past and recent torture were visible under the dirt covering their skin, including Lichtenburg figures left by shock collars.

If I'd had anything at all in my stomach, I would have lost it.

"Of course you will!" Eadgar answered brightly. "It's either you, or that girl…what was her name? Ah, yes—Alice."

"…pardon?" I narrowed my eyes.

"Alice was chosen by our gods to be their champion—but we can't let the demons obtain *their* champion, of course," Eadgar laughed. "If you refuse, Alice will take your place in the breeding pens. She *is* an elf as well, after all. If we must, we can make do with her instead of you. However, if you were to take her place, our gods will return her to Earth."

I forced myself to breathe steadily, even as my pulse raged in my ears. "If inhuman races are 'animals,' why would you willingly breed yourselves with them?"

"We are breeding them—not ourselves!" Eadgar slapped me across the face but his strength was laughable. I glared back at him in silence. "Sons become soldiers. Daughters are sent to the brothels until they are of age to return as breeding stock. Hybrids are stronger, age slower, and wield better magics. Better yet if we have pure bloodlines."

I ground my teeth together. Pure. With what I knew of Earth history, that likely meant inbreeding. My stomach lurched. "You must be confident in my personality if you're willing to show me this before I've made a decision."

"Sows always make the same choice," he cackled. "Off with you now. I have more to breed and you're off limits until the gods say otherwise. Adric, take our future sow back to her room."

I turned on my heel and stalked after the guard captain. Once outside, I took a deep breath of the fresher air outside and steeled myself. It was a terrible decision. The sort of decision that would trigger most people's desire for self-preservation. I didn't like the idea of me or any of my friends being trapped in such a wretched place for seconds, let alone possibly decades.

"I cannot say," Adric stated when I opened my mouth to question him.

"Are you allowed to tell me how long this practice has gone on for?" I sighed.

"Centuries."

So, the champions Idris mentioned... I considered, following Adric into the castle. "And this is considered acceptable in your world?"

"Anything for the glory of the empire." Adric's answer sounded tired, even if his expression gave nothing away

"I still don't understand why the empire would accept the accomplishment of their goal with tools who aren't pureblood." I noticed the captain twitch.

"All I will say is not to judge us all by the actions of others." Adric shot me a warning look. "I can say no more on the matter.

You will be safe in your rooms, for now. The gods will execute anyone who attempts to touch you prematurely. They dislike their games being meddled with.

"If you choose the empire…you will be in *that place* when you wake. If you return to Nabyr-zahn, the deities will claim this body of yours. I do not know what they will do with it."

Adric left me with a curt nod, leaving me to enter my room alone. Once inside, I locked the door and searched my room thoroughly, checking to make certain no one was hiding in the closets, under any furniture, behind curtains, or anywhere else I could think of.

Once satisfied I was truly alone, I slumped into a chair and stared at the floor, my mind reeling. Me or Alice. Eadgar had been lying when he had said that Alice would be returned to Earth, but the rest of his words rang true. My instincts told me that, if I were to take her place in the Issradian Empire, she would be sent to Nabyr-zahn. The deities wanted their champions—they would likely be willing to swap.

Alice couldn't fight. Hells, she preferred gathering and crafting in almost every game we played. She would be useless to either side in combat. The Issradians clearly only cared about 'breeding stock.' But the demons had indicated that they wished for more.

The moment I woke up in my bed, I ran past Iris before she

could say a word and into the bathroom, retching. It wasn't long before I couldn't throw up anymore. After dry heaving for a while, I brushed my teeth and got a glass of water. Iris looked at me with concern when I returned to my room.

I was surprised she was still there.

"What's wrong?" Iris probed, her brow knit with worry.

"You're seriously going to tell me you don't know?" I grimaced at how hoarse I sounded, but soon forgot it when the goddess shook her head. "The reason none of your 'champions' have sided with the demons is because of the Issradians' ultimatum!"

"Ultimatum?" Iris echoed.

I sighed and then proceeded to explain to her what had happened. She was just as pissed as I was, if not more, and I felt a little relieved to see it. The demon deities seemed more 'human' than the human deities did!

In the end, she confirmed my suspicion that Alice would be sent to Nabyr-zahn in my stead. The 'game rules' dictated that both sides *must* have a champion when new ones were brought to Jeriskyr. They couldn't simply pick yet another new replacement for the demons.

"It isn't strictly against the rules of the game...but it is in such foul taste!" Iris spat as she paced across my room. "All these millennia they accuse *us* of not playing fair, yet this is what they have been up to?! To force mortals to make such a horrendous decision... If...if you choose to save Alice..."

"If." I sighed and ran a hand through my hair as the goddess shot me a dumbfounded look. "I haven't made a decision yet. I'm still mulling it over. I don't make decisions like this on a whim. There are other factors here that I need to consider."

"Such as?" Iris turned to face me fully, her expression doubtful.

"Alice is dead weight, considering what the demons need," I replied, placing a hand on my hip. "She wouldn't be able to help them unify, let alone assist them with assaulting the Issradian Empire—and eventually rescuing me. I could...if she can survive long enough to be saved."

"I...will give you a day to process what you've learned from the empire," Iris informed me, shutting her eyes briefly. "I'm afraid I can't give you much more. I would advise against contacting Alice about this. Knowing the human gods, she won't have any idea of their tactics yet."

The goddess disappeared and I promptly collapsed on my bed. Bruce attempted to get my attention several times, but I didn't have it in me to talk. Logic told me that I shouldn't make the swap. My loyalty to my friend said otherwise. Logic said that was idiotic, that in the long-term, a better solution was needed.

Yet she would have to suffer until that 'better solution' was reached.

I didn't want her to suffer...but it was also a choice of saving one person or thousands. That complicated matters. In a way, either one seemed like a selfish choice.

I shifted when I heard a tea cup rattling in its saucer. Soon after, the smell of chocolate reached my nose. Bruce's blue light blinked at me, then slid along its track and over to my desk. A steaming cup of hot chocolate sat waiting for me. It'd been a while since I'd seen Bruce utilize the apartment's fancier features.

Then again, I did usually do things for myself.

"Thanks, Bruce," I murmured, pulling myself off the bed. Once I sat down at my desk, I took a sip of the hot chocolate and sighed.

"Miss Alice is strong," Bruce stated after a moment. *"Stronger than you credit her with."*

I must have looked awful if even my AI was trying to cheer me up. I glanced over at his light, contemplating the day I'd just had. "We only have a day to work with, Bruce. If I'm going to make the right decision, then we're going to have to make the most of it. Will you help?"

"Of course, Cerys."

Chapter Eleven
Cejari-ir

Everything smelled different.

My eyes snapped open, revealing an unfamiliar ceiling, lush emerald décor, and a pleasantly warm room. I cautiously sat up and froze when I felt my tail twist, jamming up against my spine. "Fucking hell!"

Once out of bed, I rubbed my rump and whimpered. If I hadn't been awake before, I sure as hell was now. I was beyond relieved once I realized that I was in my rooms in Nabyr-zahn and *not* in Darmos. I had no intention of going back to that damned city unless it was with an army to liberate it.

And by 'liberate,' I meant burn it to the fucking ground.

Someone had been tending to my demon body while I was gone. I was clean, as were my nightgown and bed linens. My hair was barely tangled despite having been asleep. After poking my head through a few doors, I found a handful of dresses and sandals waiting for me. I picked the closest one, dressed myself, and then made my way toward the double doors leading out.

"Lady Cerys!" An armored man looked bewildered when I opened the door.

"We were expecting her," a voice stated from my right. Emrys gave us a sheepish smile. "I was on my way to tell you. Guess the gods were impatient."

"They didn't give me any warning either." I turned to look up at him. "Did they say how long I have here?"

"They expect you to announce your decision after the tour." Emrys' pleasant expression melted away as he examined me. "You look awful. What happened?"

"You'll all find out soon enough," I sighed, crossing my arms loosely over my stomach. His frown deepened, and he looked like he intended to inquire further, but he must have changed his mind. Emrys motioned for me to follow him after giving the guard brief instructions to continue protecting my room.

"You hungry?" He glanced at me.

"I may not have an appetite for a while," I stated.

"That bad?"

"That bad," I confirmed.

"Should we be worried?"

"Assuming you don't already know, you should be pissed."

Emrys' expression became one of contemplation as we walked but he said nothing more. He could probably tell I didn't intend to say anything else. I wasn't allowed to—yet. A quick e-mail from Iris had seen to that. Besides, the fewer times I had to repeat it, the better. And…there was still the possibility that the demons were just as twisted.

"So, you came after all," Idris commented as we walked into the small garden he'd been waiting in. He paused when he turned to look at me and then smiled. "I would prefer that we didn't waste each other's time. When you return to the humans—"

"Take me on a tour of Cejari-ir," I cut him off. A subtle frown crossed his face as he examined me before he shot a questioning glance at Emrys. The demon in question only nodded once in response. "I am reserving judgment until after. You should show me the same respect."

"Even when it appears your mind is already made up?" Idris crossed his arms and planted his feet shoulder width apart. When my reply was only to sigh, he narrowed his eyes at me. "You are less fiery than before."

"You seem like the sort of man who believes actions speak louder than words, but you won't let me do either." I shot him an agitated glare. "I'm not supposed to make or announce my decision until after you've shown me your city, in case you've forgotten."

"Silas trusted her for a reason," Emrys spoke up, startling me. Not only was I surprised by the mention of Silas, but Emrys wasn't exactly the first person I'd thought would defend me. He noticed my look and shrugged. "Silas sent us a pretty portrait and your name, along with a letter about you and Ebonwing. Something about wanting to keep you safe when we invade."

"So, he was serious when he offered me help?" I arched an eyebrow.

"You're not the only one who struggles to read him," Idris remarked dryly. He raised his hands, shrugging. "Fine—you want to see the city, I will take you to see the city."

"It's not like I'm asking you to cut something off," I pointed out with a huff. Emrys snorted and quickly covered his laughter, while Idris just stared at me. "I don't understand why you're being so stubborn about this. Is it really so hard to give me the benefit of the doubt?"

"You're wasted on the humans." Idris left it at that as he passed me. When I didn't follow right away, he shot an impatient look over his shoulder.

"I'll look after the palace while you two're out," Emrys shrugged, leaving me with the king.

That struck me as odd. Emrys was meant to be one of Idris' closest companions and the one in charge of the king's protection. Yet he wasn't insisting on an escort? I looked back at the king, only to find he had wandered off without me. Pursing my lips, I picked up my pace and hurried after him.

"You will need a cloak." Idris glanced down at me as I caught up to him. "We can fetch one on the way. I would have had one prepared for you if I had realized you were so bullheaded."

"My personality *could* work in your favor, you know." I prodded him in the arm with one finger. "Look, I get your lack of trust. It's not my strong suit either. Humans suck. I'm not asking you to trust me. I just want the benefit of the doubt—and the same base respect you would give to any other new acquaintance."

"That's all?" Idris gave me a doubtful look.

"That's all," I nodded, doing my best to remain amiable. Idris was doing a *fantastic* job of agitating me despite how recently I'd arrived. His behavior struck me as illogical for someone who needed help, but I figured there had to be a reason for it—even if I wasn't privy to it yet. "Besides, I'm not allowed to tell you anything until I've been given a tour of your city."

"Unless you marry me." Idris shot me a confident smirk.

"You must be joking," I scoffed. "Granted, I can't imagine how a *king*—let alone an *incubus* king—would find himself so desperate that he'd have to chase after an Otherworlder."

"Perhaps I simply find you that beautiful?"

"Bullshit."

"At least, when you keep your mouth closed."

"I should punch you."

"Again?"

"Again."

Idris pursed his lips, before turning away and striding toward a nearby door. I heard him speak to someone briefly, and a moment later he returned with two cloaks in hand. He offered me one but didn't let go when I grabbed it.

"If you wish for me to treat you with a certain level of respect, it would help if you returned the favor." He narrowed his eyes at me.

"It's hard for me to take you seriously when first you try to kill me, and then you claim I should marry you," I countered as he finally allowed me to take the cloak.

"You would be safer if you said 'yes.'" He shrugged and strode down the hallway. "What *are* you permitted to tell me about your visit to the Issradian Empire?"

"That your company is infinitely better than theirs," I responded. *Safer?* The claim seemed so ludicrous I didn't know where to begin.

"Despite your protests?" He arched an eyebrow as I fell into step with him.

"Yes."

"What is their emperor like? I have yet to meet this one."

"Hmmm?" I glanced up at him, frowning. "I didn't meet him."

Idris stopped in his tracks and turned to furrow his brow at me. "*What?* It's the ruler's responsibility to see to the gods' champion!"

"I was shown around by his adviser and the guard captain." I shook my head slightly. "As far as I'm aware, I didn't even get a glimpse of the man. Unless…"

"Unless?"

"I'm not allowed to say yet," I grimaced. "After the tour, sure."

"Does it perhaps have something to do with your change in demeanor?" Idris' piercing gaze made me shift in discomfort and look away from him. "I suppose it can wait. What do you wish to learn of Cejari-ir?"

"All I got in Darmos was a carriage ride around the city," I murmured, my gaze flicking around the interior of the palace. There was art everywhere, but all of it was scenes of war or fantastical illustrations. Not a single portrait of Idris, former royals, or nobles. Finally, I returned my attention to Idris and said, "Given that, my expectations aren't very high, and I'm sure you have a mountain of work to attend to as well, so—"

"If there is even the slightest chance that you might choose us, then it is my duty to see that you learn all you need," Idris cut me off, raising one hand as if to silence protests. "We will walk through the city and you may ask me questions. It would be best if we are finished before nightfall."

"Why is tha—goddamn, it's cold!" I bristled the moment he opened the palace doors.

"That would be why." Idris pulled his cloak around himself. "It is autumn. Soon enough, there will be snow on the ground and it will be much colder."

I clutched my cloak tightly around myself and followed Idris out of the palace. Sandals and a lightweight gown were definitely *not* suitable for the weather, but the sudden change in temperature had given me my first question. "How is the palace so warm?"

"Do you not have heated homes in your world?" He tilted his head slightly.

"We do—I just didn't expect Jeriskyr to have them."

"Nabyr-zahn uses magitech—ah..." He glanced at me as if attempting to determine how much he needed to explain.

"I'm familiar with the concept. Machines run via magic or magical materials, right?" I offered.

"We use magitech for many things," Idris continued, nodding. "It is integral to our way of life. The lights you see, the running water within the palace, the far-more-agreeable temperature, and the kitchens are all dependent on it. The majority of Cejari-ir utilizes magitech in the same manner."

They were more advanced than I'd given them credit for. I examined my surroundings with interest. Much like the palace, the city beyond it was beautiful and alien. There were occasional patterns or other motifs that struck me as similar to things from Earth, but they were few and far between.

The city had been built around several streams, creeks, and even a river. It had been cold enough the previous night that the edges of each one had remnants of ice clinging to their banks. I spotted the glimmer of frost in many buildings' shadows.

What I didn't see much of was people.

"Why did you choose to appear in the mountains?" Idris' voice from beside me startled me into turning and looking up at him. I had no idea when he had drawn so close, and I still couldn't get a read on what he was thinking or feeling.

"The mountains? Ah…" I shook my head. "I didn't *choose* to go there—I was dropped. Literally. Up until that point they'd continued to give me the illusion that I was simply playing a new game. Your *gods* have barely given me a chance to ask about it."

"No warning whatsoever?" He gave me a skeptical look.

"None."

"Then I am even more impressed by how quickly you adapted to the situation," he remarked, rubbing his chin as he examined me. "I saw you fall from the sky. I was intrigued—until you began causing havoc, at any rate."

"I caused 'havoc' because I had a pissed-off demon king in gods know how much armor barreling after me," I pointed out with a snort.

"You are never going to let that go, are you?" There was a mildly plaintive tone to Idris' voice that I struggled to not laugh at. It was the first real indication of emotion beyond protectiveness over his city that I'd seen since my arrival.

I attempted to soften the blow, sort of. "I will eventually. Maybe. Depends on if you try it again."

He raised an eyebrow. "Then do not give me a reason to."

I didn't plan to, but I kept the thought to myself, deciding it would probably overstep the deities' stupid rules. Besides, there was still the possibility for him to show he was worse than the humans. I didn't think he was, but I preferred to make certain. Jumping to any more conclusions than I already had didn't seem good for my health.

Though it would have helped if his emotions had been clearer. While pleasant, the mask he wore let too little slip past.

"That way is the residential quarter." Idris pointed to his left, then motioned in front of us. "And this road leads to the merchants, artisans, and guilds. The road to your right would take us to more guilds and residences—the ones there are related to combat.

"Where would you like to go?"

He was being rather accommodating despite his protests, which left me wondering how he actually felt. "I'm mostly curious about your people. When I was in Darmos the first time, I got a decent handle on what the humans of the Issradian Empire are like. The same can't be said for the demons of Nabyr-zahn."

"You are interested in the people?" he murmured, before glancing down at me when I shivered. "Very well. At this time of evening they are likely in the taverns. We will go there."

I followed him through the empty streets and examined the buildings as we went. Everything appeared to be in good condition, but the scarcity of people unnerved me. By the time we reached a small plaza with a fountain in the middle, I could count the number of people we had passed on one hand.

"Oh! If it isn't His Majesty!" A man with ginger hair grinned when we entered the tavern. It didn't take long for him to notice me. "Who's this, then? I don't recall seeing any new Otherworlders coming through."

"Is it that obvious?" I wondered aloud, curious as to how they could tell, since I had a succubus' body.

"She's the new champion." Idris smirked and shot me a sideways glance. "And my new queen if she would give me the time of—"

"Do you *want* me to punch you?" I demanded. "Is it your fetish or something to get beaten up by a woman two-thirds your size?"

I took a deep breath, forcing myself to cool off. My emotions were still running high because of my experience in Darmos, but I knew better than to turn it against my tour guide—and potential ally. Bitch mode needed to power down.

"I could just command you to behave." Idris patted me between my horns and strode deeper into the tavern, pulling his cloak off. He didn't seem at all bothered that the building was jam-packed with his subjects or that they weren't prostrating themselves before him. "Bryn, I'll have my usual. Lady Cerys will have tea and stew."

"I don't—" I started to object but fell silent at the look he gave me.

"When did you last eat?" he questioned.

"Uh…" I trailed off. The genuine concern in Idris' eyes made me falter, but food and I hadn't really agreed much the past few days.

"I thought as much." Idris nodded briefly before turning his gaze to the black-haired demon named Bryn. "As I said—tea and stew for the lady."

Everyone in the tavern was male, aside from me. The patrons, the servers, the bartender, and even the few kitchen staff I caught glimpses of. It was drastically different from the corseted wenches I'd grown used to in games. While I didn't necessarily mind being surrounded by men, I had to wonder where the women who *didn't* work in the palace were.

I knew where I hoped they *weren't*.

"Now then, what's this 'queen' business?" Bryn walked over and placed a gigantic cup of tea in front of me before turning to look at Idris. He placed a large mug of something that smelled of alcohol in front of the king. "She's pretty and all, but…"

"It would have been a simple way to skip the process and secure a champion for our side, for once," Idris responded as he hefted the mug.

"Aye it would, but you needn't sacrifice—" Bryn paused and glanced over his shoulder at me. "No offense, lass. It's just…Otherworlders don't tend to stay."

"I'd have to be insane to have said 'yes,' given the circumstances." I pulled my tea closer. "From my perspective, it's just as ridiculous as a stranger on the street walking up and asking to marry me."

The two men chatted a bit longer, eventually coming to the topic of how I had arrived in Jeriskyr the first time. Idris took it upon himself to explain the battle I'd 'dropped in on,' but didn't make it past the part about me punching him in the jaw. Bryn and the men close enough to hear were soon howling with laughter.

"So, the rumors are true about Cerys here being different than the usual girls the gods choose!" Bryn cackled, though I frowned slightly.

"Do they always choose women?" I asked, a knot growing in my stomach. There were only a few possible reasons for that choice.

"Aye, always," Bryn nodded. "Ah—but I should go check on your food."

Before I could ask him anything else, the cheerful demon was off. I hesitantly raised my cup of tea to my lips, took a small sip, and found myself thankful that he'd already sweetened it for me. Maybe the demons weren't so bad after all.

I eyed Idris over the rim of my cup.

Well, the ones I could read, anyway.

"Tell me, why were you interested in the people?" Idris sat back with his mug as he examined me. The citizens seemed nice enough, but their monarch? That was up in the air.

"I wanted a better feel for how they feel about Nabyr-zahn and you," I replied honestly, setting my cup down. "Of course, I could have asked you, but you'd be biased."

"So, you wanted to see how the people act and what state the city itself is in?" Idris gave me a skeptical look.

"What better way for me to see if they respect you as their ruler and if you're a good one?" I shrugged, choosing not to take his skepticism personally. "Like I said before, we don't have kings in my world. We don't have queens, either. That manner of rule was abandoned after the last two World Wars."

"Last two?" Idris leaned forward. Of all the things to pique his interest, it figured *war* would be the most effective. "Just how many 'World Wars' has your world experienced? And are they *truly* world-wide?"

"Yes, truly world-wide," I replied dryly. "We've had four. They appear to enjoy coming in pairs. After the last one, a world-wide government was founded. Each region has a representative on the council, and the council votes on laws or anything else that would affect the world as a whole. Lesser matters are handled by the regional representatives."

"How strange," Idris remarked, shifting to cross his legs. An intrigued expression had replaced his pleasant mask, his eyes bright with curiosity. "Humans are often impatient creatures, but they also refuse to ever agree on anything. How does this 'council' of yours ever get anything done?"

"They have deadlines and there's an odd number of representatives," I began, tapping my nails against the table. "They're not allowed to abstain from voting, either. If someone refuses to vote, they're honorably removed from the council and a replacement is found. That doesn't happen often, though."

"How are councilors chosen?" Idris prompted.

"World-wide vote." *That* earned a dubious look in response.

"Sounds like a pain in the arse," Bryn remarked, setting a massive bowl of what smelled like beef stew with a beer-based stock in front of me. Next came several thick slices of steaming hot bread. My stomach rumbled loudly in response to the smell. There was *definitely* bacon in it. Excellent. "Well, don't hold back on our account then, milady!"

"So, the kitten's mouth is not the only thing that roars," Idris smirked.

"You don't want any food, Idris?" Bryn glanced at the king as I growled.

"I've already dined." Idris shook his head. "I underestimated how stubborn this one would be."

"You mean you thought I would pick the humans for stupid reasons." I pointed my spoon at him.

"Given our track record with winning over champions, can't say I blame him," Bryn remarked. He shot me a crooked grin when I shoveled a heaping spoonful of stew into my mouth. "I'll leave you to your food. He was clearly right about you not having eaten in a while."

Oh, shove it, I thought as I chowed down. It was good. Like, really good. Maybe it was because the meat and vegetables hadn't been grown in a lab somewhere, or maybe Bryn was just that amazing of a chef. Or perhaps the whole 'hunger is the best seasoning' mindset held a facet of truth.

"Just how long has it been since you've eaten?" Idris looked flabbergasted.

"Maybe a day or two," I replied, after swallowing a mouthful of food.

"…and how long since you finished your tour of Darmos?" Idris frowned, a hint of concern showing through again.

"A day or two."

"You were given time to think?" Idris looked surprised, and a moment later he tilted his head. "*They* do not usually give champions time to think before sending them our way. Did you ask for time?"

"No, I didn't." I grimaced and picked up my tea. "Sure needed it, though."

"Then why insist on your tour here?" Idris rested one elbow on the table and placed his cheek in his hand. "You appear to have made up your mind already, yet you insist that we do things the proper way. Other champions believed a walk around the palace to be sufficient before declaring their decision. You are also far more willing to converse than they ever were."

"For someone who is supposedly so smart, you are incredibly stupid." I pointed at him with my spoon again. It had to be a sin *somewhere* for such a physically attractive man to be so oblivious. Snorts of laughter erupted all around us as Idris bristled. I shot him a smug smile and decided to tease him more. "I knew you were delusional when you suggested I marry you. *This* delusional, though? I'm disappointed."

"Why you—" Idris growled, revealing his fangs.

"You two'll get along just fine!" Bryn grinned as he returned with two plates, a large slice of some type of pie on each one. He set one in front of Idris and the other near me. "Don't hold it against him, lass. We've all watched dozens of Otherworlders come and go—champion or not. It's less painful for us to believe you won't choose us."

"It's less amusing when you make sense." I shook my head. "Look at it objectively, for a moment. If you were in my situation and you were told that you had to make a decision that would potentially bring about the end of one side—what would you do?"

"Give both sides as good an inspection as I could," Bryn nodded. "New world, new people. Both mean new cultures. Just because people look like your own doesn't mean—"

"—that they are the same," Idris finished with a reluctant sigh. "I cannot fault your approach, Cerys. However, if you *do not* choose us then this has been an immense waste of my time, and I am a busy man."

"One who is pretending not to be worried about what I saw in Darmos," I pointed out, earning a crooked smile in reply. "I promise that I will tell you once we've finished with this tour. Even if I didn't, you would soon hear it from your gods."

"You told them?" Bryn arched an eyebrow at me and then looked to Idris with a stern expression. "In that case, *Your Majesty*, give her a chance! When was the last time a champion divulged anything to us or to our gods?"

"Now you are falling for her too?" Idris sighed.

"Too?" Bryn smirked, clearly getting the wrong impression.

"Silas seems to trust her as well," Idris muttered. With a look of reluctance, he turned his attention back to me. "What do you want to see after you finish eating?"

"Hmmm…" I tilted my head and pretended to think. In truth, I knew what I wanted to ask, but he had a habit of annoying me. He could wait a little for my answer. "How about your favorite place?"

"My, how bold you are to ask to see a man's bed, kitten," Idris purred. He let out a rumbling laugh when I swatted at him.

"That's not what I meant!" I snapped, attempting to fight off the way his tone and his laugh made my heart flutter.

"Of course," he chuckled, shooting me an inviting smile. "However, it *is* my favorite place. I rarely find time to rest and my bed is the only place that work does not follow."

"Okay, how about your favorite *non-bed* place?" I rolled my eyes.

"Why do you care?"

"I don't. I'm trying to get an idea of what sort of man you are,"
I replied. At least, it was half-true. The longer we talked, and the
more he teased me, the more curious I became about what made
him tick. *Caring* was too strong a word, though.

"His favorite place is the mountainside overlooking the city,"
Bryn stated. The king sighed and gave the man a frustrated look.
"You won't be going anywhere near there dressed like that, though,
lass."

"You like to look down at the city?" I asked, skeptical.

He motioned vaguely with one hand. "I am proud of what
Cejari-ir has been able to build and maintain through the centuries,
despite our troubles. You can see the entire city, and the palace,
from the mountains. It is especially beautiful at night."

"And you'd freeze if he took you up there," Bryn added, before
motioning toward my feet. "Or slice your feet to ribbons. Not sure
which would happen first."

"Speaking of the cold, we should go soon if you are finished."
Idris looked to me with a firm gaze.

"I'm finished." I nodded before looking to Bryn with a smile.
"It was delicious, Bryn. I'll have to see about coming back for
more."

"Coming back—" Idris cut himself off and darted after me as
I headed for the door. Once outside, he bristled, baring his fangs

at me again. "You should not give my people false hope!"

"Say what you want," I shrugged. "I'm learning to ignore you."

I wandered off down the road and Idris soon caught up to me, seething in what I considered unwarranted rage. He shot me an agitated glare, but his gaze softened slightly when his eyes met mine. *I* was determined, regardless of what he thought. Idris was a pain in the ass, that was certain, but it seemed to mostly be out of concern for his people. I could respect that.

Idris opened and closed his mouth a few times before finally sighing, his shoulders drooping. "I have another favorite place. It has a similar view to the mountains, but it is inside the palace where it is warm."

"Lead the way," I smiled, watching him falter.

"I… Very well." Idris straightened and then glanced down at me again. After a moment, he looked away but offered me his arm. "You should stay close."

I decided to take his arm and let him lead me back toward the palace. By now, there were no citizens on the streets, only the occasional guard or soldier. It was cold enough for our breath to fog in the air and for deep breaths to sting, yet the sun was still in the process of setting. The sky was alight with a myriad of colors, dyeing the snowy mountains nearby in pinks, oranges, and purples.

Despite the cold, there appeared to be a few plants native to the region that flowered even in such low temperatures. There were many throughout the city, sparkling in various colors beneath a growing layer of frost.

"You are more curious about us, and our city, than I expected," Idris spoke after a few minutes, looking down at me with a quizzical expression.

I studied him for a moment, attempting to read beyond his curiosity. Alas, I couldn't make out anything else. I was beginning to wish I could peek inside his head to find out what he was really thinking, and what he truly wanted.

"Cejari-ir is quite pretty and is entirely foreign to me," I stated, half-shrugging. "There are occasional elements here that remind me of my world, but overall, I can't label anything here as being distinctly from any of the civilizations on Earth. Past or present."

"There...are *some* elements?" Idris asked slowly.

"A pattern here, a painting there, a style of architecture elsewhere," I replied, thinking back on everything. "My first impression of your palace was that it was similar to at least three or four ancient styles from Earth. However, the way they meld together makes it clear that the similarities are either a coincidence, or that perhaps people from this world and others like it may have influenced Earth cultures."

"I still can't believe your people call your world *Earth*!" Idris shook his head. I couldn't help but laugh at him.

"It probably won't change any time soon," I grinned. "Can you imagine trying to get billions of people to agree on something like that?"

"Billions?" Idris stared at me, so stunned that his mask dropped entirely. Unfortunately, he soon recovered.

"Humans breed like rabbits," I pointed out.

"You seem to think poorly of your own kind," Idris commented with a reserved frown.

"Hmmm? Some of them, sure," I replied. "I'm just being realistic. My species is growing at such an unsustainable rate that we had to begin building our cities *up* instead of *out* in order to still have arable land."

"Up, you say?" Idris murmured, rubbing his chin with his free hand. Though subtle, he had the look of a man who had begun planning something.

"Was just about to come looking for you two," Emrys called, giving us a short wave as he strolled down the road toward us. He nodded toward me and added, "I'm surprised you got him to stay out as long as you did."

"She had not eaten in 'a day or two,'" Idris stated, glancing at me before looking at Emrys again. The other demon frowned and cocked his head. "I have decided we will convene in the gardens. We will not be needing tea. You may come if you like, Emrys."

"I want to hear what she has to say too," Emrys nodded.

Honestly, I hadn't expected a garden to be our destination. I accompanied the men to the palace. Once there, a servant took my cloak.

Idris and Emrys led me through the ornate corridors and then through an archway. Beyond it was a sprawling garden with blooming trees and flowers. It had been allowed to grow wild and untamed. Vines crawled across the walkways, up the walls, and around pillars. Some had even begun to creep up the legs of various benches and other seats throughout. The air smelled of fresh earth, rain, and many types of blooming flowers.

"My favorite place," Idris offered, leading me to the balcony surrounding the outer edge of the garden.

"I can see why." I leaned against the railing and looked down at the city, then turned to look at the garden. Idris perched on a nearby chair and nestled back against it, sighing. "I suppose you want my answer now?"

"It would be nice, yes." Idris' gaze flicked toward me. "Granted, I think I—"

"I choose Nabyr-zahn," I stated, watching as his eyes widened. I swallowed the urge to tease him for *still* doubting me.

After a moment, he shot to his feet again and took several steps toward me. "I refuse."

"What?" I yelped, my pulse skyrocketing and a lump forming in my throat. "You can't do that, can you? Don't make me go back—"

"Idris? What in the hells are you thinking?" Emrys demanded, grabbing me by the arm and pulling me back behind him slightly.

"*Let me finish!*" Idris exclaimed. "*Both* of you!"

"Yes, an explanation would be wise," Iris remarked as she

appeared between us. She did *not* look happy.

"I will not accept her as your champion until I have had a chance to see *her* world for myself," Idris stated, turning to look at Iris. However, he soon returned his gaze to me when I collapsed in place. "Cerys? What—"

"That was so cruel!" I pulled my knees to my chest and buried my face in my thighs. "I spent so much time agonizing over this stupid fucking choice and then you go and give me a heart attack!"

"There, there," Iris cooed, patting me on the head. "His intent wasn't to doom you, Cerys, I assure you. It will be fine. Very well, Idris. I can give you a week on Earth—no more."

"Don't I get a say in—" I started, but it was too late.

Chapter Twelve
Earth

I groaned and pulled my pillow over my head to silence the infernal alarm blaring in my room. Only a few seconds passed before my mind caught up and I realized that I heard masculine voices arguing.

"Release me, phantasm!" Idris snarled.

"Mistress Cerys, I have captured the intruder for you," Bruce stated as I sat up in bed. *"What would you like me to do with him?"*

"Oh?" I remarked, glancing over to my door. Sure enough, Idris was in human-ish form and being held captive by a cage of electricity. He was completely nude, revealing his muscular body, numerous battle scars, and his rather impressive...well. I certainly couldn't let him know I thought that.

I pulled myself out of bed and stretched, then glanced down. Oops.

"Have you no shame, woman?!" Idris demanded.

"You're the one intruding in *my* room," I pointed out, glancing over my shoulder. Shrugging, I addressed Bruce next. "You can let him go, Bruce. He's our guest—add Idris Bloodsong to our visitor list."

"As you wish." Bruce dropped the demon king on his rump as I strode across my room.

Idris looked up at me questioningly when I stopped in front of him. To his credit, he met my eyes instead of staring elsewhere.

"Scoot over." I pointed toward the door to his right. "I can't get dressed if you're blocking my way to the closet."

"Ah..." Idris cleared his throat and then pulled himself to his feet before moving out of my way. "You appeared upset with my declaration. What—"

"Upset? You scared the shit out of me!" I snapped, shooting him a sideways glare before opening my closet. "What the fuck were you thinking, pulling something like that? I was about—"

"Surely you have people you care about in this world," Idris stated, causing me to shoot him a frown. "If I had simply accepted your decision, you would not have had the opportunity to return and tell them goodbye. Even if you succeed and *want* to return to

Earth, there is no guarantee anyone you know will be alive when you do. Demons live for a long time if we are not killed."

"You were trying to be considerate?" I asked begrudgingly, my heart clenching.

He nodded.

There wasn't really anyone I wanted to talk to, let alone say goodbye to, who weren't in Ebonwing. Besides, how was I meant to say 'goodbye' to anyone when I was supposed to keep them from knowing Jeriskyr was real?

I sighed again and yanked two robes out of my closet. The second, I threw toward his groin. He was so worried about *my* nudity that he didn't seem to have noticed his, and I was beginning to feel guilty about admiring the scenery.

"What..." Idris trailed off once he looked down. "Ah."

"Hmmm, what time is it?" I muttered, striding past Idris in search of a clock. Six in the morning. Wonderful. The utter *opposite* of when I had wanted to wake up.

"This is your home?" Idris asked. I glanced over my shoulder at him to find him poking around my bedroom with undisguised curiosity. When he noticed me looking, he cast me a small frown. "You are still angry. Just what did you see in the Issradian Empire?"

"*Tch*, do you really want to know?" I grimaced, before striding toward the kitchen. "I'm going to make tea, if you want some."

"Tell me." Idris placed a hand on my shoulder. "I did not mean for you to think that I was sending you back to...whatever it is you saw. If it is truly so horrible, then I would have you tell me what it is. My intention was to be considerate."

"Something you should be pissed off about," I stated, chewing on my lower lip while I contemplated how to explain it. Finally, I pointed toward the bathroom. "If you feel like you're going to be sick, do it in there, please. You should be able to recognize the toilet."

I wasn't entirely sure just how battle-hardened the king was, but I also wasn't in the mood to clean vomit off the floor. He seemed to care greatly about his people, so I figured it was better safe than sorry.

"It is truly so appalling?" Idris watched me with a furrowed brow as I sat down in the kitchen.

I fidgeted with my hands in my lap for a moment, considering how blunt to be or how much detail to use. While it was something he needed to know, I also didn't want to convey it in a manner that turned me into the target of his anger.

"The reason that your kind haven't secured any champions is, quite simply, because of an ultimatum the humans propose when one comes to tour Darmos," I began with a heavy sigh. Idris sat across from me, his expression still one of concern. "They do take us on a carriage ride through the city, but it ends with them taking us to a dark, filthy area behind the castle. Once there, they open a hatch in the ground and lead us into a series of underground rooms that smell of sex, piss, shit, vomit, and death."

"*What*—" Idris silenced himself, a growing expression of horror creeping across his face. He looked as if he'd just had an epiphany of some kind.

"They have dozens of inhuman and mixed-breed women chained down there," I spat, interrupting the stunned king. "The bastards called it the 'breeding pens.' They think that the champion's purpose is to be bred with the human soldiers and nobles. They're trying to produce an elite bloodline.

"Sons are either killed or used as frontline fodder. Daughters are sent to the brothels to be raised. Later in life, once they're old enough, they're brought back to the breeding pens. They want a 'pure' bloodline—"

Before I could finish, Idris was out of his seat and had run to the bathroom. I rose to my feet and strode over to the kitchen sink to pour him a tall glass of water, adding honey and lemon to it. When the retching stopped, I strode over to the doorway and handed him a spare toothbrush and a tube of toothpaste from the pantry. "You can clean your mouth out with these if you want. I left water on the table for you."

Without another word, I returned to the kitchen table to wait. Comforting people was not my forte. It wasn't long before he rejoined me.

"They..." Idris faltered, then shook his head. "You spoke of an ultimatum."

"Me, or my closest friend," I stated simply, watching his eyes widen. "My choice between the empire or your kingdom determines which one of us goes to the breeding pens. The human gods appear to make their choice of champion based off whoever is close to the champion *your* gods choose."

"Then…your friend…" Idris frowned, looking at me as if he wasn't sure what to think. "You are choosing to not take her place?"

"Now you know why I needed time to think," I nodded, a knot rising in my throat. There was no 'winning' choice, but that didn't make matters better. "In a way, taking her place would be the easy way out. It would mean she would be safe. It's a trade of lives—mine for hers. She isn't capable of combat in Jeriskyr. Her specialties are gathering and making things. In the long-term she wouldn't be helpful to Nabyr-zahn at all. She would basically be seeking asylum with you.

"However, I *can* fight. I can also strategize. You intend to conquer the Issradian Empire, I intend to rescue my friend. Given what those *bastards* are doing, I can't imagine you could think of the human 'champion' as your mortal enemy."

"No… That's…" Idris shook his head hard, scowling. "The bastards have made a mockery of the god's game. Corlyotir must be furious."

"Corlyotir?" I asked, puzzled.

"The goddess who brought us here." Idris motioned to the room.

"Oh. So that's her actual name," I muttered.

"So, you thought I was dooming you to…" Idris paused, a look of regret crossing his face. He shifted to face me fully and bowed his head, startling me. "I apologize, Cerys. It was not my intent to frighten you or make you think that I would send you back to such a place. I never imagined those pigs would… I am sorry."

"What's done is done," I sighed. "I accept your apology. However, I meant what I said about rescuing Alice. I refuse to let her rot in that place. This has become about more than simply getting back home for me."

"Why?" Idris asked simply.

"Why what?" I frowned.

"Why are you so intent on returning home?" Idris challenged.

"I…" I pursed my lips. "It's all I've ever known."

"And?"

"That's it. It's what I know and am familiar with."

"Family? Friends?"

"I don't really have family." I grimaced, shaking my head. "Friends…sure."

"Then…it is possible you will choose to stay." He shot me an unreadable smile.

"Unlikely," I stated. It didn't matter how many times I'd fantasized about living in another world, or about being swept off my feet by some hot inhuman man. The reality was that I was human…and should return to where my kind belonged.

"This 'Alice' girl—you're certain that they will send her to that place?" Idris narrowed his eyes. "You do not believe they were bluffing?"

"I don't think they were, no." I shook my head. "Speaking of…she and I haven't spoken since this mess started. I should probably call her myself to inform her of my decision and why I made it."

"You would tell her yourself that you doomed her?" Idris looked baffled.

"I would prefer she hears it from me." I grimaced again, striding over to a screen embedded into a nearby wall. Whether he'd meant it to or not, that comment had stung a bit. "Bruce, open the curtains, please. See to it that Idris has whatever he needs and answer any questions he has. Honestly, please."

"Yes, Mistress Cerys."

"The curtains—" Idris started to say something but fell silent when they slid open to reveal a view of the city. Soon enough, he was out of his seat with his glass of water in hand. He didn't stop until he was at the windows, staring out at the landscape of steel and glass. "When you said your people build 'up,' I did not imagine it was on this scale."

I remained silent and flicked through several menus, shooting Alice a message to ask about her dinner plans. When she responded seconds later, she made fun of me for being awake already and seemed her usual, cheerful self. It made me feel worse. I clenched my teeth and asked her to meet me and my 'plus one' for dinner.

She immediately got the wrong idea.

However, she had a 'plus one' too.

I frowned. She never referred to Ryan like that, so I wasn't sure if she was just making fun of me or if she had a guest of her own.

"Cerys?" Idris called me like it wasn't the first time.

"Sorry, I was sending messages to Alice. What did you want?" I asked.

"How far behind your world is the Issradian Empire?"

"Several hundred years," I replied.

"Tell me... What made you decide to side with us instead of freeing your friend?" Idris looked at me with an unreadable expression. "If the past champions chose to switch places to save their friends, then what of you? Why is your choice different?"

"I'll admit that self-preservation is part of it—but I don't know why at least *some* of the other champions wouldn't have done the same." I sighed, crossing my arms over my stomach. "I grew up in a place where women are essentially slaves anyway. Except there the women are brainwashed into thinking it's their greatest joy to serve the man they were assigned to marry.

"I was a smart kid. I figured out early on it was bullshit and planned a way to escape. I've been free of those bastards for a decade or so now, and winding up in a similar, or worse, situation is something I want to avoid."

"You are not from this city, then?" Idris asked, glancing out the wall of windows.

"No." I walked over to join him. "My 'family' runs an extremist religious compound well outside of the city. The government is struggling to find legal ways to prosecute the people who run the compound. It's one of those cases where their own laws are holding them back. When I escaped, it was on foot and in the middle of the night. The police detained me when I stumbled into the city. I was an absolute mess, but I'd made it.

"This region's representative helped me get on my feet. My apartment is in one of the residential buildings he owns, and my 'allowance' comes directly from the government. It's not much, so he helps...a lot. I'm not permitted to work or attend public universities until the government finds a *legal* way to deal with the religious compound I escaped from. They're required to find a peaceable way through the mess...which they aren't going to find, I think.

"I stay here most of the time. My 'family' sends people into the city every now and then to look for me. They want to take me back."

"So, joining the Issradians would be like trading one form of slavery for another," Idris murmured mostly to himself, frowning.

"Maybe it's arrogant or delusional of me, but I think I have a good chance at saving Alice from the bastards," I added, glancing to the side at the demon king. He was a little *too* easy to talk to. "We both have good reasons for wanting to overthrow the Issradian Empire. You to save your people, me to save the first friend I made in this city. Alice comes off as dainty and fragile to most who see her...but she's not. She's strong. A survivor. However, I don't know how long she will last in those conditions."

"It is possible that our gods will be able to save her," Idris stated, turning to look at me. "At the very least, they may be able to change the game the human gods are playing. Using the champions in such a manner is sick and was never the intent of their game.

"If the humans are insistent on breeding...then our gods may be able to convince them to allow your friend to marry a noble instead. While not ideal, it wouldn't be difficult to make an improvement to her situation."

"I'd rather not get my hopes up." I shook my head. "Anyway, that's my story. My decision was made based on both self-preservation and confidence in our ability to overthrow the bastards. At any rate, your company is much better than theirs. Even without their bullshit ultimatum, I was inclined to choose Nabyr-zahn. Now then, we need to find you something to wear. I think I may have some men's clothes around here..."

"Cerys."

"What?"

"Thank you for sharing your story with me." Idris caught my hand and brought it to his lips, catching me off-guard. "I was concerned about your motives and your loyalty. If you were willing to betray your friend, then there would have been no way to trust you. However, even if you may be arrogant, it is clear you do not intend to abandon her.

"Now that you have declared your decision, you cannot go back on it, even if you change your mind about what the best course of action is. You stated your decision to me, and Corlyotir heard you. Even if I refuse you, the gods will simply send you to a different demonic kingdom."

"Can you let go of my hand now?" I shot him an irritated look.

"Why?" The corners of his mouth curled into an alluring smile.

"Because I need to go find clothes for you to wear."

"You could take me out of them instead." Idris' purring tone sent an unwelcome wave of heat through me. I'd *almost* forgotten he was an incubus.

"How about 'no?'" I shook my head and yanked my hand from his before stalking off toward the room I stored things in. Charming. Dangerously charming. I would have to be more careful than I'd first thought. "You wanted to see my world, right? We're meeting Alice for dinner tonight. You're going to need appropriate clothes."

I rummaged through the boxes in the room, listening as Idris followed. When I glanced back, he was leaning against the door and watching me with an unreadable expression. Returning to my search, I soon found a pair of men's jeans and a loose sweater I thought might fit him. Shoes would be more difficult.

"Why do you have men's clothes stashed away?" Idris asked.

"They were going to be a present to my ex before he dumped me," I stated, holding the clothes out to him. "We'll find you something more suitable downstairs, but you need to at least wear *something* on the way. Hopefully these at least kind of fit. You're tall."

"Am I?" He shot me a quizzical look.

I reexamined him. In Jeriskyr, he stood over eight feet tall, so it was a relief that his height was closer to normal on Earth. However, he was still above average.

"Yes, you are," I nodded, before turning around to search for shoes he could wear. Eventually, I found some sandals that *might* work. When I turned around, though, I stopped and just stared at him for a moment. "Weren't *you* lecturing *me* about shame just a short while ago?"

"I am an incubus—I have no shame." He smirked and pulled the jeans up his long, muscular legs. "You, however, are human, and humans are prude—"

"Oh, shove it." I stalked past him, taking the sandals with me. "Bruce, let the ladies in the boutique know I'm coming in with a male customer. Send them his measurements and have them prepare both casual and formal clothes for him to try on."

"My measurements?" Idris followed me, unfolding the sweater as he walked.

"My sensory apparatuses are capable of scanning your body and taking measurements off of purely visual information," Bruce

answered matter-of-factly.

"I don't know if these will fit—doubt it—but it's worth a shot." I held up the sandals. "If not, I guess you'll just have to go downstairs barefoot. It's a good thing that your body here doesn't have the horns and tail, but you're still going to get looks with that hair and eye color. Not sure how we're going to cover that up... Maybe claim you're a cosplayer? Hmmm..."

"Yet your hair is normal?" Idris tossed aside the sandals when it was clear they wouldn't fit and then moved to follow me to the door.

"Mine's dyed—yours isn't." I reached up and tugged at his dark, wavy blue hair. "We can probably get away with claiming yours was recently dyed but anyone who knows anything about dyeing is going to be able to tell that's a lie."

"Claim he is the official model for Idris Bloodsong," Bruce suggested. *"The* Jeriskyr Online *advertising campaign went live as of yesterday. Imagery from the game is all over the city."*

"Are you serious?!" I exclaimed, turning to look at Bruce's light. "Ugh, of all the times..."

I stalked toward the door, cursing the entire way. Just great. The possibility of us being clobbered by drooling women had just gone up by a significant percentage. Bruce was right that it'd be easier to claim that the Idris 'in-game' was based on a real Idris, but that put us in all kinds of odd situations. Grimacing, I stormed down the hallway without waiting for the demon king.

"This is bad?" Idris questioned, falling into step with me.

"Annoying more than anything," I muttered, pulling my phone out of my pocket as it buzzed. I turned on the screen and sighed in irritation. The Ebonwing members were still spamming me with messages. "Oh, come on, it's not like I haven't rolled a different faction than them before!"

"Pardon?" Idris tilted his head.

"Ebonwing members are pissed off about me 'playing' as a demon character," I replied, holding up the screen in front of his face. He frowned slightly. "I wasn't even *given* the choice of anything else. Technically, players can choose to roll a demon in the Issradian Empire and be 'owned' by their guild. They can't understand why I didn't do that since no one else is running into the 'faction lockout' issue that I did."

"It still puzzles me how you can see our world as a game." Idris' frown deepened as we strode toward the elevator.

"I'll show you when we get back to the apartment. There's some stuff you should see anyway." I pressed the button for the ground floor and grimaced when I saw how many stops the elevator had to make before it got to us.

"Warming up to me after all?" he teased.

"No. Especially not if you keep that up."

When the elevator finally made it to us, it was empty, and I sighed with relief. I walked into it and shot Idris an impatient look when he hesitated.

"What...is this?" Idris placed his toes inside and nudged at the floor in suspicion.

"An elevator. It will take us downstairs."

"What about...actual stairs?"

"Do you *see* how high up we are? I am not walking down that many stairs."

Idris glanced out the clear windows behind me and grimaced before joining me in the elevator. He gripped the railing inside so tightly that his knuckles turned white. I considered teasing him for it, but I could relate. When I'd first come to the city these things had terrified me. I still wasn't entirely fond of them.

"You said we are going to meet this 'Alice' girl for dinner?" Idris questioned, clearly attempting to take his mind off the plummeting contraption.

"Yep."

"Is it not possible to convince her to remain in this world?"

"Not really. The gods can pluck us out of it at will—we don't have to 'log in' first like normal players do." I shook my head. "I considered the option for suicide too, but was informed that they just need my soul. If I killed myself here, then I'd *really* be stuck in Jeriskyr permanently."

"There is no way out?" Idris looked surprisingly sympathetic, so I just shook my head in response.

"Ah, Ms. Cerys!" Two women greeted me the moment the elevator opened. They almost immediately turned to stare at Idris.

I glanced back over my shoulder at him as well. As much as he'd been annoying me, I could understand why they were gawking.

"As you can see, my guest needs better clothing," I spoke up when the women stared a little *too* long. They both jumped and came back to reality, turning to stare at me instead.

"Guest?"

"So, he's...*available*, then?"

"You're both incorrigible." I shooed them out of our way. Idris shot them an alluring smile that caused them both to devolve into giggles. "Alright, we need casual and formal attire for him. We're meeting some friends of mine for dinner tonight."

"Dress code? *Great.*" Caroline, the blonde, grinned. "I have the *perfect* suit in mind for Mister..."

"Call me Idris," he replied, his voice pitched slightly lower than usual.

Oh please. I resisted the urge to roll my eyes and started walking toward the boutique where the two women worked. They soon hurried to follow me as they pelted Idris with questions about his taste in fashion. They were even worse than I'd thought they'd be.

"What about you, Ms. Cerys?" Annette smiled at me. "Perhaps a dress to match your *date*?"

"I'll pass," I stated flatly.

"But you two would look so cute together!" Caroline exclaimed.

"They have excellent taste." Idris shot me an amused look

when I groaned.

"In clothing, sure." I turned to look at Annette. "Make sure he's got enough clothes for at least a week, casual and formal. I'll be in the lobby if you need me."

Without another word, I stalked out of the boutique and left the demon king in their more-than-capable hands.

Sure, he was attractive. It was too late for me to deny that, considering how enamored I had been when I'd watched the Jeriskyr anime with Alice. I'd never live it down if I tried to claim otherwise. However, he'd tried to kill me. And his behavior since then had been utterly ridiculous—especially compared to my initial impression.

Besides, I didn't intend to stay in Jeriskyr.

I didn't need to make friends, let alone anything else.

"Ms. Collins, will you be going out today?" one of the security guards asked, frowning slightly when he spotted me. "Be careful. We received word that *they* are in the city again, searching for you."

"Already?" I sighed, crossing my arms. "That's what, the fourth time in the past month? They seem like they're getting more desperate. My guest and I will be heading to dinner tonight. We'll be careful."

"Looks a lot like a younger Gwythyr, doesn't he?" the guard laughed, glancing past me. I frowned and followed his gaze. He was right. "Granted, the Councilor doesn't have any kids, far as I know."

I looked at Idris again before opening my phone. Councilor Gwythyr had given me his number for use in emergencies, such as if my family ever found me again. Along with a picture.

The resemblance was undeniable.

«Tell me, Councilor, what do you think about Jeriskyr?» I hesitated a moment before hitting send. If I was wrong, I'd sound like a damned crazy person.

«Isn't that the new game you kids are playing?» His response came a lot faster than I'd expected.

«For some people, perhaps» I responded. «Idris Bloodsong bears a striking resemblance to my FAVORITE regional representative. »

There was a pause of nearly two minutes before my phone vibrated with an incoming message.

«How is he?»

«Stuck with me for a week» I answered. «We're going to be at *Aleksander's* tonight for dinner if you want to see him»

«You...were dragged into our problems?»

«Dragged is a good word for it, yes»

«I can't make it tonight. Politics. What about tomorrow? Same place?»

«That should work» I grimaced at my phone.

Aleksander's was the restaurant my older brother ran. He had originally come to the city to look for me and take me back home. Instead, he'd let me stay, and started his own restaurant so that he'd be nearby to keep an eye on me. It wasn't the best place to go while our family was looking for me, but it was too late to change plans, and Alice loved the food there.

«Don't tell him I'm here» Gwythyr's message made me frown slightly, but another followed soon after. «If I know *Them*, my boy thinks I'm dead»

I pursed my lips. That complicated things. «Fine. See you tomorrow»

«Thank you for telling me. You've always been a bright girl»

I snorted and dropped my phone back into my pocket before turning to look for Idris. Sure enough, he was still in the boutique. When I returned, he struck a seductive pose and gave me a look that made my skin prickle into goosebumps.

"Well?" he asked with a confident smile.

"You're enjoying this a little too much," I remarked, shaking my head.

"Cery, we found this *amazing* dress!" Caroline tugged at my arm. "Look, this dark blue would look amazing on you! Are you *sure* you don't want—"

"It would look incredible on her, certainly." Idris rested his forearm on my shoulder and gave me an encouraging smile.

"Well, we will be going to dinner again tomorrow," I sighed, pressing my fingertips to my temples. "Fine, have the dress and matching shoes sent to my room. You should still have my measurements. Are you done playing dress-up with Idris yet?"

"Eager to get me away from the competition?" Idris teased.

"Where do you get so much confidence?" I gave him a baffled look.

"How about the dark blue one tonight, and this red one tomorrow?" Annette suggested, causing me to shoot her a frustrated glare. She clearly had the wrong idea about tomorrow's dinner. The red one was something I'd wear if I wanted to seduce someone. That was definitely *not* what I planned on doing.

"Not the right kind of dress for the occasion," I replied flatly. "And Idris has a lot of work to do before I'd even *consider* wearing something like that around him."

After shutting down their repeated attempts to pour me into sultry dresses, I left the boutique and checked the nearest clock for the time. We had a few hours to kill before heading to *Aleksander's* for dinner. Crossing my arms, I considered what to do. If people were out in the city looking for me, I needed to keep my excursions to a minimum.

On the other hand, Idris needed to see the city while he could.

"What's wrong?" Idris asked quietly by my ear, making me jump. He smiled slightly. "Sorry, I did not mean to startle you."

"We're going back to my apartment for a little while." I turned on my heel and strode toward the elevator.

"Decided you do not want to share me after all?" Idris backed me toward the railing once he'd joined me in the elevator.

"Can you be serious for *one minute*?" I sighed.

"I *am* being serious."

"Bullshit."

"Then what is troubling you?"

"My 'family' is in the city searching for me again," I grimaced. "It's not exactly safe for me to leave the building when they're here. At the very least, I shouldn't walk around too much. So, I'm going to get dressed for dinner now and we can drive around the city until it's time to meet Alice."

"I am confident I could deal with them for you." Idris smiled, his eyes taking on a cold sheen.

"I'm sure you could—and we would wind up in irreparable trouble for it." I prodded him in the chest and narrowed my eyes. "No killing anyone. Even injuring someone could cause a lot of problems. Violence is frowned upon severely. If it wasn't, my family and the compound they run would be a non-issue."

"Even if your life is in danger?" Idris looked genuinely baffled.

"I killed someone to protect Alice and myself, once," I offered after a moment of thought. "There was a great deal of questioning involved and I'm still under surveillance to make certain violence doesn't become a habit." Idris snorted with laughter, earning a sour look. "Anyway, I'm sure you get the point. *Behave.*"

"I will do my best," he smiled.

That fills me with so *much confidence.* I kept my sarcasm to myself and soon exited the elevator with Idris close behind. Once in my apartment again, I chewed my lip and glanced at the clock, then shifted to look up at the demon king. "Alright, how about I show you what 'players' see when they come to Jeriskyr?"

"Weren't you going to get dressed?" He arched an eyebrow at me.

"I am, and I intend to shower first." I waved dismissively as I strode into my room to fetch my VR visor. When I returned, I dragged Idris into the living room and pointed to the sofa. "Sit."

"What is this?" Idris caught me by the wrist when I went to put the visor on him.

"It's a VR, which stands for 'virtual reality,' visor. It's how we interface with games. I'm not sure if *Jeriskyr Online* will work, so I'm going to show you an older game I've played."

"You're certain it's a game?" Idris shot me a knowing look when I faltered.

"No. Got any better ideas?" I challenged him.

"A few..." he murmured, his gaze trailing down to my lips, throat, and then cleavage.

"Not happening," I stated flatly, shoving the VR visor into his hands. At least, it wasn't happening *yet*. The idea was tempting. *He* was tempting. I shoved the unhelpful thought away. "Put it on."

Without another word, I stalked back to my computer and brought up *Bengllor Online's* launcher. I navigated to the character creation menu before switching it to visor mode, then peeked into the living room to make sure Idris had obliged me. To my surprise, he had. He was collapsed back against the sofa, fully immersed in the game.

Some peace and quiet. Finally.

Chapter Thirteen
Not a Date

I decided to let Idris play *Bengllor Online* for a few hours while I collected my thoughts and sent messages out to the Ebonwing members to explain the situation. While I wasn't allowed to tell them Jeriskyr was a real world, I was able to explain that I truly had encountered a faction lockout. A quick e-mail to 'Iris' helped me to gather proof.

My guild mates were still pissed that I hadn't just sat at the creation screen for hours trying to slip in, but their concerns had been quelled for the moment. Most of them still insisted that I could reroll a demon on the Issradian side once launch came around.

Ha. No. Absolutely not.

After checking my appearance in the mirror and putting on glossy, blood-red lipstick, I made my way into my bedroom and initiated the shutdown sequence for *Bengllor Online*.

I'd never imagined I'd be using the VR safety features on someone. I'd always imagined that someone would have to use them to get *me* out of a game.

"Hey, I was in the middle of..." Idris trailed off and simply stared at me when I walked into the living room. "Are you certain you will not become my queen?"

"You need a better pickup line." I rolled my eyes and motioned to his discarded suit jacket. "We're going to be late if we don't leave soon. Let's go."

"You look incredible."

"Thanks."

"I mean it."

"I didn't say you didn't."

Idris looked puzzled, but fell silent as we walked into the hallway outside of my apartment. Unlike earlier in the day, it was no longer empty. There were people returning from work, and others heading out. My neighbors rarely saw me as it was, so my presence alone was enough to earn stares.

The fact that I had someone with me, and that he was incredibly good-looking, only made it worse.

"Ah, Miss Collins!" One of my neighbors smiled at me. "Going out on a date?"

"It's for business," I stated, watching his smile falter.

"With such a handsome man? That should be a crime." The man laughed, shooting me a knowing look. "Enjoy your date."

I wonder if I could set the building on fire and make it out of the city before the authorities caught me? I stalked toward the elevator, leaving Idris to catch up to me. *Yes, he's hot. I get it. No, I don't care. No, I'm not going to date him. Just stop trying, people!*

"Miss Collins?" Idris shot me a questioning look when we stepped into the elevator.

"Collins is my family name. I plan to change it, I'm just not sure what to."

"How about Bloodsong?"

"How about not?"

"As king, I can choose something for you," Idris continued thoughtfully, stroking his chin. "Hmmm, I will have to make certain I pick something that suits you well."

"I would really rather you not," I groaned.

"Cerys, Matriarch of the Bloodsong Clan?"

"Absolutely not."

"It was a jest!" Idris laughed, shooting me a brilliant smile. "Tell me, how are we going to get to our destination? Surely you do not intend to walk in such shoes."

"Hmmm?" I glanced down at my high heels and then up at

Idris. "Of course not. We're going to take my car."

"Car?" A mildly frustrated, impatient look spread across his face.

"Think of it as a horseless carriage," I replied dryly. "You'll see. Come on."

The elevator opened and we strode past the people waiting. I did my best to ignore the whispers. Clearly, my neighbors and the building's staff thought I'd never settle down with anyone. They weren't wrong, but I wasn't in the mood to argue with them for the next several hours about whether or not Idris was my date. Alice was probably going to give me a hard enough time about it as it was.

"Get in—that side." I pointed to the passenger door of my bright, candy apple-red car. Idris looked at the car and then at me a few times.

"Earth is a strange place," he commented, before sliding into the passenger seat.

"The feeling is mutual." I pressed my thumb against the ignition. It took so long for the fingerprint reader to scan me that I considered punching it. Not that it'd make things go any faster.

"You mentioned Alice was bringing someone—do you know who?" Idris frowned when I took a look at his chest. "What?"

"Seatbelt." I pointed to his other side, then down at the latch. "Metal bit there goes into that metal bit here. Law is that you have to have it on."

"Very well." Idris managed to fasten his seatbelt himself, then shot me a look that indicated he wanted an answer.

"I don't know who she's bringing," I offered as I selected our destination on the dashboard. "It probably isn't an Ebonwing member, given the way she worded it. That, or she was making fun of me."

"Why?"

"I called you my 'plus one' so that I didn't have to say who I was bringing." I shrugged slightly. "She took it the wrong way and knows I never have anyone over who isn't from Ebonwing. So, she either thinks I'm being cryptic or that I've suddenly found myself a boyfriend. Thus, she's going to tease me mercilessly."

"She is acting like her normal self, then?" Idris gave me a pointed look.

"Yes...she might not be aware of what those bastards plan to do." I made a sour face before pressing a final button to confirm our destination. The car whirred to life and began to move, startling the demon king into clutching his armrests. "You know, if you'd stop hitting on me this would be a lot more entertaining."

"Hitting on you? I have not struck you a single—"

"It's a turn of phrase," I interrupted him, laughing when his expression became even more confused. "Think of it as slang for flirting."

"Then why not simply *say* 'flirting?'" He released an exasperated sigh.

"Because language evolves in weird ways," I shrugged, relaxing back in my seat. "If the traffic isn't too bad, we should arrive in half an hour or so. Hope you don't get bored easily."

"You may be used to these sights, but I am not," Idris pointed out, motioning around us. "I will struggle to grow bored when surrounded by such incredibly strange things."

"Good." I pulled my phone out of my pocket when I felt it vibrate.

«I sent some of my men to keep an eye on *Aleksander's*» The message was from Idris' father, so I shifted to make certain he couldn't see the screen if he happened to look away from the passenger window. «No one from the compound is there. However, if you run into trouble, we've got a van parked outside. If you approach it, they'll know you need help»

«Thanks. I take it they're making more moves than usual?» I sent the message and attempted to keep my expression passive so that I wouldn't draw Idris' attention.

«We think they intend to take you back dead or alive» Gwythyr's reply made my stomach drop. «The drones are out and scanning everyone's faces to make sure there aren't suspicious folks in the city. We added Idris' face to the list based off the surveillance footage from your apartment building, so neither of you should get stopped.

«My meeting is about to start. I'll contact you again later»

"You can ask me questions, you know." I glanced at Idris as I put my phone away.

"I do not know where to begin." He shot me an amused smile. "I believe I am beginning to understand how you felt about the prospect of touring Darmos and Cejari-ir."

"Overwhelmed? Baffled? Awestruck?" I offered, shrugging. "It's hard to put one emotion on it and harder still to think of the appropriate questions to ask."

"At least you did not have to contend with massive images of yourself everywhere." Idris pointed toward a nearby billboard. It was a half-and-half image with his face on one side and the Issradian emperor's face on the other. "I had my doubts about my world being simply a game to you and the people from your world, but... It is difficult to deny, now that I have been here."

"When we go back home for the evening, I think I have some material that will help you grasp it better," I offered, leaning against the door. "It should give you some insight into the Issradian Empire's propaganda as well."

"That was not quite what I had in mind," Idris commented, shooting me a sultry smirk.

"You never give up, do you?"

"I would never achieve anything if I gave up easily," he replied cheerfully.

Idris was definitely going to drive me insane. I was having a hard enough time resisting him for mere hours, let alone having to do so for weeks, months, or years. I shifted to stare out of the window and told my brain to shut up.

Thankfully, Idris took the hint and spent most of the ride in silence. He was fascinated by everything around us, but knew to rein himself in when we slowed to a stop outside of *Aleksander's*. Sure enough, a large van sat outside the restaurant, disguised as an electrical technician service. My car rolled to a stop and parked in my reserved spot.

I got out of the car with ease and Idris followed, albeit with a little less grace. He wasn't at all used to such contraptions, nor could he be, so I decided not to tease him about it. Yet. Instead, I turned to walk toward the restaurant entrance.

"My lady." Idris chuckled and offered me his arm when he caught up with me.

"I can't tell if you're being polite or trying to cause me more trouble." I squinted at him.

"Both."

I sighed and took his arm, earning a brilliant smile in return. It would have been more suspicious if I hadn't taken his arm—or at least, that was what I told myself. Alice would be surprised either way, but strangers would be less likely to butt in or ask annoying questions if I kept up appearances.

"Ah, Ms. Collins," a blond man greeted us at the entrance. "Ms. Walsh is waiting for you in a private room. I will take you and your guest there."

"Thank you," I replied simply. "Is my brother in today?"

Idris shot me a subtle, questioning frown.

"Not today, I'm afraid," the server answered.

Good. I kept the thought to myself.

"Cery!" Alice exclaimed the moment we walked into the private room. "I'm *so* glad you called me to dinner! You wouldn't believe the week I've—"

Alice abruptly went silent, her mouth hanging open as she pointed at Idris. Meanwhile, my gaze was focused on *her* 'plus one.'

"Adric." I narrowed my eyes. It was unmistakably the Issradian emperor's guard captain.

"Cerys." Adric nodded to me, earning a questioning look from Alice. "We meet again. I wasn't aware it was you and *that* we would be dining with."

"That?" I questioned, following his gaze to a scowling Idris.

"Oh my god, Cery, he's so much hotter in person," Alice whispered, leaning over to me, oblivious to the fact that both men could hear her. "This must be a wet dream come true for—"

"Hush!" I clamped a hand over her mouth as she started giggling. I cut my eyes to the side at Adric. "What are you doing here?"

"Much the same as your demon, I'd imagine." Adric glanced from me to Idris and back.

"So, *you're* the demon's champion, Cerys?" Alice exclaimed, with far too much excitement. "That's so cool! I was wondering if maybe something like this had happened when you said the game was faction-locked for you. You've gotta tell me all about Nabyrzahn. I bet it's so cool—it looked so cool in the anime we watched."

"She…wasn't told?" I shot Adric a baffled look. Now I had even less of an idea how to handle the situation.

"We should order dinner, at least." Idris placed a hand on my shoulder and gave me a warning look. A moment later, a server came to ask us for our drink orders.

I sat down across from Adric and Alice at the table, glanced over the drink menu briefly, then handed it off to Idris. He could choose. My capacity for caring about beverages was at an all-time low. Once the server left, Idris pursed his lips at the bubbly woman circling him. Alice had even less respect for personal space than he did, so I couldn't blame him.

"You were wise to tell your gods," Adric stated, giving me a neutral look. "If nothing else, you bought her time."

"Time? Time for what? Party?" Alice looked over at us but faltered when she spotted my expression. "Okay, I know that look. That's a bad look. You haven't made a face like that since those bastards almost took you back to the compound. What am I missing, Cerys?"

"You're playing an elf, right?" I asked Alice, feeling Idris tense beside me as he sat down.

"Yup!" Alice grinned. "Oh, I should show you a picture. I made her real pretty."

"Lady Alice!" Adric exclaimed in a reprimanding tone, causing her to frown at him.

"Fine." She pouted and sat back down beside him. "Serious business, blah blah blah. So, what's going on?"

"You *saw* the breeding pens!" Adric exclaimed, pressing his fingers to his temples. "How can you be so carefree? Surely you've put two and two together by now and realized that Cerys has abandoned—"

"I have not!"

"She wouldn't!"

Alice and I exchanged a look.

"Besides, what do you care?" I pointed at Adric, narrowing my eyes at him. "As far as I know, you're the emperor's loyal dog."

"*As I was saying*, you've managed to buy the Lady Alice time," Adric snorted. "I have been assigned to protect her while the deities from both sides investigate. However, there is no guarantee that the activity will cease. It's entirely possible that Alice will be sent there once the investigation has concluded."

"That's okay, it won't come to that," Alice declared with confidence, putting her arms around the much bulkier man. I tilted my head, baffled by the adoring way she looked at him. "Adric will keep me safe and Cerys will come to rescue us both!"

"I... What?" I shot her a disbelieving look. "Alice, do you understand the situation you're in? We're in? This isn't—"

Idris cleared his throat and motioned subtly toward the door, causing us all to fall silent again. I couldn't parse Alice's behavior.

She should have been terrified of what might happen to her, pissed that I wasn't switching spots with her—something. Yet she was her usual self. How? It made no sense to me whatsoever.

Was it naivete? Over-confidence? Or perhaps her means of coping involved illogical cheerfulness?

"Here's your wine." The server placed two bottles of wine on the table and a glass in front of each of us before smiling. "Cerys, Alice, the usual? How about for your boyfriends?"

Please, for the love of— I took a deep breath to calm myself. There was no need for that kind of reaction. "He's not my boyfriend, and he can order for himself."

"What would you recommend—aside from yourself?" Idris questioned me, causing Alice to giggle uncontrollably. I, on the other hand, contemplated stabbing him with every fork on the damned table.

"Fiancé, then?" The server gave me a puzzled look.

"*Absolutely not!*" I exclaimed. "We have no relationship other than business acquaintances."

"For now," Idris added oh-so-helpfully.

"Everything here is good," Alice offered between giggles. "Including Cerys."

"Alice!"

After we ordered our food and the server was gone, I nestled into the corner with my arms crossed and a pout on my face. All my agonizing over such an important decision, yet Alice seemed like she didn't have a care in the world. She was even *helping* Idris tease me more. The longer it went on, the less sense it made.

"Is she always like this?" Adric asked me.

"Yes, but usually her life and freedom aren't in danger," I muttered.

"They still aren't!" Alice threw her arms around Adric's shoulders and squeezed him, eliciting heavy sighs from us all.

"Alice will be safe for as long as Ebonwing remains together," Adric spoke, giving me a threatening look. "The Issradian Empire isn't allowed to draw attention to the reality of Jeriskyr or raise suspicion among the Otherworlders. If your guild crumbles, she becomes fair game. She has taken over the guild in your stead for now, meaning any action against her would put the empire at a disadvantage."

"Cerys has been arranging a lot of stuff over the past week or two," Alice began as she poured wine for us. "It isn't unusual for her to sometimes play the opposite faction. Sometimes she takes intelligence matters into her own hands, other times it's to determine the 'right' time for the rest of the guild to switch. She's already given us a few years' worth of plans."

"Nothing sensitive, I hope." Idris shot me a wary look.

"Of course not." I glared at him before bringing my drink to my lips.

"You truly believe that Adric can keep you safe and that Cerys will rescue you?" Idris turned to look at Alice with an intensely serious gaze.

"Why wouldn't I?" Alice stared blankly at him. "Cerys has killed to protect me before. I can't think of anything more trust-earning than that."

I pressed my fingers to my temples. The people born and raised in the city had always struck me as naïve, perhaps even lacking in certain instincts. Alice's behavior didn't sit well with me, even keeping her lack of a 'danger switch' in mind.

Though she was also a smart woman. I didn't think she would trust Adric without a reason. I glanced between the two of them, releasing a soft sigh. I couldn't relate.

"I don't understand it either," Adric snorted, looking at Idris. "You must be happy to finally have gotten a champion to side with you."

"It is difficult to be happy about it, given the circumstances." Idris glanced between me and Alice, before settling on Adric. "The girl mentioned something about rescuing *both* of you."

"Indeed she did." Adric seemed content to say no more on the matter.

The rest of dinner was spent mostly in idle chatter about both Earth and Jeriskyr. Alice appeared to be completely convinced that she was safe with Adric, and that I would be able to rescue her from the Issradian Empire. While I appreciated her trust, I couldn't help but think she was foolish to trust even me so fully—let alone Adric. He was the emperor's *guard captain,* for fuck's sake.

At least Idris and Adric were predictable. They barely got along. When they did, it was regarding wine, women, Alice's naivete, and battle.

"Ms. Collins, shall I tell your brother you stopped by?" a server asked as I made my way out.

"I'd prefer you didn't." I strode into the cool night air.

"Brother, hmmm?" Idris shot me a questioning look.

"Long story," I shrugged, turning to approach my car.

One of the men standing at the back of the government van nodded subtly to me as I walked past. I glanced at him briefly before turning to walk into the parking lot. I'd hoped Idris wouldn't notice, but it was apparently too much to ask.

"What was that about?" Idris asked. "Another 'long story?'"

"Protection," I stated, before settling into the driver's seat and closing the door in his face. When he hopped into the passenger side, I glanced at his irritated expression. "They're worried about me getting snatched and taken back to the compound, so they're keeping an eye on me and my surroundings."

I slumped back in my seat with a heavy sigh. Dinner had been so damned draining. It was like the energy had been sucked right out of me. I had to wonder if matters would've been easier if Alice had been pissed off or even hated me for my decision. Her seemingly blind trust was worrisome.

"She's always like that?" Idris asked softly.

"Always." I shifted my head a little to look at him. He seemed concerned. About what, I wasn't sure. "A lot of people from here lack survival skills because of how peaceful our society is. It takes a lot to make them question their safety. Alice comes from a good home with wealthy parents. The first time she encountered any real danger was when an obsessed guy started stalking her."

"The person you slew?" Idris nodded his understanding. "She is like a baby animal. The two of you are quite different."

"Thanks. I think."

When we got back to my apartment building, I slid off my high heels the moment we were inside and opted to walk barefoot. The shoes themselves weren't uncomfortable, but the wine Idris had picked was stronger than I was used to drinking. I'd had too much of it. I *refused* to fall on my tipsy ass in front of him. He teased me too much as it was.

"Welcome home, Ms. Collins," the receptionist greeted us cheerfully. "You have a package. Shall I have your 'guest' carry it for you?"

Could people please stop insinuating things?! I kept the thought to myself and forced a friendly smile. "That's alright, I can get it later."

"I would be happy to help," Idris offered.

That was good enough for the receptionist. She handed the package to him without my consent and waved us off. I pouted and stalked toward the elevator. On the one hand, I wanted to tell him off for interfering. On the other, he was helping and being polite.

"Who's it from?" I asked begrudgingly.

"Your secret admirer."

"Come on, I'm being serious." I paused, tilting my head. Then again, that was a more modern sort of phrase, as far as I was aware. Something possibly too modern for someone from Jeriskyr.

"So am I," Idris replied, tilting the package toward me. He smiled when he saw my baffled expression. "I thought you said you did not have much in the way of family, friends, or acquaintances?"

"I don't." I frowned, rising up on my tiptoes and leaning against his arm to get a better look. "*Handwriting*? Most people just use printed labels these days. I don't recognize it, either."

"You are soft," Idris remarked, leaning down to nuzzle my hair and startling me into backing away. I hadn't realized I was practically shoving my bust into his arm. He laughed and shot me a sly look. "Come now, you needn't react as if I am made of fire."

"You will be when I finally decide to cook you!" I hissed, looking away from him. *Far too soon to be so familiar with him. Ugh. I'm gonna blame the wine. Yep. Totally the wine. I'm not attracted to him at all. Nope, not me. Nuh-uh.*

"Do you think the package might be a trap?" Idris questioned as we stepped out of the elevator and walked down the hall. "After all, you seem quite startled by it, so I have to assume something like this doesn't happen often."

"No idea." I shook my head.

Idris lifted the box to the side of his head and shook it gently as we walked down the hallway. He seemed more interested in it than I was. I just wanted to sleep and *pray* I didn't end up with a hangover.

"It sounds like fabric," he suggested.

"Mmmhmm," I muttered, half-paying attention as I fiddled with my keys.

"Here." Idris slid an arm past my waist and gripped my wrist, steadying my hand. "Perhaps a lighter wine next time, kitten?"

"Don't call me that," I grumbled, turning the key.

Once inside, I tossed my shoes into a corner and pulled the pins from my hair. Getting all dressed up was nice every now and then, but getting out of it was better.

I pursed my lips and paused mid-reach for the zipper. Right. I had an incubus staying in my apartment. Stripping in front of him wasn't a good idea…probably. I bit my lower lip, considering it. The thought of seeing his reaction was tempting, and I didn't necessarily *mind* where that could lead. I shook my head hard. That was enough of *that*.

"Shall we see what was sent to you?" Idris suggested, tilting his head slightly when I continued walking toward my room. "Are you not curious?"

"I want out of this dress first."

"Is that an invitation?"

"*No!*" I retorted, before slamming my bedroom door behind

me. However, the zipper raid boss was too much for my tipsy ass to handle and I soon came back out, sulking.

"What?" Idris questioned when I stalked over to him, pouting.

"I can't reach the zipper."

"I thought you said it was not an invitation?" Idris smirked.

"Still isn't."

"I know," he chuckled, motioning for me to turn around. "I have to 'behave' myself, after all."

"Thanks," I grumbled once he'd pulled it down for me. I retreated to my room again, clutching the dress over my chest. *That* had been more embarrassing than I wanted to admit.

I changed my clothes, opting for loose pajama pants and a tank top. After pulling on a robe, I headed toward the kitchen in search of tea. Alas, there was a half-naked demon king there.

"Aren't you going to put on a shirt?" I sighed.

"Do my scars bother you?" He frowned at me.

"Huh?" I shot him a puzzled look and then let my gaze drift down to his bare torso. He was covered in a lot of them, sure. I met his eyes again. "No. Why would they?"

"Then why should I put on a shirt?" he asked, equally puzzled.

"I— Never mind." I shook my head. Like hell I was going to explain to an *incubus* why he should put clothes on. "Want tea?"

"Certainly," Idris answered. I could *hear* the smile in his voice. I had no idea why the offer made him happy. "I'd thought you would have wanted to sleep."

"I said that I had stuff I should show you," I pointed out, dragging a stool over so that I could reach the higher shelves. Before I could step up on it, Idris put a hand on my shoulder and shot me an amused look.

"Which ones did you want?" He motioned to the open cabinet.

"...second shelf from the top, the two on the left."

Idris retrieved the tea tins with ease and placed them on the counter for me before moving away. I shot a suspicious look at his back as he walked toward the wall of windows.

"Does your world not have stars?" he asked, as I searched for a type of tea that sounded good.

"We do, you just can't see them from inside the city because of the lights." I picked up a tin of Earl Gray teabags and pried it open. If I was going to set up the anime for him to watch—or anything else, for that matter—I was going to need a spike of caffeine to keep me going.

"The package, Cerys," Idris reminded me, chuckling when I shot him a perplexed look. "We should make certain it is not dangerous, at least."

"If you wanna open it, you can." I shrugged, indifferent.

"Even if it's truly from an admirer?" Idris challenged.

I hesitated, then shook my head. With my terrible dating record, I highly doubted it. "It's not."

"You don't sound certain."

"Just open the damned thing."

It wasn't long before Idris tapped me on the shoulder and gave me a triumphant smirk. He handed me an envelope from inside the package before walking out of the room. All he said before disappearing was, "You were wrong."

Frowning, I looked at the envelope like it was a foreign object. When I opened the letter, I bit back an aggravated sigh. All it said was, *I hope you will wear this to dinner tomorrow.*

Like father, like son! I fumed, stalking over to the box. The ensemble inside had to be worth several thousand dollars. It was the sort of dress meant for a celebrity event, not for a dinner meeting at *Aleksander's.* Just what in the hell was Gwythyr plotting? *And now his son is going to think—* Oh, for fuck's sake.

I carried the box into my room and set it aside before returning to the kitchen. Once done with the tea, I arranged a variety of cookies on a plate and carried it into the living room along with Idris' cup. He looked pensive, almost disappointed.

"So, what is this about dinner tomorrow?" he questioned, his tone neutral.

"You and I were invited to another dinner at *Aleksander's*," I replied, offering him his cup. He crossed his arms loosely, his eyes narrowing and his head tilting toward me slightly. "I'm not sure why you seem so disappointed."

"I dislike competition—especially in a world that frowns upon violence." Idris gave me a chilling smile and slid his fingers along my hand before properly taking his tea. "Who is he?"

"Not competition," I replied dryly. "More like someone who is intentionally trying to rile you up. Why, I'm not sure. Why it's working, I'm even less sure."

I set down the plate of cookies and returned to the kitchen to fetch my tea, deciding to take a little longer so that I could collect myself. I knew that I was physically attractive. That Idris flirted with me was only a surprise because I thought demons would have a very different idea of what counted as pretty or interesting. Maybe it was just an incubus thing, maybe it wasn't. I didn't know.

I didn't like not knowing.

When I returned to the living room, Idris still looked to be in a foul mood. I set my tea down on the coffee table before striding over to the shelves beside the TV. I felt him watching me, but he didn't say anything this time. Once I finally found what I was looking for, I strode over to him and set the VIP basket Iris had given me in front of him.

"This is going to require a bit of explaining." I pointed down to it.

"You do not intend to answer me about this dinner invitation?" Idris narrowed his eyes at me.

"Do I owe you an explanation?" I countered.

"Ah… I suppose not." He shook his head slightly and sat back, sighing. "The invitation is for us both?"

"Yes."

"And if I decline?"

"Then I'll drag you there myself," I shrugged. "Can we focus, please?"

"Where am I going to sleep?" Idris' question threw me off and I stared at him for a moment. I hadn't considered that. He smiled. "Did you think that I was going to suggest you share your bed with me?"

"No. I forgot about the whole 'you probably need sleep' part." I shook my head and then winced when everything spun. "Okay, yeah, definitely a different wine next time...

"I have a guest room you can use. The sofa you're sitting on folds out into a bed, so that's an option too if the bed in the guest room is too small. I can show you this stuff later if you're—"

"Please, sit down before you fall down." Idris stood up and grabbed me by both shoulders.

"I'm not *that* drunk!" I protested, glaring at him. "Tipsy and tired, maybe, but I—Eek! Put me down!"

"That is not the sound a kitten makes," Idris teased as he sat me down on the couch. He laughed in response to my expression. "I labor to call that a glare, Cerys. You hardly look threatening. Now then, what were you attempting to show me?"

"That stuff." I pointed to the basket, which was now out of reach. He took the hint and handed it to me before sitting down beside me, a little too closely, on the couch. "This is stuff that Iris—Coryl...Corylo...whatever—gave me when I was done with my 'demo.' They gave things like this to all the early access players."

"Stuff." Idris gave me an amused look.

"They claim it's pictures taken from in-game and whatever." I pulled a poster of him out and shoved it toward him. "There's one of each of the demon kings and ones of the Issradian Empire's elite too."

"Unnerving," he frowned. "Go on."

"I'm going on!" I retorted, smacking him upside the head with his own poster. Next, I pulled out the two anime cases. "These are what I really wanted to show you. They're...anime. Shows. Er..." I tilted my head, trying to think of a way to explain them to him. "You have theatre in your world, right?"

"Yes."

"Okay, so shows are like recordings of theatre that you can watch whenever you want and however many times you want." I nodded slightly. "An 'anime' is one that's been animated using artwork of some variety or another. So, in short, they claim that these were created with 'game art.'"

"Except the game is real." Idris nodded, making an elegant motion with one hand. "I follow you so far, kitten."

"So, one is from—" I paused and turned to glower at him, my grip on the anime cases causing them to creak. "Don't call me kitten!"

"Why not?" Idris smiled, his gaze flicking down my torso.

"Because I'm not a kitten!" I growled.

"You could be *my* kitten," he chuckled, reaching over to brush displaced hair out of my face.

"I'd be your queen before I'd be your kitten, and no to both!" I protested, feeling my face growing hot—hopefully from the alcohol.

"Anyway, you were saying?" Idris asked, shooting me an innocent smile.

"I should fillet you."

"You cannot even hold those cases steady. I doubt you have the dexterity required to fillet even a still corpse right now, kitten."

"*I didn't say I'd do it well!*"

He laughed and caught me by the wrist when I swatted at him again. This time, he pulled me across his lap, causing me to lose my balance. I landed with my back across his thighs and just stared up at him for a moment in disbelief. If I'd known I was signing up to babysit a childish demon king, I'd have declined letting him stay here.

"This is cozy," he commented, placing his elbow on the armrest. He smiled and tracked me as I extracted myself. It would have been so easy to elbow him in the groin, and it was tempting, but instead I chose to make sure I *didn't*. "Aw, now how will I stay warm?"

"A shirt? A robe?" I suggested.

"I would prefer a Cerys."

"Well, I'm not the only person named Cerys!" I hissed, before standing up. "You should watch these. Seriously. The Issradian

Empire one might teach you something, and the Nabyr-zahn one might help you identify whether sensitive information was leaked."

"Later." Idris tilted his head to the side and examined me. "We should both get some rest. I will be here for a week, after all. I am certain there is plenty of time for me to watch both. Where is the guest room?"

"That door…er, no, that door." I pointed.

"Go get some sleep," he chuckled. "I can find my way."

That was one 'royal decree' I didn't mind obeying.

Chapter Fourteen
Also Not a Date

When I woke up, it was to the smell of fresh tea and something baking. My stomach grumbled as I sat up. It smelled *really* good. Except, obviously, I hadn't cooked anything.

Remembering the previous day, I sighed and flopped back down to the bed, groaned, then pulled my pillow over my head. Why was this my life?

"Good morning, Mistress Cerys." Bruce spoke just as I'd started to drift back to sleep, causing me to jump. *"I instructed Master Idris on how to use your kitchen. Breakfast will be ready shortly—you should get dressed."*

I groped around for my phone and checked my messages, grimacing when I saw the number of notifications on the lock screen. Almost a hundred. Most were from Alice and my guild, though a few were from Gwythyr.

Whyyy?

One would think that, after a few years of being in the guild, my guild mates would have gotten used to the way I thought. Nope. Instead, nearly everyone I had contacted with plans or other information felt the need to ask for clarification, or at least double-check to make sure they understood what I wanted. By the time I'd replied to my guildies, reiterated to Alice that I wasn't dating the demon king, and chastised said demon king's father for his games, it smelled like the food was ready. I decided to stay in my pajamas.

"Ah, did I wake you?" Idris glanced over his shoulder at me and smiled. "Your technology here is surprisingly similar to the magitech we have in Cejari-ir, despite the way it looks. Fear not, nothing is damaged."

"Bruce woke me." I pointed to the blue light, which promptly skittered away along its track to hide somewhere. "Ugh, judging by the way I feel, I should've gotten up a while ago anyway."

"You are still wearing those?" Idris glanced down at my pajamas.

"It *is* my house," I pouted. "Normally I wouldn't be wearing anything."

"Point taken," he laughed, turning back to the stove. "Would you mind if we ate in the living room? I would like to resume where we left off last night."

Does he really have to say it like that? I attempted to hide my shiver by running a hand through my hair, trying to keep myself from yawning. "Yeah, sure. I usually eat in there anyway."

"Excellent. I will bring you your food." Idris shooed me toward the door.

I plopped down on the sofa the moment I reached it and whipped out my phone. «Alice, I have a demon king in my kitchen. Making breakfast. What do I do?»

«Marry him?»

«Not you too!»

«Me too??? Wait... WHAT DO YOU MEAN, ME TOO?! »

«He keeps joking about making me his queen or something stupid»

«OMG XD»

«This isn't funny! Okay it's a little funny. Imagine if he'd been wearing an apron?»

«Naked apron?»

«No... Like, one of those frilly aprons from the 1950's»

«Oh god. I'd die»

"What are you snickering about?" Idris inquired, making me jump and hide my phone.

"Nothing!"

"That was not at all convincing." He arched an eyebrow at me before setting several plates of food on the coffee table. "I will be back with our tea. Will you watch those...anime—as I believe you called them—with me?"

"I...sure, I guess." I blinked. *Why is he asking me?*

"Excellent." He smiled at me again before returning to the kitchen.

«I don't understand this creature» I messaged Alice again, internally cursing the girlish giddiness Idris' smile made me feel. It was so not helpful. «Also, you almost got me in trouble. Enough with the visuals»

«He probably thinks the same about you» Alice pointed out.

«He asked me to watch the Jeriskyr anime with him. And he got kinda irritated when I got a package from a 'secret admirer' last night»

«Okay but he's like, really hot. I bet he's even hotter when he's jealous. Why aren't you dating him, again???»

«'Hot' isn't enough for me to date someone, Alice. Dammit, I hear him coming back. Chat later»

«MARRY HIM, CERYS»

«STFU»

I shut my phone off and shoved it in my pocket before rising to my feet and setting up the TV to play the anime. When Idris walked in, I felt his eyes on my back briefly before I heard the cups clink against the table.

"Do you need help?" he asked, earning a questioning look from me. He pointed at my feet and then at my hands. "You are on your toes again. I can reach for you if you like."

"Thanks for the offer, I think." I shook my head. "But I've lived here for years without help. I'm fine."

"You think?" Idris questioned.

"I can't decide if you're picking on me for being shorter than you." I peered at him.

"Not at all!" he exclaimed, shaking his head as I returned to the sofa. "I am your guest and you did not have a choice in the matter. The least I can do is assist you while I am here."

"I prefer to do things myself. Keeps me from getting lazy." I shrugged, returned to the sofa, and pulled my legs up beneath me before leaning forward to fix myself a plate of food. "We won't be able to watch all of it before we leave for dinner. Which one do you want to start with?"

"You insist on going to this dinner date?" Idris grimaced.

"Not a date." I shook my head. "It's business."

"Business that I am invited to?" He gave me a doubtful look. "And with you wearing a dress like that?"

"Would you rather not get to see me in it?" I decided to try leveraging his supposed attraction to me against him. See if I could throw him off balance.

"A gift from another man? Certainly not," he scoffed. "Even *if* you give me the pleasure of helping you out of it."

"I don't understand you," I remarked dryly.

"What's not to understand?" Idris huffed. "What king would approve of his future queen receiving gifts from admirers?"

"But I'm not your future queen," I groaned. "Ugh, it's too early in the morning for this. Actually, any time of day is too early for this nonsense.

"Which anime do you want to watch, damn it?"

"Nabyr-zahn," he answered begrudgingly.

Irritated, I grabbed the remote and pressed a few buttons. "I can pause it if you want to ask anything or need to do something else."

"What if... Never mind," he spoke dryly, shaking his head. He began eating his breakfast, clearly done with the matter, so I fast-forwarded to the start of the episode.

Are all incubi so ridiculously jealous? I wondered, shoving a forkful of food into my mouth. "Oh, this is good!"

"I am glad you like it."

I glanced at him, but his eyes were glued to the TV. His expression was still one of slight disappointment and reluctance. I felt a little bad that I'd soured his mood. I hadn't meant to, it was just that his behavior was so ridiculous. Besides, there was no way I'd let myself become 'his' *anything*. It simply wasn't conducive to returning home. No matter how tempting he was.

Besides, there was no reason for him to be jealous in the first place.

Especially not over some human Otherworlder.

Ouch, Cerys, ouch. I gnawed on my fork and glanced at my mostly empty plate, contemplating grabbing more food to make myself feel better. Idris, however, plucked it off my lap before I could make a decision. At first I thought he was going to take it back into the kitchen, but instead he plated more food and offered it back to me.

He didn't say anything, but he looked insistent.

"Thanks," I murmured around my fork.

All I got was a small smile before he returned his attention to the TV.

Managed to upset both myself and *the almighty Idris Bloodsong. Go me,* I sulked, shoving half a biscuit in my mouth. Idris prodded my cheek, but my mouth was full, so I just shot him an inquiring look.

"Pause?" He pointed to the screen. Once I pressed the button, he asked, "Who is your favorite?"

"Huh?" I stared at him.

"In theatre, people always have a favorite character in the story," Idris explained, and I felt my face rapidly growing hot, my heart pounding. "So, who is your—"

"I don't have one!"

"Care to try that again?" He arched an eyebrow at me.

"Nope!" I shook my head. There was no way in hell I was telling him that. Not when my favorite was him.

Oh. Shit. I could've lied. Is it too late for that? Hmmm…

"Me?" He tilted his head. When I choked on my tea and began coughing, he smirked. "You expect me to believe that with how stubborn you have been?"

"You *did* try to kill me," I deflected.

"This again?" He frowned, but it was short-lived. He broke into a massive grin, while I groaned and hid my face in my hands. "You did not deny it."

"Shut up," I grumbled.

"You should be more honest, *kitten*," he teased, tugging the strap of my tank top off my shoulder. "Perhaps the reason you claim there is no competition is because you have already fallen for me?"

"*Absolutely not!*" I protested, shifting to glare at him.

"I am already aware you find me attractive."

"Being nice to look at and being possible boyfriend material are *entirely* different things!" I informed him, prodding his bicep. "I know almost nothing about you. There's no way that I could consider you—"

"So, there is a chance." He smiled and caught my wrist before I could poke him again.

"What?" I stared at him.

"If you learn more about me," he suggested, bringing my hand to his chest, "then you might decide that you wish to be my queen after all."

"That's not—" I faltered, my mind racing to think of an argument. It was difficult to think about *anything* when he was looking at me like that. Especially not if he was going to draw my hand down his chest. Ugh. Nope. Being around him was *not* good for my health. "I already told you I have no intention of remaining in Jeriskyr. You shouldn't bother."

"That was not a denial either." He smiled playfully.

Why me?! I whined internally. "We're supposed to be watching anime, you know."

"I would rather watch you."

"I'd prefer you didn't," I grumbled, attempting to pull my hand away.

"Why?"

"Because our time here is limited, and because I'm not here for your entertainment." I mustered the courage to be stern, but even I wasn't convinced by my tone.

"Even if you are not, you are still very entertaining." He chuckled, releasing me. "I *will* win you over, Cerys."

I really hope you don't. I hit the start button on the remote again and returned my attention to my food.

He was a beautiful man, but part of me hoped that he wasn't a beautiful person. That would make it much easier to keep my distance. I didn't want anyone or anything to make me consider staying in Jeriskyr.

However, I couldn't figure out why I felt that way. There

wasn't anything concrete keeping me attached to Earth, yet I felt so strongly about returning.

Maybe I should just put on my bitch pants and make sure he doesn't want anything to do with me. I grimaced. That was ridiculous, and likely going too far. Intentionally hurting an ally wasn't something I wanted to do. He seemed nice enough to not deserve that kind of treatment, even if he drove me up the fucking wall at times.

Granted…my irritation stemmed more from the notion that I couldn't, or shouldn't, pursue him. He was decidedly off-limits, and it was mildly infuriating. Especially since it was a situation I'd imposed on myself. If I grew closer to him, it would become less likely that I'd want to return to Earth—and that seemed like a bad thing. Pity.

I glanced over at him when he placed some pastry-looking thing on my plate, but he didn't answer the look I gave him. Just a smile, before he returned to watching the anime.

Once thing was for sure—I'd never thought I'd be watching anime with a demon king. I picked up the pastry and peeled off a piece. It smelled sweet, and faintly of apples. When I took a bite, it was like *heaven.* "Okay. That is really, *really* good."

"I am glad," he chuckled, disheveling my hair.

I must have fallen asleep at some point. The next thing I knew,

Idris was gently shaking me, and I found that I was curled up against his side. He had an arm around me and it looked like he'd pulled a blanket up over my shoulders, too.

"We're going to be late if you don't go get ready," he sighed, a reluctant smile on his face.

"Mmm? Wha?" I grumbled, pawing at my eyes. Finally, it properly clicked that I was snuggling with him and I scrambled away. "Sorry! I didn't mean to… I'll go get ready!"

I fled before he could say anything.

Not…not conducive… I shut the bathroom door behind me and sunk to the floor, shaking my head hard. He smelled incredible. I growled. My brain seriously needed to learn when to stop.

Fifteen minutes or so later, I emerged from the bathroom in the expensive dress, shoes, and jewelry that Gwythyr had sent to me. I'd had to put more effort than usual into my makeup and hair just so that I wouldn't look out of place in the ensemble.

I almost wished I'd taken the dress that Annette and Caroline had tried to get me to buy the previous day. *That one* had been conservative by comparison. With a dress like this, I wouldn't even have to try to seduce someone. It was practically screaming, 'come and get me.'

"I find myself liking your suitor less and less," Idris commented, examining me from head to toe. I sighed. If only he knew how ridiculous his jealousy was.

Well, at least I looked nice.

"Not a suitor." I placed a hand on my hip.

"You are certain?"

"Quite." I tilted my head, thinking. "In fact, I'm fairly certain this dress is meant for you."

"Pardon?" He frowned.

"Never mind." I shook my head. "You'll understand soon enough."

I strode toward the door, but Idris beat me to it and held it open for me, causing me to shoot him a questioning look.

"Do men not hold the door for women in your world?"

"Not for a few decades, no." I arched an eyebrow.

"Clearly someone needs to re-teach them manners and class," Idris scoffed, before offering me his arm. When I hesitated, he gave me a firm look. "You are liable to be whisked away by some fiend if I take my eye off you."

He wasn't entirely wrong. I took his arm, noting he seemed to relax a little when I did. "You're nervous. Why?"

"Because I am with a beautiful woman and do not appear to have my usual tools with which to protect her," he responded, a little too seriously. I wanted to laugh at the ridiculousness of his statement but couldn't when he took a tone like that. "You doubt me? On which part?"

"You're difficult to read." I gave him a sideways glance.

"I am simpler than you think," Idris informed me as we strode to the elevator. "Perhaps you are attempting to read too deeply into what I say."

"I... Maybe." I tilted my head, considering it. He was right that I read a lot into most things he said, though perhaps not in the same way he was thinking. "Mostly, I can't tell when you're being serious and when you aren't."

"I *do* find you beautiful, and I cannot seem to use my powers here—or at least, not with my usual ease—and I wish to protect you from any threats you might face," he reiterated, making me frown at him. "I dislike this notion of your former family attempting to hunt you down like an animal. I also know what this manner of dress would do to human men from Jeriskyr. I cannot claim to know if humans of this world are similar."

"So, you prefer to be cautious?" I asked. He looked relieved that I understood.

"Good evening, Miss— Oh my." The receptionist's eyes widened as we passed her counter. "Cerys, you look incredible!"

"Thank you." I shot her a brief smile.

Unfortunately, most of the staff working on the main level seemed intent on complimenting us both. It was nice at first, but quickly became tedious. When we eventually made it to my car, I slumped back and sighed.

"You dislike the attention?" Idris chuckled.

"I thought we'd never get out of there!" I shook my head. "I hate being late."

"Perhaps I should have opted for a fancier suit," Idris remarked, trailing his fingers down the gap of his partially-unbuttoned dress shirt. Unfortunately, he caught me watching. "I believe I am beginning to understand why you chose to be a succubus in Jeriskyr, kitten."

"Shove it," I bristled, jamming my thumb against the car's start button.

"Why *did* you choose succubus, then?" Idris inquired, his tone genuinely curious this time.

"I usually play sexy demon women in games." I crossed my arms. "Unless the character design sucks, in which case I play a male character. That's what I did in *Bengllor Online*. Female armor choices in that game were awful."

"Yes, but there are a lot of 'sexy demon women' in Jeriskyr," Idris countered dryly. "You could have been an ifrit, a djinn, a kitsune—any number of things."

"Are you complaining?"

"No, but you are avoiding answering."

"Humph," I grumbled, looking out the window. "I usually gravitate toward succubi in games because they're powerful women and aren't ashamed to *be* sexy. Humankind has come a long way, but there's still people who think certain types of clothes or certain skirt lengths are…slutty. It's limiting. I dislike being shamed or accused of being a prostitute just for liking certain things."

"Was that so difficult?" Idris chuckled.

"Yes, it was!" I pouted.

"I am an incubus—there's no reason for you to be embarrassed."

"Has it occurred to you that maybe I'm embarrassed *because* you're an incubus?" I retorted.

"You will have to explain that one to me." He tilted his head.

"That would take forever," I groaned. "The short version is that Earth has myths and legends about incubi and succubi. They aren't favorable. How many are true, I have no idea. Thus, caution seems prudent."

"Ah, human myths and legends." Idris rolled his eyes. "I can imagine."

A while later, we arrived at *Aleksander's* and I spotted my brother's car parked outside. Great. Before I could open my door and stand up myself, Idris was there holding the door open for me and offering me his hand.

Is it wrong of me to wish he'd stop being so nice? I hesitated before taking his hand, then decided refusal would be too rude. "Thank you."

"You are nervous," he commented, concern in his eyes. "What troubles you?"

"My brother's car is here today." I glanced toward the bright, metallic-orange vehicle.

"Should I be concerned?" Idris narrowed his eyes.

"I don't know if he's still on my side...and we've never gotten along that well," I replied, hesitant to say anything else. "Be on guard, I guess. Considering who we're meeting, he shouldn't do anything even if he *isn't* on my side."

Idris and I made our way inside and, unfortunately, were greeted by my brother himself. A brother who was very clearly displeased by my dress. I gave him a warning glare the moment he opened his mouth to speak.

"You haven't been by to see me in ages, Cery!" Aleksander exclaimed, looking between me and Idris. "I heard you were dating a demon, but I thought it was just a joke! What on Earth—"

"A demon?" I asked, glancing up at Idris. No horns. No tail. Alek wasn't wrong, but Idris also didn't look like a demon on Earth. As far as I knew, my brother was clueless about games, too. "Alek, we aren't dating. We're here for a business meeting and Idris is *my potential boss*. Kindly don't flub this up?"

"He's—?" Aleksander looked suitably baffled. "You have a reservation, or you want your usual room, sis?"

"Reservation. We're meeting the Councilor." I narrowed my eyes at Alek and set my jaw.

"The Councilor, ah, there we go—Gwythyr isn't here yet, but I'll take you to your reserved room," Aleksander stated, nodding. Idris tensed beside me and shot me a questioning glance. My brother, on the other hand, gave me a cheerful look. "You should come by more often, Cery. Bet you haven't even been feeding yourself right, have you?"

"She hasn't," Idris stated when I opened my mouth to claim otherwise.

"Knew it," Alek nodded. "She gets too engrossed in those VR games and forgets to eat or sleep. Honestly, even if you are a demon, I was kind of hoping you two were dating. She needs someone to take care of her."

"*Aleksander Davis Collins!*" I exclaimed.

"Sorry, not sorry." Alek stuck his tongue out at me.

I sighed heavily. If we had really come for a business interview, I would have died on the spot.

Once we were in our reserved room and my brother had left, Idris turned to glower at me.

"*Gwythyr?*" Idris demanded. "As in—" he paused, struggling to process it. "I would like to say you should not know, but your expression is far too apologetic for me to claim otherwise."

"He asked me not to tell you." I pursed my lips, fishing my phone out of my handbag. "Speaking of, he said he's going to be five to ten minutes late due to traffic in his part of town."

"You said…he's a Councilor?" Idris paced the room.

"He's this region's representative in the global government I told you about," I replied, watching as Idris stopped to stare at me. "Yeah. It didn't occur to me that you were related to him until someone in the apartment lobby pointed out the resemblance yesterday. I messaged him after to be sure."

"You said the representative is responsible for 'saving' you."

Idris frowned, then glanced down at my dress. "And that...ah."

Idris bristled and began pacing again. I imagined that, if we were in Jeriskyr, his tail would have been twitching so violently it would have knocked over everything in the room. Not knowing what to say or do, I perched on a chair and watched him pace.

"Your brother called me a demon." Idris stopped and glanced at me.

"I don't know what that's about." I shook my head. "Our family's religion is based on a lot of former Earth belief systems. They took things they liked from history and smashed it all together. Considering that's what many religions in the past few thousand years have done...it's a total mess. Legends about demons being creatures from hell was one of the things they borrowed. Something, something, demons lure humans to sin, something, something..."

Idris went back to his silent, furious pacing. When my brother returned, it was with Gwythyr and several of his bodyguards in tow. The cheerful man instructed the bodyguards to wait outside before joining us. Before Idris could tear into him about his shenanigans, Gwythyr embraced him in a tight hug.

"I'll just be going—" I started to sneak past, attempting to leave the two men to their reunion, but Gwythyr caught me and pulled me into the warm hug.

"Nonsense, Cerys!" Gwythyr exclaimed brightly. "It isn't safe for you, and I certainly won't leave my people's champion all by her lonesome!"

"Yeah, maybe, but you two—" I tried to pull away from them again.

"He is even more stubborn than I am." Idris glanced down at me.

"But…" I sighed. It didn't feel right for me to be there. They hadn't seen each other in a long time, probably, and I didn't want to intrude. It wasn't my place to stay. "Look, nice of you to be inclusive and all, but I'm going. I'll be in my usual room— Eek!"

Idris dipped down and slid an arm beneath my knees, the other behind my shoulders, and carried me over to the table. Once there, he set me gently on a chair. When I moved to flee, he gave me a firm look.

"You're practically family as well, Cerys." Gwythyr smiled at me. "Stay."

"Fine…" I grumbled, looking away from them both. *I'm not…I don't have family. Aleksander barely counts. Okay, maybe Gwythyr counts a little for saving me and making sure I have a place to stay. But still…*

"She'll be fine, boy!" Gwythyr clapped his son on the shoulder and gave him a good looking-over. "You're here with her, so that must mean she's chosen Nabyr-zahn, yes?"

"She has. I have yet to decide if I will accept her," Idris answered, and I felt my heart drop.

"What?" Gwythyr demanded, glaring at his son. "I can think

of no one better to help restore Nabyr-zahn to its glory! She is a strong woman, Idris. Knowing you, I can see why Corlyotir and the others chose her. You would be a fool to—"

"My father really likes you, doesn't he?" Idris glanced at me, arching an eyebrow. However, he seemed to notice that I was sulking. "What is it?"

"*Nothing.*" I looked away from him with a huff. "Idiot."

"I cannot fix it if you do not tell me," Idris sighed.

"Gee, what did you do to upset me last time?" I snorted.

"I— Ah." Idris pivoted and strode over to me, taking my hand in his. "Forgive me, it was a comment in poor taste. I did not mean—"

"You got an apology out of him?" Gwythyr arched an eyebrow.

"If I explained why, it would ruin our dinner." Idris glanced at his father before turning his worried gaze to me. "Cerys, I—"

"Shove it," I pouted, yanking my hand from his. I wasn't going to accept his apology this time. That whole queen thing, then saying he might not accept me, was fucking bullshit. I wanted to hang him from my balcony by his toes.

"What'd you do to Cery?" Aleksander asked as he carried in a bottle of white wine and three glasses. I shot him a glare that made him flinch.

"I said something in poor taste," Idris replied, shaking his head slightly. "I apologized, but…"

"Poor taste? More like you're full of shit."

"Cerys! Language!" Aleksander exclaimed.

"Yes, Mother." I rolled my eyes. "Like you don't swear when you're dealing with the kitchen staff or you're with your friends. Gimme a break."

I bristled when Idris took a seat beside me and Gwythyr sat across from me. They ordered appetizers, and my brother finally left. I didn't intend to give them the satisfaction of ordering anything, but Idris took matters into his own hands. I was a little impressed he remembered my order from the prior evening—mozzarella sticks.

"How do you like the dress, Cerys?" Gwythyr asked, clearly trying to change the subject.

"It's nice, too nice for me, probably. But…this is supposed to be your happy reunion after who knows how long. Feel free to leave me out of it." I continued to stare at the wall to my left, keeping as much of my back to Idris as I could. "I shouldn't be here."

"I hope you intend to make it up to her," Gwythyr commented, arching an eyebrow. "I've never seen her so agitated."

"It is not something I can easily make up for," Idris sighed. "Cerys, at least talk to me."

Why is it so hard for them to understand? I pursed my lips and took a deep breath. "All I will say is: One, you're full of shit for claiming you won't accept me. Two, I don't belong here while the two of you catch up."

"Even if we want you here?" Gwythyr asked.

"*You* want me here," I pointed out, before glancing hesitantly at Idris. "You didn't ask your son his feelings on the matter. I'm terribly out of place."

"My son accompanied you despite a package from a 'secret admirer,'" Gwythyr smirked. "Clearly he enjoys your company."

I wasn't convinced that was a good thing.

"It *has* been a few centuries since we last spoke," Idris started, his tone hesitant. "While there is much for us to discuss, you are an important part of Nabyr-zahn now, Cerys. You should hear what we have to say."

"*If* you accept me," I snorted.

"Is this going to be the new 'you *did* try to kill me?'" Idris nudged me with his elbow.

"Maybe." I shot him a sideways glance.

"Who tried to kill who, exactly?" Gwythyr asked. After Idris explained the situation regarding our first meeting, Gwythyr howled with laughter. "The gods chose well!"

"I'm inclined to agree," Idris said, a small smile pulling at his lips.

Yeah. No. They chose terribly. I reached for my glass of wine, but Idris snatched it.

"If you start now, you won't be awake enough to start your car." He held the glass out of my reach. "How about something less potent?"

"How about I make *you* less potent?!" I growled.

"I'm glad to see you get along so well," Gwythyr commented, smiling.

"You call this getting along well?" I stared at him.

"She has warmed up to me, for certain, but I would not say this is us getting along," Idris commented, a smirk slowly spreading across his lips. "Her taking a nap on me earlier would be us 'getting along.'"

"*As far as I'm concerned, that didn't happen!*" I growled, scooting my chair away from him. Falling silent, I attempted to calm myself down. I was letting the incubus rile me up far too much. Normally, I was more collected. Hell, under *any* other circumstance I would have been delighted to have Idris interested in me.

Besides, he *was* comfy to snuggle with. I sighed. Unhelpful.

"Ah well, we should let her be for now," Gwythyr remarked, shifting his gaze to Idris. "I want to know all that has happened since the gods sent me here. I expect you to explain Cerys' reaction to your comment as well, boy."

Idris stiffened at his father's shift to a stern tone toward the end of the sentence. I glanced at him curiously, but his expression gave nothing away. If I hadn't been sitting beside him, I probably wouldn't have noticed the reaction.

Finally, the two men began to discuss the changes to Nabyr-zahn. By the sound of things, the humans had continued to grow greedier by the decade. The last champion to join the demons had been during Gwythyr's time as king—he was stunned to learn that dozens had chosen to go to the humans instead.

Despite their troubles, Nabyr-zahn had continued to advance at a rate similar to that of the humans. If they hadn't lost so many people, they would have likely been far beyond the Issradian Empire in technological capability. It was honestly impressive. A handful of demons had been able to drive progressive discoveries at a rate that was a bit faster than generations of human advancements.

I could see why Gwythyr and Idris were proud of their people. Their conversation gave me the impression that they were both good kings. They seemed to care a great deal for their subjects.

As expected, Gwythyr flew into a rage when Idris told him what I had discovered during my tour of Darmos. I was thankful that he hadn't made *me* repeat it, at least.

"Calm down," I stated, glancing up at the pacing councilor. "You didn't want to draw attention, right?"

"I...urgh." Gwythyr sat heavily in his seat and clenched his fists on top of the table. "To think that something like that has been going on for centuries—maybe even before I came to Earth. It's..."

"Inexcusable?" I offered.

"That decision is one no one should ever have to make." Gwythyr looked at me with pain in his eyes. "You are a good woman, Cerys, but Alice is far too trusting. I can't fathom how she managed to have such a favorable reaction to this."

"She was genuine in her belief that Adric would protect her and

Cerys would save her," Idris added. "She is a strange girl."

I plucked my glass of wine off the table. Dealing with the two of them made me wish I was drinking something much stronger. "It's getting late. Aleksander usually closes around this time. Should we continue this elsewhere?"

"I have more work to attend to, I'm afraid," Gwythyr replied with a reluctant smile. "I'll send someone to fetch Idris tomorrow so that he and I can talk at length, and you can see to whatever preparations you need to finalize, Cerys. For now, you should go home and get some rest while you can."

We said our goodbyes and parted ways. My brother shot me a concerned look when I left with Idris, but said nothing. Once in my car, I breathed out a heavy sigh and just stared at the bright displays for a moment.

"Now then, are you going to explain why you think I am 'full of shit?'" Idris asked, shifting in his seat to look at me.

"Well, I would *like* to think your attempts at 'wooing' me would mean you'd made up your mind," I pointed out dryly. He stared at me for a moment before giving me a sheepish smile. "Yeah. Thought so."

"You have a point," Idris nodded, settling back in his seat. However, he glanced at me when he spotted me typing in a new address on the dashboard instead of hitting the 'home' button. "Where are we going?"

"My favorite place."

Chapter Fifteen
A Demon's Rage

"This is far from the city." Idris frowned as my car slowed to a stop. In front of us was a hill covered in grass and a handful of trees. Above, the moon shone bright, close to full. When I stepped out of the car, Idris hurried to follow and shot me a concerned look before scanning our surroundings. It didn't take long for him to notice the dim glow of lights in the distance—and the razor wire fence surrounding it. "Is this…"

"Yeah—*that* place is where I grew up." I followed his gaze and shrugged before making my way up the hill to the tree at the top.

"And your favorite place?" Idris gave me a puzzled look. "You did not seem fond of them."

"That," I pointed in the direction of the compound, "is not my favorite place. This is."

I turned my finger to point at the tree, and then in the opposite direction of the compound. He'd been looking for the stars from my apartment and this was the best place I knew of from which to see them. At this time of night, I figured the people living in the area wouldn't be a problem—they'd be sleeping.

Idris opened his mouth to protest but promptly shut it when he followed my gaze. The city's massive skyscrapers shone with light in the distance, a stark contrast to the otherwise pitch-black night sky. Stars and the Milky Way shone above us, a little dimmer than I would have liked.

The demon king appeared fascinated.

It was one of the few things, or places, I knew I would miss while in Jeriskyr. Before working up the courage to run away from the compound, this place had been one of my few comforts away from my family and the other people living there. It was beautiful, peaceful, and had an incredible view of the city's skyline. Hell, the little hill and the trees on it were more of a home than the complex behind us had ever been.

"Your stars are so unfamiliar," Idris murmured. He reached to grab hold of me and quickly realized I was nowhere near him. Startled, he shifted to search for me, pausing when he spotted me leaning against the base of the tree. "This place is special to you?"

"A sanctuary of sorts," I offered.

Idris opened his mouth and promptly shut it, his gaze flicking past me somewhere. His eyes narrowed and, for a moment, I could have sworn they glowed with crimson light. He shifted to look up at the sky again, but it wasn't long before I realized what had caught his attention.

They weren't asleep at all.

"You brought a *demon* here?!" a familiar male voice demanded. I scowled and glanced over my shoulder to find my estranged father and several other men from the compound stalking toward us.

They had guns.

"Demon?" I asked, puzzled, glancing between Idris and the zealots. Were they just making strange assumptions? Was I missing something? I couldn't figure out why my brother, and now my father, had called Idris a demon. Sure, his hair and eye color were odd, but aside from that he looked human.

"You're coming back with us, Cerys." Father reached for my arm, but in an instant, Idris had pushed me behind him and used himself to shield me. "Out of our way, demon! I won't let you take my daughter!"

"Daughter... And you would greet her with weapons?" Idris' cold, murderous tone sent a chill down my spine. To my astonishment, his human disguise melted away to reveal his horns, pointed ears, and tail. One of the men panicked and lifted his gun to fire, but Idris grabbed the barrel and bent it to a ninety degree angle.

"Why would you bring a demon here, Cerys?!" Father snarled, leveling his weapon at us as well. "I knew the heathens in the city were swaying you to their ways, but a *demon*, Cerys? By the gods, if you've bred with him—"

"Your own daughter, a demon's whore," one of the other men snickered. He was younger than my father by a few years and had wanted to overthrow him for decades. "Just wait until everyone hears of this! You won't be in charge much longer if you continue failing to put her down."

"Aye, look at that dress!" Another man shot me a lecherous smirk. I bristled and curled my fingers into Idris' suit jacket. My older sister had been forced to marry the bastard when she'd hit her mid-teens. "What a disgrace. Let's just end this."

Another man, the one I would have married had I not escaped, fired a shot at us—but it stopped in the air in front of Idris. Being so close to him, I could practically feel his rage bubble over. Before I could do anything, the demon king had torn the weapon from the bastard's hands and fed it to him. Idris shoved the gun down his throat until there was a sickening crunch, and the man dropped to the ground.

The others panicked and raised their guns, but they weren't a match for a pissed-off demon. Idris' face twisted with rage. Flames engulfed one of his hands as he lashed out, grabbing a gun nearest to him and pushing it aside. A shot went off, landing harmlessly in the dirt. With a jerk of his hand, Idris sheared the barrel in two and tossed the flaming scrap aside. With the weapon rendered useless, he grabbed the man by the scruff of his neck and threw him off the hill, catching the bastard's clothes alight.

Idris engulfed one of the remaining men's weapons in a ball of flame, forcing him to drop his weapon. While the man was panicking, he chucked him off the hill as well—leaving only us and my father remaining.

The enraged incubus rounded on my father next, towering over him, an expression of pure disgust on his face.

"Filth that would harm their own child makes me sick." Idris lifted my father by the front of his shirt. "Cerys will be remaining with me—where she is safe from the likes of *you*, and these creatures you call 'allies.' Come after her again and I will wipe your little village off the map."

To emphasize his point, Idris pulled the tree's shadow to him and let it climb up my father's legs. It didn't take long for the smaller man to piss himself and start whimpering.

I stared at the pair, then glanced to where Idris had chucked the others. They were on their feet, but instead of coming to attack us again, they were hightailing it toward the compound. I didn't know how to feel about the situation. On some level, I wanted to gloat. On another, I knew I should *probably* be disturbed by the violence. A dead man, one I *knew*, laid on the ground so close— but I was *happy* about his death.

"We are leaving—and you are letting us." Idris spoke, his voice taking on a musical quality. My thoughts grew fuzzy for a brief moment, but I shook it off. My father couldn't appear to do the same. "Come along, Cerys. We have wasted enough time on these fools."

Given the circumstances, I suppose I can tolerate orders. I bit back my snark and let the fuming demon escort me back to my car. Once there, his form returned to normal and he made damned sure I was situated in the driver's seat before getting in himself. The moment he was in, I smashed my finger into the 'home' button and the car took off. "That was a little—"

"They are lucky I refrained from burning them off the face of this planet!" Idris snapped, slamming his fist into the door's armrest. "Such filthy creatures. To imagine you had to contend with such foul people for much of your life. The things they *thought*—"

"The things they thought?" I echoed, glancing over at him again.

"You did not tell me they go after underaged children," he growled.

"Ah—'of age' in the compound is stuck several centuries in the past, yes. By their laws, legal. By everyone else's…not so much." I grimaced, returning my gaze to the driver's side window. "Like I said before—I was a smart kid. I got out as fast as I could. Learning that they'd chosen my husband—"

"Who is now dead."

"Yes—thanks for that, by the way." I looked over to him and he shot me a perplexed look.

More importantly, can he read minds or something? I guess I should expect an incubus or a succubus to be capable of reading sexual thoughts. But can he read more than that? ...I almost think I'd be better off not knowing the answer.

"You asked me to refrain from violence."

"*In* the city. Out here is different."

"You could have told me that sooner." Idris narrowed his eyes.

"To be fair, they should have been asleep."

"Anyway, you were saying?" he sighed.

"I ran away when I learned they'd found a husband for me," I replied. "Because my father runs the compound, me and my siblings were safe from a lot of the nastier things that go on there. The leader's children are off limits, but the rest aren't so lucky.

"A lot of people living there, including the children, have been brainwashed to think this is how things are done. That the rest of the world lives their lives in similar ways. Most of them don't know any better."

"Then how did you learn of it?" Idris frowned at me and then paused. "Furthermore, are you alright? Did they manage to injure you? Ah, or perhaps my magic frightened—"

"Your magic that I thought you didn't have access to here?" I shot him a pointed look and his frown deepened.

"I did not think I had access to it either. I just…reacted." He shook his head slightly. "Perhaps the gods took pity on us? Or perhaps they were lying from the start about my being incapable of using magic in your world. Hmmm, or perhaps Earth's gods did not want to owe Jeriskyr's deities more souls. A king and a champion would be 'expensive' to replace…"

"I'm fine." I shrugged slightly. "Got to enjoy the stars for a little while, at least…"

"It was a dangerous risk." Idris reached toward my cheek but stopped himself, shaking his head again. "However, I can see why it is your favorite place. It *is* beautiful. It would be much better without those creatures there."

"Creatures?" I tilted my head.

"Calling them 'human' is an insult to even humans!" Idris looked out the passenger window with a huff.

"I'm human too, remember?" I remarked dryly, watching him stiffen.

"You hardly count as one. I have said it before and I will say it again: you are wasted on the humans." he shot me a sideways glance before returning his gaze to the scenery outside.

I had no idea what to make of that, so I chose to let it be.

"Why has my father not dealt with those people yet?" Idris asked, his expression troubled. "Were this Nabyr-zahn, and it was still under his rule, he would have slaughtered those implicit in such crimes and rescued the women, children, and infants."

"It isn't that simple in this world. After four World Wars, people want to avoid conflict as much as they can, even to the detriment of others," I spat, more than a decade of anger setting my blood on fire. "He's required to solve the problem peacefully. Unfortunately, that takes an obscene amount of time. The people in charge of the compound know their activities are wrong. They won't give up their positions so easily."

"Ridiculous," Idris sighed.

"Bruce, inform Gwythyr and his people what happened." I tapped the dashboard, watching a blue light flicker to life. "Have the front desk prepare some good liquor for me too, while you're at it. I'm going to need it after that mess."

"Very well, Mistress. Idris, would you care for anything?"

"No."

The rest of our drive was spent in silence. Idris silently fumed, while I simply attempted to process his behavior. I couldn't recall a time when someone had gotten so pissed off, seemingly on my behalf. By the sound of things, it was more personal than that—clearly, he'd sensed or intuited just how foul the men were. It was easier, and less complicated, to think that information had been the real reason for his rage.

When we strode into the apartment building, I collected a small box containing several types of liquor and the snacks that complimented them. By the amount, it looked like Bruce had either ordered more than necessary or the receptionists had assumed that Idris would be joining me.

Once we were in the elevator and heading up through the building, Idris let out a soft sigh and asked, "Did I frighten you?"

"Hmmm? No." I shot him an odd look. "You didn't frighten me when you *were* trying to kill me, so why would you frighten me when you were defending me?"

"Perhaps because magic isn't meant to exist in your world?" Idris suggested, narrowing his eyes. "Because you are a human and I am a demon? Because—"

"Do you *want* me to be scared of you?" I arched an eyebrow and watched him falter.

"No, but I am fairly certain you should be," he frowned.

"Sounds like a waste of energy," I shrugged, stepping out of the elevator. I wasn't sure if I should tell him his actions, such as killing my would-have-been husband, had actually come as a relief. When we got to my door, I sighed and glanced up at the brooding man beside me. "Can you hold this for a moment?"

"Of course."

I handed the box to him and pulled my keys out of my purse. Once inside, I turned to take the box from him, but he strode straight past me and carried it into the kitchen. I made a face at his back and closed the door, making certain to lock it.

"You do not intend to sleep?" Idris asked, after setting the box down on the counter. He turned to watch me as I discarded my handbag and keys in their usual place.

"After that? No. I'm going to change out of this, get a glass or four of the strongest liquor in that box, and curl up on the sofa to watch something or read a book." I shook my head as I headed toward my bedroom door. "If you're going to sleep, I'll try to be quiet."

Before he could answer, I retreated into my room and proceeded to strip off my dress. Just being *near* those bastards had made me feel like I needed to shower, so I took one. Even so, I felt…relieved, and a little confused. I had hated the people from the compound for a long time, even fantasized about getting to execute them for their crimes—or at least be responsible for their prison time.

For the past few years, I'd come to accept that neither would ever happen due to the way our government functioned. Then, Idris had come along in his demonic glory and put an end to one of the figures who had haunted me for so long.

A demon who served vigilante justice. I laughed to myself.

By the time I left my room again, almost an hour had passed, but I felt a little better.

Idris, on the other hand, looked more worried than before. At least he seemed to put two and two together once he spotted my damp hair.

I did my best not to stare at his nude torso or his too-low pants. *This man is still trying to kill me, I swear, he's just changed his approach.*

"Would it be alright if we continued watching that 'anime' we were watching earlier today?" Idris inquired as I walked past him. "Or did you perhaps have something else in mind?"

"That's fine—you should watch both as soon as possible anyway." I pulled a large wine glass down and then looked through the bottles of liquor. After brief deliberation, I pulled out the amaretto and filled my glass almost to the rim. "Help yourself to whatever you want. They sent way too much for just one person."

I strode into the living room and placed my glass on the coffee table before adjusting the curtains to block out the light. Next, I rummaged around for some blankets and tossed them on the couch. I had no intention of falling asleep beside Idris again, but I *was* cold after my shower and I *refused* to snuggle anywhere near him for warmth.

"You learn anything from the anime so far?" I asked, taking a seat on the far-left end of the sofa. My hope was that he'd get the point if I scrunched myself into the corner. The less temptation I had to deal with, the better.

"Only that I will have to revise our plans several times over when we return," Idris answered, sitting down directly beside me. So much for him taking the hint. "They leave out the strangest details. They delve into my personal life, as well as our plans for dealing with the empire, yet leave out things such as my marital status or harem—"

"You have a harem?" I turned to give him an incredulous look.

Now I was *definitely* keeping my distance. It'd be way easier than I'd thought. Ugh—harem. Maybe I should've known, medieval demon king and all. I added that to the list of reasons not to get involved. Yet it was also…disappointing.

"Jealous?" Idris smirked.

"Definitely not." I rolled my eyes.

"Is that so? You strike me as the sort of woman who would want to be my only kitten." His smirk broadened as I debated punching him.

"You're terribly mistaken if you think I want to be your *anything*."

"Even though I am your favorite?" He motioned loosely toward the TV and I twitched.

"*Were* my favorite. Not anymore," I scoffed. Even more infuriating than him, or my decision to see him as off-limits, was the fact that he seemed to reignite the childishness in me.

"I'm hurt!" he exclaimed, clutching his heart. The sultry look on his face severely dampened the effect. "You could be so much more than simply our champion, Cerys."

"I have no good reason to *want* to be 'more.'" I shot him an agitated look before plucking my glass of amaretto off the coffee table. "Now, shut up and watch the anime. I don't have the patience—"

"Perhaps I intend to give you a reason to want more?" Idris caught my free hand and kissed my knuckles, his lips curving into a smile against my skin. "I tire of Otherworlders abandoning us when they have gotten what they came for or came to do. If you need a reason to stay—I will become that reason. If I cannot, then I will *find* something that will make you wish to stay."

"...just watch the damned anime, Idris."

Chapter Sixteen
A Day In

Peace. Quiet. Thank fucking god.

I yawned widely and stretched out in my bed. How I'd gotten there escaped me, but I was content enough to see that I was still in my pajamas and alone. I reached out from under the covers and plucked my phone off the end table, pulling it under the blanket with me. Dozens of messages again—mostly Ebonwing members asking for further instructions regarding *Jeriskyr Online*.

Gwythyr had messaged me too, to inform me he'd plucked his son away for breakfast. Good. That explained the quiet. I needed a break from the tantalizing bastard.

Alice, on the other hand, had sent me thirty messages. Most of them were asking about the relationship she seemed to think I had with Idris. I groaned and sunk into my pillow. «Alice, seriously, I'm not dating him and I'm not going to. Plus, he has a harem. Definitely a no»

«But he's so pretty!» Alice responded immediately. «Did you ask *why* he has a harem?»

«A pretty big pain in the ass, sure...»

Alice expertly ignored my quip. «Adric and I are going back to Jeriskyr today, so I won't be able to come have dinner with the two of you again. Apparently we've gotta act more like mortal enemies or something. Promise me you'll reconsider about Idris? He can't be as bad as you seem to think he is»

«Alice... He's not bad. That isn't the problem» I sighed in exasperation. «I don't want to be stuck in Jeriskyr permanently. Getting involved with anyone sounds like a quick ticket to remaining there *forever*»

«And what's wrong with that?» she countered.

«It isn't home»

«It could be» Alice started typing immediately and I grimaced when the message came through. «Gotta go! See you when you come save our asses!»

I tossed my phone aside and rolled onto my back to stare at the ceiling. Conversations like that didn't help me by any stretch of the imagination. I resigned myself to getting out of bed and spent the next few hours writing up more detailed instructions for the Ebonwing members. It was difficult to give them information without putting Silas in danger or giving away anything about Idris, but I was rather satisfied with the results when all was said and done.

After staring at my screen for a few minutes, I decided to shoot an e-mail to Iris—Corlyotir. Whatever. I had no idea what I was supposed to call her anymore, but I had a question for her that had been burning in the back of my mind.

Quite simply: *Why the hell did you drop me in the middle of a battlefield for my first visit to the demons?*

I didn't really expect an answer from her, but I got one all the same. Sort of.

Good morning, Cerys!

Our intention was always to make certain you met Idris Bloodsong in a swift manner. If he had been at his palace, you would have 'spawned' there. Had he been bathing, perhaps you would have landed in the bath with him. Or if he had been at dinner, you could have landed on his table.

I'm certain you and he will continue to get along famously.

Regards,
Iris Hughes, CEO

The corner of my eye twitched, and after a moment, I sighed. All those options were significantly better than landing in the middle of a damned battlefield. Though I didn't even want to *think* about what Idris' reaction would have been if I'd 'dropped in' on his bath. Hell, I wasn't convinced the gods would've even graced me with clothes if they'd done that.

With that done, I busied myself in the kitchen next. I had no interest in leaving the apartment today, demon king or no demon king. It was a wall of rain outside and just *looking* at it made me feel cold. However, I was quickly running out of things to do on my lonesome. More correspondence with Iris sounded like a terrible idea.

I paced around the living room with my tablet in hand and flicked through page after page of Jeriskyr Studios' forum in search of class and skill information. I wasn't entirely sure if the system would apply to me or not, but my tour of Cejari-ir had given me the impression that it might. Idris had mentioned guilds related to combat. At the very least, I had to assume that I'd be able to find some manner of training within the city.

Since people *had* attempted to roll demon characters on Nabyr-zahn's side, I figured I'd be able to get details about the guilds on the forum—and perhaps figure out what skills I wanted to focus on.

"You look quite serious." Idris' voice startled me into turning around. "Were you lonely without me, kitten?"

"I've lived alone for years, so no." I rolled my eyes before turning my attention back to the tablet. "I'm reading, go find someone else to bother."

The temptation to kick myself flitted through my mind. I didn't understand why his mere presence made me so...bitchy. It was almost like a defensive reflex. But it wasn't like me. I couldn't determine if *he* caused me to act differently, or if something else was the issue. After all, I'd told myself that he didn't deserve bitch mode.

Yet...here we were.

"I will pass—the people of this world bore me," Idris replied. He brushed his fingers down my spine as he passed me, leaving a trail of goosebumps in their wake. He soon took a seat on the sofa. Something about the way he sat gave me the impression he was hoping I would hop into his lap. "What have you been brooding over?"

"Information." I attempted to force myself back into my calculated, businesslike demeanor. That way, I could be curt but lay off the bitch pants.

"About Jeriskyr?"

"Yes."

"You could have asked me," he pointed out, frowning. He looked a little hurt, but I couldn't decide if he was just faking it again.

"You were meeting with your father," I countered, arching an eyebrow at him. "Besides, I wanted the 'player' perspective—not that of the biased king."

"Are you not going to sit down?" He tilted his head.

"I think better when I pace."

"Perhaps if you show me what you are looking at, I can help?" Idris shot me an agitated look. I paused. He was sort of right, but I also didn't feel like contending with his shenanigans. Then again, we were stuck with each other for the remainder of the day.

"I prefer to do things on my own." I shut the tablet off and set it on a nearby shelf. "How much of the anime did you make it through last night?"

"You do not remember?" Idris chuckled when I twitched. "Well, you were a little too engrossed in trying to kiss me."

"Bullshit!" I whirled around to glare at him. "I don't care how drunk I may have gotten, I wouldn't—"

"You did not," he smiled. "I was teasing—but you did answer my question, at least inadvertently. You must have wondered how you got to bed, then?" When I pursed my lips, he broke into a grin and shook his head. "I carried you, Cerys—and I assure you I was a perfect gentleman."

"Perfect gentleman by human or demon standards?" I squinted at him.

"I did not press my luck." He raised his hands. "Now then, to answer your original question, I finished watching it. You said there was another version you wished for me to watch?"

Wishing wasn't what I would have called it. I held my tongue and stalked over to the TV instead, swapping the versions of the anime. "The other one is from the perspective of those who favor the Issradian Empire. I figure there's a lot you can learn from that one, too."

"Will you join me?" Idris glanced up from the seat beside him to me.

I crossed my arms and attempted to think of a way out of it, but I didn't have a good enough excuse. Telling him I wanted to avoid forming attachments would've just caused more problems. The same went for if I tried to point out our differing species. "I'm going to get food first. You can start watching without me."

"I will wait," he stated as I strode past him.

Why? I bit back a sigh and glanced over my shoulder. "While I'm at it, do you want any food or a drink?"

"Are you on the menu?"

"*No.*"

"In that case, I will have whatever you are having."

I rolled my eyes once in the kitchen. He won an award for persistence, at least, if nothing else.

When I returned a while later with food and drink, I discovered Idris had really meant it when he said he'd wait. It completely puzzled me, but I shook it off and offered him one of the two plates instead. He seemed to make a point of brushing his fingers against mine before taking it and shooting me an alluring smile.

I wasn't in the mood.

"Will we be going anywhere today?" Idris asked when I sat as far from him as possible.

"No."

"You do not wish to see Alice?"

"…she and Adric returned to Jeriskyr this morning." I glanced at Idris, catching his frown before shifting my focus to my food. "Given what she said, we won't be seeing either of them again until we 'rescue' them from the Empire."

"She is dangerously attached to that man," he grimaced.

"Finally, something we agree on," I snorted.

"Are you not going to ask how my meeting with my father went?" Idris inquired, shooting me a curious look.

"Why would I? It's none of my business." I frowned at him.

"You truly believe that?" He shifted so that he had one leg crossed over the other, his torso turned to face me.

"Absolutely. There's no reason for me to think that I have a right to know." I nudged food across my plate and focused on that so I wouldn't have to look at him.

"You are not curious?" Idris' dispirited tone made me take a peek at him after all. His expression matched his voice, leading me to believe it was genuine.

"I'm not close enough to either of you to be," I stated, hoping that would explain it better. It wasn't anything personal at all, I simply didn't think it was any of my business. "I don't like to pry."

"You could be."

"This again?" I groaned.

"Of course. I will not give up so easily." He smiled, placing an arm on the top of the sofa and resting his cheek against his fist. "Especially not after having seen your world and the place you come from. It looks like a prison rather than a home. This city is better, certainly, but the people only marginally so."

"But you have no reason to care." I shot him a baffled look.

"That is where you are wrong, kitten," he smirked, motioning to me loosely. "You chose my side—meaning you are now one of my subjects. Someone I intend to keep safe. A difficult task, no doubt, but one I intend to see through until the end."

"Haven't we been over this whole 'kitten' thing?" I whined.

"Once I have finished reviewing the two anime," Idris began, ignoring my complaint, "I would like to learn more of your world. More 'shows' are fine, as are books. I am not picky."

"Bruce can find just about anything you need—and you can read it on the tablet I was using earlier," I shrugged. A change of topic was something I could certainly get behind.

"Ah, is that what you call this contraption?" Idris tilted his head. "A 'tablet?'"

"Mmhmm." I nodded briefly, then stared at him for a moment. "Are you actually comfortable in that form?"

"Not particularly, no," he answered plainly.

"Then why not use the other one now that you know you can?" I asked, puzzled.

"I thought..." He pursed his lips for a moment, his eyes ticking back and forth while he contemplated something. "You do not mind?"

"Why would I?"

"In that case, I will gladly change."

He set his plate down, rose to his feet, pulled his pants down by another few inches, and then paused for a moment to concentrate. Within a few seconds, his tail slithered into place and the rest of his demonic form soon followed. He stretched his arms above his head and I forced myself to look away from his back.

"You were staring."

Guess I didn't look away fast enough. I grimaced at the wall before looking back at the smirking king. "Is there something wrong with being curious about this whole shapeshifting thing?"

"That was not why you were looking." Idris chuckled before taking a seat. He stretched out on his side, giving his tail plenty of room between him and the back of the sofa, then balanced his plate of food on the arm rest. "In fact, I would encourage you to look more."

"And give you the satisfaction? No." I reached for the remote, which I promptly tossed his way. "You should study, *Your Majesty.*"

Once done eating, I fetched my tablet again and resumed

searching for information online. Idris was the quietest person I'd *ever* watched anything with and that suited me just fine. For one, it meant no ridiculous flirting. For another, it meant I could focus on something I found more interesting. Thirdly, doing some manner of work meant I was less likely to find myself staring at him.

Good looks aside, the sight of a demon lounging on my couch was hilarious.

"Cerys," Idris whispered by my ear a while later, startling me. When I turned to look at him, his face was mere inches from mine. He smirked when I attempted to lean back from him.

"Haven't you ever heard of personal space?" I demanded. My stomach flipped a few times, my pulse racing. How much was caused by him startling me, and how much was because of…well, *him*, I didn't know.

"I tried to get your attention the normal way—you were too absorbed." He backed away and shot me an amused smile. "What are you studying?"

"Your world's skill system," I answered, shifting the tablet to show him a long list of professions. "Since you played *Bengllor Online* a little bit the other day…you know what a class is, right?"

"Yes."

"Most games are a one-and-done sort of deal when it comes to picking a class," I continued as Idris scooted closer to take a better look at the screen. "*Jeriskyr Online* isn't like that—we're told that the three skill sets or professions we choose are what determine our class. However, I noticed that Silas and the other men at the brothel—"

"You joined him at a brothel, yet you refuse me?" Idris stared at me in disbelief.

"I was working as a bouncer." I tensed my jaw. "*Anyway*, as I was saying, I noticed that they were all the same 'class,' but each had a different combination of skills. Sometimes games give NPCs—non-player characters—their own unique rules. Now that I know *Jeriskyr Online* isn't just a game, I'm attempting to determine if it's something else."

"Without asking me for details?" Idris moped.

"I can't really ask you or anyone from your world for details if I'm not first familiar with the way it works for normal players," I pointed out, earning a sigh. After a moment, he slipped an arm behind my back and pulled me closer. "What are you—"

"It is easier for me to see this way." He tapped the screen with his free hand and used the other to pull me tighter against him. I hoped he couldn't hear my pulse speeding up. "Now then, what other limits are imposed on 'players?'"

"Skill proficiency is judged by ranks, and the time investment to hit the maximum rank in any given skill is…well, ridiculous." I swiped one window off the screen and brought up a visual representation of the skill ranks. "Most of the Ebonwing members haven't maxed their first skill yet. My arrangements for them involve having them focus on a single class up to max proficiency before they worry about any others. In theory, a single player can master every skill. Though the time sink is unrealistic."

"For an Otherworlder." Idris shot me an odd look. "So, you need to decide what skills to choose?"

"Yes. I don't like being helpless, or bored, or useless, so I intend to work on mastering at least one class immediately," I answered, flipping to another window. "I've been narrowing down what I think I'd actually like to use."

"Cerys."

"What?"

"What usually happens to Otherworlders when they die 'in-game' in Jeriskyr?" Idris gave me a meaningful look, any hint of his teasing gone.

"They respawn wherever they made their home point, and—"

"And what do you think happens to champions when they die?"

"Oh..." I fell silent and thought for a moment. "I'm going to assume that they don't respawn. However, given what the deities said, perhaps we wake up in our original—"

"No. You do not."

"Then... We die if we are killed?" I paused, grimacing.

"I think you just answered your own question." He gave me a lopsided smile void of happiness. After a moment he sighed and sunk back against the sofa. "Jeriskyr is a dangerous world, especially for a woman. You may be expected to help us overthrow the empire, but you will require a great deal of training before you can handle yourself against them.

"Demons are naturally much stronger than humans, but the humans have other ways to make up for it. They are particularly fond of applying poison to their blades or carrying incense to disorient our senses. Their tricks are seemingly endless."

"I appreciate your concern, but—"

"I am not attempting to talk you out of it." Idris gave me a knowing look. "My intent is to help you, not impede you. Training outside of the palace will be out of the question, for a time. Once you determine what you would like to learn, I will have the appropriate tutors come to you."

"I... Thank you," I sighed.

"You dislike the idea of being a caged bird?" Idris offered, smiling.

"'Dislike' is putting it lightly."

"It is a temporary measure until you are no longer easy prey for the humans."

"I can respect your decision *and* not like it, you know."

"Of course," Idris murmured, his gaze drifting along my jawline and briefly down to my throat, before his crimson eyes flicked back up to meet my agitated glare. "You are certain you will not become my queen?"

"Quite certain."

"Perhaps one of my concubines?" He tilted his head.

"What?!" I snapped, shifting to growl directly at him. "You're demoting me now? How is 'concubine' *any* better?"

"You should reconsider either option," Idris replied, giving me an amused look. He caught my wrist when I went to punch him and held my arm out of the way with ease. "Concubine may be more fitting given just how many tails you've serviced."

"What the fuck are you on about?" I demanded, attempting to tug out of his grip. The smirk that settled onto his lips made me bristle. Whoever had decided he was allowed to look so sexy *and* arrogant at the same time deserved to be skinned.

"I am only referring to the second-most sensitive portion of a demon's body, of course," Idris answered with mock innocence. "You tugged half my army. In fact, I am a little jealous you left me out."

"You *must* be joking!" I exclaimed.

"Would you like a demonstration?" he purred, leaning toward me.

"Absolutely not!" I shot to my feet and moved several paces away from him. He laughed and sprawled out on the couch on his stomach, his tail twitching back and forth like a cat's. The look in his eyes as he watched me made me want to stomp on his face. However, at this point, I was starting to think he'd enjoy that.

"Cerys," Idris called as I stalked toward the door.

"*What?*" I snapped.

"You should contemplate why I would offer you *any* such position in my kingdom," he stated, his tone finally serious and his gaze piercing. "I assure you that I have a reason."

Yeah? Well I know where you can shove that reason. I turned my back to him again and strode through the door. "Then maybe *you* should find something better to suggest than 'the king's whore.'"

Without another word, I stalked into my room and locked the door behind me. I was pissed, frustrated, and seriously needed to kill something. Playing a VRMMO didn't seem like a good idea, so I pulled out one of my old consoles and looked for the bloodiest fighting game I could find. Once I'd finished setting it up, I pounced on my bed with the controller in hand.

Okay. Time to imagine his face on every damn monster in this game.

Chapter Seventeen
Lessons Learned, Lessons Ignored

I peered at Idris over the rim of my teacup. I wished he would learn to wear more clothes. For whatever reason, he had insisted on making breakfast this morning and seemed suspiciously cheerful. And clad only in pants…which he wore very low.

I glanced at the base of his tail and then up his muscular back again, wondering how he managed to avoid knocking anything over with the long limb.

If he hadn't infuriated me so much, if he hadn't been from a different world, and if he hadn't had a harem, I would've been content to just stare at him all day…and more. Alas, too many important check-boxes were mentally ticked with a huge 'nope.'

"We should go out today." Idris pivoted to carry two plates of food to the table. He sat across from me and gave me a charming smile. "At the very least, you should see your brother one more time before we return to Jeriskyr—and it would not be wise for me to let you go on your own."

"I dunno. Maybe," I muttered, before taking another sip of tea.

"It is not safe—"

"I meant maybe about the going out part." I shook my head. "Word of what happened at the compound has probably made it to their operatives in the city already. Even if they *weren't* here, though…going out isn't exactly something I do much."

"Would you rather leave me to my own devices?" Idris smirked.

"Ah… Definitely not." I sighed, putting down my tea. "Right. I need to play 'good hostess' while you're here. What do you want to see?"

"I simply wish to explore the city." He motioned to the windows. "On foot, if at all possible. While convenient, these 'car' contraptions do not allow me to get a feel for what the people or cultures here are like."

I had to wonder why he even cared. I shrugged. He'd probably thought similarly of me when I'd demanded to see his capital. "Okay. Since I forced you to give me a tour of Cejari-ir, it's the least I can do."

"I would prefer you join me because you want to." A small

frown flitted across his lips. "Is there something else you would rather do?"

"Normally I spend my days sleeping and gaming." I sighed, slumping back in my chair. "The latter has lost its appeal slightly."

"I would imagine so." Idris leaned forward on his elbows and peered at me for a moment. "In that case... You have no qualms about accompanying me?"

I shook my head in response and decided to eat breakfast instead of speaking.

"Tell me, Cerys," Idris began with a playful smile, "have you reconsidered becoming my queen or concubine?"

"No," I stated.

"You could be whichever you desired."

"Why would I desire either? I dislike polygamous men."

He shot me a rather frustrated look. "I am not polygamous."

"Then what are you?" I rolled my eyes and strolled toward my room. If we were going somewhere, I'd have to figure out something to wear.

"Monogamous—and available," Idris purred as he followed me. He leaned against the door frame and watched me with an amused smile.

"Yet you have a harem," I pointed out.

Idris' smirk grew. "Something that should not bother you if you are as averse to my presence as you pretend to be."

Er... Well. Hmmm. I bit my lower lip and looked through my selection of dresses while attempting to think of a retort. However, my phone practically exploding with vibrations in my pocket saved me. Frowning, I pulled out my phone and nearly dropped it on the floor as it continued to vibrate.

"Is something the matter?" Idris moved to peer over my shoulder.

"I'm guessing so," I muttered, swiping the lock screen away. The torrent of messages was mostly from Ebonwing members. Even as they streamed onto my screen, I could see they mostly said the same thing: «You abandoned us to date the model for Idris Bloodsong?!»

Sighing in agitation, I swapped over to my e-mail, and sure enough, found an e-mail from Iris waiting for me. It had actually arrived minutes *before* my guildmates started spamming me.

Miss Collins,

I am afraid your time on Earth has been cut short. We will be returning you and King Bloodsong to Jeriskyr tomorrow morning. The human gods have decided that allowing the two of you to remain on Earth longer than their *champion constitutes an unfair advantage—and they do not intend to allow Alice and Adric to return to Earth.*

By now, you have likely received many messages from Ebonwing members asking about your motives for joining the demons. You and Idris were seen by press going in and out of Aleksander's. *A few astute individuals recognized Idris from the 'game.' They believe you are dating.*

To cover, Jeriskyr Studios will be claiming that the important 'NPCs' of Jeriskyr are played by actual people—and that the Idris Bloodsong in-game is modeled after his 'real life equivalent.'

In order to pacify Ebonwing, for a time, we will be stating that we hired you to play an NPC as well.

You should spend the day and evening tending to any remaining goodbyes you have to say. It is unlikely that you will be afforded a chance to return to Earth prior to defeating the Issradian Empire.

Regards,

Iris Hughes, CEO

"This is bad?" Idris' breath tickled my ear, making me stiffen.

"You're a little too close." I edged away from him.

"Again, something that should not bother you," he smiled.

"Ugh." I rolled my eyes before turning my phone's vibration off and setting it aside. "Well, if you still intend to go into town, then I suppose I'll have to look for something discreet to wear. Hmmm…"

"How about this?" Idris asked, pulling a short crimson dress down from the rack. When I stared at him in disbelief, he gave me an equally puzzled look.

"There's nothing discreet about that," I pointed out, before snatching it and returning it to its rightful place.

"Perhaps I want to see you in it?"

"Why would you care—and why should *I* care?"

"A beautiful woman shouldn't be frightened of wearing beautiful things."

"I'm not frightened. I want to avoid us attracting the wrong kind of attention." I shook my head. "Given Iris— Corlyo...Coryl..."

"Corlyotir."

"Yeah. That." I grimaced. "Given the e-mail she sent me, we should assume that our privacy has been compromised. We may have to deal with journalists, reporters, overly excited gamers, and so on, if we're going out somewhere."

"It would be more fun to embrace it." Idris strode past me and deeper into my closet, his expression one of intrigue. "For someone so insistent on denying me, you certainly have a sultry taste in fashion. I can see why you are struggling to find something that *will not* draw attention to us.

"Now then, what is this 'dating' Corlyotir mentioned?"

"I... Are you serious?" I tilted my head.

"Quite." Idris glanced back at me. "You've used similar terms before, but I am unfamiliar with them."

"Dating is a form of modern courting," Bruce explained, causing the demon to grin. *"A 'date' is when two people who are a couple— or may become a couple—go to dinner or other special occasions*

together with the purpose of getting to know each other. Aleksander's *is a popular date spot."*

"And for some reason it matters to these people that you are dating me?" Idris asked.

"I'm not dating you." I rubbed my temples and sighed heavily. "Even if I was, it shouldn't matter to anyone. It matters to my guild mates because they think I left them to get laid. I don't know how long they'll believe Iris' story about me working for Jeriskyr Studios as an NPC.

"Why the *press* cares is what has me stumped—unless someone recognized your resemblance to Councilor Gwythyr. If they've realized he has a son, then you likely just became one of the most desired men in the city. Your father has expertly avoided forming romantic relationships while in power—meaning the people who have tried to get in with him may turn their attention to you."

"Is there a way to find out for certain?" Idris scowled. For someone so intent on chasing my skirt, he seemed surprisingly displeased with the idea of being so popular on Earth.

"Yeah but I should get dressed first—and you need to find clothes, too."

"How about this?" Idris pulled down a form-fitting black dress.

"I don't think it would fit you," I smirked.

"For you, obviously." He tossed it to me. "I will attempt to find something subtle for myself."

Idris turned and walked out of the closet, finally leaving me with a moment to gather my thoughts. I couldn't fathom where he got his confidence or balls from. He made ridiculous claims more easily than most people could make sincere gestures or comments.

Stupid demon king. Why did he have to be my type? I stalked into my room and stripped off my pajamas so that I could change into the black dress. Although I didn't want to give him the satisfaction of picking something out for me, it was the least colorful and least revealing dress I owned. It would have to do.

When I walked out of my room a few minutes later, Idris slowly examined me and shot a second glance at my high heels. "You plan to walk around in such shoes?"

"They're good shoes—I'll be fine," I shrugged, before narrowing my eyes at him. "You're supposed to button those types of shirts all the way up."

"I find this more alluring," he countered.

"Suit yourself." I shook my head. He shot me a subtle frown as I walked past him and toward the living room. When he didn't follow, I glanced over my shoulder. "You wanted to see if we could find out if they've linked you to Gwythyr, right?"

"We can do that without leaving?" Idris asked, finally moving to join me.

"Bruce, turn on a news station—I don't care which one," I instructed the AI.

"This is…news?" Idris tilted his head when the TV flickered on to show a woman getting double-teamed by two incredibly buff men.

"*Bruce!* I said *news,* not *porn!*" I snapped, turning to glower at the AI's light.

"Are you certain, Mistress? It has been a while since you asked for por—"

"Yes, I am fucking sure!" I interrupted. "*News. Now.*"

"Is that the sort of thing you typically watch?" Idris inquired, an amused smile on his face.

"*No, it is not!*"

"There's nothing to be ashamed—"

"It. Isn't. What. I. Watch." I poked his chest with each word.

"So, you do watch something?" Idris arched an eyebrow.

"Doesn't everyone?" I shot him a baffled look and then sighed. "Right. Different worlds. Jeriskyr doesn't have TV or Internet."

"It is a normal thing in this world?" Idris glanced at the TV, which still hadn't changed its picture, then pursed his lips. "That woman sounds like she is attempting to mimic a cow in heat."

"Wha—" I burst into laughter. He was absolutely right, but his confusion over it—and the blunt statement—caught me entirely off-guard.

"What?" Idris shot me an exasperated look. "Am I wrong?"

"No—you're right, and that's part of why it's funny!" I laughed, clutching my sides. "Ah... I haven't laughed like that in a while. Whew.

"Yes, porn—that is, pornography—is normal in this world. It's one of the most lucrative industries and has been for a long time. As for your complaint regarding the sounds, well…a lot of women have to fake it. Porn or otherwise."

"How terribly boring," Idris scoffed, before cutting his eyes toward Bruce's light. "I believe your mistress gave you instructions, did she not?"

After a moment, the TV channel changed, but Bruce wasn't done with his games yet. I sighed and pressed my fingers to my temples. Of course the AI had to pick a channel I did actually watch. Great. That would be more difficult to talk my way out of.

"Well, this is certainly more interesting—if not what you were asking for," Idris remarked, amused, his gaze on the screen. "However, her master has terrible technique. That crop will likely leave permanent marks."

…I'm just going to pretend he didn't say that. I strode over to the couch in search of the remote and tapped my foot when I didn't see it. "Idris, do you see the remote anywhere? Bruce obviously isn't going to cooperate. We should probably hurry a bit since we're now on a time crunch."

"Is he not an automaton? Can you not *make* him cooperate?"

"AI means artificial intelligence—he's got a mind of his own."

"Someone needs to train these people. Honestly," Idris mocked the porn stars, crossing his arms at the TV, "how can they hope to keep a lover when their technique is so atrocious?"

"They're *hired actors*, Idris," I stated, shooting him a baffled look. "It isn't meant to resemble reality. And they're not usually in a relationship with the person they're with in the videos. It's supposed to be fantasy—what people think, not what people actually do."

"No wonder it is so boring," he sniffed, turning away from the TV. "I will help you look for the remote."

Why am I even discussing porn with a demon king? I grimaced as I pulled a cushion off the sofa. At least he didn't appear aroused by it. *That* would've been a little difficult to ignore.

"In politics, singles all over the city are heartbroken after reporters captured this *picture of Councilor Gwythyr's son, Idris, entering* Aleksander's *with Cerys Collins. The woman in question is known to be in the Councilor's care and is involved with one of the top gaming guilds in the world, Ebonwing.*

"Our sources tell us that the couple are simply colleagues who work at Jeriskyr Studios, however it looks to us like they're more than that."

"Wait...that isn't right." I pursed my lips at the TV as the reporter continued to ramble on.

"What?" Idris smirked. "The part about us being a 'couple'— or the claim that we aren't?"

"*We're not.*" I shot him an agitated look. "That isn't what's wrong. They're acting like they already knew about Gwythyr's son—despite this being the first time you've come to this world."

"Ah..." Idris glanced at the TV, his expression growing serious. "Then, would it not make more sense to focus on who I am and where I have been, instead?"

"Exactly." I turned on my heel and went searching for my phone. Once I found it in my closet, I returned to the living room where Idris was still watching the TV.

"Any word from Corlyotir?" Idris looked down at me briefly.

"No. Your father messaged me, though." I scrolled through the messages and skimmed them, grimacing. My life seemed to be getting weirder by the hour. "He says Earth's gods intervened…" I trailed off, skimming more of his messages, as I tried to wrap my head around the situation. I could handle the fact that other worlds existed, I could even deal with the idea that demons and the like were real. Deities, though, and how much they were willing to manipulate? That was a hard pill to swallow. "They planted memories in the heads of the populace and edited videos, photographs, and so on *en masse* to make it look like you've always been here.

"Oh… You make a cute kid."

I regretted saying it almost immediately but kept my face passive even as Idris turned to smirk at me. He plucked my phone from my hands soon after and skimmed the messages himself, his amusement growing. I needed to learn to keep my damned mouth shut.

"That is a surprising amount of effort for them to go to if we're only allowed to remain for the remainder of the day," Idris remarked, his gaze focused on the screen. After a moment, he tilted his head and tapped something. "Ah. Corlyotir expects us to pretend that we are business colleagues. We are to claim that we will be going out of town for work."

"Well, I guess that would keep Ebonwing members and my family from trying to find me in the city," I remarked as he handed my phone back to me. Sure enough, that was exactly what Corlyotir had asked us to do. She also seemed to think we would be dropping by *Aleksander's* again sometime tonight.

"Would it be simpler to go along with the claims we are a couple?" Idris asked, his gaze focused on the TV. For once, he sounded serious and not like he was hitting on me. I fell silent and truly considered it for a moment.

"No, I don't think so." I shook my head and glanced over at Bruce's light. "Bruce, how many fan sites are there for Idris?"

"Idris Bloodsong or Idris Gwythyr?"

"Really? They went with a patronym?" I murmured. Idris shot me a questioning look. "People of this world haven't used patronymic surnames in centuries. It would have made more sense for them to call you 'Idris Cynfyn' since your father is Gwythyr Cynfyn. Bruce, give me the numbers for both."

"There are two hundred thousand, four hundred and ninety fan sites for 'Idris Bloodsong' and one million, four hundred and seventy thousand, two hundred and eighty-six for 'Idris Gwythyr.' One eighth of the combined total are dedicated to Rule 34."

"Rule 34?" Idris asked when I snorted.

"More or less: 'if it exists, there is porn of it,'" I informed him. "Meaning an eighth of those sites are dedicated to erotic stories and artwork involving *you*. What I don't understand is how it's already reached that number. Even with Earth's gods interfering, that's still—"

"Deities are powerful," Idris shrugged, crossing his arms. "Anyway, how is this relevant to my original question?"

"Ah—right." I pursed my lips, turning to face him. "Given Earth's population, those numbers may seem small, but that's simply the number of websites there are. It doesn't include how many people actually *use* those sites. We should assume that each site has several hundred, if not several thousand, users. The most popular sites could have hundreds of thousands, or millions, of members."

"...meaning there is the potential for that many people within the city to have some form of interest in me." Idris glanced toward the windows and grimaced.

"I don't particularly want to have rabid fan girls or fan boys attacking me, so it's better if we don't go along with this 'couple' nonsense," I stated flatly, earning a confused look from him. "We'll act like work colleagues. If anyone asks, I'm showing you around the city because you don't get to visit much."

"And if they continue to pry about why you get the privilege?"

Privilege, my ass. I crossed my arms. "Then we'll say it's because our bosses at Jeriskyr Studios want us to get to know each other better so we can perform our roles as NPCs. If you really want to learn about my world, we need to get going."

"Would it really be so terrible to play along with the rumors?" Idris tilted his head as I strode past him.

"Have you ever experienced human jealousy firsthand?" I asked, glancing back at him. "It would be better if we didn't give them reasons to lash out at me, because even if they do, we're limited in what we can do to defend ourselves."

"Such incredible technological advances, yet humans remain savages..." Idris sighed heavily as he followed me, then paused, shooting me an apologetic look. "Minus you, of course. I struggle to think of you as a human."

"Thanks... I think?" I shook my head slightly before turning the vibration back on for my phone and dropping it into my handbag. "You said you want to walk around the city, but is there anything more specific you want to see?"

"You, out of that dress," Idris stated simply as we walked into the hallway.

"Out of the question."

"In that case, anywhere I can learn your world's history and culture."

"Right. Museums it is, then."

Once we arrived on the ground floor, I pivoted and walked a different way than we usually went, heading for the front doors. Idris strolled alongside me with his hands in his pockets and a confident smile on his face. I got the distinct feeling that either he didn't understand the sort of attention his commanding presence attracted, or that it was exactly what he wanted. By now, I was leaning toward the latter assumption.

"Enjoy your day, Ms. Collins. Be safe." One of the guards at the door nodded to me and smiled.

"She has nothing to fear with me as her escort," Idris declared.

Oh, for the love of... I rolled my eyes and held my tongue. He was such a ridiculous man.

"Now then—Ah." Idris attempted to catch my hand in his, but I swiftly avoided him. He tilted his head, giving me a curious look. "Perhaps you would prefer my arm?"

"Either one lands us in trouble." I sighed in exasperation. "*Colleagues*, remember? Means 'hands off.' Now then, one of the bigger museums is this way."

Idris fell into step with me, a contemplative expression on his face. He seemed more intent on watching me than examining our surroundings, but I chose not to comment on the matter. My patience had been stretched thin enough for the day and we hadn't even dealt with any press yet.

"You have amazing legs," Idris remarked, a small smile curving his lips when I shot him a sideways glance. "You claimed to spend most of your time sleeping and gaming—but your physique says otherwise. It appears you are more muscular than many of the women I've seen here. What sort of training do you do?"

Training... Maybe not the best choice of words after Bruce's shenanigans. I shrugged slightly. "Martial arts, mostly. There's a gym and a swimming pool in the apartment building as well."

"Oh? Perhaps you will agree to spar with me when we return for the evening?" Idris broke into a broad, mischievous grin. "It would certainly be a good way for me to gauge how much you need to learn."

"Depends on how much I decide to drink at dinner tonight," I stated.

"Ah, will we be dining in again this evening?" Idris snuck his arm around my waist and pulled me closer. I opened my mouth to tell him off, but promptly shut it when I caught the look he shot over my head. He leaned down and spoke by my ear once he noticed my expression. "I rather dislike the way some of these men are watching you...is this normal human behavior?"

"Hmmm?" I shot him a questioning look before taking stock of our surroundings. Nothing seemed out of place to me. Sure, I got the occasional look from other people on the street, but it was nothing out of the ordinary. A glance at my ass here, a peek at my chest there, glares from occasional women. "I'm going to assume so, since I have no idea what you're talking about."

"None?" Idris frowned.

"Indeed—so you can let go of me now."

"You really are quite stubborn," he remarked as he released my waist.

"And you seem intent on skipping half the steps involved in forming *any* kind of relationship with people," I countered. "How much do you know about me, Idris?"

"That I find you attractive, that you are feisty, and that you have no qualms about attacking someone vastly stronger than you," Idris chuckled.

"And how much do I know about you?" I gave him a pointed look.

"Ah... Well, if you want to get to know me, kitten, all you have to do is ask." He shot me a brilliant smile. "I suppose that would explain much of your aversion to me. However..."

"However?" I arched an eyebrow.

"Humans are mere food more often than not," Idris informed me, a mildly quizzical expression settling onto his features. "That is why I struggle to see you as one of them—in part. Simply being in my presence does not appear to be enough to sway you. While I enjoy a challenge... I simply do not understand why you are one."

"You should probably leave getting to know me—or not—until we return to Jeriskyr," I pointed out, earning a displeased frown in reply. "Idris. You *did* say you wanted to learn about this place, and we don't know how early in the morning we're going to be sent back."

"I...suppose I did." Idris sighed, looking away from me.

"Furthermore, while we're on the topic," I started, crossing my arms, "you should stop flirting with me. Lack of knowledge about each other aside, I'm not going to Jeriskyr for romance and won't have time for it. I'm being sent there to fix your mess and earn my way back here.

"I have to learn the history of the various nations, how to protect myself, how to fight for others, hone my skills—whichever ones I choose. There's no way I will have time for—"

"Which one of us are you trying to convince—me, or yourself?" Idris tilted his head, a confident smirk spreading across his lips. I twitched. He saw through me too easily. "You are implying that I am already a distraction to you. You must be *vaguely* interested in me, or that would not be the case."

"Just because you're nice to look at doesn't mean—"

"So, you are admitting you find me attractive?"

"I don't recall claiming otherwise." Now it was my turn to be confused. "Your level of physical attractiveness was never in question. Like I said earlier, we know nothing about each other— and I'd prefer it remains that way."

"Are all Earth women so comfortable with telling a man he is attractive?" Idris asked, a mischievous smile still on his lips. "Or is this simply a quirk of yours?"

"There's all sorts. You can't generalize like that." I rolled my eyes.

"So, your boldness is unique." Idris nodded to himself. "Cerys, if you are to help me and my people you cannot avoid getting to know us. Furthermore, you chose to be a race that requires frequent intimate contact. Even if you had not…do you think that you will be able to change our lot in life in a matter of months or years? The world has been like this for centuries, and likely will be for centuries more."

"That won't stop me from trying to accomplish my goals in months." I shot him a sideways glance. "By choosing to side with you I've also shouldered the responsibility for what happens to Alice. I don't consider years, let alone centuries, to be an option."

Idris made a vague motion with one hand. "Let us pretend, for a moment, that we manage to rescue your friend from the empire's clutches and house her safely within Nabyr-zahn. For argument's sake, let us say we are able to accomplish this in a matter of months.

"What will you do then? You will still be expected to carry out your role as the gods' champion. One stubborn woman cannot do in months or years what thousands of enraged demons have failed to do for centuries."

"If saving Alice and overthrowing the empire *don't* come hand-in-hand, then my focus will shift to the latter once Alice is safe," I replied after a moment of contemplation. "Just as I don't want to be responsible for the horrors that could happen there, I also don't want to be the reason she and I are stuck in Jeriskyr. I don't want to be the cause of you or your people falling to the empire after holding out for so long, either."

"And if centuries pass, what will be left here for you?" Idris asked, motioning broadly around us with both arms. "You claim you wish to return because Earth is what you know, yet everything I have read of this world indicates that technology has advanced rapidly over the past millennium.

"Returning to Earth after a matter of centuries will be like being thrown into a new world again…if it has not been destroyed by war."

"Just how much have you read since we came here? We've only been here a few days." I arched an eyebrow at him.

"I have favored reading over sleeping," Idris shrugged, before shooting me a firm glare. "Do not avoid my question."

"That's the sort of bridge I'd prefer to cross if and when we come to it." I shook my head. "I won't deny that it'd be next to impossible for me to avoid building friendships in Jeriskyr if it truly does take centuries to accomplish my goals. Even Alice has mentioned that your world *could* become my new home. It just doesn't feel like it yet."

"But given time, your mind could change." Idris nodded, rubbing his chin.

Thankfully, arriving at the museum stopped our discussion and the demon king turned his attention to learning all he could. History, the arts, everything within the labyrinthine building appeared to fascinate him. I accompanied him in relative silence, only speaking to answer brief questions or exclamations of awe. He was filled with a similar sense of childlike wonder to what I had felt when I'd first come.

Ugh, people are starting to notice him. I glanced to my left when I spotted a woman peeking around a pillar with her phone out. The museum's security was quick to reprimand her and tell her to put her phone away, but I had a feeling the damage had already been done.

"Growing bored, kitten?" Idris slipped a finger under my chin and turned me to face him.

"No—and don't call me that!" I growled. "You're already drawing attention. We may need to cut this visit off soon if we don't want to deal with the paparazzi."

"Paparazzi?" Idris trailed his fingers along my jawline before releasing me.

"Ah...journalists, photographers, and so on—of a more annoying variety."

"Let them come," he stated, shrugging as he walked off. "I will not let fleas interrupt my more interesting pursuits."

"It's not that simple, since we walked here!" I hissed, hurrying to follow. "We can't afford to have you do anything drastic within the city, so if we get surrounded by paparazzi we're basically trapped. They're like vultures rather than 'fleas.' If they catch up to us they won't leave us alone!"

"I will protect you." Idris shrugged again.

"Protect... That isn't even the problem here!" I exclaimed.

"Come now, Cerys." Idris spoke with a smile as he pulled me to his side. "You forget who—and what—I am. Or just how charming I can be. They will not be an issue."

"But... Ugh. Fine, have it your way, but let me go first," I pouted.

"I will do no such thing. It wouldn't do for us to get separated," he replied with false innocence.

I sighed heavily and crossed my arms. He was impossible. There was a shred of truth to his statement, but his tone made it clear that wasn't his primary motive. Not by a long shot. "Then at least stop petting my hip—better yet, move your hand to my *waist* and not my *hip*."

"Can I keep petting you if I oblige your request?"

"No."

"Such a pity." Idris sighed, shifting his hand to my waist. He tilted his head slightly as he looked down at me. "I did not expect such large museums. We seem to have little daylight remaining. Where shall we go next?"

"Dinner and then sleep, most likely," I replied, glancing at the clock. However, when I felt Idris' mouth by my ear I quickly shifted to snap, "What do you think you're doing?!"

"Perhaps instead of sleep I will take you to the heights of bliss?" he whispered in a tone husky with desire. My skin prickled into goosebumps even as I attempted to shy away from him, my heart pounding.

"I don't intend to let you take me to the heights of *anything*," I retorted.

"Ah… Perhaps you prefer pain over pleasure?" Idris gripped my chin and made me look at him, a wicked smile on his lips. "Far be it for me to deny you your desires."

"T-that's not—"

"You are a terrible liar."

"Like you even gave me a chance to lie *or* be honest." I growled at him, pulling myself out of his grip. "Pain or pleasure, you won't be 'taking me to the heights' of either. Nor will anyone else in Jeriskyr."

"Do not be so sure," he chuckled, trailing his fingertips down my spine. "After all, I doubt you want your feedings to be boring, or otherwise lacking."

"That's…" I tilted my head. "Well, I'll admit I hadn't thought about that."

"Now then, what shall we do about dinner?" Idris murmured. "Perhaps *Aleksander's*? While you may be resistant to seeing those of your own blood, I did not sense the same foulness from him as I did your father. Would it not be prudent to see him one last time before we return?"

"I hate it when you make sense." I pursed my lips. "Also, didn't I tell you to stop flirting with me?"

"Not likely to happen—I adore your reactions and fully intend to win you over," Idris answered plainly. "Of course, you are correct that you will need to focus primarily on other things for a time. That *does not* mean there will not be enough time for more pleasurable pursuits."

"You're impossible." My shoulders slumped.

"I know what I want and am not afraid to chase it," he smirked. "Unlike a certain kitten. Your hunting skills require further refining.

"Now then, *Aleksander's* or dinner at 'home?'"

I sighed, crossing my arms over my stomach. "*Aleksander's* is fine, I guess, but we should go get the car first. I'm not crossing the city on foot. That said, he may not even be there today."

"If he is not, at least you will have tried."

Chapter Eighteen
Blurred Intentions

A crowd of people in varying manner of garb stood between us and *Aleksander's*. They held contraptions in their hands that flashed with bright lights. Cerys had told me they were called 'cameras' and were used to take photographs like the ones we had seen in the morning news. Each person pelted us with questions faster than we could ever hope to answer them.

They had surrounded us the moment we had gotten out of Cerys' car and left the parking lot. A few of the restaurant employees had attempted to cut us a path, but they were no match for the swarm of prying insects. While I had been disappointed by

Cerys' refusal to go along with their assumptions regarding our relationship, I could now see why she had been so adamant.

The words leaving their lips were nothing compared to the vitriol of their thoughts. I was stunned by the jealousy-turned-hatred that filled them. When Cerys had mentioned the potential for her to be attacked, and asked me if I had ever experienced human jealousy, I had not been certain what she meant. Mere seconds around the reporters was more telling than any description Cerys could have given me.

Their unwarranted, vile thoughts made me sick.

"Get out of our fucking way!" Cerys snapped, baring her teeth at the reporters. She looked ready to spring into their midst with naught but her fists at any moment. "For the last fucking time, we're *work* partners. Not dating. Speaking of *work*, we have a *work*-related dinner to see to. *Now move before I make you.*"

"Mr. Gwythyr! Mr. Gwythyr! Is that true?!" The shouted questions turned toward me next. "*Aleksander's* is a popular date spot—"

"And it is run by Ms. Collins' older brother," I stated calmly, causing the crowd to falter. "As she has stated numerous times, you are keeping us from our work.

"*Kindly move out of our way and return to your homes.*"

I channeled my ability as a spellsinger into my words, and to my surprise, it worked. The crowd collectively grew still for several long moments before moving to disperse. Out of the corner of my eye I caught Cerys shaking her head slightly. It appeared that I could not fully control my power in her world. I had not meant for it to affect her.

"Shall we?" I asked, shifting to look at her.

"I guess," she muttered, glancing away from me.

"Sometimes charm is better than threats of violence, kitten," I teased, earning a brief but fiery glare in response. "Come now, would you really have attempted to fight so many people with only your fists for weapons?"

"I have feet too!" she scoffed.

"In that dress and those shoes?" I arched an eyebrow.

"I've fought in worse!" Cerys made a dismissive motion at me before entering the restaurant. The moment we stepped inside, Aleksander stepped forward with a worried look on his face.

"Cerys? You've brought the demon with you again? But…" He shot a glare at me over his sister's head before looking down at her.

"Calling him a demon again?" Cerys tilted her head, a rather convincing look of innocence on her face. "You don't say the same about Councilor Gwythyr, Idris' father, so why do you think this one's a demon?"

"Father cursed you," Aleksander pointed out, causing his sister to groan. "When you left the compound, he said you'd never find a husband who wasn't a—"

"Okay, for one—curses aren't real," Cerys began, prodding her brother in the chest. "Two, Idris and I don't have a relationship beyond *work,* and it's going to stay that way."

"But he's your type." Aleksander glanced at me, but his attention soon returned to Cerys when she punched him square in the jaw.

"I'm her 'type,' am I?" I drawled, glancing at the petite woman briefly. "I would love to hear more. However, I am disinclined to converse with anyone with ties to *that place.*"

"That... Cerys, I know you love that tree, but—!" Aleksander exclaimed, rounding on his sister. "Going there was... How could you be so stupid? If they had noticed you—"

"They did notice us, and she would be dead had I not been there," I interjected, causing the panicked man to grow pale. "Now then, this manner of talk is likely to spoil our meal—not to mention aggravate Cerys further. It would be best if we went to her private room first, at the very least."

"I... They tried to kill the two of you?" Aleksander swallowed hard, his eyes ticking back and forth as he thought. "That's going too far. What the hell possessed them to..."

Aleksander continued to mutter to himself as he led us to Cerys' usual room. Once there, he left us with menus and Cerys promptly stretched out lengthwise on one of the plush seats, her feet up on the cushions. Despite her seeming lack of interest in her brother, she certainly made herself at home in his restaurant.

"He'll calm down eventually," she stated when she noticed me staring at her. When I did not budge, she glanced over at me again and pursed her lips. "Do you intend to stand the entire time we're here?"

"I was simply attempting to figure out the two of you." I shook my head slightly before taking a seat across from her. It would have been far easier to tease her if I had been able to sit beside her, but she had left me no room. I would have to be content with watching her instead. "Well then, with that unpleasantness aside, would you care to tell me why a 'harem' or 'concubines' are such a problem?"

"All the studying you've been doing, and you haven't checked that?" Cerys sighed and glanced over her menu at me.

"Social matters can easily be taught to me by you—history, engineering, and other such skills cannot," I pointed out. After a moment, she nodded slightly as if agreeing with my statement. "Your distaste for polygamy I can understand—it is not for everyone, myself included—but I sense that is not the only part you take issue with."

"Concubines are basically 'kept' prostitutes," Cerys stated flatly. "Any form of prostitute isn't looked on favorably in our culture, and it was worse in the past. In some parts of the world they were regarded as subhuman. In other regions, it wasn't uncommon for men of high status to have large harems of concubines or even many wives.

"Modern concubines are simply prostitutes who are kept on retainer by wealthy men or women, or are prostitutes who are trading their services for a stable place to live. Sex trade is illegal outside of very specific areas, but no one likes to be caged. If they become someone's 'concubine' they can use their proximity to their master or mistress as a shield by claiming that they're dating."

"So, to you, suggesting you become my concubine is akin to saying you should become a prostitute?" I murmured, rubbing my chin in thought. "That certainly was not my intention, but I think you know that—or at least hope you do."

"Well, *I* don't intend to have my name dragged through the mud by being considered a concubine, regardless of whatever your intentions may be!" Cerys gave me a pointed look before returning her gaze to the menu. "At least, not without knowing your reason. Until you decide to tell me the reason for your harem, I'm not changing my mind."

"I—" I fell silent and glanced toward the door when I caught the sound of footsteps. Cerys followed my gaze and snorted, shaking her head slightly.

"The two of you are truly *work* colleagues?" Aleksander asked as he returned with a tray holding Cerys' favorite alcohol and two glasses. "Didn't Cerys say you would be her potential boss? However, what Jeriskyr Studios claimed—"

"Ah… I am her boss in-game," I offered, causing her brother to grimace. "Our *mutual* bosses wanted us to get to know each other better and maintain a similar working relationship outside of the game so that we would be more convincing."

It felt so incredibly wrong to refer to my world in such a way, but I knew it was necessary. I could cause trouble for my gods and for Cerys if anyone from Earth learned the truth. Furthermore, if I wanted Cerys to remain in Jeriskyr after completing her gods-given task, I needed to refrain from causing anyone from her family to get dragged into our affairs.

"Fine, I'll give the two of you the benefit of the doubt—for now." Aleksander sighed heavily, glancing between us. "Well, then, what'll you be having?"

"Whatever the lady recommends," I answered when Cerys shot me a brief look.

"Right—two orders of all my favorites then." Cerys closed her menu and held it out to her stunned brother. "What? We're going to be gone for a while. May as well take this opportunity to indulge in your cooking."

"I…whatever you say." Aleksander gave in, took our menus, and left us in silence once more.

Cerys promptly shifted to pour herself a drink and then poured one for me as well. Once done, she settled back in her seat, breathing a heavy sigh. She slowly swirled the liquor in her glass, a faraway look in her striking amethyst eyes. I was not certain what to make of her demeanor throughout the day. She had thoroughly puzzled me.

She was more than content to look at me, watch me, and yet any attempt to lure her closer was met with resistance—if not a flat rejection. When questioned, she sounded more as if she were attempting to convince herself than anyone else. If I let matters be, she would fall into silence again and say nothing unless spoken to or questioned.

To some extent, it appeared that something was weighing on her mind. For that, I could not blame her. I could not imagine what it was like to suddenly learn that other worlds existed, or to be traded to one by your own gods. Given how different our worlds appeared, I was impressed that she had not shut down entirely.

Instead, she seemed resolved…most of the time.

"Have you given more thought to which skills you wish to train in?" I asked, earning a brief yet inquiring glance from her. "If you truly desire to focus on training and studies when we return, it is my duty to make certain you have all you need—mentors included."

"I have a few ideas, but I'll have to see whether or not I'm well-suited to magic." Cerys shook her head slightly. She left it at that and returned her attention to her drink. It was almost as if she were making a point of *not* looking at me now that we were alone in a room together.

"You do not wish to begin with a lighter drink?" I tilted my head—not even a glance from her that time.

"If this is to be my last night on Earth I may as well enjoy it," she muttered, before downing the contents of her glass in two gulps. She poured a second and released a small sigh, her eyes downcast.

"Care to share whatever is troubling you?" I offered. This time, she gave me a doubtful, suspicious look.

"Is it your duty to 'care' too?" Her blunt remark stung, but I maintained a passive expression. She was far too obvious in her half-hearted attempts to push me away.

"I haven't given up on befriending you yet—or more," I answered simply, lifting my own glass off the table. "Why would I want us to be enemies? By being chosen to save my people you have *become* one of us. Do *you* want us to be enemies?"

"Well, no, but..." Cerys faltered and then released a heavy sigh. "What *isn't* troubling me? For you, this is simply a matter of freeing your people from the Issradian Empire's oppression. It isn't that easy for me.

"I'm betraying Alice *and* my species by choosing to side with you."

"I can understand your loyalty to Alice, but not to humankind as a whole," I stated, intrigued by her admission. "You have been friends with Alice for years and have done much to protect her. However, aside from your guild, how many humans do you truly care about? I sensed your rage when we were near the compound you grew up in. You would have been more than satisfied to watch me kill *all* of our attackers."

"And more..." Cerys grimaced into her glass. "Let me ask you this, then. If you were in a similar situation and had to choose between demons and humans, and the demons were that world's equivalent of the Issradian Empire—who would you choose to help?"

"The lesser of two evils," I shrugged, leaning back in my seat. "I am not fond of the idea of becoming a human, but if posed with such a situation, I couldn't in my right mind side with the demons. It would become my hope that, after doing my duty, we would be capable of reforming the demons and their culture.

"Do you not wish to do the same with the Issradians?"

"…hardly." Cerys glanced at me with an expression that made my blood run cold, but her eyes soon flitted away from me. "I don't feel a sense of loyalty or pride in my species. Just an obligation to pretend that I do."

"Yet you insist on attempting to return here?" I asked, thoroughly baffled.

"For now," she muttered, leaving at that. I opened my mouth to question her further, but the sound of approaching footsteps silenced me.

Is she simply being more forthright because of the liquor? I wondered, frowning at her. *If this is how she truly feels, then why…*

Remaining silent, I resolved to not intrude upon her thoughts. As much as I wished to understand the strange woman, I wanted her to give me answers herself. Not make me go looking through her mind for them.

"Looks like you two are gonna need another bottle," Aleksander remarked as he wheeled in a cart with many covered platters on it. "Cerys, what do you want me to do with the leftover food?"

"Mmm?" Cerys glanced toward her brother as if he should already have the answer. "Well, I guess it *is* a lot of food. Whatever we don't eat can go to the shelters as usual. That's what you do with all your other excess, right?"

"So, you *do* listen when other people are talking." Aleksander tilted his head.

"When it suits her, perhaps." I chuckled, watching as the man laid out food for us. Once he was done, to my displeasure, he joined us.

"What are you doing, Alek?" Cerys growled.

"If you're going to disappear on me for a while, the least you can do is have dinner with me. After all, if I'm not interrupting a *date*, then you have no reason to complain," Aleksander countered. Cerys just stared at him for several long moments before releasing an agitated sigh and knocking back another glass. "Good. Now then, with that settled—how about you two tell me just what happened by the compound?"

"Simple—our father and a bunch of his cronies showed up with guns pointed at us." Cerys pointed her fork at Aleksander. "They tried to kill us, Idris managed to *discourage* them, and we were able to get in my car and leave."

"What on Earth possessed them?" Aleksander sighed, his expression wrinkled with concern. Unlike the men from the compound, he, at least, appeared to genuinely care for his sister. "I knew they'd sent more people looking for you, but going to extremes like that? What is Father thinking?"

"You mentioned something about your father 'cursing' Cerys?" I asked, earning a sour look in response.

"Look, I know most city folk don't believe in curses," Aleksander began in what he likely thought to be a diplomatic tone, "but they're a big part of Anuism—'anu' means heaven, which references all that we worship. Our pantheon consists of many deities, as well as their servants. Their enemies reside in hell, such as the demons and their leaders.

"The curses started just as a way for us to deal with enemies and slanderers. Now they target anyone they don't like—or anyone who leaves. When Cerys left, our father declared to the whole village that she'd never be able to find a human man to er...*lay with*. That a traitor like her could only ever earn the attentions of demons."

"You never told me about that." Cerys released a disgruntled snort.

"You would've just laughed in my face and gone on about how you'd find the hottest, most powerful demon to take you in," Aleksander retorted, causing his sister to stick her tongue out at him.

"Is that so?" I drawled, shooting Cerys a look.

"I'm pickier than Alek gives me credit for!" she pouted.

Clearly… I sighed, turning my attention to her brother. "And you believe in your father's curse?"

"Of course!" Aleksander nodded fervently. "I've seen firsthand what happens when he curses family enemies. They always turn up dead and mutilated, just as his hex said they would. Not the nicest thing to witness, but Father is determined to protect Anuism and his followers."

"*Alek*," Cerys began, tilting her plate forward and pouting, "where's the cake?"

"Still have a bottomless pit for a stomach, I see," Aleksander stated dryly. He rose to his feet and made his way out of the room, muttering something about bringing dessert.

"Fucking finally!" Cerys exclaimed, setting her plate down. She stretched her arms over her head, causing the skirt of her dress to rise by several tempting inches. Once settled, she turned to look at me. "We should finish up and go home before Alek starts preaching to us. Seriously. I can think of a few ways we could spend the rest of the night and all of them are better than staying here."

A few ways… I tilted my head, watching Cerys pick up her glass. For a moment, I could have sworn she had given me a rather *inviting* look. *This woman should* not *be permitted to have alcohol.*

"Here you go, *Your Highness*," Aleksander offered sarcastically when he returned, placing a large slice of cake in front of Cerys. Her eyes lit up and she promptly dove into the cake with her fork, ignoring me and her brother completely. Aleksander shrugged and placed a plate of cake in front of me as well. "So, this job of yours. You and Cerys are going to be portraying important demons in *Jeriskyr Online*?"

"Correct—I will be playing the King of Nabyr-zahn." I nodded to him before lifting my fork and cutting into the piece of cake. "I'm uncertain what role they will have Cerys filling, only that we will be working together after her initial introduction."

"Humph. Maybe you're the demon our father was talking about," Aleksander snorted.

"Pardon?" I frowned at him.

"The curses always come true, but not always in the way we expect." He shrugged and motioned to me. "Cerys doesn't make it easy to get along with her, yet you're supposed to stomach working with her. You're also playing a demon in that game—the curse doesn't necessarily mean a *real* demon. It could totally mean a fictional variety."

I glanced over at Cerys, expecting a snappy retort, but she was fully absorbed in her cake and booze. Sighing, I turned to Aleksander and replied, "You are not wrong that she makes it difficult to get along with her. However, I believe you are mistaken. As she keeps reminding me, we hardly know each other."

"Perhaps," Aleksander smirked, before turning to look at Cerys. "Sis, it's getting late. You and Idris should get going before more paparazzi—or people from the compound—show up."

"If they mess with me I'll gut them with my fork!" Cerys

snapped, waving the instrument in question around briefly before looking down at her cake. "And I wanna finish eating first. I'm not gonna go anywhere."

"I will pray for you." Aleksander shot me a sympathetic look before leaving again. I arched an eyebrow at his back, but he didn't elaborate further.

"You going to eat that?" Cerys pointed to my slice of cake.

"Yes—I was waiting for your brother to finish talking," I answered dryly, sliding my plate out of her reach.

"Alek? Pfft. He never shuts up!" she scoffed.

"I suppose this 'curse' has given you another reason to hate me," I remarked casually after taking a bite of cake.

"Huh? Hate?" Cerys set her glass down and peered at me, thoroughly confused. "I don't get what you mean. For one, that's my father's stupidity at work. Two, you're implying that I hate you."

"Don't you?"

"What? No!" Cerys shook her head hard and then winced, holding it. "I don't have any reason to hate you. Not yet, anyway. Even having a harem doesn't make me hate you. Just makes it easier to keep from getting involved or invested. Like, *maybe* if you were legitimately available. But you're not. Because, you know, the whole 'several hundred women in your harem' thing. Even if I killed them all off, that wouldn't stop you from finding more, and killing off *all* the women in Jeriskyr would be *way* too much effort."

"Cerys."

"Mmm?"

"You're rambling."

"But you asked me a question." She shot me a quizzical look.

"I would have been satisfied with a simple 'no,'" I informed her, though I could not help but chuckle. "Perhaps we should work on your drinking skill when we return to Jeriskyr."

"Drinking skill? There's a *drinking* skill?" Cerys exclaimed.

"Low skill results in a looser tongue—I doubt you wish to divulge secrets to anyone who buys you a drink," I smirked. "Unless you would prefer to focus on training more pleasurable skills instead."

"Like wha—? Wait, no. Nuh uh." Cerys grew red in the face and pouted. "No snoo-snoo with harem-owning demon kings!"

"Snoo-snoo?" The context of our conversation was enough to tell me what she meant, but the words were so ridiculous that I had to laugh.

"I'm not explaining that one!" Cerys huffed and looked away.

"Shall we return to your apartment? I doubt you wish to be here when our time comes," I offered, deciding a change of topic was in order.

"Oh. Yeah. That'd be bad." Cerys paused and then glanced down at her plate, before shoveling the remaining cake and every scrap of frosting into her mouth. "Mokay les' go!"

I chose to remain silent and helped Cerys wobble to her feet.

However, it quickly became apparent that she was in no state to walk. She was far drunker than I had first thought. After a moment of contemplation, I lifted the petite woman fully off her feet and strode out of the room with her. Cerys' attempts at complaining did not last long.

"Too drunk to walk, eh?" Aleksander glanced over the counter as we passed. "I guess I should thank you for making sure she gets home, Idris. Keep an eye on her for me, will you?"

"I will try," I answered dryly.

Despite the proximity of her car, Cerys fell asleep against my chest before we even reached it. I released a small sigh and gently shook her awake. Once she unlocked the doors, I placed her in the driver's seat and climbed into the passenger side.

"Bruce, take us home," Cerys grumbled, shifting to get comfortable in her seat.

"Detecting high levels of alcohol—very well. Taking command of your vehicle's transportation systems." A blue light flickered to life in front of Cerys and, moments later, the car began to hum. It appeared that the intoxicated woman was incapable of sleeping in a moving vehicle, however.

"Cerys, have you still not determined the purpose of my harem?" I decided to attempt that line of questioning again now that she was drunk. After all, it had clearly loosened her tongue. If I wanted a straight answer from her, I would not find a better opportunity to get one.

"No—why would I?" Cerys grumbled, crossing her arms. "It's better for me to think you're some polygamous playboy that gets his rocks off by owning women. I won't get attached to someone like that."

"And what is so wrong about becoming attached?"

"I...would be better off going back to Earth," she muttered, staring out the window. "You're a king. I'm basically a peasant. The risk isn't worth it and nothing that *could* happen between us would last. A better woman than me would say, 'oh, I'm happy as long as you're happy!' But that mindset is bullshit. It's me or no one, and in a world like Jeriskyr I don't think I'd feel bad about killing the competition."

"You almost make it sound as if you want to return to Earth as a way to punish yourself," I remarked, frowning at her. It bothered me that she did not want to *try* to understand. "What if you found a man who wanted to return with you?"

"Out of the question. I don't wanna be the reason anyone is yanked out of their world." Cerys shook her head.

"You are so difficult," I sighed.

"I have to be," she mumbled.

You do not... I held my tongue, releasing another small sigh. Cerys was such an attractive woman, despite her misguided attempts to push me away. However, it was quite clear that nothing I could say would change her mind. She had convinced herself that distance was imperative. I just hoped she would not go so far as to starve herself. Eventually, she would learn just what it meant to be one of my kind.

I remained silent for the rest of our ride back to her apartment building, uncertain of what to say or to think. Cerys appeared quite adamant that she did not hate me, that she simply wanted to erase her chances of growing attached. She had indicated similarly while sober as well. A small part of me said that I should respect her wishes and let her slip through my fingers.

The majority of my being said otherwise.

When we arrived at our destination, I climbed out of the car and strode around to Cerys' side to help her to her feet. She could barely stand. To my surprise, she did not argue when I suggested that she should allow me to carry her on my back. She seemed quite content to wrap her arms around my neck and bury her face in my shoulder.

Calm yourself. She means nothing by it, I reminded myself, taking a steadying breath even as her cheek tickled the crook of my neck. Even so, I wished she did. I couldn't deny my attraction to her, even if she seemed to think it was impossible for me to be genuinely drawn to her already.

"Oh, the poor thing!" one of the women at the front desk exclaimed as we passed through. "Do you need any help getting Ms. Collins back to her room, sir?"

"I can manage, thank you," I answered simply, making my way toward the elevator. Cerys squeezed her legs around my waist when

I stopped to press the number that would take us to her floor. "Cerys, enough of that."

"Comfy…" she muttered.

"Can you stand?" I asked several minutes later, once we had reached the door to her apartment. "You need to unlock the door."

"But you're warm." She squeezed me tighter, making my pulse quicken.

"And we have limited time."

"*Fine.*"

I eased her down, then steadied her once she was on her feet. As soon as she unlocked the door, she kicked off her high heels and sauntered into her apartment, reaching for the hem of her short dress. Before I could question her, she pulled it over her head and tossed it to the floor. Her smooth, pale skin was contrasted by the black lace undergarments she wore—a questionable choice for someone so insistent on pushing me away.

"Have you no shame?" I questioned.

"If you can walk around half naked in *my* apartment, then so can I!" she huffed, making a dismissive motion at me. She strode in the direction of the kitchen, leaving me to close and lock the door in her stead.

I made my way to the living room after locking up and settled down on the sofa. It wasn't long before Cerys joined me, but watching television didn't appear to be on her mind. Without any manner of warning, she grabbed me by the shirt collar and straddled my lap. Her lips pressed to mine with a burning hunger, luring me in, tempting me with her lust. Yet she tasted of alcohol.

"Enough, Cerys." I gripped her shoulder and gently pushed her back. "I am well aware this is not what you—*nngggh!*"

My grip faltered, freeing her, when one of her soft hands snuck down my trousers and gripped me by my manhood. Cerys kissed me again, deeper, and continued to stroke my cock. Her lust was unlike anything I had sensed in her dreams the past several days. It threatened to sweep me away—but I refused.

"*Enough.*" I gripped her by the throat and pushed her back again, applying just enough pressure to give her pause. "Not like this, Cerys. You are drunk. If I am to have you, it will be when you are sober and begging for me to pleasure you.

"*Go to sleep, Cerys.*"

As I had hoped, her drunken state left her with little willpower to resist my abilities. She immediately slumped against me, falling into a deep sleep. With some difficulty, I extracted her hand from my trousers and then carried her to her room. After tucking her into bed, I made a hasty retreat to my own room and grimaced down at myself.

Even if rejecting her advances was the right thing to do, my body certainly didn't agree with me. Cerys had left my mind confused as to her intentions and my body aching with desire. I was uncertain if I should be disappointed, or if I should count my blessings that she was not such a temptress when sober.

If she wants to push me away, return to Earth by her lonesome, and avoid growing close to anyone from Jeriskyr...then why?'

Chapter Nineteen
A King's Decision

When I opened my eyes, I found Emrys standing above me with his arms crossed and his lips pursed. Sunlight streamed in through the nearby windows. It appeared to be close to midday—and the captain of my guard was most displeased.

"What happened to being gone for a week?" Emrys demanded as I slowly sat up in bed.

"The gods cut our time on Earth short," I muttered, raising a hand to my head. "I feel awful."

"Cut it *short*? The two of you were gone for a month!" Emrys snapped, throwing his hands in the air.

"A month—then what of the Issradian bastard's tax?" I demanded, immediately pulling myself out of bed. If so much time had passed while Cerys and I were on Earth, there was no time left to lose. I had much work to do and keeping the women of Nabyr-zahn safe had just become my highest priority.

"We've got two weeks at best 'til those bastards show up demanding women they can take back to Darmos," Emrys stated, following me as I flew through my suite and headed toward the bathroom. "The gods kept their mouths shut about whatever Cerys found in the city. Care to fill me in?"

"Ah… Of course." I nodded reluctantly. "First and foremost, I will need you to make the preparations necessary for Cerys to join the harem. She will be resistant, but I do not intend to let her roam free in Nabyr-zahn. Not with the tax coming so soon, and not after what she learned of Darmos. Since she insists she will not marry me, it is the only way we can protect her from the Issradians for now. She will come to accept her place within the kingdom in time."

"If she doesn't?" Emrys frowned.

"It is a risk we must take." I shook my head. "She is sacrificing much by siding with us. We would be fools to let her fall into their hands—and further fools still if we permit her to unwittingly throw her sacrifice away.

"We can discuss where to go from here as I bathe. It is imperative we make up for lost time and I am certain you have even more to tell me than I must tell you.

"Ah—and make certain the other women are aware that Cerys is important to Nabyr-zahn. They are to treat her with respect, not as an outcast."

"You're hoping for too much there," Emrys snorted. "You're right—we've got a lot to discuss and not much time to do it. The servants are preparing breakfast for you already. We've got a lot of women to add to your harem before the Issradians get here, Idris. Other business may have to wait."

"If it has to wait, it will have to wait—protecting our people comes first."

Emrys followed me as I threw open the doors to my bathroom. As I stripped off my clothing, I chose to begin with the worst news first. "Regarding what Cerys found in Darmos, we…have been misinformed about the fate of the women taken there, champion or otherwise. The humans have built something they refer to as the *breeding pens* beneath the palace. They are attempting to create elite warriors using *our* women."

"Then…" Emrys faltered, his complexion growing pale. After a moment, he cleared his throat, but his voice still came out hoarse. "Then, the women who volunteered to willingly go to Darmos as tax and as spies… The reason we haven't heard from them…"

"Correct." I clenched my fists, nearly slicing open my palms. I battled down a wave of nausea before speaking again. "Had I known of the game the humans and their gods had chosen to play,

I never would have allowed our women to volunteer themselves as tax, or as spies. What they have had to endure—"

"You know damned well it isn't your fault," Emrys cut me off. My heart clenched, but I said nothing. "We couldn't have known. If they've managed to hide their antics for centuries, from us and from our gods, we must assume there's more going on."

"There is more," I sighed, pulling myself out of the bath. Emrys silently offered me a towel, waiting for me to continue. "Cerys determined why the champions so rarely choose to side with Nabyr-zahn. The would-be champions are given an ultimatum.

"The human gods choose *their* champion based on who is close to ours. Our champion is told that it is within their control who goes to the breeding pens. Them, or their closest friend, who has been dragged into the affair.

"I will forgo breakfast. Come, I will fill you in on the days I spent on Earth and the many things we must prepare for. The fate of Nabyr-zahn's women is but one of the troubling matters we now have to adjust for."

Emrys saluted, falling into step with me. As we made our way through my palace, I explained to him the details of the 'anime' Cerys had insisted I watch. Many of our plans had been compromised in the shows we had watched together. Now I had to make certain all of our operatives changed direction and saw to their own safety first.

Furthermore, we needed to gather what information we could

regarding the breeding pens. Not only did I feel responsible for many of the lives that had been thrown into that vile place, but I also wished to help Cerys save her friend, Alice. Mere days prior, I never would have imagined that I would feel a desire to save the humans' champion. Now, I could not fathom leaving her to her fate.

Human or otherwise, no one deserved such foul treatment.

"Emrys, brief Elidyr," I ordered as we strode into my office. Elidyr looked up from the book he was reading, shooting us a concerned frown. Near my desk was a familiar stack of parchment with written requests. "If either of you require further information, ask. While you are being briefed, I will see to our growing stack of protection pleas…"

"You're going to accept all of them?" Emrys shot me a dangerous look.

"How can I not, with what we now know?" I countered, shaking my head. "We will have to make it work. If necessary, we will trade with the other demon tribes for supplies from their regions. Our men can also hunt and fish in the foothills for the early part of winter."

"There are also the Otherworlders, Your Majesty," Elidyr spoke up, causing me to frown at him.

"What Otherworlders? Surely you do not mean Cerys."

"Since just after your departure, Otherworlders have been joining Nabyr-zahn in droves," Elidyr continued, flipping through his book. He stopped on a page and then nodded to himself. "From what my spies have overheard, humans back on 'Earth,' who are members of Ebonwing, spread details regarding how to move with a tail. Since then, the majority of new Otherworlders joining Jeriskyr have been joining the demon and beastmen tribes."

That must be Cerys' doing... An amused smile came to my face. Shaking my head, I settled into the chair behind my desk and thought for a moment. Now that Nabyr-zahn had a champion, I would have to split my time between my usual duties and making certain Cerys was provided with everything she needed for success. From food, clothing, and a bed, to training and weapons.

After making certain the drunk woman was asleep, and taking care of my own...*problem*, I had remained awake to question Bruce regarding his mistress' intentions. All the research Cerys had done into Jeriskyr and her potential specializations had been stored within Bruce's memory. She had yet to decide. However, she had been impressively thorough. I had expected brief notes, not the pages upon pages of detailed explanations. She had caught intricacies that most people required years of training to detect.

It was not difficult for me to determine why she led a successful guild, or why the gods of my world had targeted her. She had enormous potential.

"Idris?" Emrys coughed.

"My apologies—'what about the Otherworlders,' you said?" I nodded.

"We can use them to help procure food," Elidyr stated, shuffling through his notes. "Emrys proposes that we send the fresh Otherworlders out on the search for food, to fish and to hunt. This would leave our soldiers free to continue guarding Cejari-ir and our craftsmen."

"Given what we know of Otherworlders, they're always looking to increase their proficiency," Emrys added, shrugging. "Our spies in Darmos mentioned the Otherworlders are always pestering people in search of work, to the point where it has become normal for the humans to offer Otherworlders 'quests' to complete.

"We need to bring more food in anyway if we want to save more people, not to mention if Cerys really does manage to help take down the empire. Our people will work harder and grow more loyal with full bellies, too."

"We will also need to provide housing and heating." I frowned, rubbing my chin. "Very well. Elidyr, instruct the Grandmasters in the city to begin leveraging the Otherworlders. Hunters, gatherers, fishermen, and craftsmen will be required to grow the city and accommodate this influx—and anyone we rescue.

"Now then, let us see to our individual tasks. The nobles will demand an audience before long, and I wish to be done with most of the day's work before then."

Chapter Twenty
The Wager

Rough masculine hands gripped my hips, claws pricking my skin. My back arched in pleasure as his lips caressed my throat. His husky whispers sent shudders through my entire body, making me squeeze his torso tighter with my legs. When he withdrew from my throat, I saw messy dark blue hair. Crimson eyes met mine.

I jolted awake and threw my covers off, fully expecting Idris to be casually lounging in my bed or something. However, there was no one there. I covered my face and took a few deep breaths, sitting on the edge of the bed as I tried to calm my racing heart. Some part of me wanted to crawl back into bed and attempt to return to my dream.

I looked around the unfamiliar room, not sure what to do. The whole, 'you're the champion of Nabyr-zahn!' thing really could have used some sort of instruction guide. Or at least a map of the palace. Something to help me get my bearings. Instead, the room I'd woken up in looked like a communal sleeping area—and I had a distinct feeling what that meant.

I was barely awake, yet I already wanted to kick Idris' ass.

Now more awake, I decided that one of the best things about switching between worlds was that I had no hangover. I had expected to wake to a splitting headache, but nope. Clear as if I hadn't downed several bottles of hard liquor the previous night.

Memory of what happened? Not so great. I couldn't even remember leaving *Aleksander's*. I figured Idris must have managed to get me home—otherwise there probably would've been an angry deity yelling at me for failing to 'leave' Earth from my apartment.

Maybe I could go easy on him…or better yet, pretend that the dream had never happened. That sounded like a better plan. He'd have been *so* much worse if he knew what sort of places my mind went once I was asleep.

"Finally awake?" A tall woman with copper horns and a matching tail poked her head around a corner and blinked at me.

"Ah! Lady Cerys!" Drysi peered around the larger woman, smiling brightly.

"Got some guts keeping His Majesty in your world to yourself for weeks." The first woman crossed her arms and scowled.

"Weeks? We were on Earth for four days, if that." I frowned, glancing down at myself with a grimace. "Clothes...I should probably find clothes..."

"Weeks passed here, Lady Cerys." Drysi hurried over and pulled open the top drawer of a low nightstand. From within, she pulled out a simple dark dress and handed it to me. "We didn't have much that would fit you. You will have to look into acquiring more clothes from the tailors or the armor smiths when you're able."

"Thanks." I nodded to her briefly before pulling the dress on. It was a little too long for me, but it would have to do. It covered the important bits, at least. "So... What now?"

"His Majesty is quite busy, but he wants to see you for some reason." The other woman snorted and narrowed her eyes. "No idea why."

Without another word, she turned on her heel and stalked out of sight. Drysi sighed and shook her head as if such behavior was to be expected. Perhaps it was. I had no idea. The more awake I became, the more I realized I had no fucking clue what I was doing or what I was supposed to do. If I didn't figure out something soon, Idris' harem would be the *least* of my worries.

"Something I should know about?" I glanced in the direction the woman had gone and then back to Drysi, who shifted uncomfortably.

"While all of us were rescued by His Majesty, some of the women in his harem truly have feelings for him and see you as competition, Lady Cerys," Drysi answered after a moment. "Everyone has heard by now that he attempted to win your hand in marriage, and how insistent he was. They're consumed with jealousy that they received no such offer, and others are infuriated that you had the nerve to decline."

"So, I pissed off his harem—great," I muttered, pawing my hair into place. "What's this about rescuing you?"

"Did His Majesty not tell you?" Drysi shot me a puzzled look.

"No, he didn't."

"Ah... Perhaps it would be best for him to explain." Drysi bit her lip nervously. "We are his harem in name and nothing more. It would be best to get the details from His Majesty—much of it has to do with the shaky peace between the Issradian Empire and Nabyr-zahn. I am not qualified to speak on such matters."

"Then I will ask him," I replied, resigned. Even though Idris had offered to explain numerous times, I'd avoided the topic like the plague, and honestly, I felt a little guilty for it. Without that information, I couldn't *truly* determine what sort of man he was or what his intentions were. While I didn't want to risk growing attached to him, it also wasn't fair of me to foist him into the 'villain' role in my mind without all the information.

"Lady Cerys?" Drysi waved a hand in front of my face.

"Sorry. So, he wants to see me?" I grumbled.

"Yes. It would be best if we did not dawdle—he has weeks of work to catch up on." Drysi nodded and motioned for me to follow her.

Grimacing, I lifted the skirt of my dress slightly and followed the demoness through the palace. Now and then, I caught my reflection. I had a feeling it would be a long time before I got used to seeing myself with horns—if it happened at all.

Before long, Drysi led me into the open throne room. She left me to my own devices, mumbling something about her duties. Despite her claims of Idris attending to work, the room was noticeably empty aside from a tired-looking Idris, Emrys, and a demon man I had yet to meet. There didn't appear to be many guards present, either.

"Awake, are you?" Idris gave me an odd look. "What do you remember last?"

"Hmmm?" I tilted my head, confused by the question. He almost sounded as if he was implying something. "Cake."

"Cake? Ah…" Idris sighed and shook his head before sitting back in his throne. "I will have to keep this brief. The nobles will be here for our meeting soon.

"Undoubtedly, you have realized that the place in which you woke up is my harem's section of the palace. I have taken the liberty of adding you. As I warned you while we were on Earth, taking your protection into my own hands might be necessary…and it is. I would have preferred you go willingly, but the passage of time has changed things."

"You're not giving me much room to argue," I frowned.

"Because you should not be arguing with someone who is attempting to save your life and protect your decision to side with Nabyr-zahn." Idris gave me a tired smile. "Further explanations will have to wait. I have instructed the palace staff to help you learn whatever you need—and Emrys will show you to the training grounds when you are ready."

"Which should be now." Emrys took a step forward and narrowed his eyes at me. "At least, that's what I'd like to say. We're going to have to get you some more suitable clothes, girlie. Your Majesty, if I may?"

"Of course. Elidyr and your men are more than sufficient to protect her from the nobles," Idris answered dryly, nodding to Emrys. "See to it that Cerys has all she needs."

Emrys promptly grabbed me by the shoulders and pushed me out of the throne room. I gave the cranky soldier a baffled look as he pulled me through a nearby doorway and around the corner. He shushed me and moments later, a group of arrogant-sounding nobles passed by. It sounded like they weren't very happy about a *human* like myself being their gods' champion.

"What's this bullshit about protecting me by force?" I asked once Emrys breathed a sigh of relief. "Drysi had some weird claims about your king's stupid harem, too."

"He's your king now as well," Emrys pointed out, making me

grimace. "It isn't my place to say. Idris wants to explain it to you himself, so you will just have to be patient and wait until he has time for you. Now, why do you look like someone pissed in your porridge?"

"Humph, that obvious?" I shook my head slightly before looking up at him. "Drysi is nice enough, but I've already met at least one woman who doesn't like me at all. Tall, copper horns and tail, looks like she could break an anvil by arm wrestling it—ring a bell?"

"Cristyn, most like." Emrys made a sour face. "Woman fights like a bull but feels entitled to Idris for whatever damned reason. He barely speaks with them but there's more than a few who think like her. Idris gave them orders to be accommodating, but I guess it ain't gonna be that simple."

"*Tch*, just wonderful," I spat. "I'm not here to get in a pissing contest with the king's whores. Breakfast, clothes, and training. The sooner I topple the Issradian Empire for you lot, the sooner I can go back to Earth."

"You mean 'go back home?'" Emrys suggested.

"...hardly." I crossed my arms and gave the confused man an agitated glare. "I'm sure Idris has already gone on about how big of a bitch I am and how great it will be to be rid of me. How about we expedite that process, hmmm?"

"That...is definitely *not* what Idris has said about you." Emrys looked hurt on behalf of his king, for whatever reason. "I don't know what happened between the two of you while you were there, but Idris had only praise for you—and perhaps a complaint or two about stubbornness. His enraged rants were reserved for the Issradians and your so-called family."

Praise...? I really wish he wouldn't. I closed my eyes and sighed, shaking my head. "Look. I don't want to stay in Jeriskyr longer than necessary. Overthrow the Issradian Empire, rescue my friend—go back to Earth. Preferably in a short amount of time."

"I can understand your desire for haste, but it may not be that simple." Emrys motioned to me. "At the very least, we need to swing by the tailors and the leatherworkers before you can start training. You're small for a demon too, so I'm betting they won't have anything to fit you.

"Let's get our asses down into town and see about outfitting you. We can discuss your potential combat options on the way. Idris said you'd been studying what you could while in your world, but I doubt it's a good substitute for the information we have."

"I...fine." I nodded. Despite wanting to argue, I knew Emrys was right. Training was important and I sure as hell couldn't do much in a dress meant for a larger woman. "Lead the way."

Hours later, I found myself back in the harem's section of the palace. Just the thought of being part of that place made my skin crawl and my blood boil. Even if I hadn't been attracted to Idris, the idea of sharing a man made me want to punch things. I was doing what I could to rein in my curiosity about the demon king, but it didn't take me long to realize his company would have been much better than sticking around with his harem.

Whatever the original purpose had been, the women had their own ideas.

"Humph, what would His Majesty want with a runt like you?" a nearby woman muttered, shooting me a scowl as she combed her long black hair. "I bet you haven't even had a man before."

"What's he see in her, anyway?" another snorted.

Calm down. You don't care. Don't make things worse by attacking these women, I told myself. *You're here to save Alice and then go back to Earth. These women don't matter. They can have their stupid sexy demon king.*

"Come on—she's the gods' champion!" a ginger-haired, white-horned woman exclaimed. "He *needed* to save her like he saved us. Lady Cerys wouldn't be here long enough to make a difference otherwise! Besides, she's made it abundantly clear that she doesn't intend to pursue King Idris. Let her be."

Regardless of what I want, I doubt he's just going to leave me alone. I shrank back when another woman swatted at me. At least three had attempted to snip off portions of my hair already.

There was no way I'd be getting any sleep around Idris' whores. They hated me too much already, despite my attempts at playing neutral.

"Stop it!" Drysi hissed when the woman attempted to hit me again. "You're acting like the humans! Do you *want* the Issradian Empire to win? At this rate, Cerys won't have any reason to help us!"

"*She* herself is a human!" another snapped, pointing at me. "Don't let her gods-given body fool you, Drysi. This bitch will turn on us and attempt to kill Idris the moment she has a chance. We should get rid of her now while we can."

At least a dozen women raised their voices in agreement. Fed up, I stood and stalked toward the nearest door. "I'm going to get some fresh air."

Without another word, I swept through the palace and as far from those damned women as I could get. While I had expected to be met with animosity from *some* of them, I hadn't properly gauged just how bad it would be. They saw me as a threat to their chances with their precious king even though I wanted no part of him.

Maybe I'll actually believe it if I tell myself that enough. I sighed, brief pain shooting through my chest. He was a beautiful man— and a good one too, if the people of Nabyr-zahn were to be believed. They revered him and his father alike for the lengths they were willing to go to protect their kingdom and its people.

A kingdom I would never belong to.

Shaking my head, I took a sharp turn and stalked toward the training area Emrys had shown me on our return trip. It was late, and most people were heading to bed, but I refused to stay around those women. There was no way I could rest around anyone who wished me harm. That they were ballsy enough to try cutting my hair or otherwise harming me while I was awake said all I needed to know about them.

Once in the training yard, I went through a set of cautious stretches and attempted to warm up. However, refocusing my mind seemed impossible. Idris and his whores weighed on me more than I wanted to admit. I wanted to fight the Issradian Empire—not what appeared to be the entire female population of Nabyr-zahn.

I'm not going to get any training done in this state. I took a few slow breaths and then made my way back into the palace. First things were first—I needed somewhere else to rest. I refused to remain near women who meant me harm.

Since several people had mentioned how busy Idris was, I decided to swing by the throne room on the off-chance he might still be there. As luck would have it, he was—though he seemed as if he was preparing to leave for the night. When I walked into the room, I found it empty aside from Idris and Cristyn. Idris examined me slowly, a small frown replacing the briefly teasing expression that had come to his face.

At least he seemed to be able to tell when I was in a poor mood.

"I'm formally requesting that you let me have my own room—preferably with guards," I informed him, forcing my voice to remain level. Cristyn shot me a warning scowl, and I decided to ignore her. She and the others had picked a fight with the wrong woman.

"Do the harem chambers not suit your tastes?" Idris' frown deepened. "I am aware, of course, that you are used to living on your own... However—"

"If they're willing to try cutting my hair, slap me, and punch me while I'm awake—how far will they go if I try to sleep around them?" I cut him off sharply, watching as his expression darkened. He glanced at the woman by his side, who squeaked and shrank back.

"You were told not to say anything, bitch!" Cristyn snapped, flinching in response to the dangerous look Idris shot her. She turned to bow her head to him. "Your Majesty, this human whore was clearly sent to grow close to you and then stab you in the back. We're only attempting to save—"

"I gave you and the other women explicit orders to welcome Cerys with open arms and make her feel as if Nabyr-zahn is her home," Idris interrupted the woman with a deadly rumble. "Cerys is our gods' champion. Even if she has refused me, you should be treating her with the respect you would show a queen. I will not tolerate such foul behavior. *Get out of my sight.*"

Cristyn fled, tripping over her skirts in her haste to get away from the enraged king. Idris looked inclined to tear her head from her shoulders, and I couldn't pretend to be disappointed by the idea. Hell, I was almost disappointed he hadn't.

"Did they succeed?" Idris turned his enraged gaze to me next.

"No," I answered simply, watching as he rose from his throne.

"Have all of them adopted such unforgivable behavior?" Idris came to a stop in front of me and cupped my face in one hand. He looked as if he was searching for even a hair out of place. I didn't know what to make of it.

"Some of them appear to be on your side," I shrugged.

"My side? You mean, your side?" Idris tilted my head to one side, his lips pursed. "Your cheek is bruised—so they succeeded at least once. Why do you feel the need to lie to me?"

"They're only on my side because they trust your judgment implicitly," I grimaced, raising my hand to rub my bruised cheek. "Ugh, you're right. It *is* bruising. Maybe I should have kicked that whore's ass after all."

"They should be thankful that I am too kind to sell them to the Issradian Empire for their betrayal." Idris' cold, murderous tone made my skin prickle into goosebumps. I looked up at him in surprise, finding his crimson eyes filled with seething rage. "By attempting to harm you they put all of Nabyr-zahn in jeopardy! What would they have done if their actions made you decide we are not worth saving? Furthermore, that they would attempt to disfigure you... I... Are you certain you are alright, Cerys?"

"I think you're more upset about it than I am," I offered, unable to think of another way to put it. After all, I wasn't really alright—but I was nowhere near as distressed as he was. I didn't understand why he was so upset. I'd acted like such a bitch on Earth, attempting to push him away, yet he seemed unfazed. "I just want to be able to sleep without worrying about crazed, jealous harem girls stabbing me."

"You are not alright."

"Must you be so perceptive?"

"You are the sort of woman who would rather shoulder her burdens by herself, Cerys." Idris shook his head as he finally released my cheek. "I am glad they did not manage to harm you, but it troubles me that they tried at all. They will have to be punished suitably—and I will need you to divulge their names. They attempted to dissuade you from seeking aid?"

"I was told to keep quiet, but they were also quite insistent that you wouldn't want to sully your name by associating with a 'mere human,'" I spat, crossing my arms over my stomach. "They mentioned that you 'rescued' them, but that's hard to believe. I would've thought they'd be more inclined to respect your orders if you had."

"We can continue this in my rooms." Idris raised a hand to silence me.

"Wait—what?" I demanded.

"It is far too late to prepare a room for you, let alone assign men to guard it," he answered plainly. "I do not believe the women will leave you alone even if we could. If they're willing to betray me over your presence, I fear they will not cease their harassment until I can take more drastic measures.

"You will remain with me—I am in need of someone to warm my bed, anyway."

"Warm— I will not!" I exclaimed as Idris pulled me from the throne room and down the hall with him. "If I must, I'll sleep on a sofa, in a chair, or on the floor. I'm not sharing a bed with you, let alone—"

"You're letting your desires run away with you," Idris smirked. "I said warm my bed—and I meant simply that. Of course, I wouldn't complain if you offered me more. However, I'm well aware that you will not. Nor do I wish to give you a reason to *truly* hate me."

"Hate...? I don't hate you, Idris." I pursed my lips at his back. "It takes a lot more than frustrating me to make me hate someone."

"I'm aware—we discussed it while you were in your drunken stupor," Idris responded dryly. "Since you remember so little of that night, I will mention it again: we will need to work on your drinking skill. You are a rather loose-lipped drunk."

"Am I?" I tilted my head, then glanced at the wrist Idris had grabbed. "You're hurting me, by the way."

"I—?" Idris stopped in his tracks to look at me, so I pointed down at my wrist. He released me as if my skin had turned into molten rock. "I apologize. Perhaps I am letting my anger get the better of me. It is not much farther to my rooms."

Idris turned away from me with a faintly pained expression and made his way toward a nearby staircase. It seemed like the more time I spent around him, the less I understood him. For whatever reason, I hadn't expected him to be upset about the women at all— yet that couldn't have been further from the actual outcome.

"What's this about a drinking skill?" I questioned, lifting my skirt so that I could more easily keep up with him. "And 'loose lips?'"

"You are a very honest drunk." Idris glanced at me, then down to my skirt. "Did you not go into town with Emrys for clothing?"

"They didn't have anything that would fit me," I shrugged.

"If you wish to continue indulging in alcohol, you will need to raise your drinking skill so that you do not tell every secret in the kingdom to all who will listen," Idris stated plainly. He caught the glare I shot him and raised his hands. "I am not saying you would intentionally harm Nabyr-zahn, Cerys. Simply that your low drinking skill combined with the nature of your inebriated self is cause for concern."

"What else happened while I was drunk?" I pursed my lips.

"Nothing of importance." He glanced away from me.

"You're lying."

"As you do frequently."

"Hey, that's not—" I started to protest.

"Then why did you lie when I asked if the women had succeeded?" Idris motioned toward my cheek, anger glimmering in his eyes again. "I know humans lie as easily as they breathe, but as

I have said, you do not strike me as—"

"They didn't succeed by my standards. A 'success' would have been actually breaking something." I pointed to my jaw.

"If they managed *that* I would kill them." He narrowed his eyes.

"I...don't understand why you're so upset about this." I tilted my head.

"Loyalty. Trust. They have damaged both." Idris made a broad motion with both hands. "Furthermore, they risked our fragile safety. Of course I'm upset."

I'm glad that's why and not because it's...me. I clenched my jaw when I felt my chest constrict. That was a feeling I knew, and one that wasn't conducive to returning to Earth. It required a change of subject. "Maybe I should sleep in the stable, or the armory, or something."

"Like some outcast peasant? I refuse!" Idris scoffed. "You are being difficult for the sake of being difficult. Would it kill you to graciously accept my hospitality?"

"You *did* ask me to 'warm your bed,'" I pointed out.

Once at the top of the stairs, we were met by a door. Idris placed one hand flat against it and almost immediately I heard it unlock. He pushed the door open and strode inside. I hesitated to follow, but not for long. Spending the night with the demon king seemed safer than staying with the murderous harem.

I glanced around the room, noting a seating area, bookshelves, a few display cases, and several more doors. The walls were polished stone, with dark wooden beams every few yards. More exposed beams protruded from the high ceilings above us. The floor was made up of large pieces of polished stone of different varieties, used to make a repeating pattern. Thick, colorful rugs covered much of it. Much of the décor and upholstery were equally vibrant.

"I will fetch you one of my shirts and a robe," Idris stated as he strode toward one of the adjacent doors. I lingered by the entryway and glanced around, still a little uneasy. "Make yourself comfortable."

How am I supposed to be even slightly comfortable with this? I chewed on my cheek and edged toward the closest chair. Once sitting, I clenched my hands in my lap. Idris' harem had me reconsidering my decision to help Nabyr-zahn, let alone stay in it. *Maybe I should've asked the gods if there was a different kingdom I could help...though they'd probably hate me too...*

"Cerys?" Idris' proximity made me jump and I looked up, startled.

"Sorry. I was thinking." I shook my head, attempting to quickly calm myself.

"I hope you will eventually understand that I am your ally, Cerys." Idris gave me a mildly pained look. "I am well aware you did not want to join my harem, let alone become my queen, but when I said it was for your safety, I meant it. That they would then put you at risk in a different manner—"

"In a different manner?" I prompted. "So, are you going to tell me what all this is about?"

"Change first." Idris held out a long shirt and a fluffy robe. Once I took them, he motioned toward a nearby door. "In there, if you would like your privacy."

I quickly fled, changed, and then returned to the room where Idris was waiting. His robe was far too long but at least it was warm. And it smelled nice.

"Well?" I probed.

"How much did they tell you?" He offered me a cup of something that smelled vaguely of chocolate.

"Just that you rescued them from the Issradians somehow."

"I would have preferred you work it out yourself, but your loose-lipped self made it clear you weren't even trying," Idris began, making me grimace. "Our current peace with the Issradian Empire, shaky though it may be, comes at a cost. Each of the demon and beastmen lands is subjected to a tax—however, it isn't wealth or resources they take. Their tax is people. Women, if there are any available."

"*Tch*, the pigs," I muttered, bristling, before taking a sip of my drink—definitely some variation of hot chocolate. It helped a little. Idris gave me a sad smile. "How the hell do you save them *and* maintain your peace, then?"

"A king's harem is strictly off-limits," Idris answered, motioning to himself. However, his expression was bitter. "Anyone else is fair game, regardless of rank or profession. Women are necessary to our survival as a species. Most of our people understand that if we are to win against the empire—or outlive them—then we must be able to procreate.

"Every female born in Nabyr-zahn has become a member of my 'harem' in order to evade the Issradian Empire. Men, such as Silas, volunteer to take their place when the humans come to collect their twisted 'tax.' The majority of the women have husbands, or at the very least, a paramour."

"So, the ones who don't are likely the ones holding out hope of winning you over, or are too young to care about such things yet?" I asked, earning a brief nod in reply. He appeared genuinely displeased with the situation. "In that case, I can understand your insistence that I join your harem. However, it doesn't explain your 'be my queen' attempts."

"You are a strong-willed woman. You deserve better than being one of hundreds in a king's harem," Idris shrugged, glancing away from me. "Now that I have seen your world, I understand why you reacted in such a way. However, I have not changed my mind. I *will* win you over."

"Why?" I asked simply.

"What do you mean, 'why?'" Idris frowned.

"You don't have a reason to win me over, a good portion of your subjects hate me, and since I'm human you'll hate me eventually too." I counted off on my fingers, continuing, "You haven't done much, if anything, to hide your hatred of humans. Plus, I'm not staying. I've been a bitch. I'm trying my damnedest not to get to know any of you, so—"

"Hmmm, did someone slip alcohol into your drink?" Idris murmured, snatching my cup from me. He raised it to his lips and took a small sip, then tilted his head. "I certainly do not taste or smell any—"

"Hey, that was tasty! Give it back!" I reached for the cup, but Idris swiftly captured my chin with his free hand and lifted my face toward his.

"You are transparent to me, Cerys," Idris informed me, his voice much softer than his gaze and his grip. "You are attempting to protect yourself the only way you know how, with but a vague inkling that it is putting you at odds with others instead. Unless you betray the people of Nabyr-zahn, I will not hate you. Even if...even if you truly chose to leave Jeriskyr once your task is done. Help yourself to the food. I am going to prepare myself for bed."

Idris released me, set my cup on the table, and swiftly left the room, leaving me feeling more confused than before. Why did he seem so distressed whenever the topic of me leaving his world came up? Why didn't he hate me yet? Sure, I had intended to act like myself and *not* go out of my way to make him hate me...but it hadn't turned out how I'd meant it to. I'd been a bitch, and he *definitely* should have hated me for it. He didn't deserve such shitty treatment.

What confused me more was why either of us seemed to care.

We'd only known each other for a matter of days and had gotten off to a terrible start. I would've been less stumped if he'd wanted to kill me himself—or even ordered his harem to.

I heaved a sigh and picked up my cup. Idris was making it increasingly difficult for me to see him as a bad person. I didn't belong in Jeriskyr. Why I wanted to return to Earth was another question entirely, but I didn't want to make the choice a hard one.

"Still brooding, are we?" Idris walked back into the room a while later, wearing a pair of low, loose pants and an open robe. He pushed his damp hair out of his eyes and gave me a small smile. "You are staring."

"You wear less clothing than your harem does," I retorted before I was able to bite back bitch mode. Fantastic.

"I was not complaining. You are one woman whose attentions I do not mind." Idris shot me a confident grin before glancing at the food cart. "You have yet to touch anything. Are your thoughts truly so worrying?"

"Why do you—" I stopped myself and sighed heavily. "Given all that's happened, on top of my preexisting concerns, I have little appetite."

"For someone who claims she doesn't want to make friends here, you certainly do worry a lot about whether or not you'll be accepted," Idris remarked casually as he sat across from me.

"That's none of... Wait." I stared at him in disbelief, feeling myself growing hotter by the second as realization hit me. "How in the hells did you know—"

"Demons are telepathic, kitten," Idris answered with an amused chuckle. "When I said you are transparent I meant it quite literally. Another skill you will have to train, certainly. It would not do for me to spend the duration of your visit shielding your thoughts myself."

"I don't know whether to thank you or punch you," I groaned, slumping back in my seat.

"You are most welcome," he laughed, lifting the lid off one of the platters and picking up food for himself. "Perhaps we should play a game to ease your mind?"

"And how does playing a game with a telepath do anything of the sort?" I asked, grimacing when my stomach growled in response to the smell of food. Perhaps I was hungrier than I wanted to admit.

"I can effectively 'turn off' my ability to read your thoughts. While a useful skill, I try not to intrude unless I am truly baffled by someone's behavior," Idris informed me as he picked up an entire platter and set it between us. He paused long enough to give me a meaningful look, then lifted its lid. "Perhaps we can bet on our game. I cannot allow you to win freedom from my harem, as I am sure you now understand, but perhaps there is something else you would like to win?"

"Er... I like weapons?" I frowned, thinking about it for a

moment, then shrugged. *He may as well have asked me what anime I like. Whoosh. Every possible thing on the tip of my tongue—gone.*

"Cerys, I already intend to provide you with *anything* you desire," Idris stated, a little more sensuously than necessary. "I was already determined to pamper our champion before seeing your world. Now that I have seen where you come from, the life you once led, and the life you currently lead—I am even more determined. Think on a grander scale."

"What are *you* going to try to win?" I pursed my lips. I had no idea what I wanted, especially not if he was already plotting to trouble himself unnecessarily.

"It isn't a trouble—nor is it unnecessary," Idris remarked, smiling. "As for what I intend to win, I think I will claim a new part of you with each victory until you are entirely mine—or you beg me to conquer the rest. Whichever comes first."

"*What?!*" I yelped. "You can't be serious!"

"As I stated—you should think in broader terms." Idris grinned.

A piece of me? Really. Why did he want such a thing, and how was I meant to *not* jump to conclusions? I wanted to give him the benefit of the doubt, but he was also an incubus. Something naughty could have been his entire goal.

Though, if I could squeak past with some wins, I *could* leverage our games to my advantage. The problem was, nothing pertinent came to mind. I didn't know enough about Jeriskyr yet to think of anything I'd *want* or even *could* win.

"I don't… There isn't anything I want." I pressed my fingers to my temples. "We've already established that you're going to help me rescue Alice, so that's out. What you just told me means anything else I might ask for is covered already too."

"Power? Land?" Idris tilted his head.

"Being *given* power sounds boring. I'd rather earn or take it." I snorted dismissively, ignoring the mischievous grin that spread across his face.

"You could ask for me." Idris motioned to himself.

"That's basically just reversing your game on you. That's no fun, and I don't have a reason to make that kind of move. Granted, I suppose you don't either." I sighed and finally leaned forward to pluck food off the platter when I felt my stomach rumble again.

"Your own harem, perhaps?" Idris suggested.

"I've already told you I don't like polygamous men—what makes you think I'd be a hypocrite?" I arched an eyebrow at him.

"Surely you want for something."

"…not anything that can be won through a game." I shook my head, feeling my chest constrict again. It was a sensation I hated. A reminder that I had failed to fully lock off my emotions in time. Something I hoped wouldn't get in the way of my goals in Jeriskyr.

Besides, it wasn't like I could win 'a happy life' or 'freedom from being the champion' by playing a game against Idris.

"What of your training, then?" Idris rubbed his chin in

thought. "Perhaps I could reward you with something unique?"

"Maybe," I shrugged. "Aren't you putting a little too much into something you're confident of winning?"

"If you aren't fighting for something, you won't be an interesting opponent," Idris pointed out. "You're competitive. I need to find something to tantalize you with if you're to entertain me."

"And why would I care about entertaining you?" I grumbled.

"Why indeed?" Idris' knowing look made me purse my lips again.

"Fine—if I win a match, you have to help with my training."

"I was already planning to."

"…you aren't making this easy," I sighed. After thinking for a while in silence, I looked up from my food again and locked eyes with Idris. "If I win, I get to carry out the execution of the Issradian emperor, his adviser, and those loyal to them."

"*Oh*?" Idris smirked, leaning forward. "You would rob a king of his vengeance, Cerys?"

"I thought you were confident in your ability to win this game of yours?" I countered innocently, watching as Idris' tail began to switch like a mischievous cat.

"You will most *definitely* lose now." Idris rose to his feet. "We shall have our first match before bed—it will be a good chance for me to see how much I need to teach you of the game, and an excellent opportunity to conquer part of you."

"Wait. Now?" I asked in disbelief, but Idris had already disappeared into one of the adjacent rooms.

Shit.

Chapter Twenty-One
Evening Recreation

"Ah, I forgot to mention this earlier," Idris remarked as he strode into the room, carrying a large rectangular wooden case. "Our visit to your world, and Corlyotir's cover story for us, has had an interesting effect. Nabyr-zahn and some of our neighboring kingdoms have had a sudden influx of Otherworlders—and they are not struggling to manage their tails as those in the past have. Did you have something to do with this?"

"Well, who knows?" I crossed one leg over the other and smiled. "Maybe Ebonwing decided to share what I learned about managing tails."

"'Maybe,' you say." Idris shook his head, placing the wooden contraption on the table between us. "Our games are certainly not as fancy or advanced as yours, but this will have to suffice—and it will help us kill two birds with one stone."

"Let me guess," I pointed down at the lacquer inlays on the very top, "a strategy game of some kind? Even now we still have this type of game on Earth, it's just all virtual instead of utilizing a board."

"The lack of magic users in your world made me think." Idris nodded as he set up the board. "Even if you have strategized in virtual worlds, we can't be certain that magic works the same way in Jeriskyr. What you already know can be used as a foundation to strengthen your knowledge—which you will need against the Issradian Empire. Games such as this one can be excellent learning tools. I wish to discuss the matter of your training as well, if you are confident in your ability to multitask."

"It's an important topic, so sure," I replied, scooting forward so I could pick up one of the playing pieces. Wood, stone, lacquer, and paint resulted in pieces that looked more like art than part of a game. "Well, as long as you realize it means I'll be asking you even *more* questions, that is."

"I doubt I would ever complain about having more reasons to converse with you," Idris informed me with a smile. "After I saw you safely to bed, I had Bruce provide me with copies of your studies. While it appears that there is much the people of Earth do not know about Jeriskyr's skill systems, what you compiled was not wrong.

"A piece of 'missing' information would be demonkind's telepathy. While it is a skill you must train, and something that you can use for both offensive and defensive purposes, it doesn't have to be 'equipped' in the same manner as profession-related skills."

"Are other species capable of telepathy?" I handed the game piece to Idris when he motioned for me to do so.

"Not naturally, no. Elves once developed a magic that has a similar affect, as have the beast tribes more recently." Idris began placing dozens of pieces on the now-flat board. It was far, far larger than I had been expecting.

"In that case, let's call telepathy a 'racial skill' for simplicity," I suggested, earning a dubious look in response. "When you made your character in *Bengllor Online*, surely you noticed each race had specific traits? In other games, sometimes it's a skill instead of a passive bonus."

"Then it would be more accurate to say it is a 'species skill,' while the abilities of an incubus or succubus would be the 'racial skills,'" Idris pointed out. I tilted my head, considering it for a moment, then nodded my agreement. "Everything in Jeriskyr has levels indicating how proficient one is. Mundane things, such as language, speech, and drinking all progress simply by 'doing' and are available to you always. They should not be a problem for you.

"Your species, racial, and profession skills are what concern me. There is much you simply do not know because you were not raised *as* a succubus."

"And professions?" I prompted.

"It will be time consuming, but it would be best if we had the city's Grandmasters determine what you will do well with," Idris replied with a small frown. "Given the influx of fresh Otherworlders, the Grandmasters will undoubtedly be busy. Emrys, Elidyr, and myself may be able to assist some...but we are also in the process of preparing for the Issradians. We have merely a week before they come to collect their tax."

"So, I'll need to work on basic training until we can figure out what profession will suit me?" I grimaced. "Any books that will help? I can't spend *every* waking moment physically training."

"My library is at your disposal," Idris offered. A mischievous smile spread across his lips as he set the last piece into place on the board. "Now then... I believe it is high time I claim the first part of my new territory.

"Green gems indicate the unit has healing capabilities, blue means they can handle being on the front lines, red means they utilize melee weapons, yellow for long range, purple for offensive magics, and the white gems are your generals. Each piece holds multiple capabilities, as with any real soldier. Your goal is, quite simply, to eradicate my armies or take my generals."

"Are there restrictions to direction of movement or how many spaces?" I asked, looking over the pieces on my side of the board. Ten generals. There appeared to be a grid pattern as with chess or checkers, but some of the grooves on the board reminded me of Go.

"Ranged units can only be placed where the lines connect," Idris replied, pointing at a free space on the board where the grooves met, then he motioned to an empty square. "Everything else can only be placed on open tiles. There are more types of units, but this should be sufficient for a beginner. We will add flying and mounted pieces when you come to understand the game better.

"Each unit represents a full section of your army—not an individual soldier."

"And how many spaces are we allowed to move per turn?" I tilted my head.

"Ranged combatants three, frontlines one, and the rest—including both manner of magic users—two." Idris reached out a hand and beckoned briefly. "Hand me your cup. I will refill it for you."

"I can do it myself."

"I am closer."

Pursing my lips, I did as he asked and then grumbled my thanks when he returned the cup to me.

"Shall we?" Idris inquired with a devious smile.

"No listening to my thoughts, got it?" I narrowed my eyes at him.

"Of course, kitten. I intend to conquer you through entirely legitimate means," Idris chuckled, motioning toward me. "You may go first."

"I still don't understand why you want to 'conquer' me," I muttered, picking up a frontline piece.

"Because, once I have claimed you, it will be impossible for you to *willingly* leave Jeriskyr without my permission." He smirked when my fingers twitched. Irritated, I placed the unit down and crossed my arms, waiting for the king to make his move.

"And why you want *that* is also beyond me," I stated, shaking my head.

"Aside from my desire for you to remain in Jeriskyr with me," Idris began as he moved a ranged piece forward at a diagonal, "I would feel much better knowing that returning to Earth was truly your choice. There is every possibility that the gods could forcibly remove you from this world. If you were forced to leave Jeriskyr, I would know. Then, I would not think that you had betrayed m— us."

"You're a strange man," I muttered, moving a caster unit forward. *I should have known his goal was still to keep me in Jeriskyr. I get the feeling there's something more to his reason for wanting me to stay. Though…he is right when he says that the gods could force me to return against my will. Hmmm.*

I didn't want to admit it, but there was something relaxing about playing against Idris in the dim light of his suite. The low glow of magitech lamps flickered in a way reminiscent of candlelight. It was comfortably warm, especially wrapped up in his robe and drinking hot chocolate. It was so late that we were likely the only people still awake, and I could make out hints of moonlight filtering in through the windows of an adjacent room.

Idris appeared to be taking the game seriously, yet he was patient in teaching me how to play. His flirting and teasing had been replaced by careful instruction and friendly conversation. It was quite the change of pace compared to our time on Earth, but I had to admit I was enjoying seeing this different side of him. He seemed more genuine, less desperate, though still troubled.

There was no way in hell I'd win my first match against someone who clearly played the game frequently, but that didn't mean I was going to slack off either.

"Cerys, did I mention the other role my harem members serve?" Idris asked after a while, mulling over the next move he wished to make.

"I wasn't aware they served any role—so no," I shook my head.

"They are all trained in combat," Idris offered, his expression troubled. "Meaning they could have easily made good on their threats, and more than one should have managed to land a hit against you.

"Dignitaries, such as kings and nobles, are expected to attend business gatherings with an escort. Under normal circumstances, this would be their wife or their betrothed. Given these harsh times…we are escorted by beautiful but dangerous women."

I leaned back in my seat, considering it. "Pretty bodyguards who can stay closer to their king than a normal guard? It makes sense. Emrys and his men wear a hell of a lot of armor. They'd get in the way at gatherings, I'd think.

"As I told you, I do have some martial arts training from my world. That said, I don't think most of the harem women were truly trying. Well, that or their form is awful. I didn't recognize their style, so I can't say for certain."

"With the rift between you and my harem, you may have to take on the role of escort," Idris stated, his gaze flicking up to meet mine briefly before he finally placed his unit on the board. "As the gods' champion, you will be expected to make appearances at such events."

"Adding more work to my list?" I arched an eyebrow.

"Would you rather be stuck in the palace with my harem?" he countered, smiling. "Not to mention that it would not do for you to become bored—and it would be a good learning experience."

"And what's in it for you?" I asked dryly.

"The company of a beautiful woman, of course," Idris replied without hesitation. "You are quite interesting after all, and I certainly would not complain about an opportunity to make the nobility or the other kings jealous."

"They'd have to have a reason to care in order to feel even remotely jealous." I rolled my eyes and placed a piece down.

However, I immediately regretted it and cursed. My final general was in range of Idris' casters and didn't have enough infantry to protect him.

"Well, you certainly understood your mistake quickly," Idris chuckled, claiming my last piece. He set the general aside and settled back in his seat, a devious smirk on his lips. "You are a quick learner. I'll have to be more cautious in the future. Now then, I think it is time I choose where to stake my claim…hmmm…"

"You really intend to 'claim' something?" I bristled, wondering if I was going to have to stab a demon king my very first night in Jeriskyr.

Idris gracefully rose to his feet and strode around to my side of the table, stroking his chin in thought. I glared at him out of the corner of my eyes, but it had little to no effect on him. His tail swished playfully behind him, his mouth curving into another of his sinfully alluring smirks.

I fully expected Idris to choose something, or somewhere, inappropriate. So, when he reached down to grasp my right hand, I shot him a questioning look. He bowed and kissed my knuckles, his eyes locked with mine. I had no idea what to do or say. My first instinct was to pull my hand from his, but his grip was far too firm for that.

"Your right hand is now mine," Idris informed me with a triumphant smile, straightening to his full height before pulling me to my feet. "Are you disappointed?"

"I'm disappointed I lost and confused by your choice." I sighed, thoroughly baffled by his behavior. "You tend to act so...so... I really thought you were going to do something that would result in me slapping you."

"I meant it when I said that when I have you, it will be willingly," Idris smirked, stroking the back of my hand with his thumb. I tilted my head. I couldn't recall him saying that. "Alas, it is late—I did not expect you to last so long during our game. We should turn in for the night."

"I'll sleep on the cou—"

"You will do no such thing." He pulled me into another room by the hand and shot me a confident smile over his shoulder. "After all, your hand belongs to me now. If it comes with me, so must you."

"You're incorrigible!" I exclaimed as Idris sat on the edge of his bed. He grinned and pulled me with him, using his arm to lift me off the floor and onto the plush bed beside him. "I'm not sleeping with—"

"This is the safest place you could be." He stretched out on his side and pulled my right arm fully over his torso. He didn't stop until my hand was over his heart. I felt his tail coil lightly around one of my ankles. "Get some rest. You will be joining me in the throne room for my morning meeting."

Really? And I'm supposed to be the big spoon too?! I stuck my tongue out at the back of his head. *Wait. Priorities, Cerys. Be pissed that you're in this situation in the first place, regardless of spoonage. You don't want to be any spoon.*

"Keep telling yourself that, kitten," Idris murmured drowsily, nuzzling into the pillow.

I held my tongue and attempted to quiet my thoughts. Clearly, I wasn't going to get out of this situation any time soon, and despite his drowsiness, Idris' grip hadn't loosened at all. I was most definitely trapped in the bed with him. And not in the fun way. Even if he was right, and it was the safest place to be, it still felt strange to be in bed with anyone after living alone for so long.

I hoped it wouldn't turn into a common occurrence.

Chapter Twenty-Two
Reprimand

Once I sensed that Cerys had drifted off to sleep, I quietly sung a spell to make certain it remained that way, then pulled myself out of bed. I glanced back at her peaceful expression before leaving the suite and searching for a change of clothes. I couldn't simply stand by and do nothing about the way the harem had treated her.

I made my way through the palace, my blood boiling. Cerys was our gods' chosen champion. The Champion of Nabyr-zahn. Despite the human gods' foul games and their underhanded tactics, Cerys had chosen to side with us of her own accord.

A choice no one should have been forced to make. I grimaced, my thoughts shifting to Alice. *Our enemy… Hardly. That girl is harmless. I pray the gods' investigation, and that Adric fellow, can keep her from the fate the other champions have met.*

When I rounded the corner leading to the harem's section of the palace, several women looked up from their activities with surprised expressions on their faces. It did not take long for several to move toward me, offering me their company, but I raised a hand to silence them. When they spotted the expression on my face, they shrank back.

"Drysi—is it true that many of the women here have threatened our champion?" I spoke coolly, turning my gaze to the woman I had assigned to assist Cerys.

"Y-yes, Your Majesty…" Drysi turned pale and shot a nervous glance at the women near her. "Since Lady Cerys has yet to formally declare her decision, and your proposal to her…many here are concerned about her intentions."

"And you think that attempting to harm or disfigure the gods' champion will win her loyalty?" I shot a frigid glance toward Cristyn and the shivering women around her. "Drysi, you will provide me with a list of women who have acted out against Lady Cerys. It has become clear that I must revisit the loyalty of the women I chose to save.

"If any of you are thinking that you should defect to the Issradian Empire, then step forward and offer me your head now. I will not tolerate traitors."

"Y-Your Majesty, we sought to test her loyalties for your sake!" Cristyn exclaimed, shifting to prostrate herself before me. "As a human, none of us here should trust her. Furthermore, her mind is blocked off—"

"Her mind is shielded because I chose to protect her from prying individuals," I growled, taking another step forward. "Listen well: Cerys has sacrificed much by choosing to side with Nabyr-zahn. I will not have us lose our champion to petty jealousy!

"After all she has learned of Darmos for us, I cannot in my right mind send any of you to the Issradian Empire as punishment. Instead, traitors will meet death. Those of you who are still loyal will receive appropriate punishment for attacking our champion.

"Drysi."

"Yes, Your Majesty?" The woman in question dropped into a low curtsy.

"Deliver your list to Emrys and Elidyr in the morning," I ordered, before looking to the less trustworthy women. "If I find that any of you redirect your hostility toward Drysi, or to anyone else who was kind to Cerys, I will have you drawn and quartered."

Without another word, I spun on my heel and left. I scoffed when I heard several of the women break out into tears behind me. If they wanted my kindness, then they should have considered that before turning against Cerys. How they could think I would approve of such actions was beyond me.

When I returned to my suite, I changed back into a pair of

trousers and strode quietly into my room. An amused smile spread across my face when I spotted Cerys. Though still asleep, she had captured my pillow, wrapping her arms and legs around it. Her face was buried so deeply into it that I was surprised she could still breathe.

I could hardly remain angry when faced with such an adorable sight.

With some difficulty, I liberated my pillow from the slumbering demoness and slid into bed. After sinking into place, the sensation of a hand sliding over my abdomen surprised me into looking down. My breath caught as I watched Cerys wrap one arm fully over my torso and nuzzle her face into my stomach. I remained perfectly still until I was certain she was still asleep, then released a heavy sigh.

The gods had certainly chosen a confusing woman.

Chapter Twenty-Three
Moonfire

When I woke, it was to an empty bed and the smell of food. I felt like I'd slept well, which was surprising, given the circumstances. Idris' suite, Idris' bed. Not at all how I had intended to spend my first night in Nabyr-zahn. I sat up, rubbing the sleep out of my eyes. The bed was massive, but good lord was it comfortable. Despite the situation, I wasn't entirely convinced that I wanted to get out of it.

I quickly took stock of myself. My panties, Idris' shirt, and the robe he'd provided me seemed mostly in place. It appeared that I'd slid one arm out of the robe at some point during the night, but that was all that was amiss. Satisfied for the moment, I crawled over to the edge of the bed and slid off.

"Ah, you are awake—good," Idris commented when I walked through the doorway. He was already fully dressed and appeared to be reviewing a stack of documents while drinking his morning tea. "The room to your left is the bathroom if you would like to wash up before breakfast. We do not have long before my morning meetings, so I recommend you make haste."

"What about clothes?" I pointed out. "Ah, right. I'll get yesterday's—"

"You will do no such thing. I will not have my future queen dressing like a common peasant!" Idris cut me off, making a sharp motion with one hand. "You will find more suitable attire awaiting you in the bathroom."

I sighed in exasperation, unable to discern if he was serious or attempting to lighten the mood. "Too early in the morning for this…"

"Go on—there will still be food for you once you have finished." Idris shooed me away.

Too groggy too argue, I made my way into the bathroom and then shut the door behind me. Bath*room* was quite literal. Most of the room was taken up by a large, steaming pool of water that looked quite deep. Half the room was windows, which looked out over the city and landscape far below. There were potted plants all over the room, and even a man-made waterfall that fed the bath.

I shook my head and stopped gawking. After, I waded into the bath. It took most of my self-control to refrain from simply cannonballing into the deepest part. I decided to make it quick, more so that Idris wouldn't feel the urge to come check in on me than anything else. He'd already had too many victories in the past day—I couldn't allow him another.

After toweling myself dry, I stood nude by a floor length mirror and stared at the attire hanging beside it. Since there was no better option, I started dressing myself. The flowing, dark purple skirt had slits up both sides, all the way up to my hips. Its low waistband sat just beneath my tail, far lower than I would have liked, and was encrusted with beautiful silver embroidery. The fabric was so dark it was almost black. There was a faint shimmer to it, and much of it was translucent.

The bra-like top confirmed my initial impression—the entire ensemble was quite similar to those of belly dancer costumes on Earth. It was beautiful, certainly, and accentuated my *assets* quite well. However, in my mind, it was quite at odds with Idris' 'queen' claims. I took a deep breath and shoved away my agitation for the moment. I had to remind myself that such clothing could be normal in Jeriskyr, or at least in this region.

One thing was for certain: I sure as hell felt sexy wearing it.

"I question both your choices *and* why this fits me," I commented when I left the bathroom, running my fingers through my damp hair. Idris looked as if he was going to say something when he shifted toward me, but he promptly shut his mouth and simply stared at me.

"The…latter question is much simpler to answer, but I do not understand your first," Idris finally spoke, his gaze flicking up to meet mine once he'd finished examining me. "Upon our return, I enlisted the tailors to make suitable clothes for you to wear around the palace. The promise of additional coin helped hasten their task—for one set, at least. The rest will be delivered tomorrow morning at the soonest."

"And your choice of *this* kind of attire?" I prompted, watching confusion spread across his face.

"Is there something wrong with it?" Idris frowned, examining me again. "It appears to fit well and looks quite beautiful on you. What—"

"Nothing is 'wrong' with it, Idris. It's beautiful and I thank you for going to the trouble," I interjected, though that just seemed to puzzle him further. "Let me rephrase my question: Is it normal for women, especially your supposed *future queen*, to show so much skin? Though…I suppose you're showing quite a bit of skin too."

"Ah, of course." Idris nodded as if he'd realized something. "Women of high standing within the demonic kingdoms use jewelry and the showing of skin to indicate their status. Open back attire or low skirts and trousers are a staple among our kind to accommodate our tails. Further showing of skin is simply showing off.

"You mentioned before that you chose to 'play' races similar to mine due to the ability to show off your body without being judged for it. After seeing Earth, I can understand why—and sought to indulge your preferences."

"You listen better than I gave you credit for," I murmured, watching a relieved smile spread across his face. "Well, in that case I won't question you further. You said we have limited time before your meeting? Why do I need to attend?"

"I would like you to, firstly," Idris answered, motioning toward me as I sat across from him. "Furthermore, neither of us have given the gods our formal answers yet. Corlyotir will be joining us to hear our decisions, and to soothe the nobles, if necessary."

"I noticed they seemed...*displeased* about my presence," I remarked, selecting a few thick cuts of meat off a tray, as well as a few muffins. When I turned to look for tea, I found Idris already pouring a cup for me. "Ah...thank you. Though, is it normal for a king to serve himself—let alone others?"

"Only those he likes." Idris gave me a mysterious smile. "If the palace staff had their way I would do nothing for myself, let alone for others. They see danger in even the most mundane things."

"Yet you were 'allowed' to charge into the middle of a battlefield?" I gave him a doubting look.

"Believe me—Emrys and Elidyr will not let me hear the end of *that* for quite some time!" he laughed, shaking his head. "They would have me remain far from the battles, where I can oversee and direct our armies from relative safety. I prefer to have a taste of the action for myself, but with no heir and no other family who could take the throne in my stead, I must exercise a modicum of caution."

"By charging into a bloodbath to chase a mysterious girl *through enemy ranks*?" I asked dryly.

"I do not deal well with betrayal," Idris stated with a dangerous smile. "Speaking of which, I need to determine a proper punishment for the harlots who thought laying a hand on you—or on your beautiful hair—was acceptable."

"You shouldn't trouble yourself. You've done more than enough already." I shook my head, lifting my cup of tea and taking a few sips. The taste was entirely foreign, but delicious. It tasted like a blend of citrus and floral, helping perk me up for the morning.

"Nonsense—I have hardly begun!" Idris exclaimed. "Champion or not, I am fond of you and wish for you to be comfortable here. I must do more if I am to make amends for how those women treated you."

"Their behavior isn't *your* responsibility." I set my tea down and finished off my last muffin before adding, "As far as me being comfortable in Jeriskyr, that'll take time. I'm still not even used to my reflection!"

"Your reflection… Ah." Idris tilted his head slightly. "I suppose it will take time for you to grow used to it, yes. While I have taken on a human form here on Jeriskyr in order to go undetected in human lands… Well, you certainly do not have any similar option as a human on Earth.

"That said," he studied me, eyes narrowed slightly, "you hardly look different from your human form on Earth. Is it really so strange? You did mention playing inhuman characters in games before, as well."

"I didn't have 'my body' in them, and those games didn't have realistic physics for tails, if Jeriskyr is anything to go by," I replied, pointing briefly down to my tail. "Same for horns, really. Those games couldn't mimic the sensation of actually having them, nor did they have any nerve endings, like these clearly do."

"I see… I wonder if perhaps that is part of the reason you are so strangely attached to that world," Idris murmured, rubbing his chin. "Perhaps, as you grow more comfortable with your form in Jeriskyr, you will also become more inclined to remain here.

"Now then, if you are finished with your breakfast, we should make our way to the throne room. There are many other things I wish to discuss with you—and do to you—but they will have to wait."

"Then we should— Wait. *Do* to me? Just what are you scheming now?" I demanded, watching the smirking demon rise to his feet.

"Nothing unpleasant, I assure you. You are letting your mind run away with you." Idris made a dismissive gesture before turning on his heel and fetching an extravagant coat-like garment from nearby. He pulled it on and then shot me an expectant look. "Are you going to make me carry you all the way to the throne room? I was fairly certain you did not wish to remain in my rooms in the first place—which is rather surprising, given the way you clung to me when I attempted to leave bed this morning..."

"No way. I didn't." I stared at his confident grin.

"You most certainly did. Were it not for my duties, I would have gladly allowed you to remain curled against my chest." He strode toward the door, beckoning for me to follow him. "It appears that, while slumbering, you favor me more than when you are awake."

I didn't know how to respond to that, so I shut my mouth and followed him out of his suite in silence. Saying I *didn't* favor him wasn't exactly true, though I wasn't sure if our ideas of 'favoring' someone were the same. That said, I couldn't quite put my finger on why I felt the need to push him away. He was exactly the sort of man I would enjoy getting to know under most circumstances, yet my mouth seemed eager to betray me.

"Tell me... What do you know of your world's gods?" Idris asked after a few moments of uncomfortable silence.

"Nothing, as far as I'm aware," I frowned. "There are thousands of deities in Earth's history. Every few thousand years there's a new major religion that sweeps up most of the world. Some of the oldest ones had hundreds of deities in their pantheons. More recent religions were monotheistic. Others are more like spiritual practices rather than a religion—meaning they don't have a deity but are followed in a similar way."

"So, Earth's gods are an enigma to us both." Idris shook his head, sounding displeased.

"Idris, something has been bugging me—ah. Or should I say *Your Majesty?*" I asked, causing him to glance over his shoulder at me with an amused smile.

"I would prefer for my future queen to refer to me by name, of course." Idris stopped, turned to face me, and bowed, offering me his hand. "And I should be escorting you properly as well."

"You were almost easier to deal with when you were trying to kill me." I pressed my fingers to my temples.

"Capture you," he corrected with a chuckle.

I ignored him. "Where do you get that confidence? Or sense of humor, whichever it is."

"Was that what you wanted to ask me?" Idris smiled, his attentive gaze making me want to fidget.

"No," I replied with a shake of my head. "I wanted to ask you what happened to all of the human champions who came to Nabyr-zahn. After all, if this 'trading places' nonsense was an option for all of them…then your kingdom *has* had champions. Just not the ones you wanted."

"Tell me, Cerys, how concerned did the humans seem about the possibility of losing you to us?" Idris asked, taking my right hand in his. When I went to pull back, he tightened his grip and smirked. "Now, now. This belongs to me now, remember?"

"...for now." I sighed. "The Issradians didn't seem concerned at all."

"Because champions are not safe from the tax." Idris narrowed his eyes, giving my hand a brief squeeze. "Their champions were useless to us and many threatened to betray us during their every waking moment. Others begged us to allow them to return to be with 'their kind' or 'their friends.' They must not have known what awaited them.

"Whenever the Issradian Empire came to collect, the champions went with them."

"That just leaves me with more questions." I frowned as Idris led me the rest of the way downstairs and through the palace. He simply nodded to show he agreed with me. "If the former human champions didn't know, then why was Alice aware already? Why is there *any* loophole that allows you to keep people safe?"

"They likely wish for us to continue producing...breeding females." Idris shook his head, grimacing. However, a look of curiosity crossed his face soon after. "Now that I think of it—how many of the demon women you saw were pregnant?"

"Not many. It was mostly the elves, humans, and beastwomen who were."

"I see..." Idris murmured, smirking to himself. "Good. Then the humans have yet to determine how to undo such incantations."

"Incantations?" I asked, baffled.

"Ah, does your world not have a way of preventing pregnancy?" Idris looked down at me with an expression of realization on his face. "That would certainly explain your aversion to indulging in pleasure."

"We do…but it involves taking pills or injections," I replied, biting back any other remarks. Why I was discussing birth control with the demon king was just another thing I would have to add to my growing list of baffling topics. "Pills have to be taken daily, injections are every few months. Sometimes the woman takes them, sometimes the man—sometimes both. We still haven't developed anything with a one hundred percent chance of success though."

"So, people from your world turn to medicine in the absence of usable magics. I suppose that would be the next best thing," Idris nodded. "We use magic, with a perfect success rate, to prevent pregnancies. Every woman in the kingdom has the spell placed on them as a child to safeguard them against the Issradians the best we can. It is not uncommon for the bastards to attempt kidnappings between 'tax collections.'

"Speaking of which, we had best find someone to cast the spell on you as well. Sooner rather than later. There is no telling when you will begin to grow hungry."

"Is sex really the only option?" I pursed my lips.

"It is," Idris nodded.

"Then, why were the women in your harem insisting that I've

'never had a man before?'" I asked. For whatever reason, that seemed to strike a nerve. Idris' hand twitched around mine and his tail cracked into the floor.

"They insulted you in such a manner?" he demanded, fuming.

"So, it *is* an insult, then?" I tilted my head. My confusion seemed to quell Idris' rage, at least a little. I chose to preempt his inquiry. "On Earth, it's a mixed bag. Many of our cultures, for thousands of years, prized female virginity. For a long time, women who had had premarital sex couldn't get a husband—and thus had only homelessness or prostitution available to them."

"We're *sex* demons. Most people, even among our own race, find us irresistibly alluring," Idris pointed out flatly. "Saying that you have 'never had a man' insults more personal aspects than I care to list. Suffice to say, it is one of the worst ways in which they could have insulted you."

"All this because they want to 'win' you?" I laughed in disbelief. "I may not know you well, but I can't imagine what they've done has earned them any points."

"They are foolish, yes." Idris sighed. He took another deep breath, steadying himself, then glanced down at me again. "Further discussion will have to wait, and I must ask that you speak of my harem's true purpose to no one. Now that there are Otherworlders to worry about as well as the usual spies…"

"Understood," I nodded.

"Good. You have my thanks." He smiled, lured me closer, and

then released my hand to offer his arm instead. "It would be best if you allowed me to escort you as a proper gentleman should."

"Best in what way?" I countered dryly, linking my arm with his. "To go with this 'future queen' nonsense, or to further piss off your subjects?"

"Perhaps both," he laughed.

"Well, I'm not going to become your queen," I huffed. "And is pissing off your subjects really a good idea?"

"No matter how many times you say it, that will not make it the truth," Idris informed me with a smirk. His tail coiled around mine, making me stiffen. Whatever deity had decided to make it *that* sensitive needed a thorough ass-kicking. "Whatever is the matter, kitten? You are turning pink."

"You're testing my patience." I decided to take a more neutral approach, but his smirk just broadened into a grin. "Let go."

"As for your question," Idris drawled, removing his tail from mine in an agonizingly slow manner, "any of my subjects who would protest such a thing deserve to have their feathers ruffled. Nabyr-zahn has been without a queen since I was a child— centuries, so we're clear."

...I almost wish I hadn't told him to knock it off. I kept my face passive and shook out my tail briefly.

"Your Majesty," Emrys greeted the king as he approached from the other end of the hallway. He shot me a mildly baffled glance before returning his attention to Idris. "I was coming to report that

Cerys was missing—but I see that isn't the case. Dare I ask?"

"The harem women will need to be put in their place," Idris stated, narrowing his eyes. "Those who had the gall to attack our champion need to understand the error of their ways, and those considering doing the same need to see an example of why they should not."

"Attack?" Emrys frowned, glancing down at me. "Then where the hell have you been?"

"*His Majesty* decided it was too late to bother anyone, and that I should stay in his room overnight," I snorted, causing Emrys to look at Idris for confirmation.

"She is quite serious," Idris stated with a mischievous smile. "Have our guests all gathered?"

"What'd you do to her?" Emrys asked bluntly.

"We played a game and had dinner, nothing more. Yet." Idris shrugged.

"Has it occurred to you what your harem is gonna do when they catch wind of this?" Emrys sighed, crossing his arms. "They're going to be even more pissed now."

"More than if I had woken the palace staff to prepare a room of her own?" Idris countered, an amused smile on his lips. "Speaking of which—have the Queen's Tower prepared for Cerys. The enchantments on the door should remove the need for dedicated guards and allow her to sleep safely without the threat of jealous women interfering."

"I was half-expecting you to demand I continue staying with you." I arched an eyebrow at Idris.

"That can be arranged, if you prefer," Idris offered with a chuckle.

I honestly don't know what's worse—the 'Queen's Tower,' or staying in Idris' personal suite. I sighed, contemplating it. "Which one will piss off the harlots less?"

"Neither," Emrys stated before Idris could say anything.

"The Queen's Tower it is, then." I grimaced, shaking my head. "Sounds way too opulent for my blood, but I'm learning that arguing against Idris' 'hospitality' is pointless."

"Perhaps if you had a good reason for arguing it would be different," Idris smiled.

I pursed my lips at him. He wasn't wrong.

"Well, let's get to it then." Emrys shook his head. "The nobles are still suspicious of Cerys' presence. They're not happy about a human from another world being chosen as our champion, reassurances from the gods or not."

"I can confidently say that the humans of Earth are quite different from the humans of Jeriskyr," Idris began thoughtfully. "Even with that in mind, the kitten here is more like one of us than them."

"*Kitten?*" Emrys gave us a disbelieving look.

"I have no fucking idea why he's been calling me that, and he won't knock it off," I scoffed, before Idris could spout off anything else ridiculous.

"Would it kill you to refer to her by name?" Emrys glanced at Idris.

"Hardly. I do so frequently," he shrugged. "However, her false dislike of 'kitten' is much more entertaining."

"It's not *false*—" I started to protest for the sake of protesting, but both men motioned for me to be quiet, their expressions growing serious. A moment later, I registered what sounded like bickering. We were close to the throne room. "Humph."

"Oi, Elidyr, keep an eye on His Majesty." Emrys waved to the man briefly. "I've gotta go relay some orders to the palace staff. I'll try to make it quick."

"Of course." Elidyr nodded to Emrys, then shot a quizzical glance in my direction. "Your Majesty, I was not aware you would be bringing the champion with you. Would this have something to do with our divine guest?"

"Indeed it would." Idris adopted a more formal tone and expression before glancing toward the nobles, who were glaring at me from elsewhere in the room. "You would do well to remember that Corlyotir chose Cerys to be our champion and would not have done so without good reason. I suggest you remedy your behavior before it wears on my patience any further.

"Now, as for *you*..." Idris shifted his attention to the half-naked woman beside his throne. "I will not be requiring the services of anyone in the harem from now on, especially not from those who sought to disfigure or kill Cerys. *Leave.*"

"B-b-b-but I didn't—!" the woman stuttered, glancing from Idris to me and back. "Your Majesty, please, I—"

"Cerys?" Idris glanced down at me.

"She's telling the truth," I offered, after taking another look at the woman. "She and Drysi attempted to convince the others to stop."

"Very well." Idris turned his piercing gaze to the woman. "My statement still stands, and you are to relay it to the other women in the harem. Tell them that if they attempt to betray me again, I will see to it that they join the Issradians they appear so keen on assisting."

"Y-yes, Your Majesty!" The woman quickly curtsied, then fled.

He doesn't require their services? Ugh. Now they're all going to have the wrong impression. I held my tongue as Idris led me over to his throne. He sat down and then motioned beside him, earning a brief sour look from me. "I would rather stand."

"Would my lap be preferable?" He tilted his head, a mischievous twinkle in his eyes.

"You would invite a human whore—" The noble didn't even get to finish his sentence before the king was on him. He kicked the noble in the torso, sending the man crashing backward into a pillar. Before he could muster any strength to recover, Idris skewered the weaker demon's shoulder with a sword that appeared out of nowhere.

An inventory system, maybe? I wondered, examining the sword.

"Let me make this perfectly clear to all of you," Idris spoke in a calm, collected tone that made the color drain from the faces of the nobility. "Nabyr-zahn is now Cerys' home and I would have my subjects welcome her with open arms. It has been centuries since we were last blessed with a genuine champion and you would be fools to turn her against us.

"Any insults toward Cerys will be treated as insults to me and my bloodline."

That's going too far. I chewed on my lower lip and attempted not to fidget.

"Well, I take it that means you've made a decision, then?" Corlyotir giggled from the pillar she had been leaning against. She glanced over at me with an amused smile. "And you have not changed your mind?"

"Despite the number of people who have attempted to drive me off—no. I haven't changed my mind." I shook my head slightly. *Jealous women aside, I do actually like what I've seen of Nabyr-zahn so far. Idris too, if I'm being honest.*

"And I am quite willing to accept her as our champion—and more," Idris added, shooting me a suggestive smirk.

"Excellent!" Corlyotir clapped her hands together and turned to look at me. "Now then, I will finalize the incantation that will bind you to Jeriskyr. Once it's finished, you will see the world as its native citizens do—and be able to see the elements of Jeriskyr, that is, the UI, once more. Is there anything else you need while I'm here, Idris?"

"Ah, yes, while I have you here..." Idris remarked as he returned to his throne, his sword leaving a trail of blood on the floor. "Which bloodline does Cerys belong to?"

"Bloodline?" Corlyotir paused, then laughed. "Ah, of course. You're concerned about avoiding inbreeding, I'm sure.

"Cerys is the first of her bloodline. We chose not to insert her within any existing clans."

"Her own bloodline, you say?" One of the nobles spoke up, looking intrigued.

"Well then, as matriarch of your own clan, you will need a clan name." Idris tilted his head, examining me from head to toe. I could practically feel his gaze as if he was tracing me with a stick. "I suppose you still object to 'Bloodsong?'"

"Of course I do!" I snorted, crossing my arms.

"Cynfyn?"

"Practically the same thing. So, no."

"Gwythyr?"

"*Same thing*. Do you ever give up?"

"Giving up is a terrible character trait."

"I'm glad to see you two get along so well!" Corlyotir exclaimed cheerfully, looking between us both with bright eyes. "Now then, before you settle that, let me finish my business with Cerys. I have places to be."

The goddess raised her hands, summoning a faint yellow glow around them. Her power drifted over to me, enveloping me in a flash of light before disappearing. Then she disappeared without so much as another word. I stared after her for a moment—I didn't *feel* much different. An instruction manual would've been nice. Something.

Concentrating briefly, I confirmed that I could once more see information over people's heads. However, most of the people in the throne room were either at the highest tier of proficiency or had question marks for a level.

"Moonfire?" Idris suggested.

"Huh?" I shot him a questioning look.

"Yes, I think Moonfire will do." Idris nodded to himself. "Cerys Moonfire."

"Wait, don't I get any say in this?" I turned to glower at him. "And why Moonfire?"

"Because your hair reminds me of moonfire lilies," Idris remarked with a tender smile, reaching up to pull some of my hair over my shoulder. "I am decided. You will grow to like it, or you will earn a title that eventually replaces it—as I have."

"An excellent choice, Your Majesty," one of the nobles simpered, earning a glare from Idris. "Now, about her *availability*—"

"Are any of you foolish enough to compete with your king for a woman's hand?" Idris interjected, his tone cold. "If all you care about is *breeding*, save your breath.

"Elidyr, take Cerys to see Alana. We need to be certain that she is healthy before she begins her combat training, and Alana can gauge how much Cerys will be able to handle at first."

"As you wish, Your Majesty." Elidyr bowed to Idris and then looked to me. "If you would be so kind as to follow me, Lady Moonfire."

Great, am I going to have nobles after me too now? I sulked, crossing my arms. *Even if Idris makes some big show of trying to 'court' me, will it be enough? Hell, how am I supposed to tell if he's serious? I sure as hell don't want him to do it if it's just for my protection, either.*

Begrudgingly, I followed Elidyr through the palace. After fetching cloaks, we left and headed into Cejari-ir proper. Aside from checking to make certain I was still with him, Elidyr remained silent most of the way. He gave me the impression he didn't talk much.

"He's just allowed to name me like that?" I asked, once the silence had begun to gnaw at me too much. Elidyr spared me a questioning glance, so I continued, "That wouldn't have been acceptable where I'm from. Only parents have the right to name someone, and it isn't at all uncommon for people to legally change their name later in life."

"As the first of your bloodline, you are a clan leader," Elidyr frowned. "Had you been raised in Jeriskyr, you would have earned a name for yourself already and His Majesty wouldn't have needed to provide you with one. Naming oneself is frowned upon."

"So, in short—yes, he's allowed to do that." I released a heavy sigh.

"Receiving a name from His Majesty is a great honor. You should be thankful." Elidyr pursed his lips and furrowed his brow. "That His Majesty saw fit to name you, let alone spend some of his time on you, simply goes to show how important you are to Nabyr-zahn's survival. His Majesty hardly ever—"

"And what has 'His Majesty' done to gain such loyal devotion?" I interjected dryly, causing Elidyr to look at me with a perplexed expression. "You appear to hold him in high esteem."

"Without him, Nabyr-zahn would have fallen after King Gwythyr's…disappearance." Elidyr hesitated, then released a small sigh. "His Majesty, Emrys, and myself have known each other since we were children. His Majesty rarely takes interest in a woman like he has with you. If you harm him, you will answer to me."

"So, he usually takes interest in men, then?" I asked, tilting my head. Elidyr gave me a dumbfounded look, indicating that perhaps I was wrong. "Well, that's what it sounded like you were implying, at least."

"His Majesty can barely find the time to feed, let alone pursue more meaningful relationships—is that clearer?" Elidyr sighed in exasperation. "He prefers women. However, with so many of our women taken by the Issradian Empire…many of us must make do with what we can get. While the harem provides His Majesty with a stable supply of sustenance, many of us have to look elsewhere."

"Clearer, yes." I nodded, deciding to change the subject away from Idris. "So, who is this Alana woman and why is she not with the rest of the harem?"

"The Issradians take only demon women from us. Alana is an elf." Elidyr shrugged, but he caught the frown I shot him. "According to the elven gods, their kind are not ours to give. I do not know what manner of deal they struck, but we can give only demonic citizens as 'tax.' Of course, this does not stop kidnappers..."

"The more I hear about the Issradians, the more I dislike them." I sighed, shaking my head. While I didn't want to converse about Idris, I also wasn't quite prepared to dwell on the Issradians in-depth either. "If this Alana woman hasn't been kidnapped, does that mean she is guarded heavily?"

"Not quite." A small, crooked smile formed on Elidyr's lips. "That woman is like a rampaging bull. After losing many men to her...the human filth ceased their attempts to steal her. It simply isn't worth what it costs them."

I fell silent as we neared a small cottage with overgrown gardens. Outside was a woman in fur-lined leather clothing. She had fiery red hair and pale, freckled skin. A basket hanging from her arm was filled nearly to the brim with various herbs and other plant matter she had trimmed from the garden. Given the beigey color of most of the plants, I had to assume it was likely her last harvest before winter came.

"Alana," Elidyr called, causing the elf woman to turn to us. Her pitch-black eyes soon snapped to me instead of focusing on the demon man beside me. "This is Lady Cerys Moonfire, the gods' chosen champion. His Majesty—"

"Stuff it, scaly." Alana set her basket down and walked toward us, shoving the demon man out of her way with one hand. She stopped in front of me and crossed her arms, looking up at me with a piercing gaze. "I was expecting you to be taller. Not every day a woman denies *His Majesty* his desires, you know."

...I'm still way taller than you. I held my tongue.

"*Alana*," Elidyr began again, the corner of *his* eye twitching this time. "We need you to make certain Lady Moonfire is in good health and see to it that, if captured, she cannot breed with the humans."

"Do you *have* to call it 'breeding?'" I shot the demon an agitated look.

"Of course. Willing or otherwise, humans are a lesser race." Elidyr made a dismissive motion.

"Inside with you," Alana stated, grabbing me by the shoulders and pushing me toward her cottage. When Elidyr made to follow, she glared at him. "Not you! Girls only. Unless you want the king to skin you for seeing *Lady Moonfire* in all her nude glory."

"...I will wait outside." Elidyr stopped in his tracks, growing pale.

Once inside, Alana heaved a sigh and then put her hands on her hips as she looked at me.

"Let's get this over with, then," Alana remarked, pointing to a nearby bed. "Strip and sit down. I hear the gods usually give their champions a healthy body, but we'd better be damned sure. Need your clothes out of my way if I'm going to halt your ability to get pregnant, anyway. You start working with magic yet?"

"Not yet..." I replied, wary, as I obliged the straightforward woman.

"Feeding?" Alana gave me a pointed look.

"Absolutely not."

"You'd better change that, and quick." She flicked my forehead. "Succubi and incubi need to feed often. The weak, two to three days. The strong, every four or five. More often if you're using a lot of magic or fighting frequently—which you're gonna be doing since you have to train. You gotta 'recharge' often, and better to do it *before* the hunger takes over."

"Takes over?" I arched an eyebrow.

"A hungry demon of any sort is a scary one," Alana snorted, rummaging through a nearby trunk. "Your hunger ain't going to care about what the world you came from is like. You let yourself become too hungry, you're going to lose your mind to your instincts until you find someone to fuck. That simple. Better to feed on your own terms, don't you think?"

Either she's incredibly damned nosy or someone put her up to this lecture. I pursed my lips as I sat on the edge of the bed. "I'll consider it."

"What is there to 'consider' if there's no risk?" Alana thwacked me upside the head before walking past me to rummage in another trunk. "Look, I'm not one of the demons but I've lived here a long time. Everyone wants the Issradian Empire dealt with—even some of the Issradians. You're our ticket to see that happen. You feed, lose yourself to hunger, or you die."

"This also part of 'making sure I'm healthy?'" I gave her a foul look.

"Consider it friendly advice from someone who knows how far Idris will go to see the Issradian Empire conquered." Alana narrowed her eyes. "With his power as an incubus, and as a spellsinger, he could make you do anything he wanted. Maybe it wouldn't be morally right, but morals are a luxury for the strong."

"I'll keep that in mind," I muttered with distaste. "If he's so powerful, then why hasn't he just done that?"

"Beats me!" Alana threw her hands into the air before walking over to me, dragging a wheeled tray with her. Set on it were numerous crystals and some instruments I didn't recognize. "The king doesn't like forcing anyone to do his bidding, but Nabyrzahn's been without a champion for so long... A lot of us thought he'd use his power to make you comply. Seems to me he wants to stay on your good side and let you stay yourself.

"Now then, let's get this shit over with. I've got a lot more herbs to pick."

Chapter Twenty-Four
Settling In

The sun had already begun to set by the time Alana was finished with me. I hadn't been able to get any more useful information out of her. She was far too focused on my feeding— or rather, the lack thereof. Once I'd given up on questioning her, she had fallen completely silent and focused on her work. While she did so, I attempted to acquaint myself with whatever Corlyotir had done to bind me to Jeriskyr.

Aside from being able to acquire information regarding other people's skills, it looked as though I could accumulate knowledge about most things in Jeriskyr without having to write it down. The information was both acquired and stored through a skill unrelated to any class or combat professions.

Learning something allowed me to review it within the UI at any given time, meaning the skill was practically a visual memory. It reminded me of in-game encyclopedias and bestiaries from games I'd played in the past.

While useful, there was an important caveat—it could only store things I had actually *learned* myself. For example, if I wanted to study herbalism, I would have to consume different plants myself to discover their purpose—or use them on other people.

As far as I could tell, it was the same for most of the knowledge that could be stored. Furthermore, it didn't store information regarding conversations I had with people. There wasn't a file on Alana, Elidyr, or Idris. If such information could be recorded, I figured it was by some other skill or ability. Or perhaps that was left to natural memory.

The fusion between reality and game made me uneasy, but Alana and Elidyr both insisted that it was the norm for Jeriskyr. Both had been startled by my revelation that such things hadn't existed on Earth for a long time—and even now, it required special glasses or augmentation to achieve a similar effect. It bothered me that Idris had made no mention of it.

"You don't have to carry all of that for me," I spoke up, glancing over to Elidyr.

In his arms and hanging off them were dozens of boxes and

bags from the tailors in Cejari-ir. While waiting for me, he had learned that the tailors had finished their duties early and they had sent word that we could pick up my order.

At first, I had thought the elegant man might be crushed under the weight of it all. He was clearly much stronger than he looked. There was far more than I had ordered when I'd gone into town with Emrys, leading me to believe that my *favorite* king had meddled more.

"It is an honor to assist our champion," Elidyr responded simply, shooting me a sideways glance. "And a further honor to help the woman my king favors…assuming you do nothing to betray that trust."

"You're all really disinclined to trust me, aren't you?" I sighed, crossing my arms. Clearly, Elidyr wasn't going to allow me to carry my own things. With that option gone, I decided to press him for more information instead. After all, if I wasn't mistaken, he served as Idris' adviser. He'd know a lot about Nabyr-zahn and Jeriskyr as a whole. "Would it be any different if I hadn't originally been a human?"

"Unlikely." Elidyr shook his head. "Trust is a luxury we do not have. You will have to earn our trust…and learn to avoid simpering fools."

"Simpering fools?" I echoed, arching an eyebrow and watching his face contort with disgust.

"Lack of trust or not, you are the first of your bloodline and the gods' champion besides," Elidyr offered after a moment, his tone indicating he was attempting to find a polite wording. "Simply put, we have a surplus of men and not enough women. The nobility are not excluded from this conundrum.

"Nobles and commoners alike will seek to pursue you. Winning you over would provide their line with a much-needed boost in longevity, regardless of trust. Of course, I suspect they will fail to see that liberating our people from the Issradian's grasp would have much the same effect…"

"I suppose they wouldn't care about my intention to return to my own world, either," I muttered, earning a troubled look from Elidyr. "What?"

"Do you truly wish to return to Earth?" he asked, his tone hesitant and confused. "His Majesty did not divulge much, but I was under the impression that you have few reasons to be fond of that world."

"I…" I paused, pursing my lips when I felt my chest constrict. For some reason, I no longer felt as strongly about returning to Earth. While I wanted to claim that I did, simply because that was what I had been saying for at least a week, I no longer felt the same conviction toward the matter. "That will depend on how the people of Nabyr-zahn treat—or continue to treat—me. If Earth still stands out as the better choice—"

"Corlyotir must have done something to you when she bound you here." Elidyr narrowed his eyes. "You sound anything but convinced about returning to Earth. Let me guess—you are claiming you wish to return because you think it is the 'right' thing to do?"

"Not exactly… I don't have enough information yet to make a decision." I sighed and ran a hand through my hair. *That said, I definitely don't feel as strongly about returning. What did she do to me?*

"There you two are!" Emrys met us in the entry hall when we entered the palace. He shot Elidyr a knowing look before turning his attention to me. "Cerys…er, *Lady Moonfire*, His Majesty suggested I should take you to the training yards and help you narrow down your choices for combat styles. Looks like Elidyr has got your new clothes too…

"Meet me here after you've changed into something more suitable for fighting."

"You are going to make me carry these up to the Queen's Tower?" Elidyr demanded, glowering at Emrys.

"Do you *want* help?" the other man countered with a smirk.

"Hardly." Elidyr turned on his heel and stalked down the hallway. "Come along, Lady Moonfire."

"Can you *both* stop calling me that? Cerys will do!" I huffed, lifting my skirts as I hurried after the tetchy Elidyr.

Only a few moments passed before Emrys fell into step with us, and I shot him a questioning look. Instead of speaking, he reached over and plucked several boxes off the top of the stack in

Elidyr's arms.

"I want to give your accommodations another look," Emrys offered, balancing the boxes on one shoulder. "Some of the women from the harem were involved with the preparation. They're claiming that they've changed their tune now that you've given your official answer—but I know damn well some of 'em are still too attached to Idris."

"Humph. I don't really want to talk about those women," I snorted, shaking my head. "How about we discuss combat instead? The sooner we fix the 'dead weight' problem, the better."

"You truly intend to get involved?" Elidyr glanced over his shoulder at me.

"I'm not the sort that likes to sit back where it's 'safe,'" I shrugged. "Even when I've played some manner of healer in games, my builds and choices usually turn it into a short-range class."

"You heal, then?" Emrys arched an eyebrow.

"Only when I have to. I would prefer I didn't." I gave him a pointed look.

"It would be safer." Elidyr shook his head and then pivoted to look at me. "If you could get the door for us, my lady."

"There's nothing 'fun' about safe." I grimaced as I stepped past both demon men. Once the door was open, they strode through and I followed.

"Archery, perhaps?" Emrys suggested.

"Or some manner of the arcane?" Elidyr added.

"I'd rather use my fists or a sword," I informed them, eliciting sighs.

"Did Idris not explain to you what will happen if you die?" Emrys glanced at me again, his expression serious.

"I'd rather go out in a blaze of glory than die meaninglessly slinging spells or arrows!" I retorted, earning a dumbfounded look in response.

"Keep speaking in such a manner and His Majesty won't be the only one pursuing you to the ends of Jeriskyr." Elidyr glanced at me and then shot a meaningful look at Emrys before returning his attention to me. "That aside, I would advise against utilizing purely short-range skills, Lady Moonfire. Were you to focus on swordplay, your only option for ranged foes would be to throw your weapon or to charge at them."

"Aye... You'd best learn one ranged proficiency to make up for it." Emrys frowned, sinking into thought. "Fists or sword you say... Any other weapons you're keen on?"

"Well, I have limited experience with a bow." I considered the possibilities for a moment. "Most other weapons I've used either won't exist in Jeriskyr or I've only used in game worlds."

"Such as?" Emrys prompted.

"Nearly every type of melee weapon you can think of," I murmured, trying to think of anything else. "Ah, also crossbows, staves, wands, maces, books, orbs..."

"Books?" Elidyr looked thoroughly offended by the notion.

"You used *books* to fight your enemies?! The poor—"

"They were used as a medium to focus magic," I interrupted him, shaking my head. "Same for orbs and wands. I've played both offensive and supportive magic-users in games before."

"We'll see how you are with a bow, then see if we can get the Grandmasters to check you out," Emrys remarked, before motioning to the apparent dead-end at the top of the staircase. "Place yer hand against the groove there. Should already be set up to accept you."

When my hand touched the frigid stone, a spiral of glowing markings radiated across the stone from my palm. The shining black and purple markings soon sunk into the surface and the entire slab slid out of our way. It struck me as similar to the door leading to Idris' suite, but I wasn't sure why the magic was a different color.

As far as proficiencies went, I had a decent idea of what I had *wanted* to combine from when I'd still thought Jeriskyr was a game. Some combination of magic and martial arts had sounded like it would be a lot of fun. Now that I knew this world was real, I wasn't entirely sure if it was something I could pull off. With that in mind, I decided to let Emrys put me through my paces with a variety of weapons before dedicating myself to a decision.

"You two wait here, I'll check it out." Emrys placed his share of the boxes on the floor beside me before walking deeper into the suite, his hand resting on the hilt of the sword at his hip.

Elidyr released a small sigh and turned to me with a questioning look on his face. "Are you certain you can't be convinced to take on more ranged skills, or perhaps the skills of a tactician?"

"Not my style," I replied, amused. "I get that either one of those options would be safer, but neither is where I truly shine. While strategy is one of my strong suits, it's always been while in the midst of a fight. Right in the thick of it."

"Then we'd better get to work immediately," Emrys remarked as he returned, looking much more relaxed. "Nothing foul lurking anywhere. No poisons that I can detect.

"Can we leave the rest to you, Elidyr? Probably be best if I get Cerys started with basic training right away."

"At least permit her to change first!" Elidyr snorted, opening a few boxes before he found what looked like basic breeches and a tunic. He pulled it out of the box and then shoved it toward me. "Here. Change. Over there."

The luxurious feel of the fabric threw me off a little. It was smooth and soft to the touch. Inside, there was a layer of fabric that felt similar to satin but was somehow stretchy. Once changed, I followed Emrys through the palace and toward the training grounds. It was late enough that we passed few people on the way, mostly soldiers and servants. Something that surprised me was the fact that some of the harem women appeared to have male visitors. Visitors they were quite fond of.

"Their lovers and husbands," Emrys offered quietly when he noticed my confusion. "Most of the women in Idris' harem are spoken for."

"What about the female soldiers I saw during that skirmish?" I inquired, my curiosity piqued. "Are they members of the harem too, or does Nabyr-zahn have some secret female military I haven't come across yet?"

"Aye, they're part of the harem too. The ones who would rather fight instead of sit around being protected," Emrys replied dryly, nodding. "Cristyn is one of 'em. I'd wager some of the women who went after you did so because of their loyalty to the king, twisted as it may be. Lot of 'em probably see it as an insult to him that you didn't accept his proposal."

"You mean his utterly ridiculous proposal that was likely in jest anyway?" I retorted, giving Emrys a pointed look. He simply shot me a crooked grin in response. "Not to mention the last time I'd seen him, he was about to slit my throat! With you and Elidyr looking on, no less."

"Normal business in war," Emrys shrugged. "The slitting of throats, that is. Not the proposal. He surprised even me and Elidyr with that one. We're not sure how serious he was either.

"That said, it isn't hard to guess why that would ruffle the harem's feathers. Sure, some of them have genuine feelings—they think—for their king. But there's another angle for you to consider, *Lady Moonfire*."

"And what is that?" I sighed.

"Fear." Emrys narrowed his eyes. "Put bluntly, it wouldn't be appropriate for Idris to keep the harem around if he got married. Our culture doesn't allow for it and he'd have a hell of a time with the nobles if he tried. Probably why he decided you were joining the harem yourself—this way he can protect all the women, not *just you*."

"So, you think the harem women are frightened that they might lose their protection? That would make sense," I grimaced. "Granted, attacking the gods' champion…to be quite honest, I was expecting something on the opposite end of the scale regarding how people treat me."

"You'll get your share of that too," Emrys snorted. "For now, you're still going to have a rough time with the harem women. I did what I could to calm them down, but Idris' claims that he doesn't need their services… Well, they're thinking that means more than their ability as guards."

"I was afraid of that as soon as he opened his mouth!" I exclaimed in frustration, causing Emrys to snicker.

"Here, let's start you off with a bow," he suggested as we strode into the open training yard. It was lit with a mixture of torches and some form of magitech, but I was still doubtful about how well I could aim in such low lighting. Instead of commenting, I kept my mouth shut and waited for Emrys to return with a bow, quiver, and vambrace. "Don't have any longbows close to your height, so short will have to do. Put the vambrace on, then we'll see whether you can draw it."

Once the vambrace was in place, Emrys handed me the bow and a single arrow. I kept my expression passive as I notched the arrow and gave the string a tentative tug. While I couldn't quite remember the traditional draw weight for shortbows, I knew damn well it was nowhere near as kind as a compound bow. Furthermore, it had been designed for demons. Likely demon men. I doubted that my new demoness body could draw such weight.

Even so, I took the appropriate stance and attempted to draw the bow, immediately feeling the muscles and joints in my shoulder creak. Pursing my lips, I managed to pull the string back almost halfway before carefully letting it go slack and turning to look at the contemplative Emrys.

"I can't draw that much weight," I stated when he still said nothing.

"You pulled more than I expected." Emrys sounded genuine, so I decided not to contest him on the matter. "With a custom bow, you might manage. Might be easier to have you work on your strength—you're going to need to anyway. Looks like 'new body' means you've got a lot of work to do."

"It seems that way." I handed the arrow back to Emrys, followed by the bow and finally the vambrace. "What shall we try next? If I can't draw a shortbow, then crossbows and longbows are likely out of the question too—and I doubt your world has compound bows."

"Compound?" Emrys gave me a baffled look.

"Compound bows use a pulley system to divert the weight once fully drawn," I explained, following him toward the nearby armory. "You can also specify the draw weight. So, let's say the draw weight is sixty pounds—once fully drawn, the pulley system takes one or two thirds of that strain away from you, while traditional bows would saddle you with the full sixty pounds until you loose."

"Sounds convenient," he snorted, shaking his head. "I follow you, but no, we have nothing like that. Might be worth running by some of the town crafters, see if we can come up with something similar.

"With bows out of the question, that'll leave magic for ranged. I don't much like the idea of forcing you to make do with primitive weapons such as blowguns and the like. You used *some* magic when you first got to Jeriskyr, didn't you?"

"Yes, to break my fall," I nodded.

"Right. Did Alana check what you're good with?" Emrys motioned for me to follow him toward a row of striking dummies.

"Darkness. The other elements didn't seem to like me much." I shrugged, glancing at the dummies. "Weapons or magic now?"

"Have to wait for the Grandmasters who're good with shadow magic," Emrys replied, offering me a short sword hilt-first. "I'm good with fire and not much else on the magic front, so I can't really help you there. Instead, we'll work out what weapons you're comfortable with.

"Any training in your world?"

"Mostly unarmed combat training," I answered as I tested the weight of the short sword. "While there were a few weapons utilized by the martial art I took, there were significantly more unarmed techniques. I'm not sure what you would call the weapons in this world, so I'll just have to tell you if I spot one in your collection over there."

"No wonder you're partial to punching things," Emrys remarked dryly.

"I actually favor kicks," I offered, pointing down at my shin and foot. "We can still start with the weapons, though. See if we can't find something I mesh with."

Chapter Twenty-Five
Distance

I rolled my shoulders, wincing, as I made my way through the palace. The past several days had been spent on work and nothing else. My time away from Jeriskyr had resulted in piles upon piles of paperwork—which unwitting Otherworlders appeared keen to interrupt. If Nabyr-zahn had not needed their kind so greatly, I would have been happy to silence them permanently.

More troubling still, I had not seen Cerys in days. Emrys and Elidyr had both given me favorable reports regarding her accommodations, as well as informing me that she had begun basic training. Alana had even given her a clean bill of health. Yet the demoness in question was nowhere to be seen. I had to wonder if she was avoiding me.

Alas, I was doing my best not to intrude upon her thoughts.

Training, perhaps? I wondered, glancing out the nearest window. Night had fallen several hours prior, but it was not difficult for me to tell that Cerys had yet to return to the Queen's Tower. Shielding her mind at all hours of the day gave me an easy way to find her, if nothing else.

I had hoped she would come to me, but it was clear now that she was too focused on other matters. I had to go to her.

Resigned, I strode down the hallway that would lead me toward the training yard and away from my chambers.

I wanted to test the petite woman for myself. No time like the present.

However, when I arrived at the training yard, my mind quickly changed. The glimpse was brief, but I most certainly could see the blood dripping from Cerys' fist as she pulled it back to strike a dummy. Droplets of blood stained the sand around her feet and there were smears of it where she had struck the dummy.

Before I knew what I was doing, I dashed in front of her and caught her wrists. Her strike did not hit me, yet there was enough force behind it for me to feel the displacement of the air through my clothes. She was using far too much strength in simple training—as if the blood running down her hands and feet wasn't enough of an indication on its own.

"Cerys, stop," I spoke quietly when she looked up at me with an expression of both confusion and surprise.

"Why?" she frowned, attempting to pull her wrists from my grip. "If I'm going to get stronger, I need to train. I've still got a few more reps—"

"You will stop before you ruin your hands or your feet," I interjected firmly, narrowing my eyes. It took several more moments before I realized my pulse was racing. I despised the sight of her bleeding. It was utterly unacceptable. I swallowed hard before continuing, "If you insist on such forms of combat, we will find you some manner of gauntlets and boots to protect your skin."

"But I need to build up callouses!" Cerys shook her head, seemingly oblivious to my tightening grip. "Fresh body, fresh skin. No callouses to speak of. It'll take a while to build them up, of course, but—"

"I will not hear any arguments—especially not such weak ones!" I snapped, pulling her away from the dummy. My tone startled her into looking up at me in wide-eyed silence. "You are bleeding everywhere. Come. We are going to pay a visit to the healers."

"Bleed—oh." Cerys frowned when she finally glanced down at her hands.

"How could you not have noticed *that*?" I asked, exasperated, watching the troublesome demoness glance from her hands, to her feet, and then to where she had been training.

"I sort of…turn off my brain to most things when I get focused," she shrugged, before looking up at me again. "I'm sure I can find my way myself. You don't need to waste your time. Shouldn't you be heading off to— Hey! *Put me down*!"

"I cannot trust you to go to the healers on your own instead of continuing to damage yourself." I ignored her fists hitting my back as I carted her into the palace. "Honestly, Cerys. What were you thinking? What would you have done if you had harmed yourself so gravely you could no longer fight? Hands are a delicate part of the body! If you refuse to be more careful, I will have to have someone watch over you at all times!"

"Why do you care?" Cerys grumbled. Her words cut me like a knife. I forced myself to remain composed.

"You want to save Alice, I want to save my people. Neither will be achieved if you can no longer fight." I gritted my teeth, scowling at myself. Her question should not have gotten to me, nor should the sight of her bloodied hands and feet. Yet, both distressed me far more than I cared to admit. The latter made me wish I could reasonably keep her in the palace, where it was safe.

"That's it?" she asked, sounding oddly disappointed. I felt one of her fists clench around my shirt. "I'm glad it's that and not…"

Liar. I shut my eyes briefly and forced my breathing to become steady. Cerys seemed so incredibly insistent on pushing me away, yet a peek at even just her surface thoughts made it clear that it hurt her to do so. I had no idea how to approach her on the matter.

My inability to truly understand her was, in part, what had led me to make such a strange wager with her.

Alas, she seemed just as baffled by me as I was by her.

"I'm getting dizzy being upside down." Cerys tugged once on my shirt, causing me to slow to a stop. Instead of putting her down, I shifted her into my arms and held her against my chest. "That's not what I had in mind."

"You were thinking of bolting the moment I set you down." I narrowed my eyes at her, watching as she glanced away. "You will be free of my presence soon enough."

"That isn't… **Fine**." Cerys clenched her jaw, her tail twitching in agitation against my forearm. I sighed, but she refused to look at me.

"Cerys, eventually you will have to decide whether you are going to truly push me away or if you want to understand me— and my kind," I informed her, watching as she ground her teeth. "Furthermore, is it truly so horrible that someone wants you to keep you from harming yourself?"

"Not like I was doing it on purpose." She shot me a sideways glance. "That said, attempting to understand 'your kind' would be prudent since I'm also the same race now…but I'm not going to learn much if you don't try to understand *me*."

"Considering you have made yourself scarce the past few days," I began, shooting her a look as I turned a corner, "I don't think you can truly turn this back on me. If afforded the opportunity to learn about and understand you, I will. However, I am less and less inclined to do so when you continually shove back."

"Maybe that's for the best..." Cerys sighed and looked away from me again. *It's not like I deserve kindness or understanding from anyone in this world or mine. If I'm going to make up my mind, it's probably best to make the choice to isolate myself.*

That was not like her. Though I knew she was remorseful regarding her behavior—to a point—her thoughts surprised me. Had her conscience truly been wearing so harshly on her, or was something else afoot? I wished I knew. If I had, then I could have helped her.

"And how will that help you accomplish any of your goals?" I asked, feeling her stiffen in my arms. "Cerys, you have allies here. Betraying us for such poor reasons is...ill-advised."

"Just how frequently do you listen in on my thoughts?" She glared at me.

"Only when you are clearly hiding something or are distressed." I shook my head. "Incubi and succubi tend to be very honest because of our ability to read each other's minds, especially when we're younger and haven't yet learned any mental defenses.

"Your lingering penchant for human dishonesty, toward yourself and others, makes it difficult to understand you without listening to your thoughts. I am *trying* to be patient, but..."

I fell silent. Bringing up her need to feed, let alone that she would *have* to see to it soon, did not seem like a wise move when she appeared to be in such an unstable state.

"Your Majesty?" A tired man looked up from his desk when I carried Cerys into the infirmary. "Ah, and Lady Moonfire? How might I help you so late at night?"

"Her Ladyship's hands and feet require healing. She has been training too hard." I sat Cerys down, watching as she glanced away with a small pout on her face. "Cerys, once you are done here you should return to your rooms to rest. You will make yourself ill if you continue to overwork your mind and body."

Without another word, I left Cerys in the healer's capable hands and made my way toward my own rooms. Never had I encountered such an impossibly frustrating woman. Frustrating me was a feat most of the women I had known throughout the centuries had not been able to accomplish. I wanted to understand her, truly I did, but her continued brusque behavior made it difficult for me to try.

I would not have tolerated such treatment from anyone else.

Should I try harder? I wondered. *Or cease trying at all? Which is the appropriate choice with a woman who refuses to accept her own desires?*

Chapter Twenty-Six
Worries

I leaned against the chest of a training dummy, attempting to catch my breath. After I'd recovered, I moved away and went through a series of stretches to cool off before returning to the interior of the palace. My training today hadn't been as productive as I'd hoped. Idris' behavior the previous night had occupied most of my thoughts, and my libido had overtaken the rest.

It was a minor miracle I could focus on *anything*.

Tch, I really should have chosen a different race. I grimaced as I walked in the direction of the Queen's Tower. *Think I'll take a bath and then track down Idris. I need more reading material.*

When I spotted a woman approaching me from the other end of the hallway, I reflexively tensed. I didn't recognize her, so if she was a harem member I had no idea whose side she was on. The woman stopped in front of me and smiled brightly, but the expression didn't reach her eyes. None of the guards seemed bothered by her presence, so I had to assume she at least belonged there in some way.

"Ah, you must be the champion!" she spoke, giving me a very slight nod. "I was wondering what sort of woman would have declined a proposal from my fiancée.

"My name is Aeres, I've just recently arrived. I am certain you and I will become fast friends! Might you know the way to the Queen's Tower?"

"I doubt that's where you're meant to be going," I replied with a frown, watching her expression falter. "At the very least, I wasn't informed that I would be sharing a room with anyone. The harem women have been quite cruel to me, you see."

"*You* are staying in the Queen's Tower?" Aeres narrowed her eyes.

"For my protection, yes," I reiterated. She heaved a sigh.

"This would not be necessary if my husband-to-be didn't make it his mission to save every woman in the kingdom!" Aeres huffed, crossing her arms. Something about her tone and body language gave me the impression that she was quite young.

"I'm sure Emrys or Elidyr would know if we're meant to share the tower," I offered, earning a sharp glare in response. "If you'll excuse me...I'd rather get all the grime off *before* seeing to my studies. It'd be best if I didn't handle *His Majesty's* collection immediately after training."

"Of course, of course, you may leave," Aeres replied, flapping her hand.

Fiancée? Really. I strode past the woman and shot a suspicious glance over my shoulder. Her pompous attitude made me want to punch her. For the first time since coming back to Jeriskyr, I found myself wishing I knew how to read the minds of others. That'd make it easy to determine if she was telling the truth.

Once I reached the Queen's Tower, I stripped and slid into the bath. My muscles ached, telling me I'd at least made some progress—even if it didn't feel like it was enough. However, with my physical training out of the way for the day, my mind was left to ponder other topics. Why didn't I feel attached to Earth anymore? Had Corlyotir's incantation severed whatever had been making me feel like I *had* to go back to Earth once everything was over?

Earth still had *some* draw for me, but nothing like before.

Then there was Idris' behavior the previous night. I didn't have to be able to read minds to tell just how distressed he'd been. He was good at keeping his expression and body language neutral, but it did nothing to mask his tone or hide his racing pulse. He'd been more upset than I'd ever seen him. I didn't know what to make of his apparent caring, nor did I know how to deal with the knowledge that he'd heard some of my darker thoughts.

It was true that I felt like I didn't deserve any kindness from anyone in Jeriskyr, but especially not from Idris. I'd gone well out of my way in my attempts to create distance between us. But it was too late for me to deny my attraction to him, and a waste of energy to keep doing so.

To make matters worse, I knew my increasing horniness wasn't just me being me. It was an indication that I'd have to feed soon, and that...well, I had no idea how to feed. I'd had sex plenty of times back on Earth, but I imagined *feeding* on sex was likely more complicated. Incubi and succubi probably used their natural telepathy in some way, or perhaps other magic.

Even if I found a willing 'meal,' I had no idea what the fuck I was doing.

This is worse than when I was a virgin. I groaned and leaned back against the edge of the bath, staring at the ceiling. My body was so sensitive that even just the sensation of the water flowing past my tail made my body hum. I could only imagine how bad it was for incubi. Poor bastards probably had more awkward boners than a teen boy had around a hot teacher.

Shaking my head, I hurried to finish my bath. Once dressed, I left again and made my way toward the throne room. Sure, I had been avoiding him for a few days, but that wasn't like me. I usually faced my problems head-on and rationally. While Idris made that difficult in some ways, I'd identified a damned big problem and I intended to fix it—well, two problems.

Neither of us was trying to understand the other.

Fiancée.

The corner of my eye twitched. The second problem bothered me more than it should have. If she really was his fiancée—great. Easy way for me to stop caring. Or at least, I hoped it'd be easy. However, if they really were engaged and he'd been coming on to me so hard, that was a huge issue. One I couldn't ignore. It'd be utterly unacceptable behavior in my book.

When I approached the throne room, the guards looked surprised to see me but motioned subtly to indicate I could walk in through the open doors without issue. Inside, I saw a dozen or so men from the shops in Cejari-ir, plus a handful of people who were likely Otherworlders. Emrys and Elidyr stood to either side of Idris' throne. The former had his massive hammer next to him, while the latter didn't have any visible weapons to speak of.

Idris looked bored...until he spotted me skulking behind the peasants. An expression of surprise briefly crossed his face before a teasing smile took its place. He lifted a hand and motioned as he spoke. "You needn't hide back there, Cerys. Come here."

"I didn't want to intrude," I pointed out. "I can wait if it's important."

"Nonsense—you can wait up here." He motioned loosely to his side.

I didn't have an argument for that, so I walked forward and joined him. Emrys shifted to the side, giving me room to squeeze in between him and the side of the king's throne. I tucked myself slightly behind it, where the king wouldn't be able to reach me with his antics. Idris shot me a mildly intrigued glance before returning his attention to his subjects.

"Are you certain we have found every remaining girl and woman in the kingdom?" he asked, earning a slew of nods from the men gathered before us. He released a small, relieved sigh. "Good. We have a week at most before the Issradians arrive to collect their tax. See to it that the rest of our young ones do not give the humans a reason to become more troublesome. Make certain that our volunteers are prepared for what lies ahead.

"Is there anything else?"

Volunteers? I stiffened, but kept my expression passive. It didn't take much effort to figure out what Idris was referring to. Even so, the thought made my stomach turn. The remaining subjects didn't seem to have much else to say, so it was the Otherworlders who stepped forward next.

"Our guild would like a building permit," a woman spoke up, her hands resting on her hips. The motley crew of demons, beastmen, and elves around her nodded their wholehearted agreement. "We wanna set up a place to help newbies get a handle on things, help put 'em to work. Getting dropped in the middle of a forest isn't really a good learning experience."

So, the demon deities have a penchant for just dropping people into places. Lovely. I glanced at Idris when I heard him chuckle. The brief glance he shot my way made the source of his amusement clear. *What happened to not listening to my thoughts unless I was distressed?*

You are *distressed,* he stated. I bristled from head to toe and my tail snapped hard into the legs of the throne. If I never had to hear someone through telepathy again, I wouldn't mind. The sensation of someone else's voice in my head was difficult to explain beyond...I didn't like it. It felt far too intimate. My body seemed to take it as an invitation to react in all sorts of troubling ways.

When I shot the king a disgruntled glare, I could tell from his smirk that he had noticed my reaction. However, he didn't push his luck further.

"Elidyr, help our Otherworlder guests find a suitable place— assuming they have the necessary coin." Idris shifted to look off toward his left. His tone made the color drain from Elidyr's face. "And make certain that they are deserving. I do not care how you choose to test them, but I will not have disloyal subjects *or* disloyal Otherworlders building within Nabyr-zahn territory.

"Emrys, go see to the *problem* we discussed."

Once everyone was gone, Idris shifted in his throne to look over his shoulder at me, his lips curving into an amused smile as he took in my appearance. I still didn't understand what he found so damned interesting, but that wasn't what I'd come to talk with him about.

"You are done avoiding me?" he questioned, his eyes finally flicking upward to meet mine.

"For now. I can't fix your damned mess if I'm making myself scarce," I pointed out, watching as Idris rose to his feet and stretched.

"Care to join me for lunch, then?" He pivoted, offering me his hand.

"As long as I'm not on the menu." I narrowed my eyes at him.

"I am glad to see your sense of humor has improved!" Idris laughed and shook his head. "I was half-expecting that I would have to take you to the healers again, but it looks as though you did not overdo it this time.

"Now then, to what do I owe the pleasure of your company?"

"We need to discuss our plans, among other things," I answered, crossing my arms. Idris let his hand fall to his side, but his expression remained pleasant as he led me out of his throne room. "I don't like being useless, I don't like being ignorant, and if I can't spend all day training, I need something else to occupy my time. I've already finished the reading material you had Elidyr send to my rooms."

"Understandable," he nodded, leading me in the direction of his suite. "And the source of your agitation?"

"Varied," I replied dryly.

"Well, I suppose that is an improved response, at least." Idris glanced over his shoulder and then followed my gaze. When he spotted one of the harem women, a small frown tugged at his lips. *Are they troubling you again?*

"Please don't do that." I shivered and shot him a frustrated glare. "Not all of them, but I'll admit *one* of them is the reason I wanted to speak with you."

"A topic that can wait until we have retired to my rooms?" Idris suggested, rubbing his chin in thought. "Care to explain why you would prefer I refrain from using more private methods of speech?"

"It's…weird," I faltered, struggling to find a way to explain it. He shot me a questioning look but said nothing else, giving me time to think. "Telepathy doesn't exist in any form on Earth. Our private thoughts are exactly that—private thoughts. If we want to communicate, it's through speech, body language, or writing. There aren't any other options."

"You will need to get used to it," Idris informed me with a small frown. "I can see how it would strike you as strange or disconcerting, given its non-existence in your world. However, it is an integral part of our culture here and is frequently used in combat, reconnaissance missions, hunting… Any time we do not wish to draw unnecessary attention, or when we know our voices will not carry over the din of battle."

"Something else I need to learn?" I sighed heavily, crossing my arms over my stomach. "I'd rather get to the point where I'm at all useful in *any* of those situations first, if it's all the same to you."

"And if I told you that part of your training with telepathy would be to learn to shield your own mind from others?" he asked with an amused smile. "Not only would you no longer require my assistance—you might even learn to keep *me* out of your thoughts as well."

"…you have my attention," I replied doubtfully.

"Make yourself comfortable while I inform the palace cooks that you will be dining with me," Idris stated, holding the door to his rooms open. "When I return, we can address your concerns and whatever it was you wished to speak with me about."

Once I'd stepped over the threshold, he shot me a smile before closing the door and leaving. I let out a heavy sigh and moved for the nearest chair. I wasn't sure how to entertain myself while waiting for the demon king to return, but thankfully he didn't make me wait long. When he returned, he hung up his royal robes and loosened the collar of his shirt before taking a seat across from me.

"Now then," Idris began as he settled back with a contented sigh. "What troubles you?"

"I'll be blunt: I haven't been making an attempt to understand you or Jeriskyr, and it isn't conducive to my reason for being brought here," I replied flatly, earning a small smile in response. "You said it yourself. I need to understand you, and your people, if I'm meant to help Nabyr-zahn—let alone myself. Hiding off in some small portion of the palace isn't going to help me with that."

"So, you are willing to take a more active role?" Idris asked, earning a brief nod in response. "Have you managed to contact Corlyotir or any of the other gods since we returned?"

"No, not yet." I shook my head. "They didn't give me, or leave me, anything to help me understand my role here or how Jeriskyr functions differently from Earth. It seems they're content to drop me in blind."

"What else is troubling you?" Idris crossed one leg over the other, his piercing gaze fixed on me. It took more effort than I wanted to admit to not fidget.

"The volunteers... Am I right in assuming they're *volunteering* as tax?" I pursed my lips.

"They are indeed—much like Silas once did," he nodded.

"And women can't volunteer? I thought some would have, given how loyal some of your harem appears to be." I frowned slightly, watching as he grimaced.

"The female soldiers occasionally volunteer, and in the past we let them if they were truly prepared to work in brothels or as servants," he offered after a moment, his eyes flashing with anger. "After what you discovered, I cannot in good conscience allow them to go. It is likely...that many of the women you saw in Darmos were once volunteers."

"Well, all the more reason to make *quick* progress," I grimaced.

"What else is troubling you?" Idris shot me a knowing look when I hesitated. "Come now, you are doing so much better with honesty. It would be a shame for you to fail now."

"Fail?" I snorted. If nothing else, that challenge alone would help make sure I said what was on my mind. However, it took me a moment of contemplation to find a way to bring it up that *didn't* make me sound like I was jealous. "I met your 'fiancée' on my way back from training this morning. She seemed a bit..."

"My what?" Idris gave me a dumbfounded look.

"So, she *was* lying?" I asked, arching an eyebrow at him. "I thought you said succubi and incubi weren't keen on lying."

"As I mentioned before—I am not spoken for." Idris frowned. "While I was aware you were having continued trouble with some of the harem members, it did not occur to me that they might go so far. What else did this woman say?"

"She pretended like she and I would become friends, and asked me the way to the Queen's Tower. For whatever reason, she seemed to be under the impression she would be staying there." I leaned against my armrest and watched as the demon king's face twisted into an agitated scowl. "Do I need to explain why this was bothering me?"

"You have made it quite clear that you are monogamous—I have to assume that, if the woman had been telling the truth, you would be utterly disgusted by my behavior thus far." Idris grimaced, shaking his head. "Though perhaps I should refrain from making assumptions."

"No, you're correct," I replied, nodding. "There are some types of people I just can't respect, and someone who flirts with people while engaged to someone else is one of them. With you, that's just the tip of the iceberg."

"What was the woman's name?" Idris narrowed his eyes.

"Aeres," I offered, watching as he released an agitated sigh.

"Of course, a nobleman's daughter." Idris shook his head, his tone making it sound as though he were dealing with a troublesome child. "She must not understand the reality of the situation in Nabyr-zahn. I will have Elidyr assign someone to inform her, if the other women have not taken care of it already. They will not have been as patient as you."

"Patient?" I arched an eyebrow. "I wouldn't say I was patient, rather that I decided not to leap to conclusions. That hasn't been working well for me, after all."

"Indeed, it has not…" Idris chuckled, relaxing back in his seat. "Well then, with your woes out of the way, does that mean you are done with me again?"

"Only if you're busy," I replied, deciding not to take offense to the comment. After all, I *had* been avoiding him like the plague. When I couldn't avoid him, I sure as hell acted…bitchy, to say the least. Idris, however, looked skeptical. "Like I said, I think we're at odds because neither of us can quite understand the other. I'm here to learn, certainly, but learning what I need to know and coming to understand you don't have to be mutually exclusive."

"You were attempting to refrain from making any connections

in Jeriskyr," Idris pointed out, motioning loosely with one hand. "Something about it not being 'conducive' to returning to Earth, if I am not mistaken. You *do* realize that understanding any of us undermines such attempts?"

"I...am keeping my mind open to staying in Jeriskyr," I replied after a moment, watching the king freeze in his seat. His eyes widened and the only movement for several long seconds was the twitching of his tail.

"That may be the sexiest thing I have heard you say yet—say it again," he purred, leaning forward in his seat. Something akin to desire shone in his eyes, but disappeared as quickly as it had come when someone knocked on the door. "What a shame. I suppose that would be our lunch."

Idris rose gracefully to his feet and shot me a sideways glance as he passed. When I heard a cart rattling, I looked over my shoulder to see a young man pushing it into the throne room. He turned crimson to the tips of his ears when he spotted me and fled as soon as Idris let him.

"With that out of the way—do you have any idea how I can contact your gods?" I asked, deciding I'd try to change the subject.

Idris shot me a knowing smile before shaking his head. "There is no guaranteed way for us to speak with them. It is rare for them to become directly involved. They refrain from interacting with mortals unless they want something.

"I am more curious as to why you're considering remaining in

Jeriskyr. You had been quite adamant about returning to Earth—and there is our wager to keep in mind, as well."

"Elidyr thinks that Corlyotir did something," I offered after a moment, noting the way Idris' eyes narrowed when I mentioned his advisor's name. "He'd noticed that I didn't seem to have the same amount of conviction about returning as you had implied. It's possible that Corlyotir binding me to Jeriskyr meant severing some connection to Earth that I was unaware of."

"Your attachment to that world did seem odd…" Idris murmured as he set a plate in front of me. "Looking at it objectively, can you say that you have a *good* reason to return to Earth?"

"Objectively? No." I shook my head. "I knew that already. I wasn't sure why I felt so strongly about returning there either."

"Are you now attached to Jeriskyr in the same way?" Idris frowned at me.

"No, I'm not. Returning does have some draw for me still, but nothing like before." I shook my head again. "That's why I said I'm keeping my mind open and nothing more. I still think it's possible for this world to prove itself to be the worse choice between the two, so I'm not committing to anything beyond saving Alice and helping you overthrow the Issradian Empire."

"You make both sound like such trivial tasks," Idris chuckled, settling in across from me once more. "Very well. If you want us to find a way to understand each other, I am certainly willing to try. I still fully intend to win you over, both for Nabyr-zahn's longevity, and for myself.

"However, it would be best if we addressed the matter of your 'class' first. Emrys tells me that you still have not determined which skills you want to take, beyond being resistant to wholly ranged specializations."

"I was thinking about some way of combining dark magic, martial arts, and swordplay," I stated, earning an intrigued glance from the king. "I can't be sure, since your subjects all seem too scared to spar with me. They think I'm more fragile than I am, or something."

"Then I will spar with you myself." Idris' lips curved into a mischievous smirk. "If you do not mind a rough playmate, that is, *kitten*."

"Maybe my end of our wager should have been to get you to stop calling me 'kitten,'" I remarked dryly.

"It is too late to change your mind now," he chuckled, his eyes twinkling with mischief. "But we could always make another wager."

Chapter Twenty-Seven
The Grandmasters

"Now then, as much as I would like to continue with our wager," Idris began as he set his plate down, "our next match will have to wait. My first priority is to determine what specializations you will be training in. I need you to be at least somewhat capable when the Issradians arrive in a few days.

"I will escort you back to the Queen's Tower so that you may change into warmer clothing. After, we will go see the Grandmasters."

"We?" I frowned. "I'm sure you have too much work to—"

"Nothing that is more important than helping our champion,

I assure you," Idris interjected with a small smile. "It would not do for us to spar so soon after eating. Instead, I believe it is high time that you met with the Grandmasters. Since they have been too busy to come to you, we will go to them."

"You're sure?" I looked up at him as he offered me a hand.

"Is my company objectionable?" A vague expression of confusion crossed his face.

"No, it's not that." I shook my head and let him pull me to my feet. "Won't you need to summon guards and such if you're heading into the city?"

"Hardly." Idris chuckled and led me toward the door. "Tell me, Cerys, what manner of abilities are you interested in? Emrys and Elidyr may wish for you to undertake ranged specialization training, but I think it would be foolish to have you trapped in something you will not excel at."

"Hand-to-hand combat, for one," I stated, catching the knowing smile that flitted across his lips. "As I said earlier, I'm considering something that would combine the use of magic and swordplay. Some games call that a 'spellsword,' but I'm not sure what you would call it in Jeriskyr."

"What if," Idris began, his expression thoughtful, "you specialized in martial arts, swordplay, and shadow magic as you mentioned earlier? Alana's report stated that you have an affinity for such magics."

"Would I be able to use it to augment the former two skills?" I asked, watching his mouth curve into a mischievous smile.

That's what I was hoping for, though I'm not convinced it's viable—and I didn't see many such classes listed in my searching. The ones I did see sounded awful.

"It is possible, yes. Easy, certainly not," Idris chuckled. "Such a combination is rarely utilized *well*. We call them Shadowdancers. People who weave melee combat seamlessly with shadow magic. In your case, I suppose your weapon will be some manner of blade— though specializing in a martial art will give you access to other weapons as well, should you desire to learn them. That is, if you are capable of the concentration needed."

"Is that a challenge?" I arched an eyebrow at him.

"Certainly," he smirked, crossing his arms over his chest. "Shadowdancers were once the pride of Nabyr-zahn, long before my father's rule and before the Issradians betrayed us. I believe that the 'secret class' of Nabyr-zahn in your notes likely refers to Shadowdancer. We have various texts regarding its abilities, and the Grandmasters have more, but it is knowledge we would not give to just anyone. A feisty, determined champion such as yourself is a perfect candidate."

"That doesn't *sound* like a challenge, then." I tilted my head, listening to him chuckle.

"You overcame the first challenge—which is gaining enough of my trust," Idris stated, shooting me a sideways glance. "Your honesty still requires work, but I suppose that will come with time.

The next challenge is testing your concentration and your coordination. You appear to have learned as much as you are able from simply striking a dummy in the training yard."

"Dummies are a terrible substitute for real opponents," I snorted.

"Yet I can't permit you to train with just anyone." Idris rubbed his chin, then glanced down the hallway to our left, a frown spreading across his face. "Ah, Aeres. I need to have a word with you."

"Oh, there you are, dear—" Aeres stopped abruptly when she spotted me.

"For lying to the champion of Nabyr-zahn, you will be learning how to care for our military's equipment and the stables," Idris informed the delicate woman, ignoring the sound of indignation that escaped her. "I will have Emrys assign someone to teach you the proper way to clean, oil, and store the contents of our armory. If you are to remain in the palace under my protection, you will make yourself useful—and you will cease making such ridiculous claims. If anyone here were to be my fiancée, it would be Cerys."

Was that last part really necessary? I sighed and pressed my fingertips to my temples. "Which I'm not, and you have a *long* way to go before I would even take such statements from you seriously."

"Shall we go on a date after we have spoken with the Grandmasters, then?" Idris asked. His expression was so innocent and genuine, I couldn't bring myself to make fun of him—only stare.

"Why else would you accept a noblewoman into your palace?!" Aeres demanded, stomping her foot. "Unlike this trash, *I* am of high birth! Someone such as I has no place among common whores!"

Idris' shadow warped violently before lashing out, lifting Aeres from the floor by her throat. The king's menacing gaze made my skin prickle into goosebumps. He had been warm and playful moments before, yet now he was like a glacier. I had no doubts that he would snap her neck if she gave him reason to, despite his relaxed posture.

"Your father had you added to my harem for your own protection," Idris began, his voice like a blade. "If you would prefer to join the Issradian breeding pens, there is still time to change your mind. I will feel no remorse if you choose to join them yourself."

"The...what...?" Aeres grew pale and began kicking her feet. "Y-Your Majesty, please p-put me down! I apologize for my insubordination! Please, allow me to remain in the palace. I will do whatever you desire, whatever you find useful!"

"*Tch*, so weak-willed." Idris' shadow dropped the woman to the floor before returning into place beneath his feet. He pivoted and shot me an icy glance. "Come along, Cerys. We have been interrupted for long enough."

I glanced over my shoulder at the trembling Aeres before moving to follow Idris. The sheer malice wafting off the demon king gave me pause. His threat had gone too far. Furthermore, I didn't understand *why* he would be willing to go to such lengths. After all, it wasn't like Aeres had betrayed him—just insulted me. I'd heard plenty worse throughout the years.

He's kinda sexy when he's angry, though. I regretted the thought almost as quickly as it crossed my mind. Idris' tail twitched hard enough to crack into the floor, making it quite clear he'd probably heard it. The devilish smirk he shot over his shoulder was confirmation. "Well, since you so obviously were listening in, care to explain why you went so far?"

"I do not take kindly to such blatant insults toward your character, nor toward my harem. She chose to attack both." Idris made a dismissive motion with one hand. "While prostitution was once a common occupation for our kind, 'whore' is still a derogatory term. It has become synonymous with the way the Issradians treat their inhuman slaves. I…may have taken further offense on your behalf."

"That doesn't explain why you'd go *that* far," I pointed out.

"It was the quickest way to determine where her loyalties lie." Idris shrugged, stuffing his hands into his trouser pockets. "Someone who truly sympathizes with the Issradians would willingly join them regardless of the breeding pens' existence.

"Aeres' thoughts made it clear she was attempting to sow discord between us. I wanted to know if it was because her allegiance had changed, or if it was jealousy."

"Quick or not, it sure was harsh. I wasn't expecting it." I shook my head slightly when he gave me a questioning look. "In my world, that would've been considered a line you shouldn't cross, regardless of efficiency. On Earth, many people value the emotions and feelings of others over all else."

"And your personal opinion on the matter?" Idris asked dryly.

"As long as you have sound reasoning, I don't particularly care how harsh you are with your subjects," I replied, after considering it for a moment. "Furthermore, I would hope it means you are even harsher on your actual enemies. That said, subjects who are loyal out of love for their leader instead of fear are less likely to waver."

"I will keep that in mind," Idris murmured, his expression thoughtful. "Does this come from personal experience, or perhaps history?"

"A little of both," I offered, striding past Idris to ascend the stairs to the Queen's Tower ahead of him. "I won't pretend that running a guild is anything like running a kingdom, but it does require structure. A tyrant who demands their members' loyalty will see their guild crumble in months, or even weeks. A guild leader who nurtures and protects their members, but with a firm, guiding hand, will have their loyalty for years. It's similar with Earth's past leaders. Tyrants were often assassinated by subjects who felt disgruntled or betrayed."

Idris fell silent until we reached the door of the Queens' Tower. When he saw the magic extend from my hand to undo the seal, a low chuckle escaped him and he reached forward, capturing one of the shadowy butterflies. It perched on his hand and beat its wings slowly a few times before disintegrating alongside the rest of my darkness.

"I am delighted to see your magic takes such a pleasant form," he remarked as he followed me into the Queen's Tower. "Perhaps redecoration is in order? Butterflies, flowers...ah, perhaps opal inlays and moonfire lily accents? I must say, the contrast between your commanding nature and your femininity is most alluring."

"I...suppose I should just accept that as a compliment." I shook my head as Idris made himself comfortable on a nearby sofa. "You said I should dress warmly?"

"Unless you have other ideas..." he purred, with a suggestive smile.

"I don't." I stalked into the wardrobe and shut the door behind me as I fought my body's immediate response to his purring. I wasn't confident I could keep saying no, or if I even should.

Deciding not to waste any time, I yanked on a pair of fur-lined leather trousers, boots, and a warm tunic. Over the top, I pulled on an ankle-length hooded coat that buttoned from my throat down to mid-thigh. Thankfully, the fabrics were soft, unlike the scratchy wool I had been expecting. Finally, I grabbed a pair of gloves and walked out of the wardrobe.

"I never did thank you properly for going to the trouble of outfitting me, did I?" I asked when Idris looked over to me.

"You are quite welcome." he chuckled, rising to his feet. "Now then, you never did answer me about my suggestion of a date."

"You were serious?" I arched an eyebrow.

"It is an interesting concept, one I would like to learn more of," Idris replied, giving me a brief nod. "You have mentioned before that you and I need to get to know each other better, and Bruce's description of a 'date' certainly seems a good way to achieve that.

"Furthermore, I have been attempting to lead Nabyr-zahn away from things such as arranged marriages. Most of our kind detest the thought of marrying for politics, status, protection, or wealth. Perhaps learning of your world's courtship rituals will give me insight on how to better assist my people's needs."

"To be fair, marriage in my world worked that way for a long time." I shook my head. "It wasn't until Earth became…well, safer, that marriage for love became more commonplace. Marriage was almost solely a business or political contract for a long time, thus the prevalence of mistresses, concubines, and so forth."

"Good—then you can understand, to some extent, how it works here," he nodded, offering me his arm. "However, that still was not an answer."

"Ah…" I stared up at him for a moment. "I…sure. If you're certain you've got time to spare after we meet the Grandmasters."

"I will make time," he smiled. "You do not look convinced."

"I'm not," I replied dryly. "Saying you'll 'make time' doesn't instill me with confidence that you aren't shirking your duties.

You've got a lot to prepare for."

"And you need to prepare as well," Idris reminded me, reaching over to flip my hood over my hair before opening a door leading out of the palace. "We can wait to discuss such things until we have returned behind closed doors, if you will. There are too many prying ears and eyes within Cejari-ir now."

"There are?" I arched a doubtful eyebrow.

"Come, you will see," he nodded, leading me down the nearest road. "Since *someone* leaked information regarding how to cope with tails…"

"I wonder who did such a thing!"

"…*I wonder.*" Idris shot me an amused look. "Because the Otherworlders now understand how to use their additional limb, we've experienced a large influx. Even during my father's time as king, I've never seen the city bustling with so much life. We are concerned about whether or not they will stay, but…"

"They don't have much choice in the matter—they're only allowed to have one character," I replied, earning a small frown. "If they decided they wanted to change their allegiance, they would have to jump through a lot of hoops to do it. From what I understand, there is a very long, tedious questline they would have to complete. Alternately, they could delete their character and reroll…but people don't like to lose their progress, no matter how little."

"Then instead of worrying that they may not stay…" he trailed off, sinking into deep thought.

"You should be worrying about how to earn, and keep, their loyalty." I nudged him with my elbow when he was silent for too long. "They're gamers. Give them a way to make progress that benefits them *and* Nabyr-zahn, and you'll be on the right track. Furthermore, once they hear rumors about the Issradian Empire, they're gonna be more likely to become invested in your country. Outright propaganda slandering the empire, however, will not work."

"A more subtle, organic approach?" Idris murmured, before glancing at me with an unreadable expression. "And what of your loyalty? How best for me to win and keep that?"

"Don't give me a reason to hate you or your people. Simple," I shrugged. "Which is another reason I said we need to learn to understand each other."

"Give me an example."

"An example?" I echoed, thinking for a moment. "Alright, let's consider your flirtatious behavior while you were on Earth with me. While it wasn't exactly inappropriate, trustworthy men in my world don't behave like that after just meeting someone. Furthermore, people from my world don't usually call someone by a pet name until they've come to know each other well and grown close—in a platonic sense or otherwise.

"Since I decided not to press you about your behavior, I had to *assume* it was a cultural difference. That perhaps the way you conducted yourself is normal for an incubus. It usually takes weeks, at minimum, for people to earnestly begin flirting in my world. Longer to take it any further."

"Whereas asking me outright would have given you a more reliable answer." Idris nodded, an amused smile spreading across his face. "Humans choose to be hesitant about the strangest things. Incubi and succubi believe in expressing our attraction instead of hiding it. In that regard, you are correct to believe my behavior is normal for my culture. However, you are wrong in thinking that I was not earnest, or that it was mere teasing."

"That's even *more* difficult for me to understand," I complained.

"Oh wow! The king and his favorite concubine actually come out of the palace?!" a surprised male voice exclaimed. A chorus of groans followed. My companion seemingly turned to ice in an instant.

Great. So, either rumors spread that fast or we're featured in the opening cutscene, or perhaps the marketing materials... I breathed a small sigh and stepped closer to Idris.

It didn't take me long to find the owner of the voice and his frustrated companions. The motley crew consisted of three demons, an elf, an orc, and four beast-people. One of the male demons wobbled up to us with a broad grin on his face. He stunk of liquor.

"Seriously, Ed. Don't," a wolf-woman sighed. She crossed her arms and shook her head when he ignored her.

"Sooo... Since she's a concubine and all," Ed drawled, his eyes shifting between me and Idris. "If I wanted to go a few rounds with that ass, or even just her mouth, how much would it cost? Or I'll do a quest. Or—"

I felt Idris twitch moments before he released my arm and conjured a sword. In almost the same motion, he swung the flame-licked blade through Ed's torso, severing him from his right shoulder to the left side of his waist. The heat of Idris' blade seared the wounds shut before they could spray us with blood. The corpse collapsed on the cobblestones as Idris conjured a cloth to clean his blade. As he wiped it down, he shifted his dangerous gaze toward the Otherworlder's companions.

"I suggest you keep your friend somewhere secluded until he has improved his drinking skill." Idris flourished the sword before allowing it to disappear. "Furthermore, remind him that a concubine and a prostitute are *not* the same thing. If I have my way, Cerys will become the Queen of Nabyr-zahn. *I recommend treating her with the appropriate respect.*"

"**That really hurt!**" Ed yowled from somewhere nearby. Startled, I shifted to find him striding over from a large sculpture. He was patting his body as if to make sure everything was still in place, and no longer had a wobble in his step. "Fine, fine, I'm sorry! She's really a nice piece of—"

"*Ed,* go loot your corpse," the wolf woman reprimanded him

again, before turning and bowing to us. "I will try to keep my guild members better in check, Your Majesty."

"See to it that you do." Idris shot her a chilling look before putting an arm around my waist and leading me away from the group. *I wonder how many times I could kill him before he ceased returning?*

...don't do that. I tensed and shook my head. A mischievous smirk spread across his face when he glanced down at me.

You do not think I should kill him a few more times? His innocent drawl made the corner of my eye twitch, among other things. He caught my tail with his briefly, sending a shiver up my spine. "I suppose I should refrain from pushing my favorite, *hungry*, succubus further."

"For your health *and* mine, don't push me," I grimaced, shaking my head. "Better yet, direct me to whatever god needs to be beheaded for making tails so damned—"

"You will grow to love it," Idris remarked, a little *too* seriously. "Although, 'Cerys the Godslayer' certainly has a nice ring to it. However, one at a time, kitten. Such difficult prey can wait until after we have dealt with the Issradian Empire.

"I will have to determine a new title for your position. If 'concubine' makes Otherworlders react to your presence like *that*..."

"I did warn you," I pointed out.

"You did, but not all Otherworlders are from *your* world," Idris countered, shaking his head. "Ah, here we are—the first of the Grandmasters you should meet resides here. We should find him training somewhere in the back."

Instead of heading for the door of the large, six-story building, Idris led me around its side and down the path between it and its neighbor. Before I saw anyone, I heard them. The grunts of exertion and the sound of skin striking bags, wood, and other skin. Several dozen people were training in the courtyard, most of whom appeared to be Jeriskyr natives. The few Otherworlders had been set against training dummies and were proving sloppy in their strikes.

Overseeing it all was a lithe demon with short black hair and piercing orange eyes. His horns and tail were just as dark as his hair, and his tanned body had even more scars than Idris' did. When he noticed us approaching, he promptly turned and gave the king a bow reminiscent of the kind we used in martial arts on Earth.

"Be at ease, Andras," Idris chuckled, glancing toward the nearest row of trainees. "You have more Otherworlders under your wing than I expected."

"And you've brought the last person I expected to see," Andras commented, turning to look at me. He gave me a brief bow. "Am I to understand by her presence that Lady Moonfire has an interest in our art?"

"Yes. I want to take on martial arts as one of my primary specializations but am well aware I can't rely on the kind I learned on Earth," I answered, nodding to the taller man. He rubbed his chin in thought, examining me. I got the impression he was looking more at my current skill level than anything else.

"You've been training already?" Andras murmured.

"I offered the palace training grounds to her," Idris stated. "She was a little *too* eager to accept. Training dummies are no longer sufficient, but allowing her to hunt outside the city walls would be…"

"A damned stupid idea." Andras shot Idris a sharp glare before turning his attention to me. "I can lend you material to study on your own until I have the time to come by the palace. You won't be able to train *here* unless His Majesty sends a squad of guards with you. I'd rather not have such distractions around the rest of my students."

"But you *will* train her?" Idris asked pointedly.

"It'll take some work since she's small," Andras began, shooting me a troubled look. "You said you have experience with martial arts in your world? How about against people much taller than you?"

"I've sparred with people up to maybe a foot taller than me," I replied, crossing my arms. "I'm used to using speed to make up for differences in height and strength. Human women are at a disadvantage against males simply from physical ability alone."

"Demons are near equal—at least, incubi and succubi are." Andras tilted his head, reexamining me. "What will your finalized specialization be? I'll need to think of how to cover your weaknesses."

"She intends to train as a Shadowdancer," Idris answered, smirking at Andras' stunned expression. "We will be meeting the other Grandmasters from whom she will require assistance after we are finished here."

"You're confident you can make up for your size?" Andras glanced at me.

"I'm not *that* much smaller than you lot!" I sighed irritably. Most of the men I'd met in Cejari-ir were only a head or so taller than me. Even Idris was just a little more. Even if I was 'small,' I was still much taller than an average human man. "Yes, yes, I will manage. Once I've learned more, I'll be able to use speed and strategy to overwhelm my opponents. Adding what I learn from my other two specializations should help cover the issue of reach."

"And you're fine with this?" Andras arched an eyebrow at Idris.

"I know her well enough to understand I will not change her mind, nor will anyone else," Idris shrugged, an amused smile gracing his lips. "Once she is no longer distracted by hunger, I am confident she will be capable of learning the arts of a Shadowdancer."

"That's high praise coming from you." Andras cast him a doubtful look before returning his attention to me. "I'll have some books sent to the palace for you. I assume the harem—"

"The Queen's Tower," Idris corrected him before he could

even finish.

"...right. I'll send the books there and send word ahead when I have time to come by to give you lessons." Andras nodded to me, then shot Idris a look. "If Your Majesty doesn't mind, I have more work to give my students."

"Of course. We will not take up any more of your time." Idris nodded, then motioned for me to follow him.

"I'm *not* distracted by 'hunger.'" I shot Idris an agitated glare once we entered the alleyway between buildings.

"You are fooling no one—especially not me," he informed me, chuckling. However, instead of pressing the topic, he motioned loosely to me and spoke again. "The martial artist skill should be available for you now that you've spoken with Andras. You should set your specializations as you unlock them."

"I...right." I shook my head slightly when Idris shot me a questioning look. "It's still weird to me how Jeriskyr feels just as real as Earth, yet has the same mechanics as games. Might take some time to adjust."

"Ah, so you are more inclined to act and react as you would on Earth?" Idris murmured, rubbing his chin. When I caught the frigid look he cast to the side, I expected an explanation, but none came. "We shall leave such talk until later. For now, let us proceed as planned."

Prying eyes? Ears? I wondered, glancing off in the direction Idris had looked in.

The Otherworlders are too curious about us, he stated. He shot me a knowing look when I bristled. *If you insist, I will stop. However, it makes informing you of such threats more difficult. For now, set your newly acquired skill. Even at such low proficiency, it will still give you an increase of strength over the basic version you have been using.*

...how about for now we save the telepathy for emergencies only? I shook my head slightly when he shot me a questioning look. Nearly every erogenous zone throughout my body seemed to react to his telepathic speech. It wasn't conducive to me getting anything done.

"Very well," Idris answered, tilting his head. He still looked a little perplexed, but said nothing more on the matter. Instead, he changed the topic. "Next we will visit Tegau, Grandmaster of Magics."

"Not shadow magic?" I frowned.

"*All* magics," Idris replied with a smile. "Tegau is our most gifted mage. There are Grandmasters of single elements at their headquarters as well, but Tegau leads them all. If you are to become a Shadowdancer, it will be with his blessing."

As we walked, I mentally sorted through my list of skills until I found a listing that simply stated 'Fighter.' When I expanded it, I found well over a dozen words listed under it—none of which I had any inkling of how to pronounce. All but one was listed as having a value of zero out of five hundred. Pursing my lips, I selected the skill flashing as 'unlocked,' and proceeded to equip it.

«Fighter has been replaced with the Nabyr-zahn martial art, Chrastr-gok

«Chrastr-gok Proficiency: 100. Apprentice»

Heat rushed through my body, sending a twitch through my extremities. I hadn't expected a physical reaction to setting the skill, yet I felt stronger already. It was akin to the phase before drunkenness where I felt invincible. *I'll have to get* that *feeling in check quick...*

"I've been meaning to ask," I began, looking up at the smiling incubus. "During our little 'vacation,' were you able to see things in my world the way you do here?"

"No, and that is one of the reasons I did not believe I would have magic available to me whilst there." Idris shook his head, placing a hand at the small of my back and nudging me toward another building. "Here we are. Let us see how the mages are faring, shall we?"

"Ah, King Bloodsong, Lady Moonfire." A man with long white hair and vivid green eyes turned to look at us when we entered the building. He gave us a brief bow. "What can I do for you?"

"Is your brother in, Halwyn?" Idris asked, causing the graceful mage to sigh and cross his arms.

"That he is." Halwyn glanced over toward a nearby door. "He is in the yard with the Otherworlder students at the moment. This influx of would-be combatants is most vexing. The fools seem to think that they can simply be given a skill and then released into the world to hunt and kill."

"Interesting. Perhaps your gods' approach to the entry of Otherworlders is better than that of the humans," I remarked, crossing my arms as I thought. Halwyn stiffened and then bowed, as if preparing to offer an apology, but I shook my head. "I know the people of Nabyr-zahn hold little to no adoration for Otherworlders *or* humans. I've got my work cut out for me."

"What is the human approach?" Idris frowned.

"Otherworlders who choose the Issradian Empire as their 'starting faction' wake up somewhere in the Darmos barracks and are told to execute a criminal," I answered, shifting to look up at the king. "What I came across was a human man who was waiting to be executed for rather vile criminal behavior. I didn't hesitate to behead him once I saw his...*personality*.

"However, most of the Otherworlders from my world fail the test. They're incapable of killing someone else. Originally, I was told it was 'because the game is too real.' I think there's more to it than that. The sample size, if you will, is quite small—it could simply be that not enough people of the right personality type have come to Jeriskyr yet. While people from my world have lost many of their more violent instincts to the passage of time, games are typically where they let loose."

"On the other hand, perhaps the sudden confrontation with violence startles them?" Idris suggested, earning a brief nod from me. "Intriguing. Perhaps if we ease the Otherworlders into our ways, and nurture them, we will find that those who join Nabyr-zahn are more combat-inclined than those who join the Issradians."

"Do you wish to wait until my brother is finished?" Halwyn inquired, shooting us a small frown. "Furthermore, your business here...? It is unusual for you to visit the Grandmasters, Your Majesty."

"Cerys requires training in shadow magic." Idris motioned toward me, a rather proud expression on his face. "She will be training to become a Shadowdancer. It is imperative that Tegau or Cai assists her."

"Very well, this way. I am sure my brother will not mind a reprieve from his current students." Halwyn motioned for us to follow him. When we entered the courtyard, the white-haired mage made a brief motion with a folded fan, sending a pillar of earth into the air. In the next instant, wind rushed past us, followed by the entire body of a man with white and black-streaked hair. "You have guests, Tegau."

"Guests?" Tegau paused mid-punch and glanced over to Idris and myself. His expression brightened immediately. Forgetting his brother, he strode over and promptly took both of my hands in his, bringing them to his lips. "You *must* be Lady Moonfire! I had heard that your exquisite beauty had charmed King Bloodsong, but never would I have dreamed such a goddess walked among us—or that she would come looking for *me*."

...suddenly Idris' behavior seems nowhere near as bad. I attempted to pull my hands out of Tegau's, while Idris simply chuckled. "Now I'm questioning your taste *and* his. Either way... Nice to meet you, I think. We're here on business, so if you don't mind—"

Tegau ignored me and pulled lightly on my hands, turning them palm up. Warmth briefly emanated from his fingers, followed by my darkness engulfing our hands. My power morphed into butterflies, which languidly beat their wings as they perched on our skin. A few flitted away to land on both Halwyn and Idris.

"No wonder the other elements wouldn't come to you—they must be jealous of such gorgeous darkness!" Tegau exclaimed, finally releasing my hands. He gave us a hazy smile and rested his cheek in one hand. "My, so the goddess with moonfire for hair is a goddess of darkness after all? How fitting! Such lunar beauty—"

"Enough," Halwyn sighed, placing a hand on his brother's shoulder. "Have you not yet learned that women do not fall for such drivel?"

"Focus, Tegau," Idris stated in a cool rumble, causing the Grandmaster's demeanor to shift in an instant. "We are here because Cerys intends to become a Shadowdancer. I believe you have—"

"A *Shadowdancer*?!" Tegau exclaimed, turning to look at me. "While quite fitting for such a beauty, such a class is incredibly challenging—not to mention dangerous. Are you certain you are willing to put yourself in harm's way, Lady Moonfire?"

"Quite certain. Sitting back with my thumb up my ass isn't my idea of helping," I answered flatly.

"Your thumb...*where?*" Idris coughed.

"It's a figure of speech." I pressed my fingertips to my temples. *Perhaps not the best saying to use around incubi. Right.*

"Our collection is at your disposal, of course," Tegau murmured, frowning as he examined me with a more serious expression. His yellow-green eyes seemed to be looking through me, rather than *at* me. "You certainly have the potential for magecraft. I would say you've enough magic at your disposal that you could reach the rank of a Grandmaster, given time. Such potent magic will require tempering.

"What will your third and final specialization be?"

"Spellsword." Idris let out an amused chuckle when Tegau grimaced.

"In which case, you will be using shadow magic for not one but *two* of your specializations," Tegau commented, rubbing his chin as he thought. "Perhaps we should combine Lady Moonfire's magical focus with her other equipment, then. Possibly in the pommel of one of her swords, in her jewelry, or perhaps armor."

"She certainly won't be able to use a mage's wand or staff," Halwyn agreed, nodding. "I shall collect and deliver copies of our documents about Shadowdancers to the palace. Where shall I take them, Your Majesty?"

"The Queen's Tower," Idris answered, earning a distressed groan from Tegau. "Now then, will you or Cai be seeing to our champion's training? It appears you have your hands quite full with your students over there…"

I followed Idris' gaze and grimaced. They were all too busy gawking at the pillar of earth Halwyn had summoned. "Shouldn't they be practicing?"

"Indeed they should." Tegau's voice took on a dangerous tone as he pivoted and shot a blast of fire toward the students. "Back in formation! For becoming distracted, you will do another fifty repetitions. Get to it!

"As for your question, Your Majesty, Cai is currently in the mountains searching for more material we can use to make magical items and foci. I will gladly handle Lady Moonfire's instruction. Halwyn, take our beginner's tomes and a focus to the Queen's Tower for the goddess as well."

"With that, we will be going," Idris commented, sliding an arm around my waist. Tegau looked like he was going to protest, but his brother muttered something to him that made him change his mind. I glanced up at Idris, finding an agitated expression on his face. "I hope you will forgive Tegau for his…quirks."

"For now." I shook my head slightly. "Punching him didn't quite seem like the appropriate response…but I was tempted."

"Tegau meant what he said," Idris sighed, pushing stray waves of hair out of his face. "He is the sort who says anything and everything on his mind, no matter how ridiculous he may sound to others. As you may have noticed, he fuses the arcane with martial arts. His brother, on the other hand, uses a more traditional approach."

"Sounds like they're a good pair then," I shrugged. As we made our way deeper into Cejari-ir, I equipped the shadow magic specialization and felt a similar rush of power to when I had changed 'Fighter' to Chrastr-gok.

«Shadow Magic Proficiency: 1. Amateur»

This would require work.

This time there was a visible change. My darkness manifested as butterflies around my legs and feet. Once the butterflies had flitted away from us, they disintegrated. It seemed that the effect was a permanent trait to my footsteps now. I looked up at the chuckling incubus beside me and frowned. "Is that going to be a problem?"

"Not at all," Idris answered with a friendly smile. "Such an appearance is quite normal for someone who equips a purely elemental specialization. It is different from say…becoming a warlock."

"Wouldn't it put me at a tactical disadvantage?" I asked.

"If you utilized something such as wind, earth, fire, ice, and the like—yes." Idris shook his head slightly. "However, darkness and light are both neutral elements. Neither has a strength or a weakness, therefore those beautiful little butterflies of yours do not tell your enemies much."

"If you say so," I grimaced. Taking in our surroundings, I noticed only a few large buildings remained, all of which were built on a cul-de-sac. "So, *all* of the combat-related Grandmasters reside in this part of the city?"

"As do many of their students," Idris nodded, leading me toward a building with a flaming sword on its banners. "The Grandmasters of other professions have similar abodes on the other side of the city, where they train and house their apprentices. Of course, some require a forge, or gardens…they require much more room than the combat Grandmasters."

Idris led me behind the spellsword's building and toward the rows upon rows of training students. It was by far the most populated of the three schools we'd visited. On the far side, I spotted a fiery-haired man with a rapier squaring off with a much less imposing-looking man with charcoal gray hair. The man was short for a demon and quite scrawny compared to his opponent. Gaunt, even. His clothes looked they had been repaired many times over but still had holes in them, making me wonder if he was a beggar.

They were sparring and, despite his ragged appearance, the gray-haired man appeared to have the upper hand. His movements were quick and elegant, making no waste.

At first, by his skill, I thought the beggar-like man was likely to be the Grandmaster of the school. However, when his gaze met mine his spell fizzled, and the redheaded man landed a strike against him, blasting him backward into the nearest wall.

Ugh. Getting distracted by the pretty demoness and her royal escort? Definitely not the Grandmaster, then. I sighed, disappointed that the fight was already over.

"It appears I have guests, Master," the redheaded man spoke as he helped the charcoal-haired one to his feet. He bowed to the man briefly and gave him an apologetic look. "Another time, perhaps? Whenever you find the time to visit Cejari-ir again."

"Of course, of course." The quiet man nodded and turned to give us a brief bow before taking his leave.

"Be cautious, wanderer," Idris called after the man. "The Issradians will be close to Cejari-ir by now. It will be safer to stay away from the main roads."

"I appreciate your concern..." the man murmured, bowing once more before leaving. I watched him for a moment, my eyes narrowed. The redhead had called him *Master.*

Perhaps it's just like how martial arts masters refer to each other as 'Master,' but... I shook my head slightly and turned my attention to the redheaded man as he approached. He gave us a pleasant smile before bowing.

"Your Majesty, my lady," he spoke, before offering me a hand. "My name is Arawn, my lady. I am the Grandmaster of Spellswords." He paused to look over my head somewhere. "Given your other choices, and my king's presence, am I to assume that you wish to become a Shadowdancer?

"I must say, Chrastr-gok, spellsword, and shadow magic will certainly make for an interesting array of abilities. If you're capable of handling them, I will certainly wish to spar with you once we are closer in ability."

"She had already chosen such specializations—I simply suggested she combine them to become a Shadowdancer instead of Shadowfist or similar," Idris commented, a self-satisfied expression on his face. "Of course, she will need instruction."

"Of course." Arawn nodded to Idris, then returned his attention to me. "I believe we have some practice swords in the armory that you can use until you find the time and the coin to have your own forged. If you will follow me…"

We followed Arawn into a small building toward the back of the property. Inside, he rifled through the mess of blades and armor until he'd found three swords that wouldn't dwarf me. He offered them to me, making it clear he wanted me to take all three.

"As a Shadowdancer, you will not be wielding them in your hands," Arawn began, making a brief motion. An array of swords appeared behind his shoulder, hanging with the points aimed toward the ground. Another motion caused the blades to fan out around him, each aimed in a different direction. "You will need to focus on learning the flying sword style. Unfortunately, I am a very busy man, and books can only take you so far…

"Your Majesty, you were already planning to train with her to some extent, were you not? Perhaps you can use that time to cover her first few ranks of the flying sword style. After all, as a Grandmaster in the spellsword skill, you yourself have plenty of the necessary knowledge."

"While I am not against the notion…you are not the only one who is busy," Idris replied, frowning as he cast a glance toward the dozens of trainees. "However, you do appear to have many more students than the other schools…"

"The Otherworlders have flocked to us in droves. Almost all of our Masters and Grandmasters have their hands full already," Arawn sighed, crossing his arms. His swords disappeared as he, too, looked toward the students.

"I'm not surprised. Spellswords aren't an option in many games, despite how many people love them," I remarked, causing both men to look at me. "What?"

"I forgot for a moment that you too are an Otherworlder." Arawn bowed slightly, a small smile on his face. "You will have whatever you need from me, Lady Moonfire. However, it will be some time before I can find the opportunity to give you instruction in person. Until then, I hope you will find Idris to be a capable teacher."

I certainly don't have much choice on that front, I considered, watching as the Grandmaster spoke a few parting words before leaving to attend to his students.

"You are certain you do not find my presence objectionable?"

Idris frowned.

"It was an observation, not a complaint," I replied dryly. "Now then... What the hell am I supposed to do with these swords? Carry them all the way?"

"Hardly," Idris chuckled, offering me a hand. "Equip your spellsword specialization. Once done, see if you can feel the melody of my magic as I draw and sheath one of my blades."

Begrudgingly, I did as he said and placed my hand in his. I didn't expect to feel anything, but when he summoned a sword over his shoulder I felt a distinct vibration through his hand. When he dismissed the weapon, I felt it again. There was a vague feeling, similar to when I was compartmentalizing my thoughts, but I wasn't sure if I was just imagining that part.

Idris suggested that I should try next. Pursing my lips, I looked down at the three swords and then concentrated, attempting to recreate the sensations I had felt. They phased out of existence for a moment before popping back.

"You stopped too soon," Idris offered, rubbing his chin. "Essentially, you are storing them until you have use of them. Otherworlders have been known to say it is akin to something they call an 'inventory.' To the rest of us, it is a magical bag or pocket that we create. One specifically for our equipped proficiencies and separate from a more general one."

"Oh! Inventory, you say? So that's why it felt vaguely familiar. Okay. For equipped proficiencies...then it's sort of like an armory chest. Got it." It figured I'd been over-thinking it. I glanced at the swords again. This time, I concentrated harder, but with a better idea of what I was attempting to do. The swords vanished almost immediately. "A 'magical bag or pocket' is quite literally how I would describe an 'inventory' to someone who didn't know what one was."

"Now then, for the final touch," Idris murmured, lifting both hands to my face. I shot him a suspicious look, but he just shook his head and then closed his eyes. Warmth spread from his palms and through my skin. When he released me, a smile spread across his face. "There—Shadowdancer should have been added to your combined specialization list."

«Chrastr-gok Proficiency: 100. Novice»

«Shadow Magic Proficiency: 1. Amateur»

«Spellsword Proficiency: 1. Amateur»

«Shadowdancer Proficiency: 34. Amateur»

So, Shadowdancer's proficiency is the average of the other three? I wondered, willing away the notifications. *I should get shadow magic and spellsword caught up as soon as possible, then.*

An eruption of murmurs spread throughout the nearby students. They all glanced in our direction and I bit back a sigh. Even if I hadn't received the same notification, I had a feeling I knew what had happened.

"What's a Shadowdancer? That sounds super cool!" One of the students turned to plead with his master.

What... Idris trailed off when he caught the look I shot him.

"Your guess that it was one of the 'hidden' classes in my notes seems to have been right. I'd wager there was a faction-wide announcement about me hitting the requisite reputation with you—and about me acquiring or equipping the class." I grimaced, flipping my hood back into place. "Due to the nature of hidden classes, it could have been a server-wide... Well, world-wide, announcement."

"Well, thankfully it is not obvious from the name what Shadowdancer entails," Idris remarked with a sigh, shaking his head. "We should quit this place before we distract Arawn's students further. Furthermore... Where shall we go for our 'date?'"

"Ah..." I fell into silence while Idris led me back to the main street, allowing me to think in relative peace. "I really don't know the city well enough to make suggestions."

"What sort of venues are common 'date' spots in your world?" Idris gave me an encouraging smile.

I rattled off some options but had to leave many off the list since I knew they wouldn't exist in Jeriskyr. Perhaps I should have been disappointed, but I wasn't. After all, I was more interested in learning about my companion than I was in indulging in expensive foods, movies, or alcohol.

"I am flattered," Idris teased, swatting at my tail with his own. "If getting to know me is your goal, perhaps a better tour of Cejari-ir is in order. After, we can return to the palace for dinner—where we can speak more freely."

"I suppose that *would* be a problem, wouldn't it?" I considered it for a moment before nodding. "Alright, show me this city you're so proud of."

"Indeed—this time I will give you a proper tour." Idris smiled and grasped my hand in his. "I will show you what I love about this city, and why. Of course, if you spot any street food you would like to try, do let me know."

"You can ask me stuff too," I pointed out.

"I am certain your questions will provide me with many more to ask, Cerys."

Chapter Twenty-Eight
Totally a Date

Unlike my first visit to Cejari-ir, the city was bustling with life. Otherworlders and Jeriskyr natives alike filled the streets. There were people peddling their wares, selling food and drink, and many of the natives appeared to be providing quests for the Otherworlders. I had thought, perhaps, that Idris wouldn't have preempted their 'needs,' but it looked like my warning had been unnecessary. He'd been a step ahead of me.

"While we are out, perhaps we should see about having armor and weaponry made for you?" Idris suggested, gently tugging me toward a nearby smithy.

"When I can afford it myself, maybe," I protested, planting my feet. "You've already been far too generous."

"Nonsense! What is a champion without weapons and armor?" Idris countered, shooting me a brilliant smile. He gave my hand another gentle tug and continued in an encouraging tone, "While I have provided you with clothes suitable for the palace, traveling, and training, you will need other equipment before long. Especially if you are to remain by my side.

"Furthermore, how do you propose to earn your own coin when you must remain in the palace for the foreseeable future?"

"You have a point there." I pursed my lips, sinking into thought for a moment. He was right, of course. If I was supposed to act as some sort of femme fatale bodyguard while with him, I'd need weapons to do so. Without at least *basic* equipment, I couldn't expect anyone to let me out of the palace on my lonesome either. "In that case, at least let me find some way to pay you back."

"I refuse. They are a gift, Cerys." He raised his free hand to shush me. "Come, we will have them fit you for armor. The weapon smiths are next door. We will commission them to make blades suitable for a Shadowdancer."

"Are Nabyr-zahn's craftsmen another thing you're proud of?" I arched an eyebrow at Idris' back as he pulled me underneath the awning. He opened the door for me and released my hand, motioning for me to enter first.

Hopefully he doesn't think he can buy me with pretty

things...though I suppose if he was going that route, armor and weapons would be a questionable choice.

I would not dream of it, Idris answered, shooting me an amused smile. "Our artisans are extraordinary. They are responsible for outfitting our entire army, and myself, so that we might survive in our campaigns against the Issradian Empire. Without their talents, our numbers would be much lower."

The next few hours were spent split between the armor and weapon smiths. Idris insisted on commissioning several sets of armor for me, as well as far more weapons than I knew what to do with. Most of it wouldn't be ready before the Issradians arrived to claim their tax, but the weapon smiths assured us that they would focus on completing one weapon set for me before then.

"You are not accustomed to gifts?" Idris questioned as we strolled down Cejari-ir's streets once more.

"Gifts were a foreign concept to me until I ran away from the compound," I answered, shaking my head slightly. "Your fa... Perhaps I should say, 'our mutual acquaintance' was damned determined to make sure I experienced all the things that I missed by living in that place. The apartment, clothing, the hefty allowance that I rarely had reason to spend, and so on..." I tilted my head, thinking back to all the things Gwythyr had done for me. "Well, I suppose I know where you get it from, at least. That doesn't make it any less awkward for me to accept."

"Then I will have to drown you in gifts!" Idris laughed, pulling me over to a nearby food cart. Before I could even think to question him, he'd ordered two bags of steaming hot pastries from the merchant and offered me one. "I was of half a mind to take you elsewhere for dinner, but I think sampling the street merchant's wares will be far more telling."

"I'd rather you didn't drown me in gifts," I informed him as I took the bag of pastries. When the scent of marinated, slow-cooked meat hit my nose, my stomach rumbled. "I sure won't complain about food, though."

"What is wrong with gifts?" Idris murmured, perhaps more to himself than to me.

"Well, if you start giving me gifts too often, they'll lose their meaning," I suggested, not sure what else to say to him. While I had other reasons, some of which made less sense than others, my statement wasn't wrong. "Nice gestures every now and then aren't so bad, but if you do it too often it becomes expected. I'd rather not become spoiled *or* dependent on others."

"You *do* require equipment, clothing, and nourishment," Idris pointed out with an amused smile. "Very well, I will attempt to restrain myself. If 'spoiling' you is out of the question, then what should we do instead?"

I considered it for a moment, not sure what to make of having his unwavering attention. "We don't necessarily have to go anywhere special. A stroll around the city, a visit to the palace gardens—just about anything works as long as we actually *talk*."

"Ah, then permit me to show you the view Cejari-ir has of the valley below!" Idris perked up, a cheerful smile brightening his expression. He motioned for me to accompany him, so I took a bite of the savory pastry and followed. "If it is not too much to ask, might you tell me what happened between you and your previous... I believe you called him a 'boyfriend?'"

"You want to know about that?" I arched an eyebrow. "Which one?"

"There are multiple?" Idris fell silent for a moment, studying me. A reluctant smile came to his lips. "I suppose I should not be surprised. I am guessing you are more inclined to 'date' those from your own world."

Was that jealousy? I watched him in silence for a moment. "Well, they all share something in common. They all felt a little...inadequate while with me. Most of them couldn't stand the pampering I received from your—well, you know. He's a very wealthy and influential man. Most of my boyfriends either got the wrong idea or were upset they couldn't 'take care of me' better than he could.

"The others couldn't keep up with me in the—ah..."

"Keep up with you where?" Idris arched an eyebrow, but a smirk slowly spread across his face. Apparently, I hadn't cut off my train of thought fast enough. "Speaking of which, I am impressed you have lasted so long without 'food.' You must be quite powerful despite having such a new body."

"Is it really considered appropriate to ask someone that?" I shot him a foul look.

"Of course," Idris answered, nodding. He looked like he was thinking, so I remained silent and waited for an explanation. "If you were to cease eating for a few days, the people in your life who care for you would ask if everything was alright, would they not? They would try to get you to cease starving yourself.

"It is the same principle—the manner of sustenance is all that is different. I do not wish to see you harm yourself. Even if you decide I am not... Well, I suppose that is false. Of course, I would prefer you choose me."

Guess he was serious about the whole honesty thing. I just stared at him for a moment, watching as he clenched his free fist. After a moment, he buried most of his expression in his food. "Well, I don't intend to starve myself. It's just that I've never been one for casual sex, and *non*-casual sex is something I'd intended to avoid. You could say that I've backed myself into a corner and I'm not willing to compromise...yet. Obviously, I know I'll have to."

"How is it casual when it is necessary to live?" Idris frowned.

"Ah..." I sighed and thought on how to word my answer in a way he'd understand. "On Earth, you either have sex with your partner—boyfriend, girlfriend, fiancée, spouse, and so on—or on a casual 'because I'm horny' basis."

"Horny?" Idris arched an eyebrow.

"Slang for sexually aroused." I shook my head. "So, there's two main types of sex on Earth. Sex with someone you are dating or love, and sex purely for physical satisfaction. ...why I have to explain this to an incubus is a little..."

"If we were from the same world, you likely would not have to." Idris laughed and shook his head. "I understand your meaning. However, for our kind, sex is just as necessary as food and water. It is something you will have to grow accustomed to, and for your sake, I hope you adjust sooner rather than later."

"Well, since you decided to ask about *my* love life," I began, shooting him a sideways glance. "How about you? You said 'dating' isn't something that's done here, but you're also centuries old. Surely you haven't been alone all this time."

"I have been alone for the majority of my adult life," Idris replied after a moment, his expression becoming pensive. "Since I pried, and because I keep touting the importance of honesty, I suppose I can tell you more. When I was much younger, I had a fiancée. I must admit that part of my reason for attempting to make you choose to remain in Jeriskyr is because of my experience with her.

"Back then, I did not know what it truly meant for someone to be an Otherworlder. I courted her and eventually asked for her hand in marriage, and she accepted. However, a few weeks before we were to wed, she vanished. At first, we thought she had been taken by the Issradian Empire. My father and I organized search parties, but we never found a trace of her.

"Some decades later, I learned that she…had switched sides. No longer a proud demoness, she was a human at the beck and call of the Issradian Empire. We met on the battlefield, and it was left to me to slay her. Of course, she was not a champion, so it was not permanent.

"We met again and again on battlefields over the course of the next century, until one day she truly vanished from Jeriskyr, never to be seen again. The gods confirmed her to be gone for good."

That…explains a lot, actually. I searched for something to say for a moment. I hadn't expected him to respond so seriously to my inquiry. "In that case, I suppose the gods haven't done much to endear themselves to you. They could have let you know at any time instead of making you wait…"

"I was young and stupid. I likely would have demanded they prevent her from changing sides." Idris snorted and shook his head. "It was for the best, in the end. I later realized that I did not love her. That would not have helped much at the time, of course, but it did wonders for burying it all in the past."

"Sorry for bringing it up." I winced.

"Not at all. I am glad you expressed interest." He smiled, brushing a lock of loose hair from my face. "After all, you will hardly get to know me if I am the one asking all the questions. I want you to feel free to ask me anything you wish. However…for the moment, be a dear and hold this."

Idris handed me his bag of meaty pastries. The cold glint in his eyes gave me a decent enough indication of what was going on. Enemies. He shifted so that his back was against mine and pulled me closer toward him. A melody left his lips as he summoned a sword and brandished it. What I thought was going to be a harmless swing of his sword turned into a streak of crimson as the blade swung through the thigh of a human. The man screamed and fell to the ground, clutching the stump of his leg.

The air around us rippled as more humans dropped out of stealth and surrounded us. None moved to help their ally.

I scowled and quickly counted the ones I could see. Assuming the ones in front of Idris had taken a similar formation to the ones in front of me, there were at least ten of the bastards still on their feet. Idris shifted his grip on his sword and plunged it into the heart of the man he'd disabled.

"Hand over the whore," one of the men sneered, causing Idris' entire body to twitch behind me. "There's a good price on her and we intend to claim it."

"Filthy..." Idris didn't bother finishing the thought aloud. Instead, he shifted his stance and another songspell left his lips. A rush of power surged through me, sending heat through me soon after. Another spell, another rush. He didn't need to say anything for me to realize he was buffing us both in some manner.

I shifted into a defensive stance with my arms in front of me and sized up the human men. Most of them were a mix of bronze and silver levels in their proficiencies, but one was gold. I couldn't figure out if they were Jeriskyr natives. If they were Otherworlders, I hoped their respawn was far, far away from Cejari-ir.

Several of the men yelled in panic when another surge of power erupted from Idris. Startled, I glanced over my shoulder to find that much of his form had shifted. Armor-like scales covered much of his body, fused with his normal flesh elsewhere. Darkness bled into his sclera, coating them black. His tail had become more wicked, and a pair of draconic wings had sprouted from his back. What wasn't covered by blue-black scales was soon obscured by a set of the most badass plate armor I'd ever seen.

I quickly turned my attention away from Idris when I heard our attackers move. One lunged for me and I instinctively shoved his arm away with a palm-strike before kneeing him hard in the gut. His bones crunched under my knee, but I knew I didn't have time to appreciate my new body's strength just yet.

The next man who attempted to grab me received a swift axe-kick to the collarbone, shattering it. He dropped in place, unmoving. I assumed the shrapnel of his bones had likely pierced his heart. Useful.

A brief verse of song left Idris' lips, but this time it wasn't a buff. Four humans around us fell to the ground, split in half by an unseen force. Their blood sprayed into the air, coating the front of Idris' armor with red. Before I could react to another assailant, Idris' spell-touched blade swung through the man's arm. He caught the severed limb and shoved it down the man's throat.

My back prickled with the sensation of movement. I shifted, causing the man's strike to glance off my shoulder. It hurt like a motherfucker, but I'd avoided serious damage. Idris sure as hell wasn't happy about it, though. He grabbed the human's head in both hands and tore it from the man's shoulders with a sharp twist. I spotted a gleam of feral delight in Idris' eyes, moments before he dropped the head on the ground and promptly crushed it like a melon under one foot.

The three remaining men didn't look inclined to give up.

"I-I thought she was still powerless!" one of the humans hissed.

"Too late to back out now!" another snapped.

Releasing a small sigh, I reached for the tingle of magic in my mind, visualized what I wanted, and summoned darkness around my hands and feet. I landed a roundhouse kick against the closest human, knocking him clean off his feet. Another good stomp crushed the fallen man's windpipe. Idris unleashed a spell through his sword, impaling one of the remaining men on a spike of earth.

The last human standing lunged for me with a knife, but his grip was wrong. I stepped to the side and deflected his attack with a strike to his wrist before twisting in place and kicking him in Idris' direction. With a devious chuckle, the demon king cut the human down, the two halves of the dead man's body flying past him to land in the street, leaving a trail of blood and organs on the cobblestone surface.

«Chrastr-gok Proficiency has reached 102»

445

«Shadow Magic Proficiency has reached 10»

«Shadowdancer Proficiency has reached 37»

I blinked the notifications away. That was an unexpected increase. Two full points into Chrastr-gok, and nine into shadow magic, just from that? I glanced in Idris' direction, watching as he opened and closed his scale-covered fist a few times. It was a shame he'd taken out so many of the humans. I could've probably gotten a lot more skill levels if he hadn't interfered.

At least I'd gotten the Journeyman—gold proficiency—one to myself. That was likely where most of my skill-ups had come from.

"Now I find myself even more eager to spar with you," Idris remarked in an amused tone, his fully demonic form and his armor melting away. He pushed his hair back, shooting me a sultry smile. "You did not panic—good. That alone is half the battle toward making certain you become a wonderful Shadowdancer. Now then…"

Idris strode over toward one of the corpses and nudged it with his boot, grimacing. Blood from the dead men spread across the cobblestone street, giving us little clean room to stand. Deciding I didn't quite feel like getting any filthier, I tiptoed across the safe patches of street until I was clear of the gore. Thankfully, it was also upwind of the smell of vacated bowels.

"*Tch*, mere vagabonds," Idris muttered, leaping gracefully from where he stood over to my clean stretch of road. He gave me a questioning look when he caught the way I'd been watching him.

"What is it?"

"You...transformed?" I asked, tilting my head. His confusion seemed to deepen, so I continued, "I wasn't aware the demonic races had alternate forms they could take. *That* wasn't covered in any of the files I read."

"Ah, I hope I did not startle you," he murmured, a small frown settling on his lips. "If so, I apologize. Ah... You managed to get blood on you after all, I see."

Idris pulled a handkerchief out of his pocket and lifted it to my cheek, a low chuckle escaping him as he wiped blood off my skin. Once finished, he examined me and then himself, amusement clear on his face.

"I suppose we are a both a proper mess now, are we not?" he asked, laughing. "I think it may be best if we returned to the palace for now. There could be more men looking for a chance to attack us, and far be it from me to force a lady to remain in bloodstained clothes overlong. Perhaps after a bath and a change of clothes, we can play another game."

"I certainly wouldn't say no to a bath after that," I remarked, shifting to offer Idris one of the bags of pastries. "Think I saved our food from the bastards, at least."

"So you did. Thank you," he chuckled, taking the bag from me. "If that little display of yours was anything to go by, I do not think I will have to worry about whether or not you are up to the task of becoming a Shadowdancer. I hope you did not over do it."

"I feel fine," I replied dryly. "Or at least, like nothing has changed. Well, aside from the fact that I want dessert. Would it be inappropriate for us to pick up something from one of the food stalls while in this state?"

"Not at all," he replied, that devious glint returning to his gaze. "I will happily indulge such a request."

Idris offered me his hand and, after brief deliberation, I decided to take it. I couldn't keep pretending he wasn't a good or interesting man. Being stubborn without a good reason for it obviously wasn't going to work with him. Nor would acting like a bitch to push him away. I had a feeling that, even if he hadn't been able to read minds, he would have been able to tell I was just being…stupid.

Once we'd returned to the palace and reported our encounter to Emrys' soldiers, Idris and I parted ways to our separate towers to bathe. He'd suggested that afterward I should choose something comfortable, and perhaps a robe, instead of getting fully dressed again. By the time I'd finished with my bath, I found myself in full agreement with the idea. Putting on clothing beyond a short nightgown and a plush robe seemed like far too much effort. With the adrenaline from our fight gone, exhaustion wanted to set in.

Shoving my tiredness away, I padded through the palace and up to the King's Tower. I knocked twice, and soon after, Idris opened the door and ushered me in. The smell of hot tea and some manner of baked goods reached my nose the moment I stepped over the threshold.

"I thought perhaps we could continue our conversation before turning our attention to another match," he suggested, motioning me toward a seat. In front of it, a dessert plate full of cookies and a steaming cup of tea awaited me. "Unless you are too tired. I would not want you to think I am playing unfairly."

"Does war care about whether or not I'm tired?" I placed a hand on my hip.

"It certainly does not..." Idris mused as he sat across from me. He leaned against the armrest and examined me in silence before speaking again, his expression unreadable. "You are not harmed? How is your shoulder?"

"I'm fine. It will probably bruise, but I think that's to be expected," I shrugged, picking up my tea. However, Idris didn't look happy about my answer. "What about you?"

"I believe you were watching me intently enough to know the answer to that yourself," he answered, a small smile coming to his face. "You are certain I didn't startle or frighten you?"

"Well, you surprised me." I shook my head slightly. "Was that a unique ability of yours, or is there even more information I'm lacking about my new body?"

"There is *plenty* you have yet to learn about your body." Idris gave me a sultry smile, his voice a little lower than usual. He shifted in his seat to cross one leg over the other, his tail swaying upward to drape over his lap. "To answer your question, it is an ability all demon races have. It takes a great deal of specialized training to grow proficient with it. For now, you are better off focusing on Shadowdancer instead."

"I suppose our chance to spar today has come and gone, hasn't it?" I decided to steer the conversation in another direction. The damned incubus was far too alluring even under normal circumstances, let alone when I was hungry. Giving him opportunities to captivate me seemed ill-advised—especially when he seemed aware of every little movement he could use to draw my attention. "Is there anything I should know or prepare for to learn the flying sword variety of spellsword? Oh, and why did you commission so many types of weapons for me? Swords and daggers I can understand—daggers are much easier to conceal. But staves? Warfans?"

"The other weapons are utilized by the Chrastr-gok martial art," Idris answered with an elegant motion of his free hand, a satisfied, approving expression in his eyes. "They too can be utilized in your Shadowdancer abilities. Warfans will come into play when you accompany me as a bodyguard. Women of the court often carry fans with them and have little room for larger weapons. While you can conceal daggers as well, warfans will be easier to manage. Regarding your first question...might I be blunt?"

"Why stop now?" I shot back dryly.

"The amount of training you can do prior to feeding is limited." Idris frowned, his genuine look of concern and the languid swaying of his tail keeping me silent for the moment. "When you exert yourself on Earth, you grow hungry after, do you not? It is the same for our kind, except we must deal with both hungers. Working with magic further hastens the drain on our stores of energy."

"So that's why you asked me if I'd overdone it earlier," I sighed, earning a brief nod in response.

Great. So, not only are incubi and succubi naturally horny as hell, feeding is way more important than I wanted to accept. Okay, so avoiding sex is out of the question—under normal circumstances that'd be fine. Who doesn't like sex?

But...I don't want to just fuck whoever happens to be available. Casual flings really aren't my thing. I also didn't want to risk growing attached to anyone. Goddamnit. And it's already crystal clear that masturbating isn't enough. Ugh.

"Cerys?" Idris's frown deepened.

"You weren't 'listening?'" I arched an eyebrow when he shook his head. "Well, that's a small blessing, I suppose. So, what you're basically saying is, if I continue being stubborn I'll grow ill or perhaps even die?"

"Your body should not let you get to that point..." He sighed and ran his fingers through his hair, an expression of discomfort on his face when he looked at me again. "I would rather not use my power as an incubus, or as a spellsinger, to make certain you feed. However, I also have an obligation to my people to make certain our champion remains healthy and capable of taking on the Issradian Empire. Yet doing so would also be a betrayal of what little trust you have in me.

"I struggle to understand how the possibility of growing attached to your 'meal' is enough to make you deny your most basic needs. Without understanding, I cannot hope to help you realize how severely you are harming yourself."

"Well..." I murmured, sinking back against the sofa. The fact that he was even *trying* to understand won him points, especially since I hadn't done the same for him. With that in mind, I decided I owed him an explanation—but it required more information. "If you were put in a situation where you were in another world, wouldn't you want to avoid making emotional attachments there?"

"Why would I?" Idris tilted his head.

"So you could go home?" I motioned around us.

"Cerys..." Idris' face contorted with an array of emotions as he opened and closed his mouth a few times, searching to find the correct words. "Allow me to put it this way. Perhaps it will help you understand. My people have been oppressed by the Issradian Empire for centuries. Many of us do not remember a time when we were free of them." Idris paused to take a calming breath, his eyes shutting briefly before he continued. "Their kidnappings and the tax have robbed countless men and women of their chance to find their would-be life partners. If given the opportunity, many would do anything within their power to find their soulmate. Our kind cannot bear to be lonely, but mere food does not provide us with the comfort or attention we seek.

"If I found my soulmate in another world, I would not hesitate to remain there. Rather, I would do everything in my power to make certain I could stay with them in their world. In fact, I know many incubi who dream of being chosen by the gods to be traded to another world, just for the mere *possibility* that they might find a mate."

"Whereas I feel like I *should* still be attached to Earth, yet I wouldn't complain if it crashed into the Sun." I sighed heavily before pausing, a frown spreading across my face. "This 'soulmate' business aside, do you feel any attachment to Jeriskyr?"

"Attachment? Perhaps. More so, I feel an obligation to free my people," Idris offered, shooting me a troubled look. "What is it?"

"You recall how determined I was to return to Earth?" I leaned forward.

"Yes, of course." Idris gave me an unamused look.

"And that neither of us could truly understand why?" I shot his own look right back at him.

"Indeed." He waved dismissively.

"Then what could your gods have done to so suddenly change my mind?" I pointed out, narrowing my eyes. "Rationally speaking, I'm completely certain that I should still feel attached to

Earth. Nothing drastic enough to alter my decision has happened. Yet it's like someone flipped a switch and cut off my ability to care even a *little bit* about Earth."

Idris nodded his understanding. "You think that perhaps there was some unseen connection to Earth that they severed?" He switched his crossed legs and sank back in his seat, falling silent for a moment. "If that is the case, it does not sit well with me. Did they not claim that your incentive to help us would be so that you could return home? With a severed connection, you would no longer care about going back.

"Without such an incentive, the only reason you would have to help us is a desire for self-preservation and perhaps a sense of obligation. Yet most people would flee rather than involve themselves in a war, I feel."

"*Tch.* In other words, I have to work out if my connection to either world is real, or if it's being forced by their respective deities." I snorted in displeasure and sat back heavily. "I guess we've wandered off track. Back to the former topic, the idea of staying in a foreign world, especially one with so many problems, is a daunting one. That said, I've considered the possibility that allowing me to leave is a lie."

"Explain." Idris' eyes narrowed, anger tingeing them. I was just thankful his anger wasn't toward me.

"Well, let's look at my arrival here and the choice the gods posed," I offered, motioning vaguely with one hand. "I was told I had to pick between the Issradian Empire and Nabyr-zahn, despite the fact that I was specifically chosen by your gods. As far as either of us is aware, Alice wasn't given the same choice when chosen by the human gods.

"Furthermore, the human gods haven't been playing fair for centuries. They've twisted the game and manipulated the situation—probably more than we will ever know. I would think that most people would choose self-preservation over saving their chosen friend, yet Nabyr-zahn has a notable lack of champions in recent history." I motioned broadly with both hands, my tail twitching in irritation. "There's likely far more manipulation we don't know about, and I'm not convinced that I ever had a choice to begin with. Too much doesn't add up. With your spies, let alone spies from other kingdoms, stationed in the Issradian Empire…I would think that someone would have learned of the breeding pens ages ago. At the very least, your deities should have known."

"You think that all the gods may be playing unfairly?" Idris muttered, grimacing. "I will not deny that the thought has crossed my mind before…"

"It's one of the reasons that choosing the demons seemed obvious to me," I replied, nodding. "With what information I had, it didn't seem likely that Alice would be let go even if I chose to side with the Issradians. The fact that Nabyr-zahn hadn't received a proper champion in ages was a warning bell for me."

"And rightly so," Idris sighed. "You are even more observant than I gave you credit for. I am glad you are on *our* side."

"Well, that ended up being a heavier conversation than I intended it to be," I mused, earning a small smile from the king. "That said, I feel a little better now that you and I have *had* a few proper conversations."

"Something I should have done sooner," Idris acknowledged with a chuckle. "I will admit that it was a mistake for me to think that I could win you over with my behavior on Earth. However, I hope you can understand that it was driven by my intention to protect you from the tax."

"And by extension your kingdom? Yes," I replied. For a moment, I considered asking him how he managed to cope with the knowledge of what had happened to so many of his subjects. Figuring I'd pried too much for one day already, I decided against it. Happier conversation was needed. "I suppose I can forgive you for how you acted on Earth, though I think we still have a ways to go."

"Even if we originated from the same world that would be true, Cerys." He let out a low laugh, a twinkle of mischief in his eyes. "I should fetch the game board before we are both too tired for a match."

I watched Idris rise to his feet and adjust his robe, revealing a tantalizing stretch of his chest before he closed it tighter. He shot me a knowing look before leaving the room. Once he was gone, I released a heavy sigh and slumped back in my seat. Self-control was terribly overrated. Especially around someone who said my name like...that. How he managed to pour both adoration and invitation into a single word was beyond me.

Maybe it's just the hunger talking. I stared at the ceiling, attempting to gather my thoughts—and quell my libido. *Ugh. How am I supposed to learn about this stupid new body of mine anyway? Asking a possibly-hungry incubus seems like a bad idea. Asking the women of the harem seems much worse.*

He sure has a great ass, though, even in that robe. ...not helping, brain.

Deciding to distract myself, I scooted forward in my seat and poured myself a new cup of tea. Our cookies had mostly gone untouched, so I picked one up and munched on it while waiting. It tasted much like shortbread, but softer and filled with something that tasted like a cross between raspberry and strawberry jam. Eating only one would've been difficult.

"Now then, did we want to modify our wager?" Idris inquired as he returned. He paused when I glanced up at him, but I quickly returned my attention to the cookies. I had a feeling I knew just what he'd seen when I looked at him. "Ah... Have you had time to study the game further? If so, perhaps we can add more units to the board."

Yep. He definitely caught that. I kept my expression passive and sat back with another cookie in hand. The roughness in his voice made me wonder if I wasn't the only one who'd been stubborn about feeding since returning to Jeriskyr. Eventually, my curiosity got the better of me. "You actually meant it when you told your harem you wouldn't be needing them anymore?"

Idris' tail twitched hard into the back of his chair as he walked past it, causing his body to stiffen briefly. "Perhaps it was a reckless decision...but yes. I cannot stand to so much as look at them currently. Why you are asking is another matter..."

"Observation," I replied, a smile spreading across my face. Seeing the demon king lose his cool for even a moment amused me far more than I wanted to admit. "I've been sitting here weighing the pros and cons of asking you or your harem for more information about being a succubus."

"Why bother with them?" Idris shot me a frown.

"Discussing such things with the opposite sex is usually frowned upon on Earth." I laughed, shaking my head. "Oh, fuck it. The blunt approach it is, I'm tired of tiptoeing around the subject.

"How do 'our kind' feed to begin with? You've told me sex is a necessary component, but I struggle to believe it's that simple."

"How..." Idris set the game board down and sighed, shooting me a warning look. "A younger incubus would be misled as to your intentions by such a question."

And they wouldn't necessarily be wrong. I kept the thought to myself, hopefully, and let a sweet smile come to my lips instead. An expression Idris seemed unsure of how to take. "Would you rather I ask someone else?"

"You are playing a dangerous game."

"Dangerous for you, or for me?" I countered, laughing when I spotted another twitch running through him. "Besides, I'm a gamer—and safe is boring. That said, asking you seems far safer than asking your harem or random men throughout your palace."

"...you are right about that." Idris sat heavily and shot me a begrudging look. "What do you want to know?"

Aside from how to get you out of that robe? Plenty. I tapped my fingers against the armrest, letting the demon king sit in relative silence for a while. The lack of reaction made it quite clear he wasn't listening in on my thoughts. "Well, how about we start with my first question? Is it really as simple as having sex, or is there something else involved?"

"Sex is sufficient," Idris answered curtly, shooting me another warning look before beginning to set up the game board.

"How is our kind's endurance?" I asked, this time earning a puzzled look. "Never had sex with a human, I take it?"

"No, I have not. I would rather eat nails," he scoffed.

"Most human men are a 'one and done' sort when it comes to climaxing," I informed Idris. He looked stunned by the information.

"What a terrible existence!" he exclaimed, shaking his head.

"Well, I suppose that answers that question," I laughed.

"If you are attempting to win an unfair advantage in our game, it will not work." Idris shot me an agitated look. "Now then, shall I add cavalry units or not?"

"I actually had something different in mind," I remarked with a suggestive smile, watching as he seemed to freeze in place for a moment. His expression remained passive—aside from his eyes. I could practically see him attempting to determine if he'd interpreted my comment correctly. "You choose the strangest times to stop reading my mind."

"You have made it quite clear you dislike the intrusion." Idris settled his dangerous gaze on me. "Once we returned to the safety of the palace, I chose to stop 'listening.' However, you are making me second guess that decision. I did not think you were the type of woman who played this manner of game."

"Normally, I'm not. Getting a reaction out of the otherwise-composed incubus king is certainly entertaining, though." I grinned in response to his low growl. Unsure of the proper protocol on Jeriskyr, I decided to take a subtler approach first. "Is the invitation to stay with you for the night still open?"

"I... That depends on what you are implying." Idris narrowed his eyes.

"I'm implying we should satisfy our mutual hungers," I stated flatly, causing a look of surprise to cross his face. "If my choices are sex or die, the choice is pretty obvious. If my choices are someone I know and somewhat trust, or random men, then again...obvious choice. Unless *you* aren't actually interested in a tryst?"

"Again and again you manage to surprise me," he sighed, his voice strained. He tilted his head back and stared at the ceiling, running a hand through his hair. When he finally returned his gaze to me, there was a fire in his eyes that made my breath catch. "And what if you become attached, Cerys?"

"Then I'll have to deal with that hurdle if it comes," I shrugged, shaking my head. "Besides, if it isn't mutual, then there's nothing to worry about."

"Are all women from your world so blunt?" Idris arched an eyebrow.

"No. I prefer to get straight to the point, and I've expended my ability to skirt around important topics." I laughed, watching as Idris rose to his feet. This time, he motioned for me to stand up too. "Hmmm, should I have performance anxiety, *Your Majesty*? Satisfying an incubus sounds like a difficult task."

"I doubt you have anything to worry about." Idris reached out and grabbed the sash of my robe, pulling me to him. The moment I was pressed up against his torso, his tail snaked past me to coil around mine, sending jolts up my spine. "Shall we retire to bed, or do you intend for me to take you where you stand?"

"Both have their appeal," I grinned. A husky chuckle escaped him as he lured me toward the bedroom. After a moment, he glanced down at me with a questioning look in his eyes.

"You are certain about this?"

"Well, at the very least, I'm quite certain I want you out of that robe," I replied, slipping my fingers beneath the overlap and trailing them down his skin. A shiver ran through him when my fingertips traced over one of his scars. "And *that* didn't seem like a 'no.'"

"Not as much as I want you out of yours," Idris groaned, the sound of his desire sending a shiver through me. Before I could think of a teasing answer, he'd pulled off my robe and left me standing there in my short nightgown. A smirk came to my lips when I caught the way he was examining me. Moments later, his gaze met mine, even as his hands gripped my ass and squeezed me toward him. "*That* is not something an undecided woman chooses to wear."

"Maybe I just like pretty things?" I teased, as his hands slipped up under the skirt. He leaned down, his lips brushing over my throat as he slid the dress up and eventually over my head.

The dress was immediately tossed aside. He picked me up by the waist and carried me over to the bed as I wrapped my legs around his waist.

"Do you want me to get undressed or not?" he asked dryly as I gave him a firm squeeze. I bit my lower lip and stretched carefully out on my back, watching him as he examined my naked body.

"I suppose I'll allow it." I shifted, giving him room to work. He shrugged off his robe before slowly sliding his pants down. His scarred, muscular body was even more attractive than I remembered. Whether that was the hunger, or because it was his actual demon body instead of the Earth one, I wasn't sure. "How long are you going to make me wait? It's cold in here, you know."

"You seemed to be enjoying staring." Idris ran his fingers through my hair once he'd joined me on the bed. He seemed as if he was burning with desire, yet he still hesitated. "Do you have any rules that I should follow?"

"If I don't like something, I'll tell you—so listen and you'll be fine," I informed him, a grin coming to my face. "The minstrel seems to have gotten better about that as of late. No attempts to kill me either. Much better."

"And that mouth of yours is going to get you into trouble someday..." Idris murmured, before pressing his lips to mine.

What started as a soft, tentative kiss quickly evolved into a breathless dance of nibbles and tongue. His mouth soon traveled to my throat, his hands roaming everywhere he could reach. I briefly dug my nails into his chest, earning a shuddering groan as a reward. Biting my lower lip, I began to scheme more ways to get those delicious sounds out of him.

It'd been too damned long since I'd last had sex, and longer still since I'd had a vocal partner. I was damned determined to enjoy every second of it. Perhaps I'd make a game out of finding ways to make him moan. Few things were hotter to me than a man willing to lose himself totally to passion and pleasure.

Chapter Twenty-Nine
Pulsing the Brakes

The quiet rustling of sheets and a brief burst of frigid air roused me from an otherwise content slumber. It did not take long for me to remember how I had gotten there. The pleasant sting of scratches down much of my torso made certain I could not forget.

My heart fell when I heard soft footsteps. I cracked my eyes open, confirming it was still late at night. Faint moonlight filtered in through the windows, illuminating a brief glimpse of Cerys' pearlescent hair and scales as she slipped from the room. That she carried her discarded robe in her arms was quite telling—she intended to leave for the night.

With her gone, I rolled onto my back and stared at the ceiling in thought. My bed had already begun to grow colder in her absence. A sigh escaped me when I felt my chest clench. I wanted her to stay with me until morning and return to me again the following night.

Why is she attempting to sneak out? Frowning, I slowly sat up in bed, pushing my hair out of my eyes. I had not heard the door to my suite close, nor had I felt the ripple of magic to indicate it had locked. Meaning Cerys was still here, somewhere.

I slid out of bed and strode through my suite in search of the demoness in question. Lazing about would not provide me with the answers I sought.

When I found her, I was struck once more by her beauty. Her back was facing me as she sat in the bath, running her fingers through her hair. She had not lit any of the magelights or candles, leaving only moonlight to illuminate her work. Desire threatened to rise within me, but I shoved it away with practiced ease. I was there for answers, not for another tryst.

"Cerys?" I spoke softly, watching as she grew still, aside from her swaying tail.

"I'm sorry, did I wake you?" Cerys glanced over her shoulder, her expression unreadable. As I had thought, something was amiss.

"You did—I thought I might convince you to come back to bed," I replied, giving her a warm smile. My hope had been that a friendly approach would encourage her to stay, but instead her face flushed ever so slightly, and she looked away from me.

"That...probably isn't a good idea." She shook her head. My heart sank, and for a moment I could not feel my limbs. What had I done wrong? She had opened up to me and shown so much interest in the past day, yet suddenly she had become distant again. "I'm almost done here, then I'll return to my rooms. I doubt your subjects would be happy if they learned I'd spent the night with you. *Again.*"

"And why should we care what they think?" I frowned, confused, but she refused to look at me. "Furthermore, if that is your reason, don't you think sneaking back to your rooms in the middle of the night would raise further questions?"

"Wouldn't it be better for them to realize I'm just 'food?'" Cerys countered, a tinge of venom in her tone as she bristled. Taken aback, I simply stared at her for a moment. A heavy sigh left her, and her shoulders slumped. "Sorry. I know that isn't fair. It's just this...this idea of having to 'feed' in such an intimate way..."

"Did I not satisfy you?" I asked, dumbfounded by her behavior. "I thought—"

"What? No, that isn't it at all!" she yelped, finally turning to look up at me. She shook her head hard for emphasis, her cheeks rosy and her captivating amethyst gaze apologetic. "That's not what I meant to imply. It's just...uh... Well, the whole platonic sex thing..." Her cheeks grew redder and she finally released an aggravated sigh. "*Leaving* is the polite thing to do. No awkward 'thanks for the food!' No uncomfortable 'why are you still here?' No weird breakfast. No pissing off the people who actually have a right to you..."

You kissed me like that *and you* dare *claim that our night together was 'platonic?'* I paused, the last part in her train of excuses sinking in. "People who have a 'right' to me?"

"Like I've said before, Earth hasn't had royalty or nobility in a long time," Cerys muttered. She squeezed herself, her gaze downcast. "It wasn't considered proper or possible for royalty or nobility to cavort with people in the lower classes. There were plenty of affairs, but nothing good ever came of them. So, considering I am basically a peasant here and the nobles are already—"

"And what makes you think that the champion of Nabyr-zahn would be thought of as a peasant?" I asked, failing to suppress the threatening growl from my voice. If one of my subjects was responsible for her skittishness, I would have their head. Sighing, I stepped out of her way as she ascended the steps of the bath. The sight of her sent my heart racing. *Honestly, when did I become so...*

"Well, you and your subjects dislike humans—and that's what I technically am." She picked up a towel and began to dry herself, refusing to look at me again. "I can't expect anyone to think of me in a better light until I've proved that I'm on your side, and that I can be useful."

"And if I wish you to remain with me?" I asked softly. "Not

only tonight, but the next night, and the night after that, and for many more?"

This time, I was close enough to hear her heart skip several beats before beginning to race. She faltered, nearly dropping her towel. Alas, her shoulders and tail drooped and she slowly shook her head.

"It's for the best that I don't. I don't want to become attached, remember?" she muttered, reaching for her nightgown and robe. "You didn't do anything wrong, Idris. I just don't know how to make you understand why going back to the Queen's Tower is the best decision for me for now."

Oh, come on, Cerys! Her thoughts reached me as her fists briefly curled tight around her robe before pulling it on. *What are you doing? Best sex you've ever had and you're being a total cunt! You know better than to think he's just going to toss you aside. Is growing more attached really that bad?*

More attached... This woman is so unfair. I took a steadying breath and reached out to run my fingers through Cerys' damp hair. For a moment she leaned into the caress, but she soon stopped herself and looked away. "If you insist that returning to the Queen's Tower is truly what is best for you, I will not try to stop you. Know that, should you change your mind, I will always welcome you with open arms."

Her breath caught. I thought, hoped, that perhaps her mind had changed, but she slowly pulled away from me and clutched her robe shut. The color in her cheeks was the only clear indication that she had failed to keep me out. She could not meet my eyes, only succeeding in raising them to my collarbone.

"Goodnight, Idris." Her soft, sensual tone sent a shiver of desire through my body, setting me on fire. She so rarely called me by name, yet each time she did, it was if she was luring me toward a sweet trap I would never want to escape.

"Goodnight..." I turned and fell silent, finding that the vexing woman had already disappeared. "...Cerys..."

I sunk to the floor and clutched my chest as I took deep, careful breaths. My fist met the floor, causing the stone tiles to groan. I should have tried harder to understand her, perhaps. To get her to stay, or to at least make her truly understand that I *wanted* her to spend the rest of the night with me. Her departure made my heart ache in ways I had not thought possible.

"When did I..." I muttered to myself, tilting my head back to stare at the moon. "It is as they say... A woman worthy of becoming a queen can defeat a king before he even knows a battle is being waged."

Chapter Thirty
Tangled Strings

Breakfast came and went, yet I couldn't bring myself to touch my food. I felt awful. Emotionally. Fucking. Awful. I should have been nicer to Idris the previous night, or at least attempted to explain my position better. The almost reverent way he'd looked at me had shut me down. I'd heard him hit the floor as I left. Hells, that alone had almost made me stop. It was now obvious that I wasn't the only one growing dangerously attached. At the time, I'd thought it best to cut the link. Sever the chain. Free us from each other.

The hurt in his eyes and his voice haunted me.

I'm so stupid. Why do I do this to myself? I leaned back in my chair and stared at the ceiling. Sure, I'd thought with my libido most of the previous night. I wouldn't deny that. Seemed normal enough for a starved succubus. But...I hadn't anticipated how much my attraction toward Idris would increase afterward. Whatever I'd been expecting, careful, sensual sex sure hadn't been it.

And now I had to figure out how to face him again after shoving him away.

Fuck. I groaned, rising to my feet. Making him wait would be even more awkward, so I'd decided I would go to the training yard a little early. Still, I couldn't seem to quell my nerves. Going in, I'd been certain it would just be casual sex to satisfy our mutual hungers. Yet the way he'd kissed me, the way he'd spoken to me, and the way he'd touched me had all felt like more than that.

I didn't know if that was simply the 'normal' way for incubi and succubi to make love...or if there was more to it. One thing was damned sure, and that was that I didn't have the courage to ask. I wasn't ready for an answer.

Thankfully, it had been late enough that no one had seen me leave Idris' rooms. Sleep hadn't been my friend, though.

When I got to the training yard, Idris was already there and it was devoid of anyone else. He was practicing against one of the magitech dummies, shooting down the decoys it shot into the air with a variety of spellsinger and spellsword abilities. I opened my mouth to greet him but promptly closed it when my chest constricted. His rather fierce demeanor seemed like it was an indication of the frustration I had left him with.

"You did not sleep." Idris' comment came from much closer than I was expecting, startling me into looking up at him. His expression was firm for only a moment before softening. "Cerys, you needn't be frightened of me."

"What? I'm not frightened, especially not of you." I gave him a baffled look as he reached out to brush my hair from my face. His fingers slowly entwined with my hair, grazing past one of my horns. I couldn't even begin to process the way he looked at me. "I was a complete bitch for no good reason last night, but saying 'I'm sorry' doesn't seem like—"

"I forgive you." He leaned down and pressed his lips to my forehead. As suddenly as the kiss had come, he released me and turned to stride back toward the training yard. "You and I clearly have more cultural differences that need to be laid to rest. However, for now, I need to get you started on your spellsword training before I must leave for my duties.

"The Issradians will be here soon to collect their tax and you will be joining me as I oversee their collection. I need you to have your skills raised to an acceptable level by then. However, you are to refrain from harming yourself this time—*understood?*"

I don't deserve... I let out a small sigh and followed him. "I brought gloves this time. See?"

I reached into the back waistband of my trousers and pulled out the pair of training gloves. However, he wasn't satisfied until he saw me put them on. After, he told me to summon my training swords from my inventory.

"Regarding the flying sword style," Idris began, allowing one of his own weapons to float effortlessly from his hand, "you will not be able to utilize it until you have first mastered the ability to make your blades fly. They should be like extra limbs once you have grown used to them—albeit not attached.

"Most spellswords utilize multiple elements in their craft, but you will be focusing on shadow magic. Your task is to learn how to feel and control your blades without physically touching them. And without harming yourself, if you please."

"They're sharp," I pointed out.

"Then *be careful.*" Idris shot me a flat look. "It is difficult to describe the sensation with words. If there are no objections, I will show you by allowing you to feel my magic instead."

"Showing me would be more efficient than explaining anyway," I nodded.

"Then give me your hand."

I placed my hand in his and waited. It wasn't long before Idris' power coiled around me and grasped a tendril of mine. He pulled my magic with his, guiding it toward the blades floating behind him. Shadowy butterflies erupted along my arm and up his. More appeared around his four floating swords the moment he brought my power to them.

"You are certain I should not have your quarters redecorated with butterflies and moonfire lilies?" Idris chuckled, shooting me a smile.

"Honestly? I would rather you put your resources toward Nabyr-zahn's defensive and offensive capabilities." I shook my head. "While I appreciate your generosity, the Queen's Tower is already more luxurious than anything I'm used to. I wouldn't dream of asking for more—and if I did, I would want control over the changes."

"Is that because you have decided to leave? Or…" Idris averted his gaze, but his grip tightened. His magic tremored briefly before steadying.

"I'm still considering staying…if I'm welcome," I grumbled, pursing my lips. "Pampering me is illogical and inefficient. It doesn't make any strides toward conquering the Issradian Empire. *That* is why I would prefer you focused on defenses and offenses instead."

"Will that make you happy?" Idris asked, his crimson eyes unreadable.

"Happy?" I echoed, perplexed. "That doesn't have any bearing on dealing with the empire either. Access to food and a roof over my head are sufficient."

"'Sufficient' is not good enough for me." Idris shook his head and shot me a crooked smile. "Alas, you have not even noticed that you are holding the blades aloft on your own, have you?"

"Hmmm?" I glanced at his swords and then back to him. "I noticed I was holding them, but your magic didn't 'retreat' very far. The crystals in their hilts and pommels serve as magical foci or conductors, I take it?"

"You are an odd woman." Idris arched an eyebrow, then made a brief motion toward the swords. In an instant, they disappeared, causing my butterflies to disperse and wander aimlessly before disintegrating. "You mentioned the 'ranks' to proficiencies before, so I will not go into further detail regarding that for now. Simply put, I need you to train the three components of Shadowdancer against the dummies until you can no longer improve in such a fashion.

"If you are not exhausted by then, find a sparring partner later today. Otherwise, we will have to hope that there is enough time for you to continue your training tomorrow. The Issradians are due within the next three days and could arrive at any time. They are known to press their horses so that they may come and go more quickly."

"Will bronze or silver really be enough for me to be useful?" I frowned up at him as he released my hand and took a step away. "I doubt training swords will be sufficient either."

"One of your fans and two of your swords should be completed by the evening," Idris replied, making a dismissive motion as he strode across the training area and over to the dummy he had been using earlier. He pressed one of the crystals on it, turning the contraption off. "I've already tasked Elidyr with fetching them for you later tonight and he will deliver them to your quarters immediately."

"What should I do about my shadow magic?" I asked, though my brain seemed to pause when Idris stretched, his clothing pulling taut. Gritting my teeth, I attempted to ignore the gorgeous man. I wasn't even hungry anymore and I still wanted to see him out of his clothes. The look he shot me when he pushed his hair out of his face did *not* help.

"You will improve it as you use it in conjunction with your blades." Idris walked over to me and trailed his fingers down the flat of one of my swords, shooting me an alluring smirk as he passed. "*I saw you watching.*"

When I turned to give a witty retort, Idris was gone. I blinked and glanced around the training yard, attempting to figure out where he had gone. Alas, a quick search revealed he had truly left. I curled my fist around the hilt of one of the swords and ground my teeth together. *That isn't something to be upset by. I should be glad he left me to train in peace.*

I glanced down at the ground, my shoulders slumping. When it came to Idris, it seemed as if all my courage and resolve had disappeared with my hunger. Liquid courage seemed like a terrible idea. So did jumping to conclusions about however he felt about me.

Was everything I said to him before we had sex just meaningless bluster? I wondered as I loosened my grip on my sword. Concentrating briefly, I directed tendrils of shadow into the weapon's crystals and willed it to float. The blade hummed with power as butterflies swirled around its length. *Well, one thing is for sure...I was wrong in thinking that I was expected to leave after. Okay, two things. Second is that I made it worse for both of us.*

My jaw creaked, warning me to cease clenching my teeth. With a small sigh, I stopped, attempting to refocus my attention to my floating sword instead. Beginning with one seemed safer than attempting to use all three at once. Idris had asked that I be careful, and I intended to do just that. Skewering myself on my own swords seemed like a terrible way to die.

Granted, the way I'm going I'll be executed for upsetting Idris. The corner of my eye twitched and I growled. *You can shut up now, brain.*

I did what I could to turn off my emotions and settled into training for the next several hours. Once I was capable of floating three blades, I decided to integrate them into some of the martial arts forms I remembered from Earth. Stabbing and slashing with the blades, even making them swirl around me, came relatively easily with the slower-paced forms taught to white and yellow belts. The further up the ranks of forms I went, the more difficult it became to multitask with the weapons.

Keeping the swords afloat was easy enough, but keeping them

steady was another matter entirely. It was like trying to balance a sword by the flat of its blade on one finger, except I couldn't *see* what I was using to balance it. However, I quickly learned that I had to take a more measured approach when they began to rattle or wobble. If I rushed to steady them, it made it worse. If I was too slow, it worsened again.

Any form of acrobatics would have to wait until later ranks. That much was damn obvious.

"Still at it?" a sultry voice questioned. I glanced over to find Idris leaning against a nearby pillar. He wore a simple, loose shirt and a pair of trousers. Not training clothes, and certainly not royal finery. "You have not stopped even to fetch lunch or dinner yet, have you?"

"Dinner?" I frowned, then glanced up at the sky, my eyes widening. "Oh."

I sensed a ripple of magic from my left flank and immediately shifted one of my blades to intercept it. The clang of metal striking metal made me glance in Idris' direction just in time to see him disperse into shadow. His strike had sent my sword spiraling out of control and diverted the path of his. His sword sunk into the sand at my feet as he reappeared behind me, a blade to my throat.

"If you are capable of that much, then why have you not yet sought a sparring partner?" he questioned as I reached up to grab the tip of his blade. I flicked the weapon away from my throat and shot him a pointed look. He gave me a sheepish smile in response.

"It was an excellent way to test your improvement and your instincts. Had you not noticed, I would have stopped."

"I believe you." I called my sword back to me and then turned to face him fully. "The reason I haven't sought a sparring partner is because I've been going over the basics. While going through my paces, I noticed that my blades became unsteady the more I exerted myself or the quicker the movements I made."

"Well, I believe that is more than enough for one day." Idris placed a hand over mine, forcing me to lower my sword. When he looked at me this time, it was with concern in his eyes. "Let us get you into the bath first. You can join me for dinner afterward."

"Bath? Dinner? Wha—?" I tried to protest, or at least question him, as he steered me purposefully into the palace.

"I have decided that I would rather not dine alone, so I will be joining you for dinner in the Queen's Tower," he informed me. "As much as I would like to claim it is purely for the pleasure of your company, that is not the case. Our scouts have spotted the Issradian party. They will likely arrive tomorrow evening. I need to brief you and make certain you are properly prepared.

"You will be spending your time at my side until the Issradians are gone. I do hope you can put up with me until then."

"…you make it sound like I *don't* enjoy your company," I muttered, my heart falling. The corners of my eyes stung briefly but I willed my stupid emotions away.

"It is difficult to tell," he stated, his grip loosening. "I thought you enjoyed my company during our date, but…"

Fuck. I ruined our date, didn't I? When the realization hit me, I didn't know what to say. I'd thought I was done beating myself up, but that one notion was enough to start the cycle all over again. "I'm sorry, I—"

"I do not need apologies, I need answers—do you or do you not enjoy my company?" Idris fell into step with me and shot me a tired look.

"You're difficult to understand *and* deal with, but yes, I enjoy your company," I replied, releasing a heavy sigh.

"*I* am difficult?" Idris stared at me in disbelief.

"In a different way from how you find me difficult," I stated dryly, opening the door to the Queen's Tower. "For what it's worth, I am *trying* to be less…stupid. Anyway, we can worry about our lack of understanding later. Preparing for the Issradians sounds far more important and I don't feel like being partially responsible for you shirking your kingly duties."

"Take your bath first." Idris nudged me in the direction of the bathroom and gave me a small smile. "I will be satisfied with your answer—*for now.*"

For now, huh? I retreated to the bathroom, unraveling the rest of my disheveled braid along the way. *Hopefully that lasts long enough for me to get my thoughts in check. Or at least properly resolve to stop being a bitch. Pushing him away isn't doing either of us any favors, and I…don't want to push him away. Not anymore.*

Chapter Thirty-One
Marionette

Elsewhere in Jeriskyr...

Corlyotir tapped her claws on the table with impatience, gazing into the viewing window before her. Nearby, a man lazed with his back against a pillar. He watched the goddess in silence, his expression passive as Corlyotir grew more and more agitated.

Empty seats gathering dust lined the table to the goddess' left and right. The surface of the table itself was littered with books, scrolls, and broken artifacts. Remnants of a more prosperous time for Jeriskyr's demonic deities.

"I thought you said they were a perfect match?!" Corlyotir snapped, turning to glare at the bored man. "We already determined that, of the six kings, Idris is the most likely—and most worthy—to unite demonkind against the Issradian Empire. If he and the champion continue to be at odds—"

"You did a sloppy job," the man spoke. Corlyotir froze. To other observers, his tone would have sounded casual or even nonchalant. The goddess knew better. One misstep would lead her to oblivion.

"Meical, you assured me that Cerys would choose Nabyr-zahn, and you were right. She has. However, her attitude toward King Bloodsong—"

"Must you make me repeat myself?" Meical narrowed his unusual eyes at the goddess, and she gulped. Even after millennia, Corlyotir had never grown accustomed to the man she called Meical. The universe itself shone in his eyes, full of abyssal darkness with glimpses of twinkling stars.

"I cut her ties to her world, as is customary." Corlyotir adopted a careful tone and clenched her fists in her lap. "There should be nothing left to make her reject Jeriskyr, or anyone in it."

"Did you *succeed?*" Meical sighed. "The answer is that you did not. You left strings connecting her to Earth, and they are forcing her to push others away. If you had sent her to one of the other kings, her behavior would have resulted in her being cast out already.

"You're lucky your stupid mistake didn't cost you your champion."

"Well, cutting a champion's ties was once your job!" Corlyotir snapped, slamming a fist against the table. "Trusting you now is a risk We had to take. She may be the last champion Nabyr-zahn sees and We let you pick her!

"The demons are running out of time. You have been right about Cerys for the most part, but if she's still bound to Earth—"

"You want me to fix *your* mess?" Meical gave the goddess a frigid look. "I will go finish the job, but only because Cerys has the capability to end this stupid game you and the other gods insist on playing."

Meical turned on his heel. His long, serrated tail slashed the air in front of him, creating an ominous rip. He strode through it, leaving the frustrated goddess alone with her thoughts. The demon shook his head as he reappeared in the Queen's Tower in the palace of Cejari-ir, the air warping around him. Using his power, he displaced himself to keep Idris and Cerys from noticing his presence.

The two demons appeared to have ceased arguing and were instead focused on preparing for the next few days. Meical watched in silence for a while, a faint frown on his face as he observed Cerys. Never before had he seen the woman so hesitant, or so prone to making herself feel worse. Her frayed connection to Earth was negatively impacting her behavior to an extent that reflected

Corlyotir's mistakes.

It should never have become such a problem.

How many of the champions from other kingdoms were lost because of that woman's failures? Meical's eye twitched. After waiting for a while, Idris finally turned his attention away from Cerys in order to prepare more tea for them. Meical didn't waste a second. He strode across the room and over to the demoness. Once within reach, he prodded the center of her forehead once.

Cerys' eyes fluttered shut and the dark magics around her feet dissipated moments before she slumped back in her seat, sound asleep. When Idris said something to her and received no reply, the demon king turned around with a deep frown on his face. His expression softened when he realized that she had drifted into slumber. The king swiftly collected the woman in his arms and carried her to the bedroom, hesitating for only a moment before leaving her to sleep in peace.

With the king gone, Meical padded into Cerys' bedroom and allowed the distortion magics around him to fall. A simple wave of his hand revealed dozens of frayed golden threads extending from her chest and out from the ceiling of her room. Meical let out an agitated sigh. Corlyotir had done an even worse job of severing the champion's ties than he'd thought.

Meical's hand wrapped around the cluster of threads, drawing them taut. In the next instant, his tail lashed out and severed them cleanly—save for one. He frowned and plucked at it like a harp string, listening as it resonated.

Hmmm? I missed. Plucking it again, a grin slowly grew across Meical's face. *Oh, so it's tied to* that *ability…now that could be fun. Ahhh, too much effort to fix it right now. I must be losing my touch. I will leave it—at least this one will not yank her back toward Earth.*

"Now then, 'Boss,' for showing me that even humans can be good people, and because it's my fault you've come to Jeriskyr…" Meical murmured, placing a hand over Cerys' eyes. He closed his own eyes and concentrated briefly, summoning forth a portion of his own magic. "Take this gift. You will need it. Shadowdancer won't be enough, but with this…"

Meical released her, satisfied with his work, and opened another tear to transport himself through. When he came out the other side, he grimaced at the interior of an Issradian estate before shifting his form. The charcoal gray hair and night-sky eyes gave way to a human body with bright, gaudy pink hair.

"You're late, Ryan." Adric looked up from his paperwork with a grumpy expression. "How someone capable of controlling time always manages to be tardy is…"

"How's Alice?" Ryan asked, shooting Adric a cheerful grin. "Time magic? That sounds pretty awesome! Though that doesn't sound like something Jeriskyr Studios would let players have."

"Cut the act. We're alone." Adric twitched. *Of all the allies…*

"Whoa, you've got like, a *huge* stack of paperwork there. More *taxes?*" Ryan shot Adric a look that made the guard captain grow pale. "Answer the question."

"Lady Alice is fine...for now."

Chapter Thirty-Two
The Demon King's Consort

When I heard the door to my suite open, I grew still in the bath and listened for a moment. Without many other options available to me, I summoned my swords from my inventory and aimed them at the door to the bathroom whilst continuing to bathe. The low chuckle when the door swung open made me release a sigh of both relief and agitation.

"You could have knocked," I stated dryly, listening as he strode closer.

"I want you to come spar with me," Idris informed me as I stood up in the bath. I ignored his piercing gaze and walked past him to fetch a towel. "If you do not perform well enough, I will have you remain in the Queen's Tower for the next few days whilst under guard."

"Hmmm? Should I change into something else, then?" I shifted to look at Idris, noting the odd expression on his face. "What is it?"

"Something has changed." He narrowed his eyes.

"Not that I'm aware of." I shook my head, proceeding to dress myself. If he wasn't going to give me an answer, then the fancy-yet-skimpy attire he'd left hanging in the bathroom the previous night would have to do. I still wasn't quite sure if I really fit the femme fatale description, but the letter he'd left for me had seemed insistent.

"You are not feeling any different?" Idris gave me a concerned look.

"Feeling…?" I tilted my head, thinking. "Well, I feel the best I've felt since coming to Jeriskyr, though I'm not convinced that's something to be worried about."

"Compared to how you appeared to be feeling yesterday, my concern is the swiftness of this change." Idris crossed his arms, examining me again. "I would ask if you had fed in my absence, but…"

"Do biscuits and smoked meats count?" I shook my head at him. "Anyway, sparring, you said?"

"In a manner of speaking, yes." Idris fell silent and studied me while I finished dressing myself. "I will attack you, and you will fend me off with shadow magic and spellsword abilities only. Rather than asking you to defeat me, I simply wish to make certain you have enough control."

"And I'm supposed to somehow be a bodyguard in *this*?" I asked, motioning to my dress. An amused smile spread across his face, but he remained silent. "If someone seriously attacks me, or a fight breaks out—"

"You will be fine, Cerys," Idris spoke softly, cupping my face in one hand. I just stared at him. The previous day, I would have yanked away from the gesture. Today, I didn't mind his touch at all. Quite the opposite. Idris traced my lower lip with his thumb, concern returning to his gaze. "I was right. Something has changed. You would not have tolerated this yesterday."

"Yet you decided to try it again?" I deflected, crossing my arms.

"Is it truly so difficult to admit that you enjoy my touch?" Idris asked, even as he let me go.

"Yes, it is," I replied, sighing. That response was just as good as saying outright that I liked his touch. He gave me a mysterious smile and offered me his arm instead of teasing me about it, at least. "Okay, so maybe you're right that something changed. I don't know how or why—last thing I remember, we were talking in the sitting room and you'd gotten up to refill our cups with tea."

"I carried you to bed, left you a note, and laid out clothes for you before leaving," he murmured as I linked my arm with his. "Did anything appear to be out of place when you woke? No one should be able to get in, except—"

"T-that may be my fault…" Corlyotir stated meekly, appearing between us and the door leading from the tower. She looked much like a naughty child who had just received a lecture. "One of my colleagues dropped by to complete the ritual to bind Cerys to Jeriskyr. I had not done a thorough enough job."

"All is well now?" Idris gave the goddess a threatening look.

"Yes, with her ties to Earth severed she should no longer act in irrational ways." Corlyotir hesitated, glancing at me. "That is, unless you actually enjoy hurting yourself and those around you, Cerys?"

"I don't, but I might make an exception." I gave her a pointed look. "First of all, I wasn't told that my ties to Earth would be severed. Second, I've received no guidance at all regarding how Jeriskyr works or what I'm expected to do here. Third, you lot seemed to think dropping me *in the middle of a battlefield* for my first visit was a smart idea.

"Then there are the details of this game of yours, which I'm still fuzzy on. *I* was forced to pick a side, yet Alice was just dragged into this and forced to go to whichever side I didn't choose? Why don't the other champions get a choice? How in the hell did you, *as fucking gods*, not know what the Issradians were doing? Furthermore—"

"Speaking of the Issradians, I really must be going. Our investigation is nearly concluded." Without another word,

Corlyotir disappeared and I growled in frustration.

"After we conquer those Issradian bastards, I'm gonna…" I trailed off and shot Idris an agitated look when he started laughing. "What?"

"I told you before—smaller prey first." Idris shook his head, smiling. "We will have to simply trust Corlyotir for now. Come, we should hurry. If you cannot defend yourself well enough, I will make certain the Queen's Tower is well guarded for the duration of the Issradians' stay."

"You don't think the enchantments on the door are enough?" I asked, as the door in question closed behind us.

"Humans are tricky creatures," Idris murmured thoughtfully, glancing down at me. "I suppose I should be thankful that you are simply difficult rather than tricky."

I'm not usually that *difficult, though…* I decided not to say anything aloud, remaining silent as we made our way to the training yard.

When we arrived, Idris released my arm and walked a decent distance away from me before summoning a single sword. He told me to summon *all* my swords, so I did. However, he made no move to attack me. Instead, he studied me in silence for a few moments.

"What?" I finally asked, shooting him an impatient glare.

"Use your warfan too." Idris motioned to my hip, where I had tucked the closed fan. "As a Shadowdancer, you should be capable of wielding a weapon, controlling your flying swords, and weaving in both armed and unarmed strikes.

"Try to fend off my spells and my swords alike."

The moment I pulled my fan from my waistband, Idris' sword flew toward me with far greater speed than I was anticipating. I made an upward motion with my closed fan, summoning a wall of darkness between me and the sword. The translucent magic 'solidified,' trapping Idris' blade within it.

«Shadow Magic Proficiency has reached 150»

«Congratulations, you are halfway to Journeyman»

If I could have punched the vocal half of the notifications, I would have. The damned thing sounded like Corlyotir and I was still mad at her. Besides, I was practically an NPC—what did I need notifications for?

Around me, the air seemed to crackle. I summoned a vortex of shadows around me, deflecting the flames erupting from the demon king's sword. Sensing movement behind me, I directed two of my floating weapons to intercept it. The clang of metal against metal confirmed my initial thought—it was another sword, and Idris had summoned it behind *me* instead of near himself.

"You certainly do not appear to have any trouble multitasking," he murmured, appearing to my left with another sword in hand.

A smile spread across his lips when I raised my fan and blocked his strike. There was hardly any strength behind the slash, and he had turned his sword so that the blunt side was facing me. Even so,

I shot him a suspicious look.

"That can't be all you wanted to test." I kept an eye on him, tracking him with my remaining blade as he circled me. He let out a low laugh and slid an arm around my waist, pulling me closer to him. A shiver ran through me when his tail coiled around mine. I shot him an agitated glare. "Just what are you—"

"Despite that tremble, your weapons did not waver," he remarked in a conversational manner, a smile pulling at his lips. "It appears that the extra time you spent working on control has helped you a great deal...in that regard, at least."

"Does that mean I passed your little test?" I narrowed my eyes after a moment and added, "Furthermore, are you going to let me go?"

"Indeed. We can't very well make our way to the throne room like this." Idris smiled, releasing my tail and my waist alike. Once he dismissed his weapons, I returned mine to my inventory as well, save for my fan. "You look disappointed, kitten."

"Back to calling me that?" I arched an eyebrow at him.

"It would certainly lend credence to the ploy of you being my favorite concubine," he teased, twisting a lock of my hair around his fingers. "Now then, why are you disappointed? Your performance exceeded my expectations."

"I would rather not discuss it," I replied dryly, shaking my head. Like hell I was going to tell him I was missing his arm or his tail. "You look like you want to say something."

"I need…permission," he stated, a small frown on his lips.

"Permission? For?" I wasn't in the mood for hesitation.

"To kiss you, for one," Idris answered plainly, causing me to stare at him in disbelief. "As far as the Issradians are aware, you are a member of my harem, as well as First Consort. If we do not act close, they will grow suspicious of the harem's purpose."

"Weren't you trying to avoid titles similar to concubine?" I sighed.

"Is 'consort' unacceptable?" Idris' frown deepened.

"…well, I don't know how the Issradians will interpret it," I began after a moment, placing a hand on my hip. "Saying 'First Consort' or 'favorite concubine' would basically be the same thing on Earth, though." A sigh left me, and I looked up at him again. "I suppose that's kind of the point though, isn't it?"

"You *did* reject my proposal," Idris pointed out, a smile spreading across his face. "I also require permission to speak with you via telepathy. I am certain you will have questions throughout the next several days and it would be much simpler if you permitted me to answer without raising our 'guests" suspicions."

"Fine, I'll cooperate." I crossed my arms and gave him a sideways glance. "I guess telling you to remain 'appropriate' isn't enough, is it?"

"Tell me what is not appropriate, and I simply will not do it." He shrugged, clearly amused. "It is quite obvious our ideas of appropriate behavior are different, and now that you have had a change of heart...*again*, I am unaware of what boundaries you wish for me to follow."

"Right..." I pursed my lips, a spike of annoyance running through me. I still felt a strong urge to throttle Corlyotir. "By 'appropriate,' I mean you need to keep your hands and tail away from erogenous areas while in public. No groping the honkers, ass, between the legs—"

"'Honkers?'" Idris tilted his head. Sighing, I pointed to my boobs. "Ah. More Earth slang?"

"Yes," I replied dryly. "Groping of any sort in public isn't considered acceptable behavior even between couples. You'll see people grab each other's ass sometimes, or people will put their hand on their partner's hip instead of keeping it to their waist—but the people around them get huffy about it."

"I see," Idris murmured, rubbing his chin. "So, it is not necessarily that the people involved do not enjoy it, but rather it makes the people around them uncomfortable? Therefore, it is considered unacceptable behavior?"

"Exactly!" I nodded.

"You specified *in public*," Idris drawled, a flicker of intimacy in his gaze. "Was that an oversight on your part? Or..."

"It'd be stupid of me to say, 'hands off' in private when feeding is an issue," I pointed out, watching his smirk grow. "I'm...not really *against*—"

"There you two are!" a voice called from down the hall. I

promptly shut my mouth and glanced over my shoulder, finding Emrys coming toward us. He was dressed in what I could only assume was ceremonial armor of some kind. "We received confirmation that the Issradians have entered the city, Your Majesty. It appears that they are scouring Cejari-ir before coming to the palace…as usual."

"The only women they will find are Otherworlders. We shall await them in the throne room." Idris shook his head, sliding an arm behind my back. "Cerys, you did not answer me in full."

"Oh. Right." I shook my head slightly. "I'll cooperate on both counts."

"Glad am I to hear it." Idris flashed me a brilliant smile, giving me a brief squeeze before turning his attention to Emrys. "You and Elidyr are to escort us even within the palace until we are satisfied the Issradians are gone. I refuse to take any chances with Cerys' safety."

"Very well, Your Majesty." Emrys bowed briefly and then glanced down at me. "It's a shame the two of you returned so close to the tax. Looks like, at the rate you're going, you could have hit Journeyman in your specializations before they'd gotten here if you'd had a few weeks."

"Gold—er, Journeyman? So soon?" I arched a doubtful eyebrow. "I was under the impression that it takes a long time to 'level.'"

"It's the last two tiers that take a while," Emrys offered as the three of us made our way through the palace. "Give it a few weeks, maybe a month or two, and someone with talent can reach Journeyman. Expert and Master take an age."

"And Grandmaster takes longer still," Idris added, shooting me an amused glance. "You look as if you're up to something."

"Ah? No, not exactly." I shook my head. "You tell me something takes a long time, I become determined to blow that estimated timetable out of the water. Even under normal circumstances."

"And I will encourage you to do so—within reason." Idris shot me a look and lifted one of my hands in his. "Your health, safety, and learning are just as important."

"I'm not going to shred my hands and feet again," I scoffed.

"Here we are," Emrys stated, clearing his throat. He gave us a pointed look and Idris immediately adopted a dangerous, frigid mask. I tilted my head and glanced between the two of them. Maintaining a mask of any kind was *not* my forte.

Do not worry about it. Your role is to stay by my side, be beautiful, and look for threats to us both, Idris reassured me, pulling me into the throne room with him. The nobles bowed deeply to their king as we passed them. Most kept their expressions passive, but a few shot me venomous glares or lecherous looks. *Perhaps it is time I redistributed wealth and status...*

How about we worry about how we're going to deal with the Issradians first? I stated dryly, watching as Idris took a seat on his throne. He watched me with an amused smile. *And what am I supposed to do now, exactly?*

Tradition would dictate you sit at my feet, Idris replied, flicking a dangerous glare somewhere behind me. *If that is unacceptable, you may stand to my left or perhaps drape yourself over my lap.*

I bit back a snarky comment, smoothed my expression over, and took a seat on the highest step of Idris' throne. He let out a low chuckle and briefly ran his fingers along one of my horns before turning his attention toward Elidyr. A moment later, the brooding man strode over with a few cushions for me. I took them with mumbled thanks and adjusted myself so that I was sitting on one hip and facing Idris' long legs.

There were few other options without cramping my tail.

Relax, Cerys, he purred, running his fingers through my hair. *If you are too tense the Issradians will grow suspicious.*

Getting comfortable with a tail is hard, okay?! I shot him an irritated pout, causing him to pause—but it didn't last. An entertained smile spread across his face and he brushed some of my hair out of my face.

You really are more comfortable with me now, aren't you? Idris moved his hand away and shot me a small smile. *I would like to discuss the matter more with you, but perhaps it can wait. Until this business is over, I can be satisfied knowing that if you choose to push me away again…it will truly be your choice.*

Assuming this comrade of hers even did the job properly this time.

I bit back a snort.

"Your Majesty, you truly intend for this woman to be First Consort?" One of the nobles stepped forward, speaking in troubled tones. "As a champion…"

"As a champion she deserves all the help we can give her, no?" Idris shot the man an amiable smile. "Your concern is noted. However, I could not possibly allow Cerys to be assigned lower status—*because* she is our champion."

I glanced up at Idris when his tone shifted to one of menace. It wasn't directed at the noble who had approached us, nor any of those behind him. The incubi in the room tensed ever-so-slightly, shooting uneasy glances toward the door. When Idris noticed my questioning glance, a smile flitted across his lips and he slid his fingers through my hair again, taking care not to bump into my horns.

They sent scouts ahead of them into the palace, he offered, his expression pleasant but otherwise unreadable. *I would have liked to have had a proper seat prepared for you before their arrival…I hope you can forgive me for having you sit there.*

A 'proper' seat would be too suspicious if you want to maintain this harem scheme, I pointed out, turning my gaze away from him and toward the greater room. *…how long until I'm capable of detecting or seeing through stealth?*

You will be able to sense them once you reach Journeyman, but seeing them comes much later, Idris murmured, continuing to stroke my hair. I didn't want to admit it, but I enjoyed the attention. Though I probably would have enjoyed it more if I'd known whether the gesture was genuine or simply for show.

"Ahhh, the beast's cage is as extravagant as ever!" a familiar voice echoed loudly from somewhere down the hall. I tensed, instinctively clutching Idris' leg. "If the prideful creatures didn't expend so much of their resources on grandeur, perhaps they would be able to fight back!"

Cerys? Idris nudged one of my horns as my tail snapped back and forth.

I'm pretty sure that voice is Eadgar Odilo, the emperor's adviser, I hissed, doing my best to relax my grip on the king's leg. Even so, I wasn't confident that I could keep myself from launching myself at the bastard's throat if I *didn't* hold onto Idris in some manner. *Eadgar is the one I had to tour Darmos with. Adric was along to provide protection, but Eadgar is the one who did all the talking. And staring.*

Then it is not fear that is making you cling to me? Idris removed his hand from my head and motioned Emrys closer. The demon in question released a low growl before summoning a greataxe and resting it on the ground in front of him. *If the humans make one wrong move, they will not live to make another. On that you have my word, Cerys.*

I must ask that you do your best to conduct yourself in an unassuming way. Your fan should be in your hand, and it would be best if you appeared to be more interested in me *than these proceedings.*

And that is supposed to work how, *exactly?* I battled the urge to roll my eyes. *Idris, they already know I'm the champion. I've met this twisted animal before. Unassuming or not, I still want to rip his throat out.*

I took a deep breath, attempting to calm myself, before pulling my fan from my waistband and snapping it open. If all else failed, at least I could hide most of my expression behind it. The sensation of Idris' tail slinking around my torso startled me into glancing up at him. While the gesture itself hadn't flustered me, the look on his face sure as hell did.

Huffing, I turned my attention away from him and bristled when I caught the sound of his low chuckle. I'd have to figure out a way to get him back for this nonsense later, when it wouldn't get us into trouble with the Issradians or their spies.

"Ah, and there's the King of Beasts!" Eadgar exclaimed with false cheer as he and his escort entered the throne room. The fire in the nobles' eyes made it clear that the people of Cejari-ir were anything but defeated. How they managed to restrain themselves was beyond me. "You would keep your *champion* chained at your side? How very awful."

"Given the gods' investigation, I think we can all agree you have no right to talk to me about what is 'best' for a champion," Idris stated, his scimitar smile just as cold as the expression in his eyes. "The emperor's adviser has come all this way to oversee 'tax collection,' has he? To what do we owe this…pleasure?"

Pleasure, my ass. Sticking a cactus up my—

Cerys, please. Idris flicked one of my horns.

"I'm here to offer you a trade." Eadgar gave Idris a broad, greasy grin. "You give us your champion, Nabyr-zahn will no longer have to pay us tax."

I felt my heart leap into my throat. If I knew anything about gray area morality and trades, it was that a choice between one person and many often favored the many. After all, Idris cherished his people and wanted to protect them. I wasn't convinced that a champion was important enough for him to skip on such an opportunity.

Though it sounds too good to be true. I pursed my lips and forced myself to slow the pace of my fan while I considered it. We knew the humans of the Issradian Empire weren't trustworthy. Even if they didn't take any more tax, the offer could indicate that they were ready to move on to whatever the next stage of their plan was. Given what I'd heard while in Darmos, I was relatively sure that meant they would be seeking to wipe out the demonic races.

"And if we do not?" Idris questioned, his tail tightening around me.

"Then we will take our tax and return in another six months for more," Eadgar laughed. "And then in another six months, and another…"

How often do they usually come? I asked when I felt Idris tense further.

Once every human lifetime, Idris answered, with an almost inaudible growl.

"Don't you want to see the champions reunited in 'service' of our glorious emperor?" Eadgar sneered. I glanced to the side at Idris when I felt a shiver of rage run through his tail and down his leg alike. "A lunar elf and a succubus—"

"You will take your tax and then you will leave." Idris spoke in a tone that made the humans grow still like deer. "I will not have you or your tax stranded by the winter snows. Elidyr, how long do they have?"

"The first of the storms will arrive in two days, Your Majesty, perhaps sooner," Elidyr answered, bowing deeply.

"You would trade your people rather than lose *that*?" Eadgar spat, pointing at me.

Before any of us could react, Idris was out of his throne in his full demonic glory and had lifted the much-smaller human by the front of his gaudy robes. Eadgar's escort scrambled away from the pair, reaching for their swords, but stopped when Idris' guards moved toward them.

"'That' is Cerys Moonfire, Champion and First Consort to the King of Nabyr-zahn," Idris spat at the terrified man, his wings flexing as he adjusted his grip. "We would go to war for her and eviscerate every last human who dared stand in our way. *Remember that.*"

Idris tossed the soiled man into his guards and dashed forward, his sword appearing in hand. I cursed internally and summoned my own swords, one aimed at Idris and the rest at the humans who had moved to intercept him. The king grew still and shot a dangerous look at me over his shoulder.

"I think you've made your point—and they can't deliver the message if they're dead," I pointed out as Eadgar scooted backward on his ass, leaving a smear on the floor. He let out a feminine squeal when my sword drew closer to him. "And *you* lot are guests here. If you wouldn't let *us* get away with it while in your lands, you should refrain from doing similar here."

"Y-you would threaten—" Eadgar blubbered, raising his chin high into the air. "*I* am the emperor's adviser, woman!"

"Yes…hold your head high. I will have the chance to sever it before long." Idris shot the human one last glare before turning on his heel and stalking back toward me, his demonic form melting away. When I was satisfied the humans weren't going to attack his back, I returned my blades to my inventory. *That was a dangerous move, Cerys…but you are right. I should not kill them—yet.*

He trudged back to the throne with a fiery expression on his face, but it softened when his eyes met mine. Instead of speaking, he reached down and hoisted me up by the waist the moment he was close enough. I did my best not to fidget as he pulled me onto the throne with him. 'Not fidgeting' was the only way I knew how to react. I wanted to do more—embrace him, nuzzle him, *something*—but it didn't feel right to do so after I'd shoved him away so many times. Regardless of the cause.

However, that didn't stop me from shooting Eadgar a victorious sneer before reopening my fan and hiding my expression once again. Like a good little consort, of course. The *First* Consort.

"Emrys' men will make certain you and yours do not overstep the boundaries of our treaty," Idris informed the humans, his tone one of immense boredom. "If you do not wish to die in the storm, you had best make haste."

...and what you *did doesn't endanger the treaty?* I questioned, doubtful.

We have a reputation for acting before we think. It will be fine. He pulled me up so he could nuzzle into my shoulder, before releasing a heavy sigh. *You needn't be so concerned, Cerys. The fools chose an awful time to collect their tax and will be dealt with accordingly.*

Ah... I placed my hands on his shoulders and gave him a look. *That's all well and good, but won't they grow suspicious if you 'deal' with them? And...maybe you should let me off your lap.*

We cannot leave quite yet, and I intend for you to stay right where you are. Idris brought a hand up to my face and pulled me into a soft, brief kiss. The outraged snarl from somewhere behind us made it clear the humans hadn't left yet. "Silence, human. Cerys chose *us,* and you will not be changing that. Especially not with such vile, yet somehow childish, behavior.

"Or do you wish to contest the gods' decision?"

I glanced toward the human party as Idris loosened his grip enough to allow me to curl up next to him on the oversized throne. A small smirk coming to my lips, I hooked one leg over Idris' thigh and leaned into his torso with my bust, resting my right hand low against his abdomen. If I hadn't been so close to him, I never would have noticed the shiver that ran through him or the quiet groan that left his mouth.

More ways to play with and test him—excellent. I could get used to the whole 'First Consort' nonsense if it provided me with more opportunities like that.

"The gods..." Eadgar grew pale, his voice hoarse. He coughed into one hand, but it did nothing for his vocal cords. "We will leave tomorrow morning once our horses have rested."

The humans fled the throne room and Idris released a heavy sigh. Several long moments passed before the nobles and soldiers alike erupted into agitated mutters and snarls. I could only assume that meant the spies had also taken their leave, but I wasn't confident enough in the assumption to test my luck.

"Well then, Cerys." Idris trailed his fingers down my side as he spoke, not stopping until his hand rested on my hip. "What do you think we should do about our 'guests?' Aside from kill them, of course, as that is not an option."

"Give the Otherworlders a quest to protect Cejari-ir's citizens and *actual* guests," I suggested, glancing up at him. "That way, you can test their loyalty, protect your people, *and* still have the numbers required to protect the palace and its grounds. It would also make it clear to the Otherworlders what is going on."

"Ah, so it would…" Idris smirked and glanced over to Elidyr. "Have one of your men handle Lady Moonfire's 'quest.' Make certain that it is clear the Issradians are taking a portion of our population as 'tax' and that we are attempting to keep them from taking more than permitted."

"I will relay your orders at once, Your Majesty, Lady Moonfire." Elidyr bowed and then stepped out of sight, leaving me to shoot Idris a questioning look.

"Otherworlders are more likely to push themselves to perform well when the orders come from a beautiful woman," Idris answered my unasked question with a mischievous grin. When his gaze shifted to his court, the mirth disappeared from his expression and he turned to ice. "Make the necessary preparations for our guests, and for what may come after. I also want emissaries sent to the other kings.

"We need to know if the Issradians are forcing similar deals."

Chapter Thirty-Three
We Must Rebuild

I flipped through the pages of a massive tome, examining the diagrams and writing within. Until the rest of the palace woke up for the morning, I was stuck in the Queen's Tower, so I had decided to make the most of it. The previous day, I hadn't managed to get any studying in. After the Issradians had left the throne room, Idris had kept me with him throughout the entirety of his duties for the day.

Much to my surprise, he and the nobles didn't appear cross that I'd kept him from killing Eadgar. Rather, it was the opposite. They all knew how bad it would have been if Idris' actions had caused an early war and were thankful I had managed to stop him.

Unfortunately, the rest of Idris' duties for the day had been related to more mundane internal workings. With the influx of Otherworlder citizens in Cejari-ir, the demons were quick to begin expanding their infrastructure. From what I understood, much of the rush was to prepare and secure extra supplies for the winter. More homes had to be built, along with all the magitech plumbing and heating they required.

While I wanted to learn more about my new home, I'd chosen to study the documentation on Shadowdancers for the morning. To some extent, I had hoped that they would work like books in life simulators, where simply reading would gradually increase my proficiency in the topic. Alas, they were more like skill books in RPGs—except with dozens of skills within them, and requiring study.

The more I read and studied, the more knowledge I gained regarding skills past Shadowdancers had created and used. Some of it was useless to me without a different set of base proficiencies, so much of it I skipped. Nearby, I had a stack of paper and a pen so that I could transcribe what I *could* use. The organization of the tomes was utterly unacceptable to me.

"Someone is focused this morning." The comment made me glance toward my bedroom door in surprise. Idris smiled when he saw my expression, but made no effort to move from where he was leaning against the door frame. "Are you not cold?"

"No, I'm not," I replied, shifting my attention back to my pen and the nearest sheet of paper.

"And what are you studying?" he inquired, pushing away from the door frame. He strode over and laughed when I swatted at him with my tail. "You are getting used to your new body then? Good."

"Shadowdancers." I lifted one of the closed books in my left hand, offering it to him, while I continued writing with the other. "I woke up earlier than I would have liked, so I decided to spend the morning making up for yesterday's lost time. Right now, I'm working out which abilities actually matter to me. Many of these require a ranged weapon, or dual-magic specializations, and so on."

"Should I come back later?" Idris questioned, catching my tail in one hand when it swayed toward him again. I shot him a questioning look, so he continued, "It would be best if the First Consort joins me in seeing the Issradians off, but if you would rather not, excuses can be made."

"They're actually preparing to leave?" I arched an eyebrow at him, unable to read his expression. "Or are they being thrown out?"

"Throwing them out would be just as problematic as if I had taken Eadgar's head," he replied, his mouth curving into an amused smile. "You were right to suggest we give the Otherworlders a 'quest' to protect the city from the Issradians. My men report that all the Otherworlder spies have been dealt with, leaving only the natives. The Otherworlders were furious to learn of the tax.

"While I am glad…I do not understand why they would react in such a way if they believe our world is a fictional one."

"I'm not sure how to explain that one to you," I remarked, scooting toward the edge of the bed. When Idris didn't move, I nudged the side of his thigh with one foot. When he only shot me a questioning look, I prodded him in the chest. "If I'm going to come along and play 'First Consort,' I'll need to get dressed."

"Ah, so you will join me?" He smiled and took a step away, giving me just enough room to climb out of the bed. I sure didn't miss the glint in his gaze while he looked down at me. Whether or not he was *too* interested, I had yet to decide. "The Otherworlders do have a reason to care, at least?"

"Well… Have you heard of a concept called 'role-playing?'" I asked, glancing back at him briefly before walking into the wardrobe.

"No, but the term sounds self-explanatory," Idris answered as he leaned against the door frame to watch me.

"Let's take *Bengllor Online* as an example, since you played that," I began, sorting through a drawer of undergarments. "That type of game is called a VRMMORPG—which stands for 'Virtual Reality Massively Multiplayer Online Role-Playing Game.' VRMMO or MMO for short. 'Role-Playing Games' all have a common thread of really in-depth world building and story for the players to get involved in. Your standard player won't get too hardcore into the role-playing side of things, but when a game is faction-based, just about everyone forms loyalties and emotional investments in the side they picked.

"So, with *Jeriskyr Online*, the Issradian Empire is a dominant faction with questionable morality at best. Many people play games to escape reality or, 'being human,' so even if the Otherworlders currently in Cejari-ir aren't role players at heart, they still have an emotional attachment to the faction they chose to play with their friends."

"A bond which can be strengthened?" Idris murmured, his gaze flicking briefly down to my legs when I bent over to pull up my panties. "Then, even though they are unaware that Jeriskyr is real, it is possible to get the Otherworlders just as invested as we are."

"Maybe even more." I shot him an amused smile before turning away to look for something suitable to wear. "Otherworlders respawn. In games with difficult content, if the game's systems allow it, you'll often find that large guilds will employ death rush strategies against difficult foes."

"Death rush?" Idris arched an eyebrow, then shook his head. "You will want to dress more warmly than that, kitten. It is snowing."

"Oh." I glanced at the skimpy dress in my hands and pouted before returning it to its hanger. "A death rush is where people will die and immediately run back to whatever they're fighting, often with some form of coordinated effort or strategic value. For example, in *Bengllor Online,* mages and healers have a limited pool of mana to cast spells with. When you die and respawn, it's refilled back to full.

"So, mana-using classes will sometimes strategically rotate their deaths and run back to the boss. In some cases, death rushes are combined with zergs—a zerg being such a massive number of people that you can get away with ignoring most mechanics."

"Mechanics?" Idris echoed.

"Ah—different sorts of attacks and such. You played the tutorial, right? So, you saw the indicators for the tutorial boss' huge swings." I crossed my arms while looking at my selection of clothes. 'Stay warm' and 'First Consort' were completely opposite notions in my mind. "Anyway, the point is, if a battle takes place close enough to a respawn point or they have a way to travel quickly, it's akin to having an immortal army.

"Have the Issradians not employed such tactics in your skirmishes?"

"No…but perhaps that is because they are few in number?" Idris offered, his expression contemplative. "You mentioned that there weren't many Issradian 'players' capable of killing—and that it may be due to how the Issradians test the Otherworlders. As far as I am aware, there have never been enough of them. The few who are capable are often relegated to the rear guard."

"The Issradian military is likely what, a few tens of thousands in strength?" I murmured, mostly to myself, but Idris voiced his agreement as he strode over to me. "Okay, I don't know how many Otherworlders have purchased the game yet or how many will, so take these numbers with a grain of salt.

"Let's say that two million players roll characters in the Issradian faction and only two percent are capable of combat. That's still forty thousand potential soldiers for the Issradians to utilize. However, it's unlikely *that* many people will be online at any given time."

"Here." Idris pulled a pair of leggings out of a nearby drawer, followed by an elaborate dress with long sleeves. It certainly looked warm, at least. "Given your numbers, we can expect a large boost in the Issradian military's strength." He paused when he noticed me wince. "What is it?"

"Well... The numbers could be much higher than that." I sighed, tugging the leggings on. "Let's take one of the most popular early MMOs. Its peak subscriber count was around twelve million—with some uneven split between the game's two factions.

"Jeriskyr has more than two factions, and Earth's population is several billion larger than it was back then. Right now, the game is probably still in beta, so what we see in Cejari-ir right now is a fraction of what we're going to see when the game officially launches. That's probably part of the reason you've got Otherworlders asking for building permits, people who want to make the Veilwood Forest a little better, and so on."

"That is..." Idris fell silent and sunk into deep thought while I finished getting dressed. Instead of pestering him, I poked around in search of gloves and knee-high boots. "I am uncertain how we're meant to support so many people."

"Manipulate the system," I suggested, pulling my gloves on as I walked over to him. "Instead of telling Otherworlders there's no room for them, give them quests to gather and hunt for supplies to *make* room. Players love housing—especially if they can build and then keep their own. Guilds also like having guild manors or other such communal buildings where they can house their entire guild instead of requiring individual houses for hundreds of people.

"You have city planners, architects, and engineers, right?"

"Of course," he nodded.

"Then have them begin making preparations for Cejari-ir to expand by several times its current size," I suggested. "The city's current position is easily defendable due to its mountainous location, but that also means you'll need careful planning for the city to grow. It's going to need new tiers, new districts, and some new infrastructure may need to be relocated underground. Large constructions such as guild manors may need to be built outside of the city somewhere instead of in it."

"Regardless, we will have to hope that the Otherworlder craftsmen learn quickly," Idris pointed out, crossing his arms as he examined me. "Will you continue helping me to understand the Otherworlders and their needs? If we are to keep them, and ask them to help us against the Issradians, it would be best if their loyalty is genuine."

"Hmmm? Of course I will." I shot him a perplexed look. "Should we get going?"

"Perhaps so. The sooner we make them leave, the sooner you can have breakfast," he remarked, shooting me a knowing smile. "I wish to show you the view of the valley below, as well."

"I also need to train, though," I pointed out, following him through the suite and out of the Queen's Tower.

"We can find breakfast in the city and continue where our date left off," Idris suggested, chuckling. "Of course, it will not be much of a date with Elidyr and Emrys escorting us—but that is a necessary evil. There could be more filth lying in wait."

"That doesn't cover the training problem." I rolled my eyes at his back.

"By the time we return to the palace, our food should have settled and we can spar together if nothing else comes up," Idris offered. "Perhaps I should think of a reward for you as well."

"A reward? For what?" I released an exasperated sigh. *Okay, he's right that we shouldn't train immediately after eating. Even so, why does he want to show me the view from Cejari-ir's outskirts so much? That doesn't seem like something I would need to know unless there's military significance—or perhaps he just wants to show off?*

"Your Majesty, Lady Moonfire," Emrys acknowledged us when we reached the bottom of the tower's stairs. "The Issradians are impatient to leave. Looks like the threat of the storm—and your combined threats—put them in their place."

Combined threats? I wondered, before glancing at the chuckling Idris.

Swaying the decision of an enemy they fear means only one thing to them, Idris commented as we followed Emrys. *To them, it means that you have some manner of power over me—a power that you could turn against them if they cross you.*

"We have finished our preparations and we have men on their way to speak with the other kings and their courts as we speak," Elidyr informed us as he joined us. "The Otherworlders loyal to us have unearthed more spies within Cejari-ir's walls, as have our men. We have taken the Jeriskyr natives elsewhere for...*questioning.*"

"And the Issradians are none the wiser?" Idris smirked.

"We believe so, Your Majesty," Elidyr nodded. "The Otherworlders are already clamoring for more work."

"Good—we will be addressing that soon enough." Idris nodded his approval, glancing down at me. "What do you think, Cerys? What manner of task shall we give them next?"

"Dangerous ones, if this storm is as problematic as you made it seem," I answered pointedly. "Since they can respawn, and the temperatures won't affect 'players' to the same degree as they will you, they shouldn't have any issues working in the cold. Hunting, foraging, quarrying—there should be a decent number of Otherworlders who've decided to focus on those types of proficiencies. Your citizens *and* the Otherworlders alike are going to need resources.

"I've never been the best when it comes to economy, but with the information I gave you earlier, building up Cejari-ir's stores as well as providing the craftsmen with what they need seems prudent."

"Your Majesty?" Elidyr tilted his head, looking to Idris.

"I will brief you later—suffice to say we should expect a drastic increase in our Otherworlder population soon, and we must prepare," Idris answered, narrowing his eyes at his aide. "Send your men to consult with the Grandmasters, craftsmen, and combatants alike. We will likely need our combat-ready Otherworlders to procure materials for us as well."

"Monster drops?" I inquired, feeling a familiar itch. "So—"

"Once the Issradians are gone, and you have reached your next tier of proficiency, I will *consider* bringing you on a hunt—if the weather holds." Idris shot me a knowing look. "My men and I will not be idle either. There are some marks that we cannot expect the Otherworlders to handle so soon, and we will need the hides, horns, claws, fangs, and other parts of such beasts."

"Good eats, too." Emrys grinned broadly.

"That was a lot of 'ifs,'" I grumbled.

The four of us made our way down the road and into the city proper, surrounded by a slow but steady drift of small snowflakes. Only a dusting had coated the ground thus far, yet everywhere I looked, people appeared to be preparing for much more than that. There were people ferrying logs, others chopping them, and some appeared to be making certain their windows were properly sealed.

It didn't take long for us to find the Issradians and the incubi they would be taking to Darmos with them. I had expected the volunteers to look depressed, broken, or at least something unpleasant. Instead, they stood tall and proud, towering over their human captors. Many of the Issradians barely came up to the chests of the demons, and most were shorter than that.

Hell, most of the human soldiers only came up to my tits and I was supposedly 'short' for a succubus.

"Humph, the 'First Consort' has clothing on this time," one of the human soldiers muttered, earning snickers from his comrades. The demons, on the other hand, looked much like they were dealing with testy children.

"You really won't trade us the woman?" Eadgar crossed his arms, giving us an impatient look as we approached. "One woman, or—"

"You are asking us to trade *our champion*, knowing full well what would happen to her if we did." Idris spoke in a level tone that seemed to scare the humans even more than his outburst the previous day. "With no guarantee that you or your gods will change your ways. We will not accept your 'offer.' Cerys will be remaining here."

"You've got balls of steel, lad," Eadgar gaped, glancing at the chained demons near him. "Flat out telling these *poor* boys you're throwing them away? *Tch*, it's no wonder your kind—"

"They made their choice and I will not dishonor them by nullifying it." Idris tucked me slightly behind him. He glanced briefly to his left when thunder rumbled in the distance, then settled his dangerous gaze on the humans. "You have what you came for. *Leave.*"

"Bastard…" Eadgar scowled, curling his hands into fists before turning to give his men their orders. "We will be back in another six months."

"My lord, that isn't what the emperor…" a guard spoke quietly, seeming to think we couldn't hear him. The fat man hurriedly shushed him before clambering into his carriage. The rest of the escort mounted their horses and soon began to move off at a slow pace.

The demons who had volunteered as 'tax' gave us subtle nods and bows as they shambled after the carriage. I clenched my teeth, unsure how to feel about the situation. Sure, they had volunteered with full knowledge of what they were getting themselves into…but that didn't make it any less difficult to watch the humans march them off toward the city gates.

You needn't be so concerned. Idris slid an arm behind my back, but his gaze was still on the caravan. *The men who volunteered did so to act as informants. They are fully prepared to serve Nabyr-zahn from within the empire's borders.*

If the weather does not kill their captors, that is.

"Shall I investigate, Your Majesty?" Elidyr bowed to Idris, an insidious smile on his lips.

"Once we have returned to the palace for the day, yes," Idris nodded. "For now, it is high time Lady Moonfire had breakfast and saw the valley below. Let us be off."

By the time we reached the park at the city's edge, I had something in my hand that could only be described as breakfast in a cone. A pancake cone. Well, it tasted better than a pancake really—and it was thicker. Inside were fresh berries, savory meats, and a drizzle of a sweet sauce. I'd been skeptical at first, but after the first two bites, I'd decided I could live on this sort of food alone if I had to. It was like dipping bacon in maple syrup, but better.

Even Elidyr seemed less cranky as he ate his.

"So, the entire outer rim of the city is a park? Or garden?" I asked as we walked down a cobblestone pathway. Many of the shrubs appeared to be speckled with vibrantly-colored berries beneath a dusting of snow. Some of the evergreen trees appeared to have some manner of large fruit hanging from them as well.

"The parks throughout Cejari-ir are home to cultivated varieties of edible plants, Lady Moonfire," Elidyr offered, motioning to a fruit almost the size of his head. "Due to the danger of allowing our citizens to roam outside the city on their own, we chose to bring many of the otherwise-wild flora within our walls. Other tiers of the city house farmland, livestock, and other sources of food."

"Other sources?" I arched an eyebrow.

"Hothouses," Idris answered, drawing my attention to him.

"Oh. We call those greenhouses sometimes, but same thing." I tilted my head in thought. "So, do you use those to grow out of season crops, or ones from other regions?"

"Both." Elidyr looked relieved that I understood the concept. "With this influx you spoke of, we will have to calculate how much expansion must be done. Hunting will only cover so much, and then there's the issue of lumber..."

"The Veilwood Forest is off limits," Idris stated when he caught my puzzled expression. "We should avoid conflict with the forest's protectors."

"So, trees don't respawn, then?" I pursed my lips, ignoring their dubious glances. "Well, that confirms what I was told before coming to Jeriskyr at least. Doesn't help much with the lumber issue, though..."

"Another quirk of games?" Idris sighed at me.

"Yes, most games don't have realistic growth cycles. Resources usually respawn in five to ten minutes. Rare ones take longer, or only at certain times of day," I nodded, watching him grimace. "Right now, most of Nabyr-zahn's population lives within Cejari-ir, right? Perhaps instead of attempting to expand the city to accommodate the equivalent of an entire country's worth of Otherworlders, you should permit them to establish towns and villages throughout Nabyr-zahn."

"Lady Moonfire has a point," Elidyr murmured, rubbing his chin as Idris frowned. "The abandoned villages will need to be rebuilt if we intend to take back our people from the Issradians, and the Otherworlders are thirsty for work."

"And Otherworlders can't be taken by the 'tax,' right?" I pointed out.

"We will go over it during tonight's meeting," Idris nodded, nudging me with his tail. "For now, turn your attention away from work and gaze upon Nabyr-zahn, Cerys. You have seen our city, but not our lands."

I glanced at him briefly, but he prodded me in the direction of a nearby stone railing instead. Before I had even reached it fully I realized why he'd seemed so insistent on showing me.

Below us sprawled a wide gap between two mountains and a perilous, winding road leading to the city itself. Several more circular tiers of Cejari-ir rested below us, filled to the brim with agriculture, places for processing materials, and other important industry that would have otherwise bothered the city's inhabitants with noise or fumes.

Beyond Cejari-ir's final tier, a series of waterfalls gushed from beneath it to feed the valley the mountains bordered. Despite the accumulating snow, I could make out dark purple foliage peeking out between many rivers and streams. At the base of one of the mountains was what I could only assume was the beginning of the

Veilwood Forest. Its ancient trees rose high into the air, shedding the last of their autumn leaves.

Deeper into the valley, I thought I could make out large stone formations, but I couldn't be sure. It was too far. The snow and clouds both obscured my vision any further.

"If *this* is what your home looks like, then I'm fairly certain you should've been in far more shock during your visit to Earth," I stated, shifting to look up at Idris. When I saw the look on his face, I tilted my head slightly and studied him. His expression was pleasant, soft...perhaps even adoring. Why he was looking at *me* like *that* when there was such incredible scenery to look at instead was difficult for me to process.

I knew what that sort of expression meant from a human man on Earth. But from an incubus who lived on Jeriskyr? Even if it was the same...well, if I was being honest, I didn't know what to do about it. Cultural protocols and all that.

"Your world shares similarities with Issradian lands," Idris offered, his mouth quirking into an amused smile. "Many of our skirmishes and other conflicts have occurred on their soil. Earth's buildings and technology were what startled me, more than anything."

"Here, a moonfire lily for Lady Moonfire."

Idris shifted to face me fully and offered me a single flower. I took the large flower and looked down at it with surprise. His reasoning for giving me that name finally made sense. Its petals were a brilliant opal and each was streaked with a splash of color down its center. The strong citrusy scent wafting from it would have made a *fantastic* perfume.

"You weren't kidding." I arched an eyebrow at him before remembering my manners and shooting him a small smile. "Thank you for the flower—and for the food too, of course."

"You are quite welcome." Idris chuckled and leaned down to kiss my forehead briefly before putting an arm around me, leading me down the path once more. *It would have been much better if we did not have company, but alas…*

"We should be returning to the palace, Your Majesty." Emrys cleared his throat and shot us a pointed look. "That goes double if you still want to give Lady Moonfire a sparring lesson before seeing to your appointments."

"Yes, yes, of course." Idris released a reluctant sigh. "Cerys, after our lesson is concluded I want you to continue training. After we spar I will have more detailed instructions for what you need to work on—be it sparring with my men or working on the skills you were studying this morning."

"We're going to change clothes first, right?" I glanced down at my dress and then at his heavy royal finery.

"Aye, you two've got plenty of time—if we head back now." Emrys shot Idris another look before returning his attention to me. "I'll be assigning someone to keep watch while you train until we're satisfied the Issradians and their spies are truly gone."

Bleh. I bit back a grimace and simply nodded to him instead. *Okay, so heavy focus on training. Let's see if I can make it so being babysat isn't a necessity.*

Cerys, I am a Grandmaster *and they still insist on protecting me in much the same way.* A low chuckle escaped Idris as he gave me a brief squeeze. *It is Emrys' job to worry about us both. Try not to be too harsh on him.*

...so, if we kill all the threats... I suggested.

You are getting ahead of yourself, he reprimanded me, but his expression was full of mirth and admiration. *We shall focus on securing Alice's safety first. Then we can consider our long-term plans.*

Any word on Alice yet? I prompted, glancing up at him again.

Only that she and Ryan are continuing to run Ebonwing in your absence, and that she is being protected by the guild—some manner of quest they were assigned, Idris offered, his expression contemplative. *The gods should be concluding their investigation soon. Whether or not the humans will do as they're told, however...*

Right. So, we need to figure out a sneaky way to remove her, and maybe all of Ebonwing, from the empire. I pursed my lips, considering it. That could be difficult, but not at all impossible as far as I was concerned. Convincing Ebonwing to change sides would be fairly easy.

You are ambitious, Idris remarked dryly.

Of course! As First Consort *I have to make a name for myself.* I smirked when I felt him twitch.

You have already achieved that, I assure you, Idris chuckled. *It is not every day that someone is capable of stopping King Bloodsong. For better or for worse, you will have gotten the attention of many with your behavior during yesterday's meeting.*

King Bloodsong *included,* I pointed out.

Indeed—something you had *been against drawing.* Idris remarked.

Silly me! I exclaimed sarcastically, before giving him a sultry smile. *I've decided having your attention isn't bad at all—when it's focused on me, at least.*

I will keep that in mind. Idris smirked, his tail brushing against mine briefly before he turned to glance over his shoulder at his guard and his aide. "The two of you are dawdling. I can hardly give you further instructions when you linger so far behind."

"Our apologies, Your Majesty," they replied in unison, soon hurrying to fall into step with us.

"Good. I am going to give you both more details from the conversation Cerys and I had this morning. Tomorrow, I expect you to both provide me with proposals for more quests we can assign the Otherworlders." Idris paused to give them a pointed look. "We will rebuild Nabyr-zahn, even if it requires their help. It would not do for our captured people to have no homes to return to."

Chapter Thirty-Four
A Slime is Fine Too

Idris' sword flew past my face, leaving the air sizzling in its wake. I shoved his sword arm away with one hand, grabbed his wrist, and jammed the ridge of one foot into his ribs. Dark butterflies exploded outward from my foot when the strike connected. He bent over from the force, but I didn't let him pull his wrist out of my grip. Instead, I shifted, using his momentum and a burst of shadow magic to toss him.

My three practice swords whirled around me, deflecting the quick jabs of one of his blades. Two of my commissioned swords sped toward Idris, piercing the spot where I had landed. When I felt the air ripple in front of me, I brought up my warfan and intercepted his downward strike.

"You are much better at this than I expected," Idris remarked, his lips pulling into a lazy smile. "In a few years, perhaps, you will be able to hold your own against my full strength."

"A few years?" I sighed. "I know you're holding back because this is just practice and I've just begun, but—"

"Should I show you just how much you have yet to overcome?" Idris chuckled, gripping my chin in a movement faster than I could follow. "*On your knees.*"

Everything ground to a halt. Vaguely, I was aware of the sound of my weapons clattering to the ground and of my knees sinking into the sand. I could feel Idris' presence, but it was like all thought processes beyond physical touch had stopped. My eyes were open, yet I couldn't register anything they saw. It was all just…blank, awaiting another command.

One that never came.

Idris' fingers slid through my hair, pushing it back between my horns as he sung a few brief words in a foreign language. The moment the last word left his tongue, my senses returned, and I looked up to give him an indignant glare.

"Dirgeweavers such as myself are far more dangerous than you give us credit for, Cerys." Idris chuckled, dismissed his sword, then offered me his hand. "You are a woman who learns best through action, and such a power is difficult to explain through words besides."

"Oh yes, the spellsinger-bard-king-whatever can tell his consort to get on her knees, yet he couldn't have simply said, 'certain proficiencies are capable of rendering your mind useless, kitten.'" I snorted, allowing him to pull me to my feet.

"Perhaps I will make it up to you," he remarked, a suggestive smile on his face as he brushed my hair back again. "Once I am done with my duties for the day, and once you have finished with your training, that is."

"Make it up to me *how*?" I gave him a suspicious look as he gripped my hips and pulled me closer. He bit his lower lip, glancing at my mouth then back up to my eyes.

"I believe you understood me perfectly." He leaned down and pressed his lips against mine. Just when I started to kiss him back, he pulled away with a teasing smile on his lips. Instead of moving away, he shifted to whisper in my ear, "Perhaps we can break in *your* bed next…"

His husky tone sent a shiver down my spine. I caught a glimmer of enticing mischief in his eyes as he turned to leave the sparring area. Shaking my head, I reclaimed my weapons and dismissed them to my inventory before following him.

"Now that you've fought me yourself, what sort of training do you want me to focus on?" I asked, stretching my arms above my head. Despite holding back, he'd gotten me good a few times. I could tell I was going to be sore soon enough.

"You are not going to give me an answer now?" Idris shot me a subtle smile.

"…I'm withholding judgment."

"Would another night with me be unpleasant?"

"No, quite the opposite, I'm sure," I replied dryly, crossing my arms when he shot me a questioning look. "It's a question of whether I'll still feel like it, and whether I'll be too sore, by the time you come by."

"I will not have you go easy on your training just because you 'might' be too sore to indulge later," Idris informed me, laughing. "Alas, duty calls, and I will need to bathe before I join my subjects.

"You should experiment with your skills for the remainder of the afternoon, and you have my permission to use the magitech targets for additional challenge. Since you do not flinch when attacked, you are quick, and you have good instincts, I am comfortable having you familiarize yourself with specific techniques instead of sparring away bad habits."

"Okay, for the afternoon, you said?" I murmured.

"*Within reason.*" Idris gave me a sharp look. "I intend to join you for dinner once my meetings are finished. Perhaps another game while we wind down for the night…assuming you decide you do not mind company."

"Company does sound nice." I tilted my head. "I do want to play another match or two of that game as well."

"Then I will see you later tonight," Idris stated, a warm,

relieved smile spreading across his face. He glanced toward a pair of nearby guards next. "Once Lady Moonfire is finished with her training, escort her back to the Queen's Tower. I am not convinced that all the Issradian and Otherworlder spies are gone."

Once Idris had departed, I strode from the sparring area over to where rows of training dummies sat. With no idea how the magitech ones worked, I soon found myself waving the guards over to help me set them up.

"Is there anything else you require, Lady Moonfire?" one of them asked, hesitating to return to his post once they had finished.

"Well, if I'm going to be training for the remainder of the afternoon... Water." I flung one of my floating swords at the moving target and released a sigh when it only grazed the edge. My concentration and control over magic seemed to be better when I was in danger—or at least while sparring. "I'm going to need to do a lot of work, it seems."

"You will be fine, Lady Moonfire!" one of the guards asserted, a bright smile on his face. "If you need anything at all, simply call and we will be happy to assist you. After all, you will soon need actual opponents. Dummies are good practice, but you have moved beyond increasing your proficiency against them."

"Then I may ask you to spar with me later, or to find someone who will." I looked between the two guards, sizing them up. They were smaller than Idris, but only by a few inches. If I were to spar with them, I'd be at a disadvantage regarding reach. Even if incubi and succubi were close in physical ability, trained soldiers would obviously be stronger than my 'new' body.

They both bowed to me before returning to their posts. After exchanging a few words, one went to look for water or a servant, leaving the other to keep an eye on me. I wasn't happy with the idea of being watched at all times, but there was little I could do about it. Even if I didn't like the situation, I knew it was for my own safety and that their concern was warranted. After all, even if the Issradians themselves couldn't easily sneak into the palace, Otherworlders likely could.

Sighing, I turned my focus to the spinning discs above one of the training dummies. It seemed like an utter pain, but I didn't have a better idea. I needed to be capable under any circumstances, not just when I felt threatened. After all, if I wanted to ambush or otherwise catch someone unaware, I needed to be able to aim properly. A twitch ran through me and I flung one of my swords at the discs again. This time, it landed closer to my target but not in the center like I'd wanted.

Either way, it didn't *feel* like progress to me. Playing with magitech dummies was incredibly dissatisfying. Sure, it was good target practice and much safer than aiming my pointy swords at an actual person…but good lord, was it boring. Frustrated, I decided to try multitasking instead. Float all my swords, go through my martial arts forms, and weave both spells and my blades toward the targets.

"How graceful!" a voice exclaimed from nearby. I whirled around, aiming all my swords at the voice's owner. It took me a moment to place his face, but I chose not to lower my weapons. Tegau, Grandmaster of Magics, simply grinned at me and clapped his hands together in delight. "You are doing well, I see, Lady Moonfire! I simply couldn't resist the urge to come check in on your progress any longer. Not after hearing about your display in court."

"You've heard about that?" I grimaced.

"Darling, *everyone* has heard about it!" Tegau laughed. He pushed away from the wall and strode toward me. "His Majesty should be ashamed of himself, trapping the beautiful butterfly here where she can't truly spread her wings."

"My lord, His Majesty's chief concern is Lady Moonfire's safety," one of my guards sighed at the Grandmaster. "The Issradians—"

"And what could their spies do against a champion and a Grandmaster?" Tegau scoffed, waving a dismissive hand. "Lady Moonfire requires real opponents. That much is clear from watching her. We can hardly have our champion die from boredom."

"While I don't disagree—" I started to protest.

"Put away your weapons, Lady Moonfire!" Tegau gave me a broad, mischievous grin. "We are going to go test your abilities against something with a little more oomph. You hardly need His

Majesty's coddling."

The moment my weapons disappeared, the Grandmaster sprang forward and pulled me into a pillar of light with him. When my vision recovered, I shivered and glanced up with a sharp glare. Tegau's cheerful expression didn't falter. Instead, he procured a cloak from his inventory and offered it to me. I set aside my indignation for the moment and examined our surroundings. We were in a forest somewhere and there was no snow on the ground. It was cold, but sunny. However, there were no birds chirping or any other sounds to indicate animals.

"Where are we?" I frowned at Tegau, watching as he pulled on a pair of thick leather gloves.

"The southern reaches of the Veilwood Forest," Tegau began, flexing his fingers a few times. "The Mages' Guild received a request to clear out monsters who have been making it difficult for Otherworlders to build nearby. Normally I'd send some of our recruits to deal with it, but this seemed like an excellent opportunity to test the *famed* First Consort."

"So...you want me to kill stuff?" I tilted my head, watching the incubus grin cheerfully. "And you somehow thought whisking me away without His Majesty's permission was a good idea?"

"You will be fine!" Tegau laughed. "Here, draw your swords. We are looking for wood slimes. More often than not, we use fire to hunt such creatures. However, you have chosen to use shadow magic and a less traditional form of spellsword. You need to learn to make your darkness mimic other elements."

"…slimes. Okay." I chewed on the inside of my cheek and followed the incubus as he skipped through the underbrush. *I've seen way too much hentai. Hopefully not* that *kind of slimes, as funny as that could be. I wonder…if they* are *that kind of slime, could I tame one and keep it as a pet? To use in 'questioning' people, of course.*

I didn't have any other brilliant options, so I followed Tegau through the forest and kept my attention on our surroundings. The silence of the forest made me uneasy, though the Grandmaster appeared completely at ease. He juggled several balls of flame in one hand as we walked, his expression infuriatingly cheerful. Whatever his relationship with Idris was, I couldn't believe Tegau might consider his behavior acceptable. Given how intent Idris was on protecting me, I had a feeling he'd tear into Tegau once he realized who was responsible for whisking me away from the palace. Though I hoped he wouldn't punish my guards too badly.

"Ahhh, there's one!" Tegau exclaimed, putting an arm around my shoulders. He pointed toward a clearing, while I just stared in disbelief. "There, a wood slime. I could kill it with ease, but that wouldn't be of any use to you. Fight it, and I will observe. If it becomes too dangerous, I will kill the creature for you, darling."

"And you want me to kill this with shadow…flames?" I sighed in exasperation. "How am I supposed to do that? It's the size of a house!"

"Easily! You summon your shadows with the intent to inflict

burns on your foe." Tegau gave me an encouraging smile. "Perhaps you shall become Cerys Shadowflame if you perfect the art? Ah! Or if you are *truly* talented, you will learn to make your shadows mimic any number of elements. Now then, shoo! Show the wood slime what Lady Moonfire is capable of!"

Of all the instructors... I sighed and settled my gaze on the gargantuan slime. A mere thought was all it took to make darkness engulf my floating blades, but I had no idea how I was meant to turn the shadows into flames. Willing them to burn seemed too simple and I doubted whether the Grandmaster was truly the straightforward sort. After all, he was even more ridiculous than Idris had been on Earth.

Even so, I decided to take the chance and do as Tegau had said. I didn't have a better idea of how to make shadows take on flame-like properties, so why not give him the benefit of doubt, right? I redirected one of my swords to float in front of me before concentrating on the desire to burn the wood slime into oblivion.

The creature was dark brown and covered in what looked to be moss, mushrooms, and broken pieces of trees. It appeared to be eating a fallen tree, though I saw what looked to be humanoid bones floating inside its body. Good enough reason to kill it. My butterflies swirled more quickly around my sword, leaving threads of flame-like darkness in their wake. When I was satisfied with the amount, I shot the sword through the slime's body.

The creature squealed in pain, briefly forming spikes on the surface of its body before firing them outward. I motioned with one hand, summoning a wall of darkness in front of me while calling my weapon back with the other. Grimacing, I summoned shadowy flames around both my swords and struck the creature again. This time, it rolled toward me. I leapt out of its way and summoned my warfan from my inventory, calling forth a blast of darkness as I waited for my swords to return to me. The darkness struck the moss on the slime's back and caught it alight with black flames. However, that wasn't enough to kill the creature. Instead, it split into dozens of smaller slimes, shedding the burning moss.

«You have successfully learned Darkflame Flourish»

«Shadow Magic Proficiency has increased to 160»

«Shadowdancer proficiency has reached 148»

Ugh, I'm doing a terrible job of keeping all three skills even! I whined internally. Shadow magic was now my highest at a hundred and sixty, while spellsword was a hundred and fifty-five and Chrastr-gok had stalled out at a hundred and thirty. I'd originally wanted to keep them even, yet I'd had to focus harder on shadow magic and spellsword because they were so…new. Chrastr-gok, at least, shared similarities with Earth martial arts.

"Okay…and how do I kill the baby ones?" I asked, but no answer came. Tegau just grinned from where he'd hopped onto a tree branch and continued swinging his legs back and forth like a child. Sighing, I quickly counted the slimes, losing track around thirty. I definitely did *not* have thirty swords. Instead, I needed a way to bunch them up and execute them all at once.

Okay, Cerys, think. Darkness in most games usually has certain properties attached to it, right? Flames, ice, lightning, whatever, are all common forms for darkness to take on. What else can it do?

A grin spread across my face when it came to me. Gravity, gravity was what it could do. Spells and skills that could pull in or move targets were often dark-aspect spells in some form or another. Even if that wouldn't work, making it act like ice could potentially slow the creatures down long enough for me to kill them off. I decided to take the gravity approach first and made a downward sweeping motion with my closed fan. The ground beneath the slimes fell in on itself, creating a small 'dent' nearly the breadth of the original slime creature. The slimes attempted to roll up the edges but couldn't gain enough momentum. However, they soon began attempting to push each other up the walls.

Another motion with my fan created an orb of darkness at the center of the dent. A third swipe of my fan, and butterflies exploded outward from the sphere to form a vortex, sucking the wood slimes away from the rim and toward the orb.

Calling my swords, I summoned intense heat around them and plunged them both into the orb, creating an explosion. The slimes popped like superheated oil and soaked into the disrupted soil. Grinning, I brought my swords back to me and let them hover behind my right shoulder.

«Shadow Magic Proficiency has reached 173»

«Spellsword Proficiency has reached 172»

«Shadowdancer proficiency has reached 158»

Really? That much experience? Well, I suppose it was *a lot of monsters,* I considered, staring at the hole for a moment. *Maybe this is a 'higher level' area? Or is it from using new spells? Hmmm…*

I glanced up at Tegau as he dropped from the tree and landed next to me, a rather serious look on his face.

"Where did you learn that?" Tegau frowned at me.

"Hmmm? Learn what?" I stared at him.

"That was not standard usage of shadow magic." Tegau narrowed his eyes at me, then sighed, shaking his head. "Would this be some Otherworlder trick?"

"Well, I *was* thinking about what darkness in games can do," I offered, making him grimace. "It varies by game, but there are a lot of games where darkness is a utility element rather than an offensive one. I didn't want to be dog-piled by all those slimes, so making them stay put seemed like a good idea."

"You did a fine job, Lady Moonfire," Tegau nodded. "It is simply an odd choice of strategy. In Jeriskyr, shadow magic is almost solely used for offense or for healing. Natives certainly wouldn't have thought to use it in such a way."

"Well, if you can use it to mimic flames, then you can use it to mimic ice—and ice can be used to bind things in place, right?" I pointed out.

"Wind would have normally been used for what you just did,

but that was most certainly pure darkness. Neither fire nor wind nor ice." Tegau tilted his head for a moment, then walked over to the crater I'd left. He nudged the soil, his expression skeptical. "And you most certainly destroyed them in one blow. I see Idris has been underestimating you a great deal if he thinks you require protection."

"Underestimating me?" I gave him a doubtful look.

"Yes. Your proficiencies may be low, but your mind for strategy is clearly higher than a mere Novice or Apprentice." Tegau summoned a large jar from his inventory and scooped some of the slime-stained soil into it. "Furthermore, an Apprentice wouldn't have thought to combine their spells in such a way. Or, at least, a Jeriskyr native would not have. Otherworlders often come up with odd strategies, but I was not expecting it from you, my lady."

"Well, I *am* originally an Otherworlder," I pointed out, shrugging. "That said, most games I've played rely on combining skills or chaining them in order to kill something. You can't just use one or two skills and hope the thing is dead, unless you're much stronger than the target. Though I get the feeling HP doesn't work quite the same here as it does in games…"

"HP?" Tegau shot me a puzzled look.

"Health points." I shrugged again and walked over to him. "It's how you track whether or not you need healing during a fight. Strikes you take chip away at your HP, and eventually you die if your health goes to zero. Of course, since they're just a game, you respawn…well, unless it's a permadeath game. Since I'm a champion, we can think of that as permadeath mode, apparently…"

"Otherworlder or not, a blade through the heart will kill anyone," Tegau stated, shooting me another frown. "Clearly you need to learn far more about this world than I expected. Has His Majesty not yet provided you with books regarding monsters and their weaknesses?"

"He has, but I've been studying culture and Shadowdancer abilities," I replied, before pointing toward his jar. "What are you going to do with that?"

"Wood slimes do not usually grow so large. I'm going to take these samples back to my guild hall in order to study them," Tegau replied, a brilliant grin spreading across his face. "Since His Majesty has neglected such an important part of our world, I will instruct someone to bring monster guides to you. You will soon have no choice but to hunt to increase your proficiency, and it would be foolish to send such a beauty against monsters without knowledge of their weaknesses! Had I known about His Majesty's failings, I never would have allowed you to attack a wood slime all by your lonesome."

"You made it sound like there's more than one that needs to die," I pointed out, watching as Tegau quickly shook his head.

"I have learned what I needed of you," he stated. "I will return you to the palace and send some of my students to finish off the rest. While effective, it looks like that spell combination of yours took a great deal of power to execute. Frankly, I'm surprised you are still standing. Do you feel any negative impact? Anything at all?"

"Hmmm? I feel fine." I blinked up at him. He looked genuinely worried, though I had a feeling it was more that he was thinking about what Idris would do to him if I had hurt myself somehow. "If we're going back to the palace, sooner rather than later seems like a good idea. It's getting dark."

"Of course, I wouldn't want to be responsible for Lady Moonfire becoming lost in the woods," Tegau exclaimed, realization crossing his face. He quickly dismissed his jar into his inventory and instructed me to do the same with my weapons. Once finished, the Grandmaster carefully grabbed my shoulders and the world spun.

When everything stopped spinning, a familiar scent made me tense. The rumbling growl that followed caused me to snap my eyes open. With a startled squeak, I darted out of the way as Idris lunged for Tegau, grabbing him by the throat. I stumbled over the edge of the training area in my haste to get away, but an agitated Emrys promptly caught and steadied me.

"Your Majesty, wait!" Tegau yelped, gripping Idris' wrist with both hands. "I assure you the First Consort is—"

"Where did the two of you go?" Idris snarled, his form rippling briefly in his anger. "I assigned Cerys to remain in the palace for a reason, you fool! Regardless of how powerful you are, if you two had been outnumbered—"

"Veilwood Forest," I offered when I realized Tegau couldn't speak around the pressure Idris was exerting. "I killed a really huge wood slime while Tegau watched. He has samples he needs to study since it was unusual, so it would probably be best if you didn't kill him."

I paused for a moment and continued when he didn't let go, "Also, I'm hungry. So, if you still plan to join me for dinner..."

Idris' grip on Tegau twitched, as did his tail. He glanced at me in a questioning manner, but I just smiled. I would make him wait for an answer, especially if he didn't let go of his subject soon. Even if I couldn't yet beat Idris in a fight , I still had plenty of ways to make certain he didn't do anything he'd regret later.

"What was unusual about this wood slime?" Idris set Tegau down carefully and sighed.

"It was large, Your Majesty." Tegau paused to clear his throat before continuing, "When Lady Moonfire's shadows set the creature on fire, it split itself into dozens of smaller slimes. Her rather unusual manner of thinking resulted in her victory."

"Explain," Idris commanded, narrowing his eyes.

"Lady Moonfire used darkness to create a small crater around the slimes, and then created an orb which caused the slimes to become trapped within it, Your Majesty." Tegau bowed deeply and stayed that way. "Her swords, surrounded with shadowflames, pierced the orb, resulting in an explosion that wiped the creatures out."

"I see. You were expecting Cerys to think as dully as your typical Apprentice?" Idris looked down at the Grandmaster with a bemused expression on his face. Sighing, he crossed his arms. "Next time you decide to bring Lady Moonfire on a training excursion, you are to ask permission first—and bring an escort. I will not have her safety compromised simply because you believe yourself capable of wiping out full guilds on your own."

"I have done it before." Tegau pursed his lips.

"And if they take Lady Moonfire as a hostage first?" Idris gave him a pointed look before turning to walk over to me. "Tegau, obey my orders if you wish to continue serving as Cejari-ir's Grandmaster of Magics. Cerys, and her safety, are not to be toyed with. No matter your curiosity, and no matter how proficient she is."

"Orders?" Emrys shot Idris a knowing look.

"Make certain Tegau returns to his guild hall," Idris stated. "While you're there, see how the Otherworlders are faring. I would like to know if they will be of any use to us."

"Not quite what I was expecting." Emrys arched an eyebrow and then shrugged, turning his gaze to Tegau. "You heard His Majesty. Let's go."

I watched the two incubi wander off for a moment before turning my attention to Idris. He had a contemplative-yet-hesitant look on his face.

"Might I convince you to allow me to converse with you while you bathe?" Idris finally asked, his gaze unreadable. "I would know more of Tegau's little excursion...but I doubt you wish to lounge in your rooms while covered in dirt."

"That's fine. Should make my bath less boring, anyway," I shrugged. "Shall we? Or would you rather stay here and stare at me some more?"

"I can stare at you anywhere," Idris smirked, shaking his head. "Yes...we can retire to your rooms for now. I have much to ask you about this little adventure that bastard took you on..."

"Ah, there you are, Your Majesty!" Drysi barreled down the hallway and stopped in front of us, placing her hands on her knees as she attempted to catch her breath. "I've finished distributing your orders. The men manning the guardhouse by the city gates asked me to bring you this report."

"Now?" Idris arched an eyebrow as he took an envelope from the exhausted woman.

"A messenger had just brought it by a short while before I arrived, Your Majesty." Drysi nodded quickly, then looked toward me with a smile. "Good evening, Cerys! You seem tired. Should I have something brought to the Queen's Tower to help you sleep?"

"No, no thank you." I blinked at her, a little surprised, before shaking my head. "I just need a bath and dinner. Getting to sleep shouldn't be an issue."

"Should I—" Drysi began to ask something, but she fell silent and shot Idris a puzzled look when he chuckled. "Your Majesty?"

"Cerys will be quite fine. I will make certain she does nothing to strain herself further." Idris grinned when the succubus turned pink. "Good work, Drysi. We will not be needing any further assistance for the evening, and I have already asked the palace chefs to have dinner brought to the Queen's Tower."

"O-of course." Drysi curtsied to us and fled.

"She appears fond of you," Idris remarked once the woman was gone.

"Huh? Me?" I shook my head. "She's one of the few who's nice to me, sure."

When we arrived at the Queen's Tower, I headed for the wardrobe and rummaged around for something to wear after my bath. Idris followed in silence and leaned against the doorway, his expression unreadable. I forced myself to take a slower pace while gathering my things. *He* didn't need to know I was anticipating spending the night with him again.

"So, you wanted to ask me about Tegau's shenanigans?" I asked, turning away from a rack of clothes so I could approach the door. However, Idris didn't move out of my way.

"Firstly, are you injured?" Idris waited until I'd shaken my head to continue, "Did Tegau make any advances on you?"

"Well, he's a flirt, but I'm pretty sure he wasn't serious." I tilted my head, thinking about it. Idris sighed and moved out of my way before following me in the direction of the bath. "If he *was* serious, he's terrible at showing it."

"It is quite likely that he meant every word," he stated dryly. "You are certain you do not mind if I join you?"

"I don't plan to start being bashful about nudity now, of all times." I shot him a look over my shoulder before pulling my tunic over my head. "Especially not if you intend to stay the night."

"...I was under the impression you had yet to decide." Idris faltered when I gave him a brief smirk.

"That was *hours* ago," I answered innocently, as I waded into the bath. "I was already hungry after sparring with you earlier. After fighting that slime? Well..."

"You do not intend to be...difficult?" Idris asked. The way his voice caught made me smirk again, but I kept my back to him.

"Would you prefer I kept playing hard to get?" I glanced back at him before grinning and batting at the water with my tail, splashing him. "Oops... Well, you weren't planning to stay in those clothes for long anyway, were you?"

"Tell me about the slime, Cerys." Idris shot me an amused smile that didn't match his firm tone. I watched him for a moment as he began to pull off his clothes, then released a sigh and leaned back against the edge of the bath.

"Well, from what I understand, the Mages' Guild received a request to deal with the growing population of wood slimes in the Veilwood Forest," I began, pulling my hair over one shoulder.

"Tegau wanted to test me instead of sending his usual recruits to do it. I wasn't aware it was different from other slimes until after I'd started fighting it. What size are they *supposed* to be?"

"Perhaps…this big?" Idris held his hands apart, roughly the size of a bowling ball. He kept my attention for perhaps a few seconds before my gaze drifted downward. A chuckle escaped him as he joined me. "I am not going anywhere. You can wait until after dinner, and after we have played another match of our game."

"This slime was closer to the size of a house and had people bones floating in it," I replied, feeling Idris grow still beside me. "Tegau taught me how to make my shadow magic mimic other elements, so I set the moss and such on fire. It divided into many smaller slimes closer to the size you suggested."

"You then did…*something* to them, and killed them?" Idris muttered, rubbing his chin. While he was thinking, I scooted closer to him and coiled my tail around his. I grinned when I felt him shudder and caught the sound of a suppressed sound of pleasure. "*Cerys…*"

"What?" I shifted so I was pressed up against his side and trailed my fingers down his abdomen. "If I'm going to play First Consort, I may as well be convincing, right?"

"You know full well that title is for your protection and not because—" Idris caught my hand in his when it threatened to creep lower, settling his fiery gaze on me. "I want you to show me what it is you did to defeat the slimes."

"Hmmm..." I glanced across the pool of water, then made a brief upward motion. In response, the water toward the middle of the pool dipped. "And then I did...this."

An orb of darkness appeared, sucking all the water toward it. When the vortex began to grow too strong, I made another motion and popped the orb. I shifted to look up at Idris when he didn't say anything, finding a contemplative expression on his face.

"You skipped a step, given what Tegau mentioned." Idris gave me a pointed look.

"Do you *want* me to cause an explosion in the bath with us?" I paused, grinning, and gave his tail a firm yank with mine. "Well, some varieties of 'explosion' might be acceptable."

"*Nnngh...* What will it take to make you behave?" Idris growled.

"That didn't sound like you *want* me to behave." I gave him a sweet smile and traced one of my nails along a scar by his waist, watching him shiver. "How about a kiss to hold me over?"

Idris' mouth met mine with surprising ferocity. He picked me up with ease, bringing my face level with his, giving me few options other than wrapping my legs around his torso. Just when I'd begun to get lost in our kiss, I heard a knock at the door and Idris pulled back just enough to let his lips wander to my throat. I shivered when he planted a kiss on the side of my neck, trailing his claws down my spine.

"You are going to have to let me go," Idris purred, his voice rough with desire.

"I don't *have* to," I countered, squeezing him briefly with my legs. "But I will."

He gave me a mildly frustrated look before pulling himself out of the bath and wrapping himself in a towel. I suppressed a giggle when he glanced down at himself with a grimace. Idris pulled on a fluffy robe as well, further hiding his interrupted 'problem.'

Hmmm, this whole 'casual' thing is still kind of weird, I thought, quickly washing my hair. *The way he kisses me...none of my boyfriends ever kissed me like that. He's hard to figure out, but I don't even know what to ask.*

"Our food is here," Idris informed me as he returned to the bathroom, but he paused to stare at me as I pulled myself out of the bath. "You are bruised."

"Of course I am. I've been training, and we sparred." I shrugged and picked up a towel. "A handful of bruises and some sore muscles aren't going to stop me, they're just a sign of progress."

"I...just do not want to see you hurt," Idris murmured, running his fingers down my spine. I shot him a questioning look, but he shook his head and changed the subject instead. "Come, let us dine and see to our match."

"What do you intend to conquer this time?" I asked, laughing, as I shrugged a robe on over my nightgown.

"Nothing, we shall use this as a learning experience." Idris cupped my face briefly, tilting my head back so that I was looking at him, his fingertips tangling in my hair. "Before that... I wish to ask for clarity. Do you truly intend to allow me to remain the night? The Queen's Tower is yours, meaning there is nowhere for you to sneak off to this time."

"Oh." I stared at him for a moment. The thought of sneaking off, or kicking him out after we were done, hadn't even occurred to me. "I was already operating under the assumption that you'd stay—if you want to. Sneaking out hadn't crossed my mind."

"Good..." Idris leaned down to give me a tender kiss and then smiled, looking incredibly relieved. "Let us enjoy our evening then. There is no need to rush."

Chapter Thirty-Five
Worms

I stroked Cerys' back in silence while she slept against my chest, her breathing slow but steady. It had taken quite some time, but she had finally relaxed enough to sleep. I glanced toward the envelope sitting on the nightstand, releasing a small sigh. Lounging in bed would have to wait. A murmured spell made certain Cerys would remain asleep.

After gently moving her off me and sliding out of bed, I covered her with the blankets. Stretching, I made my way from her room with purpose and hastily dressed myself before leaving the Queen's Tower, summoning pieces of armor into place as I went.

When I reached the bottom of the steps, I found Emrys already clad in armor, waiting for me.

"Elidyr will keep watch to make sure no one goes up the stairs uninvited," Emrys offered, glancing past me briefly. "You sure about this, Idris? The human's a pig, sure, but..."

"He is the one who showed Cerys around Darmos. I am not letting him live even a moment longer," I stated, taking off through the palace at a brisk stride. "If we leave now, we should catch them before they are out of the Veilwood Forest. They have likely been going in circles for hours now."

"The storm arrived a few hours ago, too." Emrys fell into step with me. "*Tch*, I guess we should be thankful Cerys hasn't learned to read thoughts yet. She'd have killed him herself if she'd heard the things he was thinking."

"I am more concerned with the fact we could hear him at all." I shook my head. "It is unusual for the Issradians to come into our lands without some manner of protection. They are usually not so careless."

"Thus the high alert for all our soldiers?" Emrys sighed. "Odd to see you *this* worried about a woman."

"Are you implying something?" I cut my eyes to the side.

"I seem to recall something about you not wanting to grow attached, *Your Majesty*." Emrys gave me a pointed look. "'Because she will not be staying.'"

"...I lost that battle before I knew it had begun." I shook my head. "The gods knew what they were doing when they chose her. Whether she stays is another matter...but she is coming around to the idea."

"Better than I expected, then." Emrys raised an eyebrow but soon adopted a more formal demeanor. "The rest of our men are waiting by Cejari-ir's western gate, Your Majesty. Veilwood's dryads have already vowed to show us the direct route to our prey."

"Good," I muttered, pulling myself into the saddle of a large black cauchemar stallion. "Let us not waste time. I would rather we return before my spell on Cerys wears off."

"Spell?" Emrys cocked his head.

"To make certain she remains asleep. It would be best if she did not discover me sneaking out of her rooms." I grimaced. *Especially not after what I said to her. She will have my hide...*

Emrys and I rode quickly through Cejari-ir's streets and soon met up with our small contingent of soldiers. We made our way out of the city, heading for the Veilwood Forest as fast as we could safely guide our steeds through the heavy snow. The biting wind made me miss Cerys' warmth, but I refused to allow Eadgar to escape to Darmos. He and his men would die for their behavior in my palace, in my city, and toward Cerys.

It would not be difficult to make it look like an accident.

When we reached the Veilwood Forest, the trees and roots twisted, changing shape to guide us. We slowed our cauchemars, horse-like monsters large enough to carry our kind, to a trot, then again to a walk the nearer we drew to the Issradians. Eventually, we dismounted our cauchemars and continued on foot, spreading throughout the underbrush.

Soon, we caught the sound of fighting. Yet as far as I knew, there should have been no one else tracking the humans. Scowling, I ordered my men forward and rushed to join them. We discovered the human caravan where it had stopped in a snow-covered clearing. Their horses had been driven off and some of the soldiers were already dead.

"Silas?!" I exclaimed, catching a flash of dark green hair across the clearing. A growl escaped me when I saw Eadgar cowering in front of my ally.

"Oh, a welcoming party?" Silas placed his boot against the human's shoulder, forcing him to stay in place, before grinning and waving his long, smoldering pipe in my direction. "I thought I wouldn't see you until reaching the city."

"That one is mine." I narrowed my eyes.

Silas' grin faltered, his expression growing serious. He looked at the cowering human, then returned his gaze to me. "You've never stopped the tax collectors before, due to the war it would lead to. Why now?"

"He is the one responsible for taking Cerys on a tour of Darmos, and for showing her the atrocities his kind have committed," I spat, placing a hand on the hilt of my sword. Around us, the remaining human soldiers fell one after the other to Emrys and my escort. "Furthermore, he must pay for the crimes he was planning to commit against our champion. The other nobles and I will not rest until such a foul creature has been dealt with."

"What crimes?" Silas' tail snapped behind him as he shifted to look down at the human. "It's been a long time since I've seen Emrys or Elidyr enable you to take a target out yourself. You make it sound like the nobles demanded his blood."

"Because they did." I strode forward, stopping a foot away from Silas. Eadgar flinched and tried to pull away from his captor. "The Issradians wish to see the First Consort become a plaything of the Imperial court, to be bred with humans and beasts alike. It appears that they desire to breed halfling soldiers as well as monsters."

"First Consort?" Silas arched an eyebrow at me.

"She would not 'settle' for concubine, and the Otherworlders have made it clear as to why," I answered dryly, shaking my head. "We will make it look like an accident. You and your companions did not ruin that plan, at least…but why are you here? Your last missive stated you would remain in Darmos to gather information."

"Ebonwing has a hand in my being here—among other things." Silas paused, glancing toward several demons standing off to the side. They looked to have lost whatever was in their stomachs. "First Consort, and you're calling her by name… Guess it isn't going to be easy for me to make her one of mine, is it?"

"I will kill you if you try," I stated, watching as he released Eadgar and moved several steps away. The human attempted to flee but a mangled ankle kept him from getting far. With a derisive snort, I strode over to the remnants of his carriage and hefted the most jagged beam of wood I could find. "I would have liked to torture this creature, but doing so would ruin our plan to make this appear an accident."

"You won't get to sever my—" Eadgar's feeble attempt to taunt me ended with a sickening squelch. Humans were such fragile creatures. It did not take much for me to pierce his neck with the broken beam, separating his head from his shoulders.

"Not a blade, but it will do." I pivoted to look for Emrys. "Have the rest of our men begin their work while I question Silas as to his presence. Inform me the moment you are finished."

"Yes, Your Majesty." Emrys bowed briefly and then began barking orders.

"Now, what is this about Ebonwing?" I gave Silas a warning look. "I intend to return to Cerys sooner rather than later. Make your answers quick."

"Lady Alice and her co-leader, Ryan, have been maneuvering Ebonwing to help free nonhumans from the Issradian Empire's service," Silas began with a sigh, crossing his arms over his chest. "I do not know the details, but they have liberated several brothels of all their workers—including mine. I've heard mention that much of their work is related to a long list of tasks given to them by Cerys, but that Alice and Ryan are fully in charge during her absence.

"Most of the men you see with me were employed at the same establishment as I. The rest of the men you see with me, the sickened ones...they are Ebonwing members."

"What?" I stared at Silas for a moment and then looked toward the men he had motioned to. They were not incubi, but they were still most certainly demons. Furthermore, a mere glance was all it took for me to understand that they were not Otherworlders. At least, not anymore.

"By their accounts, they overheard something not meant for them and were pulled into our affairs." Silas grimaced, shooting a sympathetic look toward the men. "The gods swore them to secrecy and insisted they are no longer permitted to remain in Issradian lands."

"Then they have been plucked from their guild and their world both?" A sigh escaped me as I turned to look toward them. "You are friends of Cerys?"

"Y-yes..." The male lamia of the group swallowed hard before continuing, "She...is stuck here too?"

"The gods chose her as Nabyr-zahn's champion, yes." I studied the handful of demons for a moment. "She will not be afforded the opportunity to return to Earth until she has helped us overthrow the Issradian Empire—and even then, it will be up to her whether or not she goes."

"What class has the little minx decided to pick up?" An

intrigued smile spread across Silas' face when I twitched. "Got under your skin already, did she?"

"The First Consort is training as a Shadowdancer," Emrys stated as he approached us. Silas fell silent in response to Emrys' warning look. "Your Majesty, if you wish to return to the palace, our men here are more than capable of finishing this work. You should get at least *some* rest before tending your duties tomorrow."

"If my estate is still in order, and you have no objections, I will take in our displaced Otherworlder friends and my former...*colleagues*," Silas offered, motioning with his pipe. "They cannot fight, but I'm certain we can find a use for them."

"Cerys will know how best to utilize our new guests." I sighed, resigned. "If we must, we can help them become capable warriors. Now that we know what causes Otherworlders from the Issradian Empire to shun battle, I believe we may be able to reverse the effects."

"We do?" Silas raised an eyebrow.

"Almost certainly," I nodded. "Cerys informed us that the Otherworlders' first introduction to the Issradian Empire is to be taken to the execution grounds, where they are told to execute a waiting criminal. They receive no training and are not eased into such matters. We believe that this shocks them."

"Humans *are*...delicate," Silas murmured. "If our little minx is right, we can build ourselves an advantage by taking our time and properly training the Otherworlders..."

"Is Mistress Cerys well?" The vaguely familiar voice gave me pause. Given what the woman in question had told me in her world, it did not make sense for *that* voice to be here.

"...Bruce?" I frowned, turning to look at the incubus as he stepped forward. The lithe man stood a little shorter than me and had pitch black hair. His bright green eyes held a hint of concern.

"Ah, of course, you did not see me in this form while on Earth." A look of recognition crossed Bruce's face. "I was growing terribly bored during Mistress Cerys' absence. This world's gods permitted me to join Jeriskyr as one of its 'players.' I convinced them that it is only proper for a 'champion' to have servants."

"And he's been wandering lost in the woods for days," Silas added dryly, pointing his pipe at Bruce. "We came across him while tracking these bastards. Hearing he knew Cerys, I figured we could bring him along."

"Cerys is...doing better." I pursed my lips, unable to say for certain if she was well. "She is displeased with the gods for their lack of communication and lack of honesty. They have provided her with no guidance and had not told her that her ties to Earth would be severed."

"They did *what*?" Silas stared in disbelief. "What sort of game are they playing? I thought the promise to return 'home' was how they chose to leverage champions into doing their bidding."

"As did I," I nodded. "Corlyotir fled when Cerys confronted her."

"Did she now?" Silas arched an eyebrow, pausing to puff his pipe. "That pretty little thing ran off a goddess?"

"Little? Ah…yes, she was a human when you met her, wasn't she?" I laughed.

"We should get going, Your Majesty," Emrys prompted.

"I've got more news, some of which Cerys would want to hear," Silas called as I turned to walk away.

"You think I should bring her to the morning council?" I shot him a suspicious look over my shoulder. "Cerys has yet to win over *all* of the nobles. Some are still far too suspicious of her."

"Her reaction to my news should help make up their minds," Silas grinned, crossing his arms.

"Might I accompany you?" Bruce asked. "Mistress Cerys—"

"You will see her soon enough. My soldiers will escort you, Silas, and the others to Cejari-ir once they are finished here." I shook my head, beckoning to Emrys. "Come, we shall fetch our cauchemars and return to the city."

You're worried. Emrys glanced at me as we disappeared into the trees.

This 'Bruce' creature is indeed like a servant to Cerys, I answered, frowning deeply. *He is what is known as an 'AI' in their world. Artificial Intelligence. In a way, he is like a remarkably advanced automaton.*

Artificial… So, he has his own mind, but he isn't really a person? Emrys' face twisted as he thought on it.

I trust his loyalty to Cerys, but I do not trust the gods who brought him here. I mounted my cauchemar and pulled a hood over my head. *Furthermore, for them to trap some of her guild members here...*

Based on to the stories your father used to tell us of the champions, it seems like the gods have deviated from their original games. Emrys narrowed his eyes, scowling. *What do you want to do?*

Increase the palace guard, warn the Grandmasters, and have Elidyr's web of informants broaden their search for information, I answered as our cauchemars trotted through the forest. *I want to know if the other kings have experienced similar oddities with their champions. Furthermore, we should contact the elves, the beastmen...they may not be inclined to talk to us, but I want to know if their gods have been acting strange as well.*

And what are we going to do about Cerys' guild members? Emrys pointed out. *The gods could very well hang them over her head somehow. I can't think of many things that would be better leverage.*

We will keep them close, and safe, in Cejari-ir. For now. I grimaced. *It is my hope that she will help us find a use for them.*

By the time we returned to the palace, the snow was coming down in a thick blanket and most of the city's roads were coated in a pristine white sheet. An eerie silence hung over it all. I spent almost the entire ride to the city attempting to think of a way to broach the topic of Cerys' guildmates with her, let alone inform her of Bruce's presence, yet I could not think of a way to bring either up without shocking her.

When I entered the Queen's Tower, I paused in the doorway. A trail of disintegrating butterflies leading to the bedroom made it quite clear that Cerys was no longer asleep.

I steeled myself before shutting the door and making my way to her room.

"You came back?" Cerys arched an eyebrow at me when I came into view. I simply stared at her for a moment. She sat nude on the edge of the bed, her arms crossed under her full bosom. Her right leg hooked over her left, and her luxurious tail swayed beside her as she studied me in turn. "Armor?"

"I was called out on business," I finally answered. "Clearly, if you are awake, I was gone for longer than I thought."

"Business?" Cerys probed, before sighing and glancing down at my feet. "You are getting blood on the floor. I hope you weren't planning to come back to bed wearing *that*."

I looked down as well and sighed. She was right. The blood frozen to my armor was melting, leaving stains on the floor. "So much happened that I forgot about *that*. I suppose I will bathe first, if you will permit me."

"The *king* is asking the *First Consort* for permission?" Cerys asked sarcastically, before releasing an amused laugh. "Well, if you're planning to join me, you should *definitely* go take a bath first. Since you weren't attempting to play turnabout, I won't throw you out."

The glimmer of a threat was delivered with a sultry smile. I did not know what to make of her. With her ties to Earth severed, I had to assume that this was the real Cerys. While it was a vast improvement over her prior behavior, it was far different from what I had come to expect from most women. As king, I had grown accustomed to people seeking me out of a desire for power and status. Cerys seemed much different from them.

"There is much I should tell you," I began, remaining rooted in place. "If you join me—"

"You can tell me in the morning." Cerys tilted her head, examining me again. "I've got a good enough idea of where you went, given the blood. Can't say I blame you, but it was a risky move. For now, I just want to sleep."

"Morning... Very well." I sighed, too tired to argue. "You will be joining me at the morning council. It *would* be best if we both got some rest before then."

"It's important?" she asked, as I turned to make my way to the bathroom.

"Would you rather not accompany me?" I shot her a frown.

"Well, I thought I was supposed to be focusing on training," she pointed out, shaking her head. "I don't have anything against accompanying you. Just wanted to make sure it wouldn't be a problem. Plus, I know the nobles don't like me much."

"I have been assured this meeting will afford you an opportunity to win their genuine favor," I informed her. "Furthermore, you need to learn how my kingdom operates.

Joining me while I tend to my duties will help with that far more than simply telling you what I do."

"It's a date, then!" Cerys laughed as I stepped out of the room.

Does that even count as a 'date?' I wondered, tilting my head. *Or is that another Earth saying… At any rate, I hope she can maintain a pleasant mood once I tell her all that has happened.*

Chapter Thirty-Six
Morning Council

"The hell do you mean, 'Bruce and several Ebonwing members are stuck in Jeriskyr?!'" I demanded, baring my fangs at Idris as I pushed him back into the mattress. "You should have told me—"

"You said to wait until morning to discuss it," Idris pointed out, his tone neutral. He glanced down at where our bodies met, then back up to my face. "This could be a rather entertaining position if you would stop attempting to strangle me."

"I'm not trying to strangle you." The corner of my eye twitched. He was right, I had told him to wait until morning, and he'd done just that. I took a deep breath and loosened my grip on his shirt. "I expect an explanation."

"But I've already told you all that I know." Idris frowned at me, but it didn't last long. His back arched and a shiver ran through his body the moment my tail slipped into his pants. "I've gone over this before! Our kind are not wont to lie. If I knew more...*nnngh*!"

I bit my lower lip, but it did nothing to stop my grin as I watched him writhe. He was *definitely* fun to play with, and I was overdue for a bit of revenge. When I withdrew my tail, he shuddered, a groan escaping him. His hands found my hips and gripped them tight, pulling me against him.

"If *that* is your idea of revenge..."

"Don't get any smart ideas. If you push, I'll stop playing nice." I gave the front of his shirt a brief tug. "That's really all you know?"

"I may have been eager to return to bed with you," Idris informed me, sitting up. He cupped my face in one hand, drawing close. His mouth met mine, briefly, but I soon pulled away and pressed a hand against his chest. The disappointed, searching expression in his eyes gave me pause. "Is it not enjoyable?"

"I'm not going to be responsible for you missing your morning council," I pointed out, eliciting a heavy sigh. "There's really nothing else for you to tell me about where you went last night?"

"I told you all that happened." Idris trailed his fingers down one of my legs as I got off him. "You know, I am not against being late."

I glanced over my shoulder at him as I straightened my clothes. He shot me an inviting smile, but I wasn't going to give in that easily. "Idris, it's high time I got involved with the workings of your kingdom and preparations for dealing with the Issradians. Indulging can wait until the end of the day, when your responsibilities are done and my training is out of the way."

"Tonight?" Idris prompted when I walked away from the bed and over to a nearby dresser. I shot him a questioning look. "Or...would you prefer to be free of my company until you need to feed again?"

That...is actually a good question. I crossed my arms, mulling it over. Whatever our relationship was, I didn't quite have a name for it. We weren't exactly dating, we weren't boyfriend and girlfriend, and we certainly weren't engaged or married. Mutually beneficial didn't seem to quite fit either. I was fairly certain Idris' attraction toward me ran deeper than that, even if I wasn't yet sure what *my* feelings were. I doubted he would have put up with my behavior for so long if he wasn't genuinely drawn to me. "I enjoy your company, so I don't want to be 'free' of it, as you put it. That said, is it appropriate?"

"If you have no objections, then yes, it is," Idris answered as he pulled himself off the bed. He pushed back his disheveled hair and shot me another smile. "You look surprised."

"That was a much, *much* simpler answer than I was expecting." I stared at him for a moment, shaking my head. "I should keep up this femme fatale facade even at a meeting of nobles, right? Can I at least do that while wearing pants?"

"Pants? Perhaps..." Idris tilted his head, studying the revealing dress I wore. "Can I not convince you to wear that? It looks beautiful on you."

"It's pretty, sure, but it doesn't give me enough movement. Too tight through the torso." I strode in the direction of the wardrobe, Idris following close behind. "I think I saw something akin to harem pants in here..."

"Harem pants?" Idris arched an eyebrow. When I lifted a pair of sheer lavender ones, a smile came to his face. "Ah, you mean sarouel. I see."

After quickly changing, I summoned a matching fan from my inventory and tucked it into the waistband of my pants. With that done, Idris and I made our way out of the Queen's Tower together. It felt incredibly freeing to no longer be bound to Earth, but it was clear that my behavior toward Idris while I was still tied had had an adverse effect. I wasn't sure how to address the problem either, aside from just being...nicer. Though perhaps that wasn't quite the right word for it. Being 'nice' wasn't the issue, it was acting like myself that was important.

"Alright, business," I began, glancing briefly at Idris. "Did my guild members introduce themselves? What race are they?"

"They did not introduce themselves, as they were too frightened...and a touch disturbed by our brutality," Idris stated, offering me his arm. "As a replacement for your combat training for the morning, perhaps it would be best if you learned to conduct yourself as the First Consort. Remaining close to my side and having your fan out at all times would be a start."

"Well, it's a type of progress," I agreed, taking his arm in mine and opening my fan with the other.

"As for their race," Idris continued, "they are a varied manner of demons. Bruce is an incubus, but the rest are not."

"Bruce is...are you serious?" I stared at him.

"Quite." Idris nodded. I couldn't suppress my laughter. "I take it that I was right to assume an automaton—AI—would make a poor incubus?"

"This should make for an interesting meeting, at least!" I shook my head, grinning. "You should know that I still have reservations about getting involved with your court or the way you run things. I doubt running a guild is much like running a kingdom. For one, there are far more lives at stake. For two, the monetary and resource costs of changes were never my forte."

"How does Ebonwing handle expansion of territory, then?" Idris shot me a doubtful look. "From what I understand, your guild is a successful one. Even Otherworlders who joined Nabyr-zahn speak of your guild."

"Mmm? I come up with plans, strategies, and defensive layouts. Then the officers of Ebonwing work out how much money and materials are needed to make it all come together." I shrugged, shooting him a brief smile. "Once all the costs are worked out, the various branches of the guild reach out and work on specified projects. We have gatherers, makers, and hunters. They band together and coordinate their efforts to procure resources as quickly as possible. If an area or specific item is contested, then our combat-oriented members swoop in and eliminate the competition—and protect our gatherers in case other guilds attempt the same.

"Many of our competitors take the approach of only doing what they think they can afford. Ebonwing makes grand plans and moves its parts as necessary to achieve those goals."

"Which is why you suggested we leverage the Otherworlders to acquire the materials and food we need?" Idris murmured, a contemplative expression passing across his face. "I see. So, you create a plan or design, your members work out the logistics, and then the guild as a whole works to gather resources. When do you spend them?"

"Not until we have everything necessary." I snapped my fan shut and tapped his chest with it. "In many games, an in-progress construction can be attacked by other guilds and destroyed. Creating a guild hall or city in pieces as materials are gathered would result in bleeding resources. So instead, we get everything together and then make a large event out of building our home or city. The guild splits into groups of guards, scouts, builders, runners, and so on."

"And which portion do you assist?" Idris glanced down at me with a truly curious expression on his face. I was honestly a little surprised he was taking interest. After all, a game and the real world were two different things. Sort of.

"I was usually with the groups engaging attackers," I replied after a moment, eliciting a low chuckle from the incubus. "Strategy comes quickest to me in the middle of a fight. People can plot and plan all they want but fail to realize their opponent has done the same. We come up with intricate plans and choose favorable terrain, sure, but flexibility is necessary as well."

"And not everyone is suited to making snap decisions," Idris nodded, smiling. "I can see why you were against a fully-ranged class. By taking on a hybrid combination, you can learn the needs of both, which will help you make informed decisions in battle."

"Good morning Your Majesty, Lady Moonfire." Elidyr greeted us at the doors to the throne room, bowing briefly. "The two of you are the last to arrive. Shall I send the servants to fetch anything for you?"

"Tea and breakfast for us both," Idris answered, giving Elidyr a brief nod. *As for your concerns, Cerys, you will not learn if you do not join me. If you are not confident in your input, then wait until we are in private to give it, if you wish. I will not fault you for being cautious.*

"Ah, Cerys!" Silas exclaimed, a cheerful grin spreading across his face when we entered the room. "My, becoming a succubus seems to have agreed with you. Beautiful as ever, but far less fragile. Human bodies seem so incredibly frustrating."

"Cery? It really is you!" a familiar voice exclaimed. I glanced in its direction to find a handful of demons who looked very out of place in Idris' court. Their unease and lack of confidence showed clearly in their body language and on their faces. "We're so sorry! We were trying to continue following your orders, but when we realized how weird Alice was acting we tried to eavesdrop and learn more."

"Our stealth was nowhere near high enough to fool one of the human gods," another added, sighing. "They stripped us of our levels, forced us to become demons, and made Silas bring us with him. We're glad he agreed to help us, don't get me wrong, but..."

"Do you think the gods cut their ties?" I glanced up at Idris briefly, noting the displeased way he was looking at my guild members.

"I do not care either way, as long as there is a use for them while they are here," Idris informed me, giving me a pointed look. "You would know their strengths best. How can they best serve Nabyr-zahn?"

Straight to work with them, is it? I arched an eyebrow and looked toward the Ebonwing members. "Their strengths revolve around information. Gathering it, sorting it, coming up with ways to utilize it, and spreading what information we want others to know."

"We were sworn to secrecy by the gods, so we can't give you any of the information we learned while in the Issradian Empire," Ivan spoke up, slithering forward. While his face was what I had expected...the body was not. He grinned when he saw my expression. "Come on, Cery. How many games have let me play a naga or lamia before? If I'm going to be stuck here, at least I can be something cool."

"Right..." I tilted my head. "So, you're sworn to secrecy. Great. Okay. What if you 'learn' what you've already heard while sourcing info for us?"

"That should be kosher. If not, we've got crafting and gathering classes we're interested in," he shrugged. "What's this you were saying about cut ties?"

"Otherworlders are connected to their home world by invisible threads. Mine were cut." I crossed my arms, tapping the air absentmindedly with my fan. "I'd say we should find out if your connection to Earth was cut before letting you do any work. Idris had a hard enough time dealing with me while my 'strings' were still in place. A group of you could be a huge problem."

"That's *His Majesty* to you, woman," a blond incubus snarled, rising to his feet. He placed his palms on the table before him and leaned against it, shooting me what he probably thought was a threatening look. "Champion or not, you are being far too familiar—"

"She has my permission to be as familiar as she desires," Idris cut him off, pulling me closer. His tail coiled around my upper thigh, one of his hands resting low on my hip. I twitched when a few of his fingertips came to rest just under the waistband of my low sarouel. "Cerys is our champion, and the First Consort. I have not given up on making her my queen, and I expect you to treat her as if she has already acquired such status. If you do not, I will not hesitate to take your head and distribute your wealth to someone more loyal."

"I'd be happy to take in Cerys' guild mates until we've confirmed their ties," Silas offered, an amused smile on his face. "Alas, all here should settle down or His Majesty and the First Consort will never reach their seats."

"Very well," Idris sighed, shifting to look toward Emrys. "Have your men escort Silas' guests to his estate. They do not need to be here for this meeting and Cerys can catch up with them later."

"Your Majesty, I must echo Cadfael on this matter. Are you not being too quick to trust this champion?" A ginger-haired incubus rose from his seat next. To his credit, he didn't flinch in response to the glare Idris settled on him. "The gods have done little to gain our trust over the past several centuries. Even during your father's time, they were of little aid. How can we be certain this woman can help us?"

"Are you suggesting that her fate should be left to the empire, simply because she may not be capable of overthrowing them?" Idris' low, dangerous tone made many of the nobles grow still.

Silas, however, simply smirked and crossed his arms, looking much like he'd just had a thought confirmed. "Regardless of her ability, Cerys was given no choice with regards to coming to Jeriskyr. When posed with a choice between us or the Issradians, she made the decision to side with us in the hopes she could save her friend and because she doubts the gods' game just as much as we do.

"*Furthermore*, she joined us because the Issradians are foul. She wishes to see them slain just as much as we do."

I can speak for myself, you know. I smacked Idris' ass with my tail and then gave him an innocent smile when he shot me a reprimanding look. *My, my, this tail is so incredibly hard to control! How* do *you manage?*

"Silas, I believe you mentioned you have some manner of news to report," Idris began as he settled onto his throne. His gaze returned to me briefly, an expectant gleam in his eyes. Smirking, I perched beside him on the throne and threw both my legs over his thighs, letting one dangle between his legs and the other rest over them entirely. *...you are enjoying this too much.*

As are you. I flicked open my fan and glanced out across the throne room, delighted to note that several of the nobles were red with rage. Until I could beat them into place, playing good little consort would have to suffice. Plus, it had the added benefit of flustering Idris.

"As I mentioned last night, Ebonwing has been working to free nonhumans from their service in Darmos," Silas began as he walked forward, coming closer to the throne. "Lady Alice and her co-leader, Ryan, have been helping to evacuate the freed workers in secret. Mirela, their spymaster, has secured Darmos' waterways as a safe passage out of the city. Many of our kind were suspicious as to why the human champion was going to such great lengths to free the 'slave races,' as the Issradians call us."

"Do you know all of this because they've grown careless in my absence, or because your own informants are so good?" I frowned at him and he shot me a quizzical look. "When you told me before about Ebonwing's reputation, and I returned to Earth, I drafted detailed plans for them to follow in Jeriskyr. After learning the world was real, and during Idris' stay on Earth, I fleshed out those plans further. Mirela has worked as my 'spymaster' for a long time, and we work well together. She's usually not careless, and information typically doesn't make it outside of her unit."

"It is, or was, my job to learn all that I could of Darmos and the workings of the people in it." Silas gave me a crooked grin. "Otherworlders believe me to be an information broker, and Mirela was one of my best customers. It's because of my connections, and my working relationship with her, that I know why Lady Alice has put such a heavy focus on 'saving' the nonhuman inhabitants of Darmos."

"You mean a reason aside from the girl being hopelessly naive and far too innocent to have been dragged into a world like ours?" Idris snorted, earning throaty laughter from Silas.

"That's my impression of the girl too, aye." Silas shook his head, still chuckling. "Alas, her reasoning is far less pleasant. Allow me to start from the relative beginning: When Alice first came to Darmos for good, the investigation into the breeding pens was already well under way. However, the humans were not fighting to keep the pens as much as one might think. Rather, they have been acting like they do not care if they get to keep the breeding pens.

"Innocent as she may be, Lady Alice is no fool. She had Mirela investigate the humans' behavior, and Adric appears to have become Ebonwing's ally. What we discovered is that the Issradians are fully prepared to abandon their 'breeding project.' They were not bothered by the lunar elves' deities threatening them, nor were they concerned with the possibility of being forced to surrender the women from the pens to their rightful kingdoms. The Issradians are acting from a place of power like we have never seen, and with unprecedented confidence.

"Before I left, Mirela passed me a missive confirming my fears: The Issradians are preparing to destroy all nonhuman races, and they intend to start from within their own borders first."

"They what?!" I snarled, my amusement disappearing. "Those fucking bastards are going to kill off everyone who isn't human? Even their servants? Then there's the tax. That slimy, fat bastard said they would be coming every six months from here on out to take people!" I stopped, turning to look at Idris. "You better have made sure he died like the pig he is. Even if you did, I think I may go find his corpse and feed him his own—"

"Ahem," Silas coughed, an amused smile on his face when I glared at him. "Yes, the humans intend to kill even their slaves and servants. Lady Alice's focus on evacuating the brothels comes from the humans' plans to torch both red-light districts. She is doing what she can to leverage your guild and save as many lives as possible from her precarious position."

"And how is Ebonwing keeping her safe?" Idris questioned, while I crossed my arms and silently fumed.

"The answer to that is twofold," Silas offered, motioning with both hands. "First, the Ebonwing members were given some manner of 'escort quest.' Lady Alice has several Ebonwing members who are capable of combat with her at all times. Second, she and Adric are currently engaged. None of the nobles dare touch her while she's engaged to the emperor's guard captain. Due to his bloodline, he holds a great deal of power within Darmos."

"His bloodline?" I asked begrudgingly. *Alice is engaged? Seriously? Now that is definitely for show.*

"Ah... Adric is the bastard of the last emperor and one of the Issradian champions." Silas grimaced, shaking his head. "He is an incredibly talented warrior and strategist. While he has no right to the throne, the humans see him as proof of the pens' success..."

"Well then, Lady Moonfire, what do you think?" Idris shot me an entertained look when I glared back at him. He tucked some of my disheveled curls behind one ear while I continued to sulk.

"With the immediate threat to Alice's innocence gone, what do you think we should do?"

"Prepare for refugees, see if the other kingdoms are willing to coordinate to evacuate their people?" I sighed heavily. "It's a shame your world doesn't have nukes. I'd like to drop a few on the Issradians right about now."

"Nukes?" Idris tilted his head.

"Short for 'nuclear.' I'd imagine you found some reference to nuclear missiles or bombs while researching Earth," I huffed. "Point is, I'd like to see their asses wiped off the face of the planet and wouldn't mind if it made the area uninhabitable for a few decades, either. I suppose killing them the old-fashioned way will have to suffice, but most of them would die of old age if we killed them *properly*. Feeding them pieces of their bodies, torturing them, perhaps burying them alive."

"...you are certain this woman comes from a human world?" Cadfael, the blond noble from earlier, spoke in a strained tone. The color drained from his face when I glanced toward him.

"I have told you before and I will tell you again: Cerys is one of us." Idris released an agitated sigh, his gaze settling on the noble. "Cerys wishes to see them punished just as much as we do. Even on Earth, her experiences with humans did nothing to endear them to her. While she has friends among them, certainly, she is not the sort to stand by and let such vile actions go unpunished."

"Guilt by inaction," I offered, looking toward Cadfael as well.

"I would happily eradicate Darmos if it was within my power. If all the Issradian natives died, this world would be better off. Of course, it's *not* within my power, and we should get our people out of there if we can. I doubt anyone in this room wants to see the humans execute all the people who've been taken as 'tax,' and I doubt any of you are stupid enough to think that Ebonwing or Nabyr-zahn alone is capable of evacuating everyone in time. Plus, if the Issradians are going to make such a big move, they won't remain within their borders for long."

"I have already reached out to the other demon kings, and this will give us more fuel for discussion if nothing else." Idris sighed, settling back in his throne. He studied me briefly, before looking toward the seated nobles. "If you are quite finished doubting the First Consort, then we should move on to discussions and plans. With Ebonwing making efforts to evacuate so many people, and with the predicted influx of Otherworlders in Nabyr-zahn, we are going to have to reevaluate our plans for accommodations and expansion. Has anyone brought Silas up to speed?"

"Elidyr briefed me," Silas offered, glancing my way. "Has Bruce found his way to you yet, 'Lady Moonfire?'"

"No, I was wondering where he was." I shook my head.

"He mentioned something about 'studying his strange, fleshy body,'" Silas remarked with a lopsided grin. "Perhaps he took a stroll around town?"

"Cerys will be remaining here, for now," Idris interjected,

narrowing his eyes at Silas. "She cannot be allowed to wander Cejari-ir on her own yet, and those capable of escorting her are currently busy with other matters."

And you want to keep me on your lap, I'm guessing, I added, squeezing his leg with mine briefly. *At least you and your throne are comfy.*

Perhaps we can break the throne in next, Idris suggested, sliding his tail around mine. "Have you more to report, Silas?"

"Not at all. We can move to the next topic of discussion if you like." Silas returned to his seat and placed a book in his lap before lifting a quill from the table. "I will take notes and determine if there is any way for me and mine to help regarding expansion."

Breakfast and lunch passed before we were free of the morning council. Idris insisted that he had no other responsibilities to tend to in the throne room for the day, so we soon found ourselves wandering in the direction of the training yard. A guard had mentioned in passing that they'd seen someone matching Bruce's description heading the same way, so it seemed like a good way to kill two birds with one stone. I wanted to know what in the hell Bruce was doing in Jeriskyr, the how of it, and whether he was a 'player.'

"Ah, Drysi," Idris called as we neared the harem's part of the palace. "Have you seen an incubus with black hair and green eyes walk past? He is an acquaintance of Cerys' and we have been searching everywhere for him."

"O-oh, you mean Bruce?" Drysi grew pink in the face, then coughed into one hand. "He was...um...*struggling* with his new body. He insisted he was male in his home world as well, yet he was walking around with an uncontrolled erection!"

"...and where is he now?" I arched an eyebrow.

"Well, you see..." Drysi inched toward the door behind her and tugged at it as if to make certain it was fully shut. "I suggested he 'take care' of the problem but had to explain the matter of privacy. He just pulled it out the moment I said anything!"

"So, you had him go to one of the empty guest rooms?" Idris asked, the corner of his eye twitching.

"Oh! It's my duty to clean the rooms in this section of the palace today, so I was planning to do so once he's finished!" she exclaimed, flinching and tightening her grip on the door handle behind her. Alas, the 'incubus' in question was stronger and easily pulled the door open. Drysi stumbled and Bruce easily caught her, shooting her a confused look before returning his attention to Idris and me.

"Ah, I thought I heard your voice, Mistress Cerys." Bruce's bright green eyes snapped to me after studying Idris. "I was searching for you so that I might serve you, yet I appeared to have lost my way."

"Serve her in what manner?" Idris growled, tucking me behind him.

"In whatever manner Mistress Cerys requires of me, of course." Bruce tilted his head, clearly confused. "As her servant, I will help her with anything."

"Bruce, why did you choose an *incubus* of all things?" I interjected before Idris could question the AI again.

"Given a succubus' needs, it appeared to be the most rational choice." Bruce frowned at me. "Jeriskyr lacks the systems required for me to provide you with porn, yet I have learned plenty about sex from your queries on Earth."

"...I don't recall modding you to 'learn' about sex." I stared at him. "Besides, that isn't how it works! First of all, I didn't ask for you to tend to *those* needs. Second, watching porn isn't a substitute for having sex! That's not how any of this works!"

"You gave me access to your bank account and did not tell me I couldn't spend money. I modded myself," Bruce shrugged. "Jeriskyr's deities decided that my level of intelligence is sufficient to justify providing me with a corporeal body. Now that I have one, I will be able to accrue knowledge while serving you."

"Cerys will not be needing to feed from you." Idris bared his fangs at Bruce. "As First Consort, she is mine and no one else may touch her."

Bruce tilted his head and remained silent for a moment before speaking. "You are effectively Mistress Cerys' boss, meaning you are my boss as well. I will adhere to any parameters my masters set for me. However, this corporeal body requires sustenance. If I am not permitted to feed with Mistress Cerys, am I to understand that I should service Master Idris instead?"

"No." Idris twitched.

"Then how should I care for this body?" Bruce's mouth turned downward into a deep, quizzical frown.

"Bruce, are you able to log out?" I asked, crossing my arms. The glance he shot down at my chest briefly before looking up at my face gave me the impression he wasn't merely mimicking 'people behavior.'

"I am incapable of logging out. My directive is to remain by your side and make certain you have all that you require." Bruce shook his head. "The gods did not want me acting as a messenger between you and Miss Alice. I may only log out when you do."

"Drysi," Idris called with a tired sigh.

"Yes, Your Majesty?" Drysi gulped.

"Teach Bruce about our race, our city, and our kingdom." Idris placed a hand on his hip and looked from Drysi to Bruce and back. "Perhaps find someone willing to feed with him, as well. It wouldn't do—"

"I will!" Drysi volunteered a little too enthusiastically. She seemed to realize how eager she'd seemed and turned bright crimson. "I-I mean, if there are no complaints, I would not mind teaching him about his new body."

"As you wish." Idris shook his head in disbelief before pivoting to look down at me. "Let us go get some training in before dinner, now that the matter is settled. You need more practical experience with Shadowdancer, and I would rather you get it by sparring with me for now."

"Am I permitted to continue acting as Cerys' servant?" Bruce called after us when we started to move away.

"With Drysi's supervision, I suppose." Idris grimaced before glancing back over his shoulder. "Drysi, source several more men and women from around the palace who can act as Cerys' servants and guards. It's high time the First Consort was treated *as* the First Consort. I trust you know who might still be at odds with Cerys' presence."

"They are coming around to the idea, Your Majesty," Drysi offered quietly. "Some of them truly believe themselves to be in love with you, however. They will continue to be difficult."

"Compile a list. I have no qualms about making my position clear to them." Idris shot her a chilling look before leading me off. However, we didn't get far before running into a very serious-looking Emrys and a relaxed Silas.

"Just the two people I hoped to find!" Silas grinned. "Idris, we should hold a feast."

"...a feast?" Idris sighed, pressing his fingers to his temples. "Why?"

"To celebrate our champion, my return, and the beginning of our movements against the Issradians, of course!" Silas laughed.

"Even Emrys agrees. Go on, tell him."

"It would be good for morale," Emrys relented, his tone flat. "With the rest of the nobles finally scrounging up some respect for Cerys, it would be prudent to improve morale among your troops, vassals, and the nobles."

"A feast would certainly be the quicker option..." Idris murmured, rubbing his chin. Soon, a smile slowly spread across his face and his eyes cut toward me. "And it would be an excellent opportunity for Cerys to work on her drinking skill."

"What's wrong with her drinking?" Silas arched an eyebrow when I growled at the king.

"Something about honesty and loose lips," I snorted.

"Ah, then I will have my men make certain any spies who attempt to enter the palace or the feast hall die on the spot," Silas remarked with a warm smile. "They will be happy to have the work. Any objections, Your Majesty?"

"None at all," Idris laughed. "Emrys, has Elidyr determined where the Issradian Otherworlders 'respawn' when killed in Cejari-ir?"

"Not yet. He's looking for some more to kill," Emrys shrugged. "You're really going to go with this feast idea?"

"It will be an excellent opportunity to boost morale and to announce our formal preparations for war." Idris smirked, squeezing me closer to him. "Of course, I would like to see Cerys here enjoy herself in the palace for once.'

You've already seen me enjoy myself, in both your rooms and mine, I pointed out, earning a brief but sultry glance in reply.

"Make the preparations to hold the feast for tomorrow night. We should give the rumors time to spread." A mischievous grin replaced Idris' smirk. "It would not do for Silas' men to trouble themselves with guarding the palace if there are no threats for them to eliminate."

"We'll go inform the palace staff, then." Emrys grabbed Silas by the collar of his shirt. "Let's go. We're getting in their way."

Chapter Thirty-Seven
Additional Responsibility

"Is this really necessary?" I crossed my arms.

"The feast, or your dress?" Idris glanced over his shoulder, shrugging on a button-down shirt.

"Both." I glanced toward a nearby mirror and then back to Idris. "The idea of 'protecting' you while wearing a dress instead of armor still strikes me as incredibly strange. As for the feast, I can understand the idea that it will help improve morale, but I'm not convinced I should be attending."

"My subjects are eager to celebrate the acquisition of our first champion in centuries," Idris pointed out. I grimaced. That was something I couldn't argue with. "Such obvious matters aside, I wish for you to join me. I will not force you to attend if you would rather remain here, but..."

"You don't have to tell me that'd be a stupid move," I snorted. Shaking my head, I uncrossed my arms and fidgeted with the loop of decorative silver chains around my waist. They were all that kept the dress's hip-high slits from gaping too far. Much of my chest and back were also exposed. The dress was gorgeous, certainly, and something I would've picked in a heartbeat in any game. Picking it for the real me to wear, though? That was still difficult.

"You are overthinking it." Idris tugged gently at one of the chains, an amused smile spreading across his lips. "Of course, if you would be more comfortable in something else, I will wait for you to change."

"This is fine. I need to get used to the clothes in this world anyway." I sighed heavily. Under other circumstances, I might have balked about wearing the revealing dress. However, I'd been in Jeriskyr long enough to have noticed that revealing attire was the norm for both incubi and succubi. They liked to show off, and they had to make certain their tails had free range of movement.

"Relax and enjoy yourself, Cerys." Idris slid an arm behind my back and led me toward the door. "This is an opportunity for you to work on your drinking skill and enjoy a quieter life while you can. We should soon hear from the other kingdoms and tribes who have been oppressed by the Issradians. Once we have, there will be little time for such simple indulgences."

"Have you learned anything about Eadgar's claim about the tax coming every six months?" I asked, glancing up when Idris paused. He let go of me and strode over to a nearby dresser, his expression indicating he'd remembered something.

"Nothing beyond the soldiers' thoughts," Idris answered, pulling an ornate crown from one of the drawers and putting it on. "We can't be certain that they are privy to such information, but some believed that the emperor had ordered Eadgar to cease collecting tax altogether."

"*What?*" I stared at him in disbelief. "Any indication as to why?"

"None. Elidyr's men will find more information for us soon." Idris shook his head briefly before crossing his arms, stroking his chin while he examined me. "Tell me, how do consorts from your world show their status? Perhaps I should have a crown or something else made for you?"

"Don't worry about it," I replied with a snort. "Consorts on Earth haven't had 'status' for centuries, and I don't want you wasting more resources on frivolous things either."

"Frivolous?" Idris arched an eyebrow at me as we left his rooms. "Hardly. When we meet the other kings, I refuse to let them mistake you for someone of lower status. They need to understand that, aside from being our champion, you are also an important member of Nabyr-zahn society."

"I've already got fancy dresses for that!" I shook my head. "Look, I'm not budging on this one. I appreciate your gifts, but I'd prefer to earn anything else myself, whether that's by finding a way to earn money or hunting for the materials. I don't want to be coddled."

"Coddled?" Idris looked thoroughly confused this time. "That was not at all my intention. I simply wish to...provide for you, if you will."

Provide for me? I glanced up at him briefly, noting his hesitation and averted gaze. Whatever his intentions were, he seemed to be struggling with them himself. "Let's pretend our positions were reversed, and you were Earth's champion. What would you do if I started showering you with gifts?"

"I couldn't possibly accept—" Idris trailed off and heaved an agitated sigh. "I see. It is not that you dislike my gifts. I understand.

"However, you know full well that I cannot permit you to hunt for materials yourself. You speak of redirecting my resources...soldiers to act as guards or as an escort are also a resource."

"...I didn't think of that." I sighed again. "You can't keep me locked up in the castle forever."

"Then come hunt with me tomorrow," Idris offered, a mischievous smile spreading across his face. "You require more experience, you are growing bored, and I intend to venture to the Veilwood Forest to investigate the growing number of monsters.

None of which must be mutually exclusive."

"Promise?" I gave him a pointed look.

"Absolutely. My hunt will be far more enjoyable for your presence." Idris smiled, squeezing me toward him. "Now then, enough of that for now. Today, we are to put on a good show and increase my subjects' morale. I want you to relax and enjoy yourself."

Easier said than done, I thought as we neared one of the largest palace gardens.

When we arrived, I found myself staring at the scene in awe. The entire green space was alight with small, sparkling lanterns shaped like stars. Numerous tables and seats had been set up among the various flowers and trees. Ornaments, clan banners, and other decor hung from the trees, the palace walls, and on the stone retaining wall on the far edge of the garden.

On that far edge sat the longest table, with a throne centered across from us. Beside it were three slightly smaller seats, followed by numerous seats of normal size. Nearby, men and women danced, played instruments, or performed athletic feats. Nobles, soldiers, merchants, and many other people I had met throughout my stay in Cejari-ir were in attendance. Even Bruce and the members from Ebonwing were there. Many of the women I recognized from the palace's harem.

Idris led me to the table and insisted I sit in the chair to his left. I chose to comply rather than make a scene, even if the extravagant chair and its proximity to Idris' throne made me uncomfortable, given the circumstances. Hell, I still wasn't sure if Idris' behavior toward me was because of my status as champion. Perhaps I just wasn't ready to accept that his apparent feelings for me were genuine. Sighing, I shifted so that I was leaning against one arm rest and draped my tail over my lap.

"Your Majesty, Lady Moonfire." Elidyr acknowledged us with a subtle nod before taking a seat to Idris' right. "I have finished carrying out your orders for the day, Your Majesty. Many Otherworlders are eager to perform more quests for you, Lady Moonfire."

"I've finished my duties as well," Emrys declared, taking the seat to my left. He grinned, grabbed the nearest tankard, and filled it nearly to the brim with a dark blue alcohol.

"More quests?" I looked toward Elidyr again, suspicious. "*From me?*"

"They are eager to gain your favor," Idris stated with amusement. "We discovered that they finish their tasks much more quickly when they believe it is for you. For us, they are inclined to dawdle unless they are attracted to men."

I sighed. I should have expected as much from gamers. After all, I was guilty of it myself. Whenever I found a hot and interesting character in a game, I usually prioritized doing their questline first. Between 'Jeriskyr Studios" claim that I was playing an NPC, and whatever marketing plan they had launched after we'd returned to

Jeriskyr, I could only imagine what sorts of things were running through the player base's minds. I'd have bet money that the ones who weren't attempting to appease me had focused on Idris.

I don't see Silas anywhere. I nudged Idris briefly, eliciting a grimace.

Silas wanted to deal with any spies making their way onto palace grounds, Idris answered, a mildly displeased frown settling onto his lips. *Was there something you wanted from him?*

No, I just found it strange. He did suggest the feast to begin with. I shrugged, then glanced at him when I caught the low sigh of relief that escaped him. *Dealing with intruders, hmmm?*

Elidyr and Silas had their men spread rumors of the First Consort's trouble with alcohol, he answered with a mischievous laugh. *It is an excellent way to lure our enemies into our claws.*

So, you're using me as bait. I refrained from rolling my eyes. *Can't say I blame you, it's an easy-to-execute sort of plan. I still expect you to make it up to me, of course.*

You needn't search so hard for reasons to indulge, Idris informed me, chuckling again.

"Lady Moonfire," a vaguely familiar voice addressed me. I glanced to my left and found Cadfael taking a seat near us. "I am surprised you chose to join us, and that you continue to permit us to keep our king."

"Permit... What?" I stared at Cadfael. He frowned at me, his gaze soon flicking to Elidyr and then to Idris.

"No one has told her?" Cadfael narrowed his eyes.

"I was under the impression it was the gods' duty to do so." Elidyr frowned at me as well.

Idris and Emrys echoed his sentiments.

"Care to explain?" I shifted so that I was leaning on the armrest closest to Idris and settled my gaze on him.

"Champions are permitted to choose a new ruler in their allied kingdom," Idris began, releasing a heavy sigh. "It is how my clan came into power. Nabyr-zahn's original rulers were deemed corrupt and incapable long ago by an early champion. My bloodline was chosen to replace them, and we have ruled ever since."

"The gods are growing lax," Cadfael scoffed, crossing one leg over the other. He took a sip of wine before shifting his attention to me again. "What *did* the gods tell you, then?"

"Only that they expect me to overthrow the Issradians," I grimaced. "When I attempted to get more information out of Corlyotir, she fled with the excuse of concluding other investigations."

"They've told you naught else?" Cadfael sat back in his seat, troubled. "In which case, you have yet to decide if you will allow us to keep Idris as our king."

"Well... I haven't been given a reason to think he shouldn't be king." I tilted my head, glancing at the incubus in question. He looked even more uncomfortable and troubled than our companions did. "I'm under the impression that the gods favor him. If they didn't, they wouldn't have allowed him to visit my world. Besides, I want to deal with the Issradians. I have no interest in forcing Nabyr-zahn to find a new ruler or to change its existing structure."

"Yet you are the driving force behind our sudden focus on expansion and our reclamation of lost holds." Cadfael eyed me suspiciously. "The others will remain silent, but I will not. I am not fond of this notion that our holds will be repaired and inhabited by Otherworlders. While many of us abandoned them for the safety of Cejari-ir, we wished to reclaim our former territories in our own time."

"And what's that, a few decades? Centuries?" I shot back, narrowing my eyes at Cadfael. "The incoming tide of Otherworlders aside, retreating behind Cejari-ir's walls gives you little strategic advantage in the coming war. The Issradians can freely traverse into your lands and cross them. As it stands, the city's mountainous location is its only line of defense. By retaking your holds and having them both rebuilt and staffed by Otherworlders, you give yourself a better grasp on *your own territory*. Furthermore, Otherworlders are essentially immortal soldiers, allowing you to continue keeping most of your manpower within Cejari-ir itself."

"You know full well that she is right." Idris made a loose motion with one hand. "Should her estimates be accurate, millions of Otherworlders shall soon be joining Jeriskyr."

"Let me put it this way," I stopped Cadfael when he opened his mouth to protest again, "even if Nabyr-zahn receives only ten percent of the inbound Otherworlders, you could easily be looking at a million or more people. Can Cejari-ir house one million new citizens?"

"...no," Cadfael relented.

"By my estimates, Mistress, the city could not hold even ten percent of one million," Bruce informed me as he strode toward our table. After looking to Idris briefly, as if for permission, the AI-turned-incubus sat across from us. "Launch was perhaps a day away when I left Earth. It would be prudent to provide the early access players with quests to keep the influx of new players in line. If Master Idris' vassals are concerned about the Otherworlders running their holds, perhaps they should retake their rightful positions."

"For now, I have no intention of stripping Idris of his title," I stated, shooting Cadfael a sharp look when he opened his mouth to speak. "If he wasn't a good king, you and the others wouldn't follow him as loyally as you do. I'm confident that Idris will weigh any information or suggestions I give him appropriately. Having good ideas is one thing, but finding a way to realistically implement them is another—and I simply don't have enough knowledge of this world yet.

"As for the Otherworlders, it's either expand Cejari-ir's

capacity many times over, allow the Otherworlders to take up residence in other parts of Nabyr-zahn, or deal with them taking up space in the streets and taverns."

"Need I remind you both that this is meant to be a feast, not a meeting?" Elidyr spoke up, lifting a glass of wine off the table. He cut his eyes to the side when Cadfael huffed. "Unless you wish for our guests, invited or otherwise, to learn of our plans?"

"I see." Cadfael nodded to Elidyr after a moment of thought. "In that case, I will withhold judgment for now."

Right. For now. I refrained from rolling my eyes, instead glancing toward Idris when I heard a low chuckle escape him. *Care to explain what this nonsense regarding removing you from the throne is about?*

There is little else to say that hasn't already been said, Idris offered, reaching over to brush loose hair out of my face. *It is true that, as champion, it is within your right to choose another ruler for Nabyr-zahn. That the gods did not tell you as much troubles me. I find it unlikely they withheld the information purely because they favor me. In the past, they have always left such decisions to the discretion of champions.*

"Your Majesty, I've brought your favorite wine!" A beaming succubus approached the table. She stopped next to Bruce and set the bottle on the table, one hand on the seal. "May I pour for you, Your Majesty?"

"Certainly." Idris withdrew his hand from my hair and lifted a nearby glass, moving it across the table. "It has been some time since I last visited the harem chambers. Tell me, is there anything you or the others require?"

Require? I glanced between them briefly before picking up a biscuit and taking a large bite out of it. *Hmmm, I wonder if I could get away with taking out some of the harem members.*

"Hardly, Your Majesty!" The woman shook her head firmly. "We want for nothing. Anything we could ask for, you and Lady Moonfire are already making strides toward."

"Speaking of Lady Moonfire," another woman spoke up, approaching with a platter of food balanced on one hand. Her pink eyes settled on me with a questioning, almost worried look in them. "How are you holding up, my lady? This beast isn't being too rough with you, is he?"

Beast? I followed her gaze, finding Idris was indeed who she was looking at. "That isn't how I'd describe him, but is that really an appropriate topic?"

"It is the *only* way to describe His Majesty's performance in bed." The woman stared at me in disbelief. "I struggle to believe he's finally found his match. You needn't lie simply because of his presence here. Should you need a rest from his attentions, there are a few of us he has yet to break in."

"I'm not lying, and I don't need 'replacements.'" The corner of my eye twitched as I attempted to shelve my rising jealousy. After all, I didn't even have a name for our relationship. There wasn't a reason for me to feel such an ugly emotion. *Even so...perhaps I should consider getting rid of* all *the harem members instead?*

"Cerys is being quite honest." Idris reached over to grip my chin, turned my face to face his, and gave me a mischievous smirk. "I believe this may be a case where actions speak louder than words."

His lips met mine with slow, deliberate passion. He lured me into desiring more, yet withheld it from me. When he withdrew, I had half a mind to climb onto his lap and have my way with him.

You will have to wait. Idris gave me another brief kiss before turning his attention to our stunned companions. "Does that answer your question?"

"Y-yes, Your Majesty." Both women nodded hurriedly.

"Good. Then I suggest you pour Lady Moonfire a drink, and you set down that platter. Once you are finished, rejoin your companions." Idris let go of me and settled in his throne, crossing one leg over the other. "Bruce."

"Yes, Master Idris?" Bruce gave the king a quizzical look.

"Fetch *that* for me." Idris made a motion with one hand, sending one of his swords arcing through the air. The blade pierced a shadow, eliciting a pained yowl from the person it had struck.

Within moments, Bruce had left his seat and wandered over to the hiding human. I watched as he lifted the bleeding man off the ground by the tunic and carried him over to us. The bastard wore

Issradian colors, drawing the lethal attentions of nearly every incubus and succubus in the gardens.

"Good, it is not an Otherworlder," Idris remarked, a dangerous smile spreading across his face. "Take him to the dungeons. We can deal with him later. Make certain he cannot take his own life. Drysi, show Bruce the way."

"Yes, Your Majesty!" The succubus in question hurried over with a bright smile and eagerly tugged on Bruce's arm. Bruce, however, shot me a questioning look as if he needed my approval as well.

"I'm sure I'm in capable hands," I stated dryly. "Best not to keep *His Majesty* waiting."

"Very well. I will return soon." Bruce nodded to me and then pivoted to look down at the excited succubus. "Lead on."

"Yes!" Drysi excitedly pulled him back toward the palace.

You needn't be so jealous of my harem, Idris drawled, tugging at my hair briefly. He smirked when I spared him an agitated glance. *Now then, pace yourself while drinking your wine, kitten. It is quite strong—especially for someone with no tolerance. For now, we enjoy ourselves. Tomorrow, we hunt.*

Chapter Thirty-Eight
Excursion

I watched Cerys with a critical eye as she tore through slimes and root golems in the Veilwood Forest. The creatures were small, but Otherworlders often fell to even such simple creatures. Given the growing reports of monster attacks in the forest, I could not permit myself to relax while Cerys fought them. I had promised not to intervene unless she was in danger, yet it did not feel right to do nothing.

Alas, I could not bring myself to take my eyes off her either.

She is beautiful... I let my gaze travel down her torso to her long legs and tail. She did not appear to struggle with the extra limb despite her origins. In fact, she excelled at managing it. *I believe she is ready to learn how to use her tail in combat. Perhaps she could wield one of her swords with her tail? No, no... I cannot have her tail harmed. Perhaps I should have armor commissioned for it.*

My eyes narrowed when the earth before Cerys trembled and then dropped by several feet. She took on a more relaxed stance, her swords coming to float peacefully behind her before she pivoted to shoot an amused smirk my way. When I did nothing, she raised a hand and beckoned me with one finger, her voice carrying to me. "I learned a new trick!"

"A new trick?" I frowned at her. "From what I understand, you have dented the earth befo..."

My words left me once I drew near enough to see the bottom of the pit she had created. The bottom was blanketed with darkness that absorbed all light, save for the glowing purple edges. Cerys' prey struggled to free themselves from it, looking much as if they were wading through a substance thicker than molasses. The thick strands of darkness stuck to them, weighing them down and fully immobilizing the smaller creatures.

I couldn't tear my eyes off the strange magic until Cerys leaned up against my side, her plush chest pressing into my ribs. When I looked down at her, I found a delighted, mischievous grin plastered on her face. Yet there was a glimmer in her eyes which indicated she was seeking approval or praise. A smile came to my face and I ran my fingers through her hair.

"And what gave you the idea for such a useful spell, hmmm?" I questioned, glancing away from her and toward the unnerving darkness again. *I am beginning to understand how Tegau felt about her techniques. It certainly appears to be a form of shadow magic. However, she is not yet at the level to be creating her own spells.*

"I thought it'd be amusing to drown them in darkness and I got that instead," she shrugged, one of her swords floating past to point at the pit. "I figured that shadow magic should be capable of mimicking water if it can imitate fire. Not quite the result I was expecting, but still useful."

No, that is certainly not water. I kept my expression pleasant and stroked her hair again. "Do you intend to keep them alive, or will you finish them off?"

Her expression fell slightly, a look of disappointment coming to her face. "You don't approve?"

She truly desires validation from me? I wondered. Chuckling, I smiled and leaned down to kiss the top of her head. "It is a wonderful spell, Cerys, and it will be incredibly useful should you master it. However, we have more monsters to kill before we return, so it is best not to play with them overlong."

Cerys pursed her lips briefly, shifting her gaze to the trapped creatures. I spotted a deadly glint in her eyes moments before the entire pit was engulfed in black and amethyst flames. Sighing, she brushed loose hair out of her eyes and began to search for more prey. If she was aware of my intent stare, she was choosing to ignore it. She seemed entirely unaware of just how strange her spellcraft truly was.

At any rate, such spells will certainly be useful. I cocked my head, my gaze dropping to Cerys' round bottom and the playful swishing of her tail. "Perhaps that is enough for the day, Cerys. If you go on much longer you may cause yourself harm."

"Hmmm? But I'm almost to Journeyman!" she huffed, pivoting to glare and pout at me. "One more level each in shadow magic and spellsword, two levels in martial arts, and I'll be a fully Journeyman Shadowdancer. That's when it slows down, right? So, if I get to that level now it'll mean the next time we go out I'll be working through the new proficiency range. That would be more efficient than leaving now."

"I suppose we can remain for a while longer, within reason," I relented with a heavy sigh. "This area appears to be clear, so we shall move on to the next. The reports regarding the increase in monsters were true…and I would like to know what is causing this phenomenon."

"Maybe your 'gods' are preparing for the influx of Otherworlders," Cerys suggested, causing me to frown at her. "The 'starting zone' in new 'games' usually suffers an issue of too many people and not enough things to kill. All the Otherworlders who side with Nabyr-zahn are going to spawn in the Veilwood Forest.

"Oh, speaking of starting zones, I didn't expect I'd be able to make this much progress in the forest itself. Once I'm a

Journeyman, will we be venturing somewhere else?"

"We're near to where you will continue your training," I murmured, rubbing my chin in thought. After a moment, I motioned for her to follow me and led her toward the south. "You will kill more monsters on our way to the forest's edge. Since we are so close to the valley proper, I see no harm in letting you look."

Cerys beamed and wrapped both of her arms around one of mine. I felt my pulse quicken as she squeezed my arm against her chest. Forcing my expression to remain passive, we walked through the forest that way. As much as I enjoyed her change in behavior, I wished to remain cautious. It was difficult for me to accept the change at face value, no matter how much I desired her actions to be genuine. I was pinned between my interest in her and my crumbling belief in the gods' competence.

It was not long before Cerys found more prey and released my arm to focus on her hunt. As she strode away from me, I made a subtle motion to indicate I wanted our stealthed escort to stay out of her fight. The air rippled near me as our guards took a step back and fanned out around us. Cerys was still incapable of detecting stealth, but her other senses appeared to be functioning well. Several times throughout the day, she had stopped to examine our surroundings, clearly aware that we were being watched.

"Where'd she learn that magic?" Silas kept his voice low as he allowed his stealth ability to dissipate. He stood a few feet away from me, his arms crossed over the front of his leather armor. The brief glance he shot my way made it clear that Tegau and I were not the only ones who felt uneasy.

"She began using it out of nowhere, according to Tegau." I shook my head slightly, returning my gaze to Cerys.

The woman in question spun her swords around her body with a flourish, adding blades made of pure darkness to the array. If the number of weapons, magical or otherwise, were indicative of her capabilities, she needed another eight or more swords commissioned soon. I had hoped that Shadowdancer would suit her, but never had I expected that she would utilize it so well, so soon. There were still numerous techniques for her to learn, and then master, but her progress thus far had already demolished my expectations.

Cerys' blades scattered, each piercing a different target and ripping them in two. With her swords gone, she attacked the nearest root golem with a savage-yet-graceful kick. Within minutes, she had cleared out the lurking monsters. She sauntered back over to me with a cocky smile on her lips, her gaze only briefly lingering on Silas before returning to me.

"Is there anything special I need to do after hitting Journeyman in any of my proficiencies?" Cerys crossed her arms over her stomach, her tail swaying lazily behind her.

"I will have to have more reading material delivered to you," I answered, examining her briefly. The golden medallions shining over her head indicated that she truly had moved on to the next tier in each of her chosen proficiencies. After blinking away the information, I contemplated how to approach her on the matter of her odd usage of magic.

"Have you unlocked any other magic skills, Lady Moonfire?" Silas spoke up, shooting me a brief, knowing, look.

"Other magic skills?" Cerys pivoted to look at Silas, her mouth curving into a subtle frown. She fell silent for a moment, her gaze going unfocused. "Not that I can see. Why?"

"Because shadow magic is certainly not all that you have been utilizing." I rubbed my chin and glanced toward a nearby section of dented soil. "In fact, it does not appear to be a form of elemental magic at all."

"Yet there's nothing to indicate you have a fourth skill 'equipped,'" Silas added, pointing above Cerys' head. "I've heard of champions receiving a gift in the form of additional skills from the gods before. However, such abilities still require training."

"I believe Mistress Cerys is utilizing gravity magic," Bruce stated, approaching us from the nearby underbrush. Drysi, Emrys, and a handful of soldiers followed close behind him. "The plant matter and soil in the craters she created are utterly flattened. Compacted, as if a great weight had rested there."

"Gravity?" Cerys arched an eyebrow but fell silent, contemplation written on her face.

"What other feats have you managed?" I crossed my arms. "The way you 'drowned' the monsters seemed to lock them in place. Tegau suggested that there is much else you have managed."

"I can create an orb of darkness that pulls in nearby objects." Cerys glanced around, then motioned toward a nearby fallen tree. One of her swords lashed out and drew a circle, summoning a light-eating orb. Within seconds, the broken pieces of the tree, stone, and other debris began to spin around it.

"Gravity magic would *have* to be a gift from the gods." Emrys hefted his hammer, resting it on one shoulder. "How's she meant to train in something we can't teach her?"

"Mistress, you should find another section in your UI dedicated to special skills," Bruce stated, striding toward Cerys. "If your ability is a 'gift from the gods' it should reveal itself there."

"UI?" I frowned.

"User interface." Bruce glanced toward me. "Jeriskyr natives are capable of examining information and knowledge in a visual manner, yes? In games, such things are called a user interface— UI—or a heads up display—HUD."

"He's right," Cerys murmured, tilting her head. "I've got a new section in my 'UI' for special skills, and gravity magic is there. Looks like there's only five levels, though."

"And what level are you at?" I prompted.

"Zero." Cerys grimaced. "There's only a sliver of experience in the bar. I don't see anything indicating a list of abilities related to gravity magic, either."

"Of course not," I sighed.

"We could scrounge around in the Hall of the Gods," Silas pointed out with a grin.

"Cerys is not ready to fight the guardians there." I gave Silas a foul look. "When we return, I will instruct Tegau to have Halwyn, Cai, and Seren search their library for references to gravity magic."

"Not ready?" Cerys echoed. "Are you underestimating me, or is it filled with super high-level monsters?"

"It is somewhere you should not go until you are a Master, and only with Master or higher companions." I gave her a firm look when I spotted the amused grin spreading across her face. "Come along. I told you we could look at the next place where you will be training, and I meant it. After, we will return to the palace for dinner and rest.

"Emrys, how did Bruce perform?"

"He's got potential, but can't seem to make up his mind on what skills to focus on," Emrys shrugged.

"What is it, Cerys?" I frowned at her, having noticed the piercing gaze she'd settled on her former AI.

"Bruce, how did you know about the special skill tab?" Cerys prodded him in the chest.

"One of the gods responsible for my appearance here gifted me with space magic," Bruce stated with a small, nonchalant shrug.

"Space...magic?" Cerys stared at him.

"Space?" Silas echoed before glancing up at the sky. "You couldn't possibly mean *that* manner of space?"

"Perhaps dimensional magic would be a better term?" Bruce offered. Spotting our dumbfounded expressions, he frowned before making a motion. A small, flat circle of pitch blackness appeared near us, and he directed his attention to Cerys. "Mistress, please send one of your swords through the portal."

"One of my... Okay, maybe a practice one," Cerys grumbled, summoning one of her practice swords from her inventory. The moment it flew through the portal, a second one appeared dozens of feet away. Her sword emerged almost immediately and buried itself into a tree.

"It is called 'space magic' in my UI, but 'dimensional magic' appears more fitting," Bruce offered when we turned to look at him. "I am uncertain of what proficiencies would synergize well with such an ability."

"Emrys." I glanced toward him.

"I'll help him find something." Emrys sighed heavily. "You said you wanted to show them Caradoc's Pillars before leaving, Your Majesty? If so, we should get moving. It'll be sundown soon."

After reclaiming her practice sword, Cerys rejoined us and we set off toward the forest's edge as a group. She remained silent as we walked, her expression contemplative. I worried that she might become too absorbed in her thoughts and walk into a tree, but she wove through the underbrush and around trees with surprising grace.

You are shivering. I flipped her hood up over her head. She shot me a disgruntled look before sliding her horns into place and readjusting her coat. *Shall we hasten our pace in order to return sooner?*

As long as the wind doesn't pick up, I'll be fine. She shook her head.

"Here we are, Caradoc's Pillars!" Silas motioned broadly with both arms as we left the forest.

Cerys grew still, her eyes widening slightly as she looked out over the scenery before us. Tall pillars of stone, or perhaps eroded mountainous formations, dotted the valley before us. Rivers and streams cut through much of the valley, resulting in a patchwork of small-to-medium landmasses akin to islands. The largest pieces of land were flower-filled meadows during warmer months, but now the dark purple foliage was covered in a dusting of snow. If the weather remained on course, it would be buried in white within the next few days.

Soon, Cerys' stance shifted to a more menacing one and she reached for the fan tucked into her belt. I followed her gaze, only to find a group of kitsune approaching us upon cauchemars at a cautious pace. Most of the men among them were armored soldiers, but the one on the largest steed was a man I had fought both with *and* against many times in the past. His hair, furry ears, and tail were pitch black, his eyes a piercing yellow. Unlike his armed escort, he wore mage's attire suitable for the winter months.

"I wasn't expecting the King of Nabyr-zahn to greet me

personally—nor did I ask for an escort to Cejari-ir." The kitsune narrowed his eyes as I moved to tuck Cerys behind me.

"*We* heard nothing of your arrival, Eifion." I kept my tone neutral as I focused my senses. Other than his armored guards, he had a dozen or more hidden companions as well.

"Then my missing messenger isn't your doing." Eifion frowned, before glancing to my right. A subtle expression of surprise, followed by an amiable smile, spread across his features. "And this must be the 'Lady Moonfire' I've heard so much about. Pray, forgive me if I have interrupted your training session, my lady."

"What is your business in Nabyr-zahn?" Emrys placed the head of his hammer against the ground with a loud *thud*, moving so that he was between Eifion and myself.

"I received King Bloodsong's missive regarding the Issradian's claim of taxing you every six months," Eifion stated, his mouth twisting into a feral scowl. "The humans came to us with a similar threat. However, instead of taking a champion from us, as we have none, they wanted to task us with stealing yours and selling her to them.

"We declined. I sent one of my men to inform you I would be coming to talk business with your king, but…"

He is telling the truth. Silas glanced toward me.

I sighed heavily, forcing my posture to relax. Cerys took the opportunity to step around me, her arms crossed. She tapped her closed fan against her upper arm as she examined Eifion and his escort. After a moment, she looked back at me with a small smirk. *I'm hungry. Are you going to let them come to Cejari-ir or not?*

"I am to understand you wish to have amiable discussions with my kingdom?" I returned my attention to the kitsune king.

"Indeed," Eifion smiled. "It's been too long since we were on the same side. As you know, my kind have always preferred to side with whomever has a champion. I'm told some of the beastmen are looking to join you as well."

"I will not ask you and yours to surrender your weapons," I informed him, placing a hand on my hip. "The Issradians have been sending far too many spies into our city. You're welcome to capture, interrogate, and/or kill them. I simply ask that you do not harm my subjects or our champion, and that you share anything you learn with us while you remain within our walls."

"Reasonable enough!" Eifion laughed. "Shall we? It is a long ride back to your capital from here, is it not?"

"I can expedite our travel if you wish, Master Idris," Bruce offered with a slight bow. Cerys sighed heavily and gave the AI an uneasy look. "I assure you, it is quite safe, Mistress Cerys. The gods taught me how to use the skill before dropping me into this world. It is akin to a warp, return, hearth, or home point skill in games.

"It takes a great deal of energy, of course, but I do not think Drysi will mind helping me replenish."

"Absolutely!" the demoness squeaked, promptly latching onto

621

Bruce's arm. A brilliant smile came to her face as she squeezed his arm into her bust. "Oh, but I should heal you first once we get back. You have some nasty bruises and scratches from fighting!"

Bruises? Scratches? Cerys tilted her head, examining Bruce for a moment before looking toward me. ...*I don't see any. Do you?*

I do not, I replied dryly. *Bruce may have gotten more than he bargained for with this one.*

"I'll have some of my men look for your missing messenger," Silas stated, making a motion with one hand. Soon after, half a dozen pairs of footprints sped across the snow. "It is possible that he got lost while navigating the far side of Caradoc's Pillars."

"I thank you for your efforts." Eifion nodded to Silas, then addressed Bruce next. "You said you have some gods-given ability to hasten our travel?"

Without a word, Bruce summoned a portal twice the size of the mounted kitsune party. Drysi pranced through it after an encouraging nudge from him.

"This will take us to the palace's courtyard," Bruce offered when the rest of us hesitated. "I assure you it is safe."

"Such an ability... Why, the applications in combat—" I began, but Bruce quickly shook his head and raised a hand to stop me.

"It is a one-way portal, Master Idris," he stated. "It makes use of the bind points Otherworlders use to respawn for fast travel. As such, I can only teleport to ones I've visited and am attuned to. I am also limited by distance. My hope is that the range will increase with training.

"I request you hurry. We are near my maximum distance and keeping the portal open is a great strain."

Learning of his limitations disappointed me, but perhaps I had been too hopeful. A long-range transportation system that could carry an army into a suitable place for an ambush or a battle would have been far too powerful, at least without training. Shelving my disappointment, I chose to risk taking the portal back to Cejari-ir.

"Very well," I nodded, pulling Cerys close to my side. The moment I touched her, I felt just how strongly she was shivering. My—I paused. *My what? I can hardly call her 'my champion,' or my anything else, for that matter.*

"Emrys, you and Elidyr see to our guests while I take care of the last of Cerys' lessons for the day," I ordered, leading Cerys past my companion. He bowed, but they all disappeared the moment we entered Bruce's portal. It felt like cold, thick liquid. The sensation was over in seconds, and we found ourselves in the courtyard of my palace. Drysi appeared to have run off somewhere already.

"Looks like everything is in its proper place," Cerys remarked, giving herself a quick once-over. "So, where to?"

"Bath, dinner, a game, perhaps some studying…" I murmured, an amused smile coming to my lips when I spotted her tail twitching. "Did you have something else in mind, Cerys?"

"Gee, I wonder." She gave me an impatient look. "Or would the 'beast' prefer I find someone else to sate my appetite for a few nights?"

My tail twitched into the ground hard, a low growl escaping me. An unapologetically self-satisfied smile spread across her mouth as she turned to face me fully.

"Oh? Was that a 'no?'" Cerys took a step forward and gripped the front of my coat in both her hands, tugging me toward her. "If you want to bait me into saying what you want to hear, you will have to try harder or be less obvious. Now then, you never answered me—your bed or mine?"

"…mine. However, I still insist on dinner and a bath first."

Chapter Thirty-Nine
Making Plans

I strolled into the palace library in search of my guild mates. A few guards had mentioned seeing them go that way, and sure enough, I found two of them by a table the moment I entered.

"Oh hey, boss." Ivan looked up from a map, surprise on his face. "The palace library is crazy, right?"

"And here I thought you were being kept prisoner in the Queen's Tower," Joel snorted, snapping his book shut.

"I'm not a prisoner," I stated dryly. "Where's Declan?"

"Buried in a pile of books somewhere." Ivan glanced over his shoulder, then pointed deeper into the library. "You looking for him, or all of us?"

"All of you. Our hosts want me to find you work," I shrugged, striding toward the back of the library in search of Declan. When I found him, I had to stifle my laughter. He'd picked the kitsune race and appeared to be struggling to keep a pair of glasses on his nose. Furthermore, his fluffy reddish-brown ears kept twitching in agitation or interest as he quickly skimmed the pages of a massive tome. "Declan? *Declan!*"

"Oh, sorry, Cery!" Declan yelped when I pulled on one of his ears. He looked up finally, then stopped when he spotted me. "What the hell are you wearing?"

"Normal demoness attire." I flicked his forehead. "Come on. I need to talk to the three of you about how you're going to make yourselves useful while you're stuck here."

Once we'd rejoined Ivan and Joel, I perched on a chair and examined the three men for a moment. Ivan had chosen to become a naga, Declan a kitsune, and Joel was...something. Of the three of them, Joel blended in best with the people of Cejari-ir—but I got the feeling he wasn't an incubus. There was something different about him, though I couldn't put my finger on what.

"So, our demon overlords want us to work?" Joel scoffed.

"Even the harem members earn their keep," I shrugged. "From what I hear, the three of you weren't capable of combat while on the Issradians' side, right?"

"Ugh, don't get me started on that." Ivan held up a hand,

grimacing. "Silas has me practicing archery and some other useful skills, but I'd rather not have to use them."

"Same here," Declan sighed, his ears drooping. "I wanted to become some sort of magic user, but I'm not cut out for fighting."

"And you, Joel?" I looked toward the cranky man.

"I'd rather keep my hide in place while waiting to go back to Earth, if it's all the same to you." Joel made a sour face. "Not against working, mind you. Just keep me far from anything that will result in an arrow to the knee—or anywhere else, for that matter."

"...Joel, that game came out decades ago," I groaned, rubbing my temples. "Or has it been a century now? Longer? Hell, even the remake may as well be ancient."

"Like that'll stop him from milking it," Declan muttered.

"I'm going to keep training in archery so I can defend myself or hunt if I have to," Ivan interjected, making a loose motion. "Regarding work, though, I think most of us would prefer something along the crafter-gatherer line of thinking."

"Cejari-ir needs many more of both." I tapped my claws against the table as I considered it, then shifted my attention to Declan. "For you, I think I have an idea how you can still be a magic user."

"Go on," Declan urged, leaning forward.

"First of all, healing magic. As the city's population increases, we're going to need more healers in the palace and in the city itself," I offered, watching as he grimaced. "Second option, I found references to rune and emblem crafting earlier today in one of my new Shadowdancer books. They require magical skill to craft, calligraphy proficiency, and engraving or carving proficiency. It sounds like there's a few ways you can build the class, and magic is a core component."

"Runes and emblems?" Declan frowned. "We've seen stuff like that in games, but how's it work here?"

"I think one of my swords has a rune, hold on." I summoned one of my weapons from my inventory and set it flat on the table. "Here, look at the hilt. These gems have what look like symbols suspended inside of them. 'Emblems' sounded like some sort of carving or embossing that goes on clothes and armor. They don't give stats, seeing as Jeriskyr doesn't have things like strength or intelligence. What they *do* give are augments to existing abilities. Siphons, like drain or leech, shields, and so on. I saw some references to ones that keep weapons from growing dull or breaking as easily, too."

"Word! I'll go into the city and see if I can learn more," Declan grinned.

"I'm going to pick up tailoring and leatherworking," Joel stated flatly. "I should be able to help design more practical clothes and armor. I plan to find a solution to the 'tail' problem, too. Having our pants hanging so low shouldn't be necessary."

"Well, you were studying fashion and the like on Earth, so I suppose that makes sense." I tilted my head, thinking on it. "I could definitely do with more practical clothes. Especially pants. Incubi and succubi like showing off skin, though, so you may run into resistance."

"I've already started sketching designs." Joel lifted a sheet of paper and turned it toward me. Most of the page was covered with sketches of different ways to handle 'tail holes.'

"How about you, Ivan?" I glanced toward the snakeman.

"So, one of the perks of being a naga is immunity to naturally occurring poisons and venom." Ivan stroked his chin. "I'm thinking of becoming a botanist of some sort, maybe pair it with alchemy or cooking. Or both. This body gives me some interesting advantages, and poison resistance means I can safely 'test' plants myself."

"Sounds like you're all set, then." I nodded to them.

"What about you, Cery? What's a 'Shadowdancer?'" Declan tilted his head and pointed to me. "We all saw the server-wide...err, worldwide, announcement when you earned it. I've seen plenty of people with those class picks though, and none of them were a Shadowdancer. Hell, how are you a Journeyman in all those skills already?"

"Lots of training," I shrugged, sitting back in my seat. "Shadowdancer is Nabyr-zahn's hidden class; you have to get a ton of reputation with Idris to have it unlocked, I'm assuming. At least, he's the one who unlocked it for me. It can be made from a few different skill combos, these are just what I chose. I could have picked just about any melee weapon-type instead of martial arts. Spellsword could've been replaced too."

"If we're going to be useful, we should get going." Joel gave the other two men agitated looks. "Not all of us have fur, and I'm pretty sure snakes don't do well in the snow. Cery probably has a lot of work to see to, too."

They all bid me farewell, leaving me alone in the library. After a few moments of silence, I rose from my seat and strode from the library at a leisurely pace. I wasn't in any particular rush to get anywhere, even though I knew my presence had been requested elsewhere once I was finished with the Ebonwing members. My idea of taking a slower pace was soon interrupted by an amused chuckle.

"You were taking too long," Idris stated from my left when I pivoted to glare at him. "However, I did not want to interrupt your conversation with your 'subjects.' They seemed surprisingly eager to get to work."

"They're active sorts. If they stayed in Silas' manor doing nothing they'd go crazy." I shook my head. "I looked around for Bruce as well but couldn't find him anywhere. Any idea where he went?"

"Emrys took him into the city to learn his skills," Idris replied with an amused grin. "Now then, are you finished with your tasks? It would be best if we rejoined our guests and the nobles sooner rather than later."

"I'm ready," I nodded, moving to accompany him down the hallway. "Do you think the other kings are going to send envoys, or will they come themselves, like Eifion has?"

"Unlikely. Eifion is one of the more amiable kings," Idris answered dryly. "Demon or otherwise, he allies himself with whichever kingdom or tribe has a champion seeking to overthrow the Issradians. We will learn soon enough if the other kingdoms are willing to entertain an alliance, or at least friendlier terms. Currently, none of the demon kingdoms have so much as a trade agreement."

"Sounds like a hot mess," I sighed, crossing my arms over my stomach. "So, Eifion's 'quirk' is why you need me to join you instead of working on my training or studying? I guess that makes sense. My presence gives you leverage, right?"

"Leverage is merely a bonus." Idris gave me a charming smile. "Your company is what I find most desirable."

"If you say so." I tilted my head. "Still no word regarding Alice?"

"Nothing we have not heard before." He glanced at me. "You are worried?"

"Of course I am," I nodded. "I trust this world's gods about as far as I can throw them."

"I was just about to come looking for the two of you." Elidyr stood before the throne room doors with his arms crossed and an irritated look on his face. "What took you so long?"

"Cerys was giving the displaced Ebonwing members tasks to focus on," Idris answered. "With that finished, there should be no further distractions. Shall we?"

"Please. Before the fox grows any more impatient." Elidyr sighed, his mouth twisting in distaste.

The three of us entered the throne room to find the Nabyrzahn nobles looking quite cranky and the party of kitsunes standing on the opposite side of the room. Eifion looked right at home, but most of his men appeared uneasy. Nearby, several men of various demonic races waited in a corner. They had seen better days. Their leather armor was torn in places and several of the men had bandaged cuts or gashes.

"More guests?" I asked.

"Messengers, my lady," Eifion answered, following my gaze. "Lord Silas found more than my missing man hiding within Caradoc's Pillars."

"Monsters are an issue in more places than the Veilwood Forest, it seems." Silas moved his kiseru away from his mouth and shot us an amused grin. "What do you want us to do about it, Your Majesty? Shall we thin them out?"

"No. If Cerys is right and the increased monster activity is the gods' doing, we will only make it worse if we interfere." Idris grimaced as he made himself comfortable on his throne. When I opted to lean up against the side of his throne, his attention shifted in my direction. *You will not join me?*

I've been sitting for most of the day. I'd rather stand. I opened my fan with a flourish and brought it up so that I could lightly fan myself—something that seemed to mesmerize several of Eifion's men. *The messengers are bleeding all over your floor.*

"Four messengers, four kings who are not present in this room…" Idris tilted his head as he examined the men. "Deliver your messages quickly. Then you may seek out the infirmary and a hot meal."

"I am come at the behest of King Silverscale, Your Majesty." One of the men moved forward and bowed as far as he could with wounded ribs. "My master proposes a meeting in neutral territory, that the kings might come together and discuss how best to deal with the Issradian blight. We too were threatened with a tax occurring every six months. Furthermore, our spies in Darmos have made us aware that the humans seek to wipe out the non-human races once and for all. King Silverscale believes it in our best interests to come to some manner of agreement."

The messengers behind the first all voiced similar statements from their kings. A meeting of kings, their most trusted men, and me. Far from the border with the Issradian Empire, in unclaimed territory. Eifion soon voiced his agreement as well.

"Silas, assign them guides," Idris ordered, turning his gaze to the smirking incubus. "We will have this meeting, but it would be foolish to send the messengers back on their own. They managed to get lost once already. Let us not have a repeat occurrence."

"Of course, Your Majesty." Silas nodded, grinning, before turning to look at the messengers. "Go get yourselves checked out and have a hot meal. I'll come find you once this business is over."

"With that out of the way..." Eifion moved forward by a few paces. "Regardless of what the other kings choose, I wish to draft a formal alliance between Nabyr-zahn and **Dynim-tor**."

I listened in silence while the kings and their respective advisers discussed the possibilities of peace, trade routes, and waging war in tandem. It wasn't long before I realized that I was well and truly out of my element among these men. While I was capable of vaguely following their discussion and intentions thanks to civilization building games, running my own guild, and so on, those had all lacked an important element—real lives to protect and provide for.

For real rulers, it wasn't as simple as signing an agreement or giving orders. They spent the next several hours discussing what Nabyr-zahn and Dynim-tor could provide each other with, what their respective lands needed, and what luxuries their subjects would desire from foreign lands. Then there was the matter of battle and overthrowing the Issradians. Both countries had lost lands to the humans and wanted their territories back. Of course, they wanted to rescue their people as well.

"Your tea, Lady Moonfire." Elidyr offered me a cup, rousing me from my thoughts. He continued in a low, almost imperceptible voice, "Would you like me to fetch a chair for you,

Cerys? You have been standing for quite some time."

"I'm alright, thank you." I took the tea cup and saucer from Elidyr, giving him a small, thankful smile. *Though, that said, my presence really does seem to serve as leverage and little else. This may be the first time I've seen Idris focus so completely on something that he's paid no attention to me. Not sure how to feel about that.*

"Ah, are we boring you, Lady Moonfire?" Eifion shifted to look at me, an apologetic smile set on his lips.

"Not at all, I'm learning quite a bit," I answered, shaking my head. "Running a country is beyond my expertise, so this conversation has been enlightening. Don't let me get in your way."

"You are certain?" Idris glanced toward me, frowning.

"Quite. Unless my presence is no longer wanted or welcome, in which case I will take my leave." I looked down at the seated king, noting that he appeared taken aback for a moment before smoothing his expression over.

"So, it's true what they say. Lady Moonfire says whatever is on her mind." Eifion tilted his head and rubbed his chin while examining me. "You haven't put her in her place yet, Idris?"

"Hmmm?" I gave Eifion a baffled look. "What? I got the impression you two didn't need me here anymore, so—"

I would like you to remain, Idris stated quietly. I glanced toward him again, finding a determined glint in his eyes. *Furthermore, I insist that you sit down. You have been standing for hours. If you will not sit on my lap, I will scoot over to make room.*

...alright. I'll try not to spill tea on either of us. I decided to relent, and soon perched on the edge of Idris' throne, crossing my legs. He was quick to slide his fingers along my back, eventually resting his hand on my hip. He scooted me over a few inches so that my hip was pressed into his leg. I spared him a brief, questioning look before returning my attention to our 'guests.'

What troubles you? Idris gave me a brief squeeze before addressing Eifion, "Regarding wares to trade, perhaps you should see for yourself what manner of goods Cejari-ir might offer you. Our countries reside in very different climates...perhaps artisan goods?"

"Exploring the city sounds like a wonderful idea!" Eifion beamed. "It has been far too long since I was last in Cejari-ir. Your city appears much larger than it was when we were boys."

I'm out of my element, and I find it strange that the gods would choose someone with no clue about running countries for the role of 'champion,' I answered flatly. *It's true that I find your discussion interesting, though, despite feeling so incredibly out of place.*

What can I do to make you more comfortable? Idris inquired, his tail weaving around mine behind the throne. I forced myself to remain composed and took a sip of my tea, earning a low chuckle. *You are right to be cautious regarding the gods. However, knowing how to run a country is not a requirement for champions. If you wish to learn...you are more than welcome to accompany me more often.*

"You lot are still at it?" Emrys released a disgruntled snort as he threw open the throne room doors and strode in with Bruce close behind him. I blinked at the pair a few times, surprised to find the former AI carrying a longsword and a shield. "It's well past time for dinner. Why not continue this over food?"

"That sounds like an excellent idea," Idris remarked, smiling as he turned to face me. "Will you join us, Cerys?"

"If it's all the same to you, I'd like to get my training for the day in." I shook my head, then pursed my lips when his smile faltered.

"You really intend to let her fight?" Eifion questioned, his expression troubled. "If she's a strategist, as you say, would it not be safer to have her direct our troops' movements from the safety of your palace?"

"Safer, yes. Possible? No," Idris answered dryly. *This may be our only chance to enjoy each other's company for a while, Cerys. Are you certain you would rather not join us?*

I'm not in the mood to be around people I don't know, nor am I in the mood to put on airs, I replied, letting out a small sigh. *If it was just us, it'd be fine.*

"You won't be getting any training in tonight. Whole place is occupied by my men and Eifion's," Emrys informed me before Idris could relent. "Like it or not, you're stuck with us or with going back to your rooms. Which would you prefer?"

...well, shit. I pursed my lips and gave Emrys a foul look. "In that case, I suppose I will join you all for dinner after all."

"Excellent. Bruce will be using this opportunity to learn how he should guard you." Emrys grinned broadly before patting the man in question on the back, hard.

I will endeavor to be better company, Idris offered, rising to his feet with feline grace. He pivoted and offered me his hand, but the melancholy in his gaze made me pause.

Your company isn't the problem, I decided explaining now, or at least attempting to, was better than leaving him to sulk all night. *Do you ever have one of those moods where you would rather not be around most people? Just have yourself, a good drink, and silence, or the sound of a crackling fire? That's how I feel right now. Your company, or maybe even Bruce's, is about all I can tolerate right now.*

Idris' grip on my hand tensed as he pulled me to my feet.

Not that kind of company. I gave him a knowing look. *Drysi can keep the Sexbot 3000 to herself.*

The…what? Idris shook his head subtly. *Never mind. I understand what you are suggesting, at least. If you would rather return to the Queen's Tower…I will not stop you, but your presence will be missed.*

I thought about it while Idris turned away from me to converse with Emrys and Eifion. The decision between much-needed solitude and having Idris' company was a surprisingly difficult one. It wasn't long before I realized I'd come to enjoy his company and his attention, even if he was a bit over the top at times. I could tell that some repairs had yet to be made to our relationship, as well.

He'd become hesitant or cautious with me, as if I might revert to bitch mode at any moment. It was…understandable.

When Idris pivoted to offer me his arm, he kept his expression passive and waited in silence. His body seemed tense, like he was expecting me to lash out verbally, or even physically. Withholding a sigh, I accepted his arm and leaned up against his side, gently swatting at his tail with mine.

I suppose I can suffer through the company of others if it means indulging in your company when I wouldn't otherwise be able to. I paused, not quite sure if the statement conveyed my meaning correctly. In hindsight, it sounded a little passive aggressive. *That is to say—*

I am delighted to know you find my company so desirable, Idris beamed, his tone far more cheerful than I'd expected. *We shall entertain our guests for a while, then we can retire for the evening. Since we will both be so busy for the next few weeks, we should enjoy what time we have together as best we can.*

Idris, Eifion, Emrys, Elidyr, Bruce, and a variety of guards and nobles joined us as we made our way out of the throne room. I contemplated our coming separation as we went. The idea of rarely seeing Idris for more than a few days, if at all, made me crankier than expected. While I didn't want to get in his way, I also didn't want to be completely without his company. Furthermore, I had no idea how I was meant to be useful—or act as a bodyguard—if we wouldn't be near each other. The more I thought about it, the sourer I grew.

So, you won't be needing a bodyguard? I prompted, deciding I'd had enough.

I will be sequestered away in my study, writing messages, signing contracts, writing out instructions, accepting or declining building proposals... Idris made a loose motion with his free hand. *You should use the time for training. The Grandmasters have expressed interest in helping you advance, and it would be prudent for you to assist Bruce in acclimating to this world as well. I would have suggested you do the same for the Ebonwing members, but it is clear they will not be participating in combat.*

Well, let me know if I can help. I released a dejected sigh, earning an odd glance from him. He looked as if he were about to say something aloud, but our companions beckoning us to hurry up made him shut his mouth and hasten his pace.

"Mistress, I will be learning how to 'tank,'" Bruce informed me as we all settled in at a large banquet table. "After reviewing the possibilities, I have concluded that learning a protective class first would make the most sense when paired with your less-defensive choices. My abilities should assist me in enabling you to tear through your foes with little danger to your person."

"That should be useful," I murmured.

Idris paused mid-reach for his goblet to shoot me a concerned look. I shook my head in reply before shifting in my seat so that I was leaning closer to him, crossing one leg over the other. Good food and good drink sounded nice, but my mind didn't want to focus on either. There were too many other things for me to consider. Alice and the lack of information around her, Idris' upcoming work schedule, my training, and of course, the meeting with the demon kings. We would be traveling in the opposite direction of the Issradian Empire, yet I felt apprehension about the journey. I wasn't convinced that we would be without attackers, monsters or otherwise.

Monsters, I figured, were a given. I had a feeling the same was likely true for Issradians or Otherworlders.

"Such a beautiful woman should not make such a scary face," Eifion remarked with a bright smile, lifting his goblet in my direction. "What troubles my lady?"

I'm not 'your' anything, fluffy. I heard muffled laughter escape Idris, but he was quick to compose himself. "I was considering my training. If we're going to travel, I want to make damned sure I can deal with any monsters or *other threats* we might come across."

"Worrying about those is my job," Emrys pointed out.

"I'm not going to play damsel in distress and just *let* you lot have all the fun!" I scoffed, waving one hand. "If I don't get my share of monster slaying, I'll skin some of you instead."

"We will keep that in mind," Idris stated dryly, lifting a bottle of lavender-colored wine off the table and pulling my goblet toward him. *You should find that this wine pairs beautifully with what we shall be enjoying for dinner. Perhaps, if you exercise moderation, I will treat you to another of my favorites with dessert.*

No promises. I shot him a sideways glance. *I might need a lot more than one bottle to put up with our guests.*

Chapter Forty
Kids Say the Darnedest Things

"Mirela, you still haven't heard anything about Cery?" Alice pestered the fiery-haired woman, her face painted with worry.

All Ryan could do was sigh. Alice was doing her best to learn about Cerys, Idris, and their allies, but most of the Ebonwing members were growing suspicious. As they should have. They all knew Alice and Cerys often hung out together in real life, yet Alice asked almost daily if Mirela or her spies had heard anything new. Even the most brainless guild members had begun to question what Alice was on about.

"Alice, chill!" Mirela finally exclaimed. "I don't know how you expect me to find out all that while also dealing with what you want us to do in Darmos!"

"I… Sorry." Alice sighed, crestfallen.

"I did get one piece of info you might find interesting," Mirela offered, shooting her friend a grin. "Oh, but first…you want a report on that dungeon we cleared?"

"Oh, yes." Alice nodded, a look of recognition crossing her face. "Did everyone make it back okay?"

"We're all fine!" Mirela scoffed. "While our 'brave adventurers' were killing off the beasts inside, my men and I scoured every nook and cranny for treasure—and man, did we find a lot of it. My crew should be coming back with the last of our finds soon.

"Get this, though—we found relics!"

"Relics?" Ryan perked up, his interest truly piqued—if not for the reasons his guild mates thought. "Are any of them pink?"

"What is it with you and pink?" Mirela squinted at him. "No. No, none of them are pink. Looks like they're all super powerful, though. I did some quick item identifications, and most of them are one-time use."

"If they're one-time use, store them in the vault for now." Ryan crossed his arms when several of Mirela's squad groaned behind her. "Do a thorough inspection of them once they're all in the vault, then organize them by use."

"I agree," Alice echoed, nodding quickly. "They're probably super OP if you can only use them once. We can't have anyone just using them on a whim!"

"And if some would help us level faster?" Mirela sighed.

"If any of 'em have a nice use like that, Alice or I will use them to boost the guild," Ryan shrugged. "No using rare shit for stupid purposes, got it?"

"Fine, fine." Mirela flapped her hand. "We'll go store everything and get started on identifying them all."

"So, you said you learned something new about Cerys?" Alice asked hopefully.

"Sure did!" Mirela grinned from ear-to-ear. "Got word that Idris, his nobles, and the *First Consort* are gonna be heading east of Nabyr-zahn for some special meeting. Sounds like they're trying to strike some kinda deal with the other demon kings."

Already? Ryan frowned. *I thought they'd be 'dining' on each other for a while longer before getting around to anything useful. Honestly. Who do they think they're fooling?*

"First...*what*?" Alice burst into laughter. "Oh Cery. And she was so insistent that she wouldn't get attached to that man!"

"Well, she *is* just playing an NPC," Mirela pointed out with a frown.

"Er, of course," Alice coughed. "Well, we'll just have to go to Cery then!"

"Lady Alice..." Adric sighed heavily at the bubbly girl. "There are only a few places they could be going if they are heading east, and all of them are weeks away from here."

"The demons aren't going to make their move for a few weeks, so we've got time," Mirela shrugged, crossing her arms over her stomach. "I'll get started on identifying all the relics and gear we picked up in the dungeon. If we're going to take a vacation across demon lands, we'd better make damned sure we've got some useful stuff for it. I'll start poking people to see who can stay online to fulfill the escort quest positions, too."

Mirela left, leaving Alice, Ryan, and Adric standing in silence. Several moments passed before Alice let out a sigh, her cheerful mask fading. She glanced over at Ryan with a small, weak smile. "Can I get you to finish up our leader duties for the day? I think I want to go back to my rooms and rest...er, log out, for a bit."

"Sure thing!" Ryan grinned, nodding. Once Alice was gone, Ryan cut his eyes to the side and settled them on Adric, who shifted uncomfortably. "The emperor still wants to see you?"

"Yes," Adric answered with a brief nod.

"Okay. Bring me along as your squire. I'll change my specs real quick." Ryan shrugged and opened his UI, swiftly sorting through his windows while Adric stared at him in disbelief.

"My lord—" Adric was silenced with another sharp look and sighed. "Very well. His Excellency has been eager to meet Ebonwing's other leader, anyway..."

Ryan summoned armor suitable for a squire from his inventory and wiggled into it before following Adric across the palace grounds and to the main building. He adopted his amiable

Otherworlder facade, grinning like a fool at anyone they passed by. When they arrived outside the council chambers, Adric quickly explained Ryan's presence to the waiting guards, who soon allowed them through. Several nobles looked at the pair with distaste before turning their attention to the throne at one end of the long table.

"Your Excellency," Adric murmured, bowing in the direction of the throne.

A subtle frown settled on Ryan's face as he looked in the same direction and heard the high voice that came from it.

"I've told you before! We're brothers! You don't need to be so stiff." The young boy pouted at Adric. "Did you hear back from that stupid Eadgar yet?"

"No, but I did discover what happened to him." Adric straightened, keeping his expression passive. "He acted against your orders and took a party of tax collectors to the Kingdom of Nabyrzahn. On his return trip, they were killed by one of the infamous winter storms of the region."

"*What*?!" the boy emperor demanded. "I told him we're not taking taxes anymore! He was supposed to return the demons to their rightful kingdoms—*after* winter was over!"

Seriously? Ryan tilted his head, examining the child. There was certainly some resemblance between him and Adric, except the boy appeared to be full-blooded human. *Huh. Am I in the wrong decade? I thought Wullfric was still around. And what's this nonsense about returning the demons to their kingdoms? It would be wonderful if that were true, but…*

"Your Excellency, why would we send the creatures back to their own kingdoms?" A noble sighed heavily. "Without slaves—"

"Would you wanna be a slave?!" The child pouted defiantly at the older man. "You treat them so mean. They're people with families too! If you want the Issradian Empire to be great, it needs to be built with our own hands. Human hands! There's nothing 'great' about forcing the other races to do things for us. Just makes it look like we can't do anything for ourselves."

"You're certain it was the storm that killed Eadgar?" Another noble turned to look at Adric.

"Quite. The region is experiencing harsher weather than usual." Adric nodded to the noble, then turned his attention to his half-brother. "However, Eadgar's death should be the least of our worries. My spies informed me that, whilst in Cejari-ir, Eadgar attempted to force the demons to give up their champion. He told them that, if they did, they would no longer face a tax. If they refused, the tax would return every six months from now.

"The parties he sent to each of the other inhuman kingdoms offered similar terms—except each was aimed to encourage the other tribes to steal Nabyr-zahn's champion and sell her to us."

"Such blatant disregard of our emperor's wishes…" one of the nobles murmured, frowning. "I will not pretend to understand our emperor's plan, but acting against him is punishable by death. Eadgar got what he deserved. Only it would have been better if the demons had killed him themselves."

"If I might change the conversation for a moment, Your Excellency," Adric began, making a brief motion toward Ryan. "This is my squire, Ryan—"

"Just 'Ryan' is fine." Ryan grinned, shrugging.

"I was going to say, 'the co-leader of Ebonwing.'" The corner of Adric's eye twitched.

"Oh, excellent!" The boy emperor leaned forward in his throne, excited. "My impression of Lady Alice was that she's too sweet to run a guild herself. So, you must be the stern one."

"You could say that." Ryan tilted his head. "I heard you wanted to meet me... Your Excellency?"

"My advisers said women aren't fit to lead, so I wanted to make sure someone more capable was at the head of Ebonwing." The boy nodded quickly.

Internally, Ryan twitched. Alice wasn't to be underestimated. As far as he was concerned, anyone else would have broken under similar circumstances. Yet, she spent most of her time worrying about Cerys instead of herself. The boy probably wouldn't understand that—but the nobles would. They didn't need encouragement to explore their boundaries with the woman.

"Each of Ebonwing's officers holds a specific role." Ryan shrugged again. "We all have our specializations, including Alice. Just as each of your nobles here have a specialty, I'm sure."

"Ah, I see," the boy murmured, thinking. "I'll call for you when

I have need of you. For now, I wanna hear more of Adric's reports."

"Ryan has duties to attend to. If you will permit him to leave, Your Excellency?" Adric coughed, glancing at Ryan briefly before returning his attention to his half-brother.

"Oh, sure." The child nodded. "Bye-bye!"

…what happened to Wullfric? Ryan asked, turning on his heel to leave the room.

While you were off playing human on Earth, he disappeared. I thought you'd know that, Adric huffed in reply. *Wulfy—that is, Wullfric the…Eighth? Ninth? Was secretly made emperor a year ago. The public thinks our damnable father is still in power. We still haven't found him, remains or otherwise.*

After leaving the room, Ryan shifted time around himself before opening a portal to the gods' domain. When he arrived, Corlyotir glanced up in surprise, then tilted her head, looking him up and down.

"You are late." The gruff male voice caused Ryan to glance off to the left, finding a silver-haired demon leaning back against a wall.

"Huh. Caradoc's here too?" Meical asked, as his human disguise and bright pink hair melted away. He yawned, feigning boredom.

"Meical, I have great news!" Corlyotir exclaimed, her face bright with excitement. "With all the investigations concluded, we've been given permission to open more dungeons in the demon lands! The gods all agreed that the human gods were cheating and misplaying the game. To counteract it, demon lands will have triple the number of dungeons and relics!"

'Triple?' Meical tilted his head, his eyes darting to the once-cluttered table nearby. "So…"

"I just finished distributing the relics," Caradoc shrugged. "Better still, the dungeons are protected from the other races. Only demons can enter."

"Oh, I hope Cerys finds some of the swords!" Corlyotir beamed, turning to spread a map out across the table. "Her proficiency as a Shadowdancer has been coming along quite well. The swords Idris had made for her are wonderful quality, of course, but she needs more. He underestimated her abilities!"

"Either of you know what happened to Wullfric?" Meical interjected, causing the other two gods to turn and frown at him.

"What do you mean?" Caradoc spoke, narrowing his eyes. "That old bastard—"

"—is missing," Meical interjected. "A child sits on the Issradian throne. I just met him."

The two deities stared at Meical in disbelief before disappearing into black smoke. Sighing, Meical strode over to the map Corlyotir had been looking at and spread it out further. Dozens of marks in fresh, golden ink indicated dungeons across the fractured demonic countryside. Quickly-scribbled symbols indicated their strengths, hidden treasures, and the races allowed to enter. Meical skimmed the list of relics, his displeasure mounting.

"That little brat is supposed to be running an *empire?*" Corlyotir snorted when she and Caradoc returned.

"Let's not worry about him for now." Caradoc shook his head. "We need to continue watching Cerys' progress and make certain nothing impedes her journey to the eastern reaches."

"Mirela found out about their trip and informed Alice, so we're getting dragged out there too." Meical crossed his arms and grimaced. "If they run into trouble during their travels you can contact me. Otherwise, I'll be playing good little escort to Alice. Adric will be coming along as well."

"Alice is determined to see Cerys?" Caradoc sighed heavily. "These women…"

"As if your favorite is any better!" Corlyotir scoffed. "He's been chasing Cerys' tail since meeting her! It's a wonder they've made any progress at all."

"Told you they were perfect for each other," Meical smirked, eliciting groans from the other two deities. "Don't worry so much. Cerys is a hard-ass. If Idris doesn't focus soon, or she isn't given the opportunity to work, she'll jump on him in a very different, less fun, way."

"I hope you're right," Corlyotir sighed.

"Of course I'm right." Meical waved dismissively. "Enough of that. I want the details regarding the new dungeons you've opened, and what relics you've put in them."

Chapter Forty-One
Ice & Snow

"Mistress, shouldn't you rest?" Bruce matched my brisk pace through the palace with ease, his tone a mixture of concern and curiosity. "By my calculations, it has been at least a week since you last fed. With Master Idris too busy, perhaps I should fill his role until he has time for you?"

"No." The corner of my eye twitched.

"If I am not mistaken, you and Master Idris were feeding frequently. Was this not out of necessity?" Bruce probed. I glanced at him, unable to tell from his expression if he was genuine or fishing for information. "Or were you sharing rooms for some other reason?"

"I'm the 'First Consort.' It would be weird if we *didn't* share rooms frequently." I shrugged, turning a corner and picking up my pace. The sooner we got to the training yard, the sooner he'd stop pestering me with stupid questions. "Neither of us are so weak that we need to feed daily."

"Ah. So, your frequent mating resulted in energy reserves?" Bruce murmured, tilting his head. "There is merit to that idea. Perhaps I should not wait until I feel the need to feed, and instead seek out frequent feeding so that I require it less often…"

Whichever god is responsible for Bruce coming here needs an ass kicking. I stalked into the training yard, yanking on my gloves as I went. *There's no way they brought him here for his usefulness. Someone is* definitely *trolling me.*

"Morning, Cerys." Emrys glanced over at us as he exited the nearby armory. "You two still going at it, huh? Sorry I couldn't convince Idris to let you go on a training excursion."

"It's fine." I shook my head. "The snow *is* coming down like crazy. I can understand not wanting to dedicate a bunch of people as an escort *and* to carve a path through the snow and ice."

"Sparring will be sufficient for now," Bruce added. "Now that I have caught up to Mistress Cerys, we are able to learn much from each other."

Caught up? The stupid AI will pass me at this rate! I crossed my arms and watched Bruce out of the corner of my eye. He had yet to beat me in sparring, but every fight was more challenging than the last. Fighting him was a test of both mental and physical endurance.

"Well, don't push yourself too hard." Emrys patted my shoulder and walked past me, heading into the palace.

I wish people would stop telling me that. I sighed heavily, turning my attention to Bruce. "Let's warm up and then do some target practice. We should work on some of our combos in case we find ourselves in any fights on our trip."

"Yes, Mistress," Bruce nodded.

"...are you ever going to call me 'Cerys?'" I pursed my lips. "*Just* Cerys, I mean. We're not on Earth anymore, and you actually have a physical body now."

"I am still your butler," Bruce countered, shooting me a puzzled look.

"Okay, while that may be true..." I pressed my fingers to my temples, "...I would prefer you just call me Cerys. The whole formality thing everyone is doing drives me nuts. You've known me even longer than Alice has."

"As you wish...Cerys." Bruce nodded to me, breaking into a convincing smile. "You said you want to practice our combination attacks?"

"Yeah. I'm having a hard time controlling my swords once they've gone through your portals," I answered, summoning all my weapons from my inventory. A flourish of my hand made the weapons fan out in front of me, tendrils of darkness coating their hilts. *Training isn't really what I want to be doing right now, but it will have to suffice.*

"Very well." Bruce nodded and strode toward the magitech dummies at the other end of the training yard.

"What do *you* want to do?" I asked after a moment, causing the black-haired incubus to stop in his tracks and turn to look at me. He opened his mouth to respond but promptly shut it again, his gaze shifting to narrow in on something behind me. Without moving, I willed my weapons to point at the presence behind me.

"My apologies, Lady Moonfire," Eifion chuckled. His ears twitched briefly when I shifted to shoot him a cold look, his mouth curving into a delighted smile. "I was hoping you and your servant might permit me to observe. Witnessing a champion in action is a rare treat indeed!"

"That is quite enough, Eifion." That threatening growl could only belong to one person. I kept my expression passive and glanced to my left, finding Idris walking toward us. He had a cold, stormy air about him. Emrys and Elidyr flanked him, wearing formal armor. "I will not have you disrupting my subjects whilst they train. Come along."

"Oh? But I want to see what manner of abilities our precious champion is capable of!" Eifion gave Idris a sly smile.

I glanced between them, debating whether I should intervene. Eventually, I decided to keep my mouth shut and let them settle the matter as the kings they were. It came with the bonus of examining, or rather 'admiring,' the attire Idris had clad himself in. The mix of leather, furs, and plate came together to create a rather alluring set of armor that was tight in all the right places. His plate-covered long boots had what appeared to be small daggers for heels.

Never thought I'd dig heels on a man, but with those? It works. I shifted my attention back to Bruce. He looked just as uncertain about the situation as I did.

"You have other matters to attend to." Idris stalked toward Eifion, grabbing the kitsune by the shoulders. "Do not make me repeat myself."

I watched the two kings disappear into the palace, not sure what to make of the exchange.

"My apologies, Lady Moonfire." Elidyr bowed briefly. "They are being far too troublesome... If you will excuse us."

Once they were all gone, I let out a small sigh and shrugged.

"I do not understand their behavior." Bruce frowned after the kings, then looked at me, recognition crossing his features. "You do not know what it was about either?"

"No idea." I shook my head. "Shall we?"

"Gladly." Bruce smiled brightly.

Bruce leaned back against a nearby pillar and summoned three portals in front of me. I examined the lightless black holes for a moment before letting out a small sigh. One by one, I sent swords into the portals. The moment they disappeared, they reappeared by the magitech dummies at the far end of the training yard, their connection to me severed. They clattered to the ground before I could grasp them again.

«Azimuth Sword—failed»

The notification spammed my peripheral vision twice more before fading away. I tilted my head, wracking my brain. The word 'azimuth' sounded familiar, but I couldn't place it off-hand.

"Mistress?" Bruce prompted.

"You didn't get that notification?" I asked. He shook his head. "It said, 'Azimuth Sword: failed.'"

"Ah." Bruce's bright green eyes widened slightly. He made a short motion with one hand, turning the portals slightly. "Try again, Cerys. 'Azimuth' refers to an object's cardinal direction. Perhaps if my portals and your blades are properly aligned, you will not lose control over them?"

"Worth a shot." I sighed, calling my swords back to me. This time, the connection to the blades weakened but didn't break completely. When they exited near the dummies, they grazed past extremities or otherwise pierced the dummies' arms.

«Progress toward unlocking Azimuth Sword: 3/10»

"Seven more times." I glanced toward Bruce, earning a nod in reply.

With each new volley, my connection to my flying swords strengthened. By the last, their erratic wobbling had subsided to a minute wiggle. It was still enough to throw my aim off by several inches, but I was no longer missing the targets entirely.

«Congratulations. Azimuth Sword has been unlocked»

Nnngh, that takes more concentration than I'd like... I suppressed a grimace and recalled my swords yet again. "Bruce, what other utilizations do you think your portals have?"

"I believe it will be possible to send spells and other projectiles through them," Bruce offered after a moment, allowing his portals to dissipate. "However, I am not certain if there is any synergy with your gravity magic. You are able to summon gravity wells wherever you wish, are you not?"

"Seems that way so far, within reason." I crossed my arms, letting my swords orbit around me while I thought. "It seems like a form of utility magic, at least at my current proficiency. Most of what I've been able to do is bring monsters all to one central point or slow them down. I can crush terrain with gravity, but not opponents—yet."

"You *have* combined it with your other skills to result in damage-dealing abilities, however." The voice from behind me made me whirl around to find Tegau and an unfamiliar incubus walking toward us—well, Tegau was walking, at least. His companion was *floating*. Tegau shot us a cheerful smile, stopping a safe distance from me and my swords. "His Majesty tasked me with finding a way to help you train, Lady Moonfire. Of course, he also stated that allowing you out of the palace is simply not happening."

"He's being *too* cautious," the other incubus snorted, shaking his head.

This new man was almost as pale as the snow falling around the palace. The white scales of his tail and his horns gradated to a frosty blue at the tips. His hair was bright white and layered at the top, falling in longer, straight layers around his shoulders. Sky blue eyes flicked between me and Bruce, clearly measuring us.

"This is Seren, our resident Grandmaster of Ice and Light Magics," Tegau offered when the other demon didn't introduce himself. "I figured that, if you aren't allowed out of the palace, we could have you spar against your opposing element instead."

"A demon with light magic?" I arched an eyebrow.

"According to my studies, demonkind is not restricted in the manner our world's folklore indicates," Bruce offered, walking over to join us.

"So, no leaving palace grounds?" Seren shifted to look at Tegau.

"That's right." Tegau shrugged, his smile sheepish. "While I agree with His Majesty's assessment of the storm, I had thought warping to Caradoc's Pillars might be an option. Alas, he won't let her go anywhere without a sizable escort."

"I'm pretty sure you contributed to that problem." I gave Tegau a pointed look.

"I'm sure he did," Seren sighed, crossing his arms. "Sparring isn't going to make much progress toward your next 'level' but if it'll assist you in some other way, I'll help...once you've fed. Isn't

His Majesty supposed to be taking care of you?"

"Er…" I wasn't sure what to say to that.

"She does seem much weaker than last I saw her, indeed." Tegau nodded, rubbing his chin. "Our king is drowning himself in work again, isn't he?"

"Master Idris has been working late into the night for over a week." Bruce nodded as well, confirming the Grandmaster's observation. "Mistress Cerys is too stubborn to go to him."

"Can we *not* discuss my sex life? Or lack thereof? Whichever," I huffed.

"Men," Seren sighed, causing me to tilt my head. He seemed not to notice my questioning look. "Well, Bruce seems healthy enough to spar. Now that I'm back in Cejari-ir, there's no need to rush. I'll be around whenever Cer…Lady Moonfire?"

"Cerys is fine," I answered. "Preferred, actually."

"Right." Seren nodded. "Once you're feeling better, we can spar too. Given what I've heard about His Majesty's protectiveness, I'd rather not risk pissing him off, if it's all the same to you."

"I can respect that." I pouted slightly, dismissing my swords.

"I am uncertain of how I am meant to combat a mage." Bruce frowned, looking a little concerned as I walked a few yards away to perch on a bench.

"That's what I'm here for," Seren pointed out.

"Do I really look *that* unwell?" I grumbled, glancing at Tegau when he perched next to me on the bench. He crossed one leg over the other and chuckled.

"It isn't that you *look* ill, Lady Moonfire." Tegau shook his head. "Incubi and succubi can tell, by instinct, when someone's power is weakening. Mages excel at such. If I had to hazard a guess, it would be that whatever technique you were practicing today requires much of your power."

"Close," I murmured, earning a questioning glance. "We were practicing sending my swords through Bruce's portals. My connection to the blades weakens when they go through one, forcing me to adjust quickly once they come out the other side."

"Perhaps an issue of your skills being 'new' to the both of you," Tegau offered. "Bruce has to keep the portals stable for you, which would take a great deal of concentration. The integrity of his portals likely translates to how strong your connection to your weapons remains."

"In other words, practice makes perfect," I grimaced.

"His Majesty truly hasn't been making time for you?" Tegau frowned slightly. "I know you said you don't want to discuss it, but you're Nabyr-zahn's champion. Your wellbeing is everyone's concern."

"What, do you expect me to intrude on his work and demand he bend me over the nearest surface?" I scoffed.

"Yes," Tegau stated flatly. "If not His Majesty, then perhaps someone else you trust. Or you could 'hunt' for a partner. It won't be long before others notice your needs are going unfulfilled."

"I'll keep that in mind," I sighed. Saying I wasn't keen on the idea would have been a gross understatement. Thankfully, it was enough to make Tegau drop the subject. It wasn't that I *didn't* want to feed. The problem was that I didn't want to interrupt Idris when he was so busy.

Bruce summoned his sword, shield, and armor before taking his place across from Seren in the sparring area. The mage made a sharp motion to either side, summoning two orbs floating above his palms—one pale blue, the other white with prismatic glints of light shining from it. After confirming Bruce was ready, Seren made another motion with one hand, splitting the orb of ice into six. The orbs flew toward Bruce and exploded with frost when they impacted his shield.

"That's an odd weapon." I tilted my head, watching Seren fly after Bruce. "He's a mage, but that range…"

"It's unique to his class," Tegau offered, grinning. "Seren has some truly long-range spells, but most of his abilities are mid-range. He's got a few melee abilities too, of course."

Even if I hadn't known Seren was a Grandmaster, it would have been obvious that Bruce was outclassed. Seren's spells came in quick succession, beating against Bruce's shield and armor with little mercy. Bruce attached darkness to the rim of his shield, spreading it to form a bubble around himself, but Seren's light magic tore it open with ease.

Seren was going easy on Bruce, but that didn't stop his armor and shield from gaining some new dents. The former AI sustained several cuts to his face as well. Why he hadn't put on some kind of helmet was beyond me. Considering his intelligence, I had to assume he didn't have one—or that he hadn't yet adapted to his 'fleshy body' yet.

If it was an issue with his body, I hoped it would be resolved soon. There wasn't much time left before we were supposed to leave to meet the other kings. I didn't want Bruce to put himself in unnecessary danger whenever we ended up fighting monsters— or anything else, for that matter.

"You look bored." Tegau nudged me with one elbow.

"There's no real danger in sparring," I shrugged.

"You're sulking," Tegau stated pointedly.

"I was thinking about this upcoming trip." I shot Tegau an annoyed look. It wasn't entirely untrue, after all.

"You needn't worry. I'll be sending Seren with you." Tegau smiled, his tone cheerful once again. "Drysi, Emrys, and Elidyr will be there as well, of course. With them, and many soldiers as an escort, there is little for you or Idris to fear. Where you're going, demons won't fight each other. It is a sacred place. The escort is more for the monsters and any unfavorable company you might happen across."

Unfavorable company is exactly what I'm worried about. I kept the thought to myself and pretended to watch Bruce's sparring match.

Sure, we would have ample protection in the form of dedicated guards and a small army…but I didn't want to *require* protection. If shit went down, I wanted to be useful *and* be able to protect myself. Yet all our companions were centuries-old Jeriskyr natives who had been living and breathing their proficiencies since they'd been young.

Bruce and I were mere Journeymen. How we were meant to be useful was beyond me, and that came with an added irritation: How was a champion supposed to *do* anything the gods wanted? Idris had suggested it might take me years before I could overthrow the Issradian Empire, and that prediction was becoming more and more real to me all the time.

"I think I've beaten up your butler enough for the day," Seren remarked, turning to look at me. Behind him, Bruce was doubled over, attempting to regain his breath. "I'll be staying in the palace, Cerys, so come find me once you've fed."

"I could remedy that issue—" Tegau didn't get to finish his sentence before Seren covered the man's mouth in ice.

"Do you *want* Idris to almost kill you? Again?" Seren gave Tegau a condescending glare before glancing toward me. "Let me know if Tegau is being too much for you, at any time. I'll handle him."

Seren waved to us briefly before dragging Tegau out of the training yard. I watched them in confusion for a moment before returning my attention to the exhausted Bruce. Clearly, I wouldn't be getting more training of any sort in for the day.

"You gonna be okay?" I arched an eyebrow at Bruce, watching as he finally straightened.

"Once I find Drysi, yes…" Bruce cleared his throat and bowed slightly. "If I might have your permission to leave, Cerys…"

After a few more words, we parted ways. When I returned to the Queen's Tower, I simply stood in the doorway and stared for a while. There were potted flowers and other plants *everywhere*. Roses, moonfire lilies, and dozens of other types I couldn't name. My suite had practically been turned into a miniature indoor garden. It smelled heavenly, but I wasn't sure of the purpose.

The origins were easy enough to guess at, though.

I closed the door behind me and strode into the main room, soon finding an envelope sitting on a table. Idris' handwriting. Shaking my head, I picked it up and walked into my wardrobe to pick out a change of clothes. Once that was done, I set them aside in the bathroom and stripped before getting around to opening the letter.

An apology for ignoring me earlier today? I arched an eyebrow, skimming the letter again and then checking the back to make certain I hadn't missed anything. *He sure doesn't do anything by halves, does he?*

I set the letter aside, took a swift bath, got dressed, and left my rooms again. The evening was still young, and I didn't feel like sitting around doing nothing. Though I didn't have the drive to wander down to the kitchens in search of food, either. Or to seek out Idris for a 'tryst.' Grimacing, I took a sharp turn and headed into the nearest courtyard.

A few minutes and some climbing later, I sat down on a secluded pathway behind the palace. My breath fogged in the air and snow drifted down around me freely. I let out a contented sigh and rested my back against the granite cliff face.

Time alone with my thoughts was what I needed. More than training, food, or anything else, for that matter. I had been settling into my new life well enough, but I hadn't been afforded much time—if any—to think on what to do, or where to go from here.

My primary goals were clear enough: Rescue Alice, overthrow the Issradian Empire.

But what came next? Before? Between? Those were all things I hadn't wanted to consider when I'd first come to Jeriskyr as the Champion of Nabyr-zahn. With my connection to Earth severed, those were questions I needed to give deeper thought to. It was true that I had come to enjoy Idris' company, and even pined over his absence to some extent.

However, I wasn't convinced I wanted to see where things could go with him. Before the Ebonwing members and Bruce had shown up, sure. I'd been giving in to my interest in Idris. With their arrival, however, I was concerned that their return to Earth might be tied to what *I* chose to do after fulfilling my role.

I wasn't sure what I would do if they wanted to return to Earth but couldn't because I wanted to stay in Jeriskyr. Typically, I took the approach of 'the needs of the many outweigh the needs of a few.' Even if that meant my own wants had to be put on the backburner.

If I grew closer to Idris…I wouldn't want to make that kind of decision. Even if it meant 'dooming' my guildmates and Bruce to living out their lives in Jeriskyr.

Well, I suppose Bruce probably wouldn't mind. I tilted my head. *He seems to like Drysi, or at least finds her useful. I suppose, for an AI, that's about as close to 'liking' someone as he's ever gotten. Hmmm… I wonder, is he* really *a 'person' now? Do this world's gods really have that kind of power?*

I was glad to have a familiar-ish face on my side, but I couldn't bring myself to trust the gods that had brought either of us to Jeriskyr. I wasn't sure if knowing what the gods were scheming would help with that, though. If anything, it'd probably make things worse.

Pushing the thoughts from my mind, I looked down at the palace, and at Cejari-ir beyond that. Overhead, a full moon hung bright in the sky, illuminating the snow-covered city. Thunder rumbled in the distance, though I couldn't see any clouds yet. A contented sigh escaped me.

Cejari-ir was truly beautiful, as was the snow. It didn't snow much where I'd grown up, and the cities on Earth were close to snow-free due to all the maintenance machinery necessary to keep things running. Both worlds had their own unique beauty, but Jeriskyr was quickly surpassing Earth in my mind.

When I heard the crunch of footsteps in the snow nearby, I grew still and listened more deeply for a moment, allowing my senses to hone in on the intruder. His alluring scent reached me next, and I released a small sigh. Considering I'd been missing his company, I couldn't rightly complain about the interruption of my solitude.

"Well, I certainly did not think I would need to trudge through the snow to come find you," Idris remarked, a relieved smile settling on his lips when he crested the hill and spotted me.

"I came up here to think. Stayed for the scenery," I offered, motioning to the moon and then down at the sprawling city below. "Can't see Caradoc's Pillars from here in this weather, but the city is plenty pretty."

"I would ask to join you, but I came to bring you back to the palace." Idris shook his head slightly before following my gaze. "Though I must admit, I am glad my city is growing on you."

"Back to the palace?" I murmured, tilting my head as I examined the king. His gaze was still fixated on Cejari-ir, though he probably felt me watching him. He still wore the same formal attire I'd spotted him wearing earlier in the day. "How's your work going?"

"I have almost finished, thankfully." Idris turned to look down at me. "I was hoping that I could convince you to dine with me.

Alas, you appear reluctant to leave this place."

"If I won't be getting in your way or keeping you from your duties, sure. I'll join you." I nodded to him, before remembering my manners and smiling. "Oh right—and I wanted to thank you for the plants you had brought to my rooms. Though I'm not sure how I'm supposed to care for them all."

"Your servants will handle that." Idris shook his head slightly before offering me a hand. "And you are more than welcome. If I am being honest, I was uncertain of how else to make amends for neglecting you as of late."

Neglect? I wondered, allowing him to pull me to my feet. Any reply I had escaped me when Idris' mouth shifted into a small frown, and he reached up to brush snow out of my hair. His concerned gaze soon shifted to my eyes as he cupped my face in his hand.

"It would appear that you have been out here for quite some time." He pulled me closer. "Come, let us return to the palace where it is warm."

"Have you heard back from the other kings yet?" I decided to shift the topic away from his worry as he tucked me against his side and escorted me down the path he had come from. "Or have you been focused more on Nabyr-zahn's affairs?"

"They have each agreed to meet." Idris squeezed me closer, his frown deepening. "You should have worn more if you intended to venture into the cold."

"I'm fine," I replied, making a dismissive gesture. "On Earth I didn't get to enjoy the snow, or the moon, often. Especially not in the city."

"Ah…" Idris glanced up at the moon. "Perhaps I should have an observatory built atop the Queen's Tower?"

"I can't tell if you're serious," I sighed.

"Of course I am. I will not give up on determining how to make you happy while you remain here." Idris lifted me up without warning, causing me to cling to his shoulders with minor panic. "You are too busy watching me and not paying enough attention to where you are going. Has your training truly been so tiring? You have not been feeding?"

"Training has been exhausting!" I huffed, frowning slightly. *Feeding? Who would I even be feeding on if not him?*

"You did not even consider it to be an option?" Idris asked, his tone doubtful.

"Still more than happy to listen in on my thoughts, I see." I stuck my tongue out at him. "But no. I didn't. I had offers—one out of genuine concern, the other…well. Tegau was put in his place quickly enough."

"And you entertained neither option?" Idris arched an eyebrow.

"Is that really so surprising?" I narrowed my eyes.

"Only because you expressed a desire to not grow close to anyone." Idris shook his head, sadness in his eyes. "I hope you will forgive me for misjudging you, but I assumed that you would seek out multiple feeding partners in order to reduce your chances of forming a bond."

"Did *you* feed on anyone else?" I countered, shooting him a sharp look. My senses weren't as good as the natives' were, but they were good enough for me to know the answer to the question already. He wasn't quite as drained as I was—but he definitely hadn't fed either.

"Certainly not!" Idris exclaimed, shaking his head. "While I *was* worried, I did not wish to act based on mere assumptions. I would not have been able to forgive myself if..." He paused, clearing his throat. "I will have hot food and drink brought to the Queen's Tower."

"Make sure you bring yourself too." I swatted at his backside when he turned to walk through the palace. "If you want to 'make it up to me,' you can do so by keeping me company."

"Gladly." Idris shot me a sultry smile before disappearing down the corridor.

Once I was satisfied he was out of earshot, I let out a sigh and headed up the stairs to my rooms. My feelings regarding that man were a mess, and it seemed like his weren't much better.

I stripped out of my snow-soaked clothes and pulled on a short nightgown instead, followed by a robe. *For now, I'll just enjoy and observe. We have too many important things to focus on. It would be bad if our relationship became so awkward that we couldn't work together.*

Even though I told myself that, and I *did* believe it, I still wanted to know for certain what Idris' feelings were. Except that came with the danger of having to explore and determine mine. That wasn't something I was prepared to do. Not when it could interfere with progress toward rescuing Alice or conquering the Issradian Empire.

Just be content with…whatever this is, for now, I told myself, shutting my eyes briefly. *Don't complicate it.*

I perched on the sofa in my sitting room and took a deep, calming breath. Soon, weather permitting, we'd leave with a contingent of soldiers escorting our main party. Finally, I would get a better look at the world of Jeriskyr. With luck, we'd even make some headway in forging an alliance with the other demon kings.

Romance could wait until I'd saved *at least* Alice.

There's nothing wrong with semi-platonic feeding…right?

Chapter Forty-Two
Rehlr-saffir

"Hey. Feeling better?" Seren called as he walked into the training yard. Frost and prisms of light lingered where his feet touched, with more floating around his ankles.

"Yeah, a bit." I finished re-lacing my boots and stood. "You sure we have time to do a little sparring before we have to leave?"

"We should. Just have to be careful to make sure we still have plenty of energy left for the trip." Seren stretched his arms above his head. "Where's that butler of yours? I'd have thought he'd want to go another round or two."

"He and Drysi are helping everyone get ready for the journey,"

I sighed, crossing my arms over my stomach. "I offered to help too, but apparently 'that's beneath me' or something."

"I'm sure they appreciated the offer." Seren shrugged and walked past me, summoning his ice and light cores. "Since you're the champion, they're not going to want to 'bother' you with those sorts of tasks. Of course, it doesn't help that *everyone* knows Idris tried to make you his queen."

"Still can't believe he did that," I snorted, snapping my fan open. "Okay, so. Sparring...with magic. I'm not entirely sure how this is supposed to go. Neither of us has armor, unlike Bruce."

"You should use all your abilities against me." Seren lifted into the air by a good foot or so and spun his elemental cores above one hand. "I *am* wearing armor, even if it doesn't look like it. Ice magic gives me defensive spells as well as the offensive ones, and my clothing has further enchantments.

"We're supposed to work together, and that means I should know what you're capable of. Emrys and Bruce will be our tanks, Drysi is a healer, Idris can provide support and damage—you, me, and Elidyr will be most of the damage in a fight."

"And coordinated attacks will be the most efficient against a lot of foes?" I offered, nodding to him. "Well, sparring is definitely the simplest way to show you what my abilities are."

"Ready?" Seren gave me a pointed look.

Right. Short on time. I nodded to him. In the next moment, his ice core split into multiples and flew toward me.

I darted away from two, then deflected three more with my flying swords. The remaining one exploded against my shoulder. It felt like being hit with a paintball. Ice spread from the impact point, but a sharp motion with my shoulder cracked it. Seren didn't hesitate to send several orbs of light flying toward me next.

A flourish of my fan created a speck of gravity between us, dragging his orbs off course. While Seren attempted to reclaim his weapons, I darted forward with my fan open and sliced toward his torso. He levitated out of reach, but I had an idea how to drag him back down.

I shut my fan and summoned darkness, making a sharp downward motion. However, Seren only lost a few inches of altitude. Sensing magic accumulating behind me, I sprang forward whilst conjuring a shield of shadows to protect my back at the same time. Large icicles pierced the ground I had been standing on, and moments later, they burst, sending smaller ice shards pelting into the training area.

My shield deflected them, but by now my gravity sphere had dissipated. Seren's light orbs flew at me again. I flooded the area around me with darkness, dimming his weapons just enough to see that they had formed into needle-like spears. I wasn't sure how to deal with *that*, so I had to guess—and fast.

Without many other ideas, I spun into a roundhouse kick, knocking two of the orbs off their paths. Their explosion was delayed, giving me time to move away and deflect the next two with my flying swords. A small gravity well trapped the remaining ones, which exploded in place several feet away from me.

That wouldn't work a second time. I grimaced, watching Seren 'juggle' his orbs in one hand, his expression thoughtful. If he hadn't staggered them, I wouldn't have been able to deal with them all. He'd waited before detonating them, too.

My swords flew at Seren. He spread his arms out, creating a wall of ice in front of him. I directed my swords to fly around it, but the wall extended in line with the motion of his hands. His next movement formed the surface into spikes, which soon launched toward me.

However, before I could react, flames erupted between us and evaporated Seren's spell.

"That is enough for the day," Idris called from somewhere nearby. I glanced to my right to find him lounging against the exterior wall. "Everyone is finished with their preparations. We are just waiting on the two of you."

Idris shifted to walk away as Seren put away his weapons and floated over to me. I sighed, a little disappointed that the sparring match had been cut short. Fighting against Seren's unusual skills was a fun challenge. A puzzle I wanted to work on more.

I tilted my head, my gaze drifting down Idris' back.

"He's really got a nice ass, doesn't he?" Seren nudged me, grinning.

"I wasn't looking!" I sighed and crossed my arms, tapping my fan against my hip. "Okay, maybe I was. Those pants…"

"Nothing wrong with looking, right?" Seren laughed.

"Maybe not." I considered it briefly.

"Are you coming?" Idris shifted to look back at us.

Not yet I'm not. Judging by the twitch of his tail, I hadn't kept the thought as private as I'd hoped. "You, me, Seren, Bruce, Elidyr, Emrys, and Drysi will be working as a 'party?'"

"Silas will be our eighth." Idris waited for us to fully catch up to him before walking again. "We will be traveling at the center of our formation, where it is safest. Should all go well, there will be no need for our party to intervene with any fights during our journey—though we will need to help hunt once we have made camp."

"Did you pack everything, Cerys?" Seren chimed in, causing Idris to pause.

"I think so," I nodded.

"Your guild members sent additional armor for you," Idris stated, glancing down at me. "I had the packages stored with our things for now."

"Our things?" I echoed.

"Our escort is an army of mostly male soldiers, you're the First Consort…" Seren made a vague motion with one hand. "Or should I say, 'future queen,' hmmm? You two are friendlier than I expected."

"In other words, you are safest with me." Idris nudged my tail with his.

"You don't trust your soldiers?" I arched an eyebrow at him.

"Mmhmm, overprotective." Seren nodded to himself, before shifting his eyes to the side to look at Idris. "Or are you just making an excuse?"

"You…" Idris growled, before letting out a heavy sigh. "It is true that she will be safest in my tent."

"*But* that's not the real reason you want her there." Seren laughed.

You let him act so casually with you? I glanced up at Idris.

"I have plenty of reasons—all of which are no one's business aside from mine and Cerys'," Idris stated, settling his firm gaze on Seren. "Now then, go find Silas. You and he should determine how you will handle your duties."

Seren laughed again and bid us farewell for the moment, leaving me alone with the agitated king. I looked at Idris thoughtfully but remained silent. With how tense he appeared, rushing him didn't seem like a good idea.

"I need you to promise me something." Idris kept his voice low as he turned to gaze down at me. I couldn't read his expression or tone of voice at all.

"And that is?" I prompted, tapping my fan against my hip again.

"That you exercise caution while we are away from Cejari-ir." Idris narrowed his eyes at me. "We will be traveling through places that someone of your skill level should not go near."

"Aren't we riding at the center of our escort?" I frowned. "I'm not sure how you expect me to find some magical level of caution that surpasses that."

"If we are attacked, most of my soldiers will have to separate to slay the monsters," he informed me. "There is every possibility that we will have to fend for ourselves in the event of an attack. We will be taking the route least likely to result in crossing paths with the creatures, but it is their mating season in the warmer regions we will pass through."

"So they're pissy," I sighed. "Don't worry. I have no interest in an early death. That said, I'm more concerned about humans than I am monsters. Though in this world, I suppose the words are synonymous."

"*Promise me.*" Idris brought his hands up to gently cup my face. "Emrys and Elidyr will likely focus their efforts on protecting me, should push come to shove."

"I promise to be careful," I relented. It was difficult for me to say no to that face, and dying wasn't on my agenda anyway. "What about the humans? Do you really think we aren't going to run into any?"

"You needn't fear them," Idris murmured, tracing my lower lip with his thumb, his gaze flicking down to my mouth. *That* behavior wasn't conducive to leaving.

With difficulty, I pulled out of his grip and gave him a pointed look. "We shouldn't keep everyone waiting, should we?"

"I suppose not." He released a disappointed sigh. "You choose the most frustrating times to be elusive."

"Or perhaps you just choose bad times to get distracted," I countered, whacking his upper arm lightly with my fan.

"Are you claiming innocence?" Idris shot me a sideways look.

"Of course," I replied, snapping my fan open and hiding the lower half of my face behind it. I batted my eyelashes at him for good measure. "I wouldn't *dream* of distracting you, *Your Majesty*. I—ah!"

"That should put you in your place, for now," Idris commented dryly, releasing my tail from his firm grip. He shot me a triumphant smirk when he spotted my expression. "Perhaps you should stick to battles you know you can win, Cerys."

"Maybe my goal wasn't to win?" I stuck my tongue out at him and danced out of reach when he shifted to grab me again. "Tsk, tsk, tsk! You'll have to be quicker than that!"

Smirking right back at him, I made a motion with my fan and summoned a pool of gravity magic around his feet, locking him in place. He growled at me and strained forward against the magic when I turned to shake my butt and tail at him. I darted down the hallway, away from him, before letting my magic dissipate.

It didn't take long for Idris to catch me, but that was fine. I laughed and coiled my tail around his when he lifted me off the floor by my waist. He nuzzled into my neck with a low, warning growl and gave me a brief squeeze.

"Unless you want to experiment with making love in a saddle—*behave.*" He squeezed me again before setting me down. When I didn't release his tail immediately, he gave me an agitated glare.

"That sounds like it would be terribly uncomfortable for you." I arched an eyebrow at him, considering it for a moment. "Well, I suppose that's enough playing around for now. How long do you think it will take for us to reach... You know, you never told me where we're going."

"Ah, I neglected to tell you?" Idris seemed a little *too* eager to change the subject. "Rehlr-saffir. I'm afraid the meaning of the name has been lost to time, but it is a sacred place for demonkind."

"Lost to time?" I frowned at his back as I followed him through the palace.

"It is ancient. Our cultures and languages have changed many times over since Rehlr-saffir's prime," he shrugged. "In fact, our language is so different now that we are incapable of reading the inscriptions there. We have priests and priestesses dedicated to maintaining the temple complex, of course, but the knowledge is lost to even them. We hope to find some way to decipher the texts. Alas..."

"Sounds like an interesting place," I murmured. *Seriously sounds like a place that should have a dungeon. A high-level one.*

"Your Majesty, my lady." Elidyr was the first to spot our

approach. "I have prepared Lady Moonfire's stallion as you directed, Your Majesty. Our men are eager to leave. We have only a small window before the next storm arrives in Cejari-ir."

My stallion? I tilted my head slightly, then looked at Idris when he stopped beside me.

"You will need a traveling cloak, and gloves," Idris stated pointedly. "Put those on first, then we will introduce you to your steed."

I did as he bid me, choosing to dismiss my fan to my inventory entirely in the process. While I tugged on my gloves, Elidyr led a massive black stallion over to us. There was an otherworldly air to the horse, though that didn't surprise me too much. I wasn't so naive as to think that demons of our size could ride an average horse. The bright white eyes were another indication.

"Arion will be yours," Idris informed me, patting the creature on the neck. "Upon our return, I will have better tack made for you. For now, we found a saddle that should be comfortable for you."

"Mine?" I questioned, raising an eyebrow.

"Yes, yours." He looked perplexed by my question. "Does he not please you?"

"So, *mine*-mine. Not 'just for this trip' mine?" I prompted, attempting to stifle my growing excitement.

"Ah, yes. A gift—"

"Yay!" I threw my arms around Idris' torso and hugged him

tight. "You said his name is Arion? So, what do I need to know? I assume he isn't a 'normal' horse by human standards. Diet? Grooming? Commands? How much attention will he need? Is he technically a 'warhorse?' Armor? How about—"

"I believe that answers your concern, Your Majesty." Elidyr coughed pointedly into his hand. "We are running late, Lady Moonfire. You will have to forgive me for interrupting your...celebration."

"Humph." I shot *Eliderp* a glare over my shoulder before looking up at Idris. He looked thoroughly flustered by my behavior. "Answer some of the questions, at least?"

"Ah..." Idris paused to clear his throat. "Arion and others like him are known as 'cauchemars.' They are still a manner of horse...but significantly more intelligent. It would be best if you did not treat him like a 'pet.'"

"Oh..." I pursed my lips, not sure whether to be disappointed or not. "How intelligent?"

"They understand our speech fully and are capable of telepathy. You will require further practice before you can communicate with him in that manner," he shrugged. "Some are capable of magic. Unlike the horses humans ride, you merely need to think of the speed you wish for Arion to take. 'Warhorse' would be accurate as well."

"And Arion does have armor," Elidyr added. "However, it is far too heavy for how long we will ride today. Nor should it be necessary. Once we are past Caradoc's Pillars, however, it will be needed."

Arion yanked his reins out of Elidyr's hands and moved closer to me, butting my shoulder lightly with his massive head. I immediately reached up to stroke his muzzle and then his cheeks. Even if Idris said that I shouldn't treat Arion like a pet, there was no way I *wasn't* petting that gorgeous fur.

He reminded me of a Friesian, but with a thicker coat. Like a Friesian, his long mane and tail were wavy.

"Anything else I should know?" I asked, glancing over my shoulder at the dumbfounded demon king. "Any 'rules' for how to get into the saddle, and so on?"

"None to speak of..." Idris shifted his gaze to Arion and released a small sigh. "Take care of her well, Arion. She is important to m—us."

I watched Idris out of the corner of my eyes as he walked away to speak with Emrys. Maybe he thought he'd caught himself fast enough, but I hadn't missed that. What I wanted to do with the information was another matter. It was a confirmation, in a way, of what I'd already suspected.

Though there were different types of 'important.'

"You can pet him from his back, Lady Moonfire," Elidyr sighed. He flinched in response to the look I shot him.

Tch. I guess none of these people realize how much this means to me. I bit back my frustration and strode around to Arion's sides to adjust the stirrups. Once they seemed long enough, I put my left foot in one and pulled myself onto his back. The saddle shared similarities with many of the ones from Earth, but had a V-shaped opening in the back to accommodate a rider's tail. *Did my excitement really not make it obvious enough?*

"Is everyone ready?" Idris cast his voice over everyone once he'd settled into the saddle of his own steed. Once a cacophony of affirmative answers erupted around us, we began to make our way out of the city.

I felt a little deflated as Arion fell into stride with Idris' cauchemar. While I knew I couldn't expect him or the others to understand my initial elation, having my reaction swept aside and ignored bothered me. Alas, Idris had taken on a serious demeanor. I didn't want to sound ungrateful, either.

"You have ridden before," he commented once we had left the city behind us.

"You couldn't see it from where we were, but the compound I grew up in has horses." I pulled my hood further over my head. "The people there swore off any technology that removes the need to do work. So, we had horses for herding, to carry us hunting, and so on."

"Let me guess—you have not seen a horse since leaving?" He chuckled. "That would explain your reaction, perhaps."

"Well, I also never had *my own* horse." I attempted to suppress an agitated pout and failed. Sighing, I continued, "I'll put it this way: Animals are much more pleasant to be around than most humans are. Oh. Not that I'm implying cauchemars are—"

"They are technically classified as monsters," Idris offered, earning a disbelieving stare from me. "Animals in our world are unintelligent beings with no affinity for magic. Monsters vary in intelligence, but most have magic or some other ability that sets them apart from animals."

"So, if you had two different bunnies and one had magic but the other didn't—" I stopped to growl at Idris. "What's so funny?"

"*Bunnies?*" he laughed. "So, Lady Moonfire has a weakness for animals, does she?"

"...please don't flood the Queen's Tower with rabbits next." I gave Idris a foul look.

"I will do whatever it takes to elicit such a joyous reaction from you again," he informed me, growing serious. "That is the closest to truly happy I have seen you since coming to Jeriskyr."

On about happiness again? I wondered, tilting my head slightly. Given his slip up earlier, I had a decent enough idea as to *why* he seemed so fixated on my happiness. Maybe a change of subject was in order. "Speaking of monsters and animals, I see we have a lot of supplies with us...but nothing that strikes me as 'food.'"

"We will hunt monsters for dinner once we have made camp." Idris shrugged as if it was the most natural thing in the world. "There has never been a dearth of monsters to hunt, and that has only become more true now that the gods have increased the monster populations."

"Eat...monsters?" I blinked at him.

"What did you *think* you've been eating since your arrival?" He gave me a doubtful look.

"I dunno. Beef? Pork? Chicken? Fish?" I sighed. "Eating *monsters* sounds...dangerous."

"Only if prepared poorly." Idris shrugged again.

He clearly didn't get my meaning.

"So, eating magical or intelligent creatures isn't an issue?" I prompted.

"Of course not." He shook his head.

...*right*. I had no idea how to explain my unease to him, especially not if it was truly that normal. Silence fell around us again while I considered the issue. A few minutes later, I decided to question him about it again. "Do humans eat monsters too?"

"No, they cannot," he answered. "Their digestive systems are too sensitive to magical elements. Humans grow ill if they eat monster meat and run the risk of becoming twisted if they do so frequently."

"I believe that's what she's worried about, Idris," Silas commented, bringing his cauchemar closer. "You're a demon now, Cerys. If eating monsters was a danger to you, it would have made you ill the first time you ate it."

"Do demons not eat animals at all?" I inquired.

"You're over-complicating this!" Drysi piped up, shooting Idris and Silas a reprimanding look before turning her attention to me. "Demons treat monsters the way humans treat animals. A lot of animals wouldn't do well in Nabyr-zahn's climate. The ones that do are hunted by monsters."

"Ah, so if demons hunted animals as well, they would soon disappear entirely." Bruce nodded to himself.

"I guess that makes sense," I grimaced, still not convinced. "What is the 'right' way to prepare monster meat?"

"Some have venom sacs that must be carefully removed," Silas offered with a grin. "Others have spines, exoskeletons, or other nuances that have to be removed in precise ways. Do it the wrong way, you'll end up with ruined meat."

"Some just aren't good eats," Emrys added. "Can we not talk about food? I'm getting hungry just thinking about it."

I'm really out of my element here. I reached forward to stroke Arion's neck. *I get the feeling I've only scratched the surface of Jeriskyr, if that. Guess I'm going to have to up my game if I'm to learn everything necessary about my class, this world, our allies, and our enemies. Ugh.*

You cannot rush such things, Idris commented, eliciting an aggravated sigh from me. *Would you feel better if you read while we travel?*

No. I looked away from Idris and out at the opening to Caradoc's Pillars far ahead of us. *If I do that, I won't memorize the route we're taking. Plus, that's not conducive to the whole 'be cautious' thing you asked me to do.*

"Well, shall we pick up the pace once we're out in the Pillars?" Emrys asked, looking over to Idris for approval. "We wanted to be the first ones to get to the temple, right?"

"Yes." Idris' simple response earned a frown from our companions. Even I wasn't sure what to make of it.

You seem troubled. I decided to pry.

I was wondering what I would do if you told me you refused to dine on monster meat. He glanced toward me.

What? If you tell me it's safe to eat, that's enough. I stared at him. *We have a saying on Earth: 'When in Rome, do as the Romans do.' In other words, when in a foreign place, follow the lead of someone from that culture. Plus, I trust you wouldn't let me eat something that would* literally *kill me.*

Point taken. He sighed in relief. *That is a good saying. Perhaps your world has its occasional merits.*

Occasional? You're being too generous.

Despite Idris making me promise to be cautious, we ran into no trouble on our journey to Rehlr-saffir. Dilapidated towns and other ruins dotted the landscape during our fortnight-long trip into neutral territory. The only travelers we encountered were the occasional wandering elf or beastman merchants. Most of the trip was done at a walk, with occasional breaks.

"Kings Bloodsong and Ebonmaw, welcome." A demoness moved to block our path into a crevasse. "You are the first to arrive. Have you brought your offerings?"

I watched in silence as the kings motioned some of their soldiers forward. The men promptly carried two large trunks to the woman and opened them. She was silent for a few moments before shutting the lids and nodding to us.

What are the offerings? I asked, unable to contain my curiosity.

Various goods that don't occur naturally in this region, Idris replied, a relaxed smile on his face. *You should pay more attention to our surroundings, Cerys. Chances to journey to the birthplace of demonkind are rare. Enjoy it.*

I shifted my attention away from him reluctantly and scanned the tall stone cliffs surrounding us. The crevasse was so narrow that we could only fit two cauchemars side-by-side within it. I wasn't sure what I was supposed to be admiring. Maybe the mild weather? The colorful striations in the stone?

It became much more obvious when we approached the stories-high statues at the end. Beyond them sprawled a lush valley dotted with trees and ornate buildings. Elegant statues of demons, plus some more abstract ones, rested between buildings. Carved stone arches with inlays of crystal wove in and out of the rim surrounding the valley.

Upon closer inspection, I realized the 'arches' were in fact parts of a continuous dragon sculpture that wrapped around the entire valley. Waterfalls poured over the rim in several places, feeding the rivers that flowed to the central point.

"Is this...a crater?" I quickly examined the cardinal directions again, noting the unusual formation of the valley's 'rim.'

"It is," Idris nodded. "And a natural fortress, if you will. Attackers would have to scale the cliffs to reach this place. Only demons can see the crevasse we just traversed."

"We should meet with the priests sooner rather than later," Eifion spoke up, bringing his cauchemar closer to us.

"Indeed..." Idris shifted to look from Emrys to me and back. "Take Cerys with you to set up camp. I would rather not expose her to Rehlr-saffir's caretakers just yet. We shall return to you soon."

"That was an odd choice of words." I frowned at the kings' backs as they rode away, then shifted my attention to Emrys when he snorted.

"They're an eccentric bunch. Been here for centuries. Some longer," he grimaced.

"Eccentric is putting it nicely," Seren stated dryly. "Add to that your status as champion, Idris' obvious infatuation—"

"Obvious? Why, what*ever* are you talking about?" Silas commented as we followed Emrys across the valley.

"Hmmm? You didn't notice?" Drysi inquired in disbelief.

"I believe it was sarcasm." Bruce tilted his head.

"I am surrounded by idiots." Elidyr sighed heavily, then

glanced at me. "Or rather, 'we' are, my lady."

"Maybe we're the 'eccentric bunch,'" I snorted.

"It'll be night in a few hours. Let's get camp set up!" Emrys roared to everyone. He began barking orders rapid-fire, leaving no more room for discussion.

I pitched in where I could, but I couldn't shake the feeling that we were being watched. Soon enough, my observation resulted in Silas and Elidyr sending some of their men to investigate the valley to make sure—though they assured me that Rehlr-saffir was always 'strange.'

Let's hope it's that. I'd rather not get eaten by a sandworm or something while trying to sleep. I shivered at the thought, then pursed my lips. *Would it even be called a sandworm when there's no sand here? Hmmm...landworm? Earthworm? Ah. No, probably not that last one. Though that'd be amusing.*

Shaking the thought from my head, I resumed unpacking my inventory in the tent I'd be sharing with Idris.

"We need to find an outlet for that nervous energy of yours," Idris commented from somewhere behind me, causing me to whirl around. He smirked, rubbing his chin, as he slowly examined me. "Though perhaps you already had something in mind?"

"Sleep. *Actual* sleep." I placed a hand on my hip. "I don't think I got *any* last night! The roaring from those—"

"You should have plenty of time to catch up on sleep while we wait for the other kings to arrive. The priests said that their scouts have yet to spot them." Idris strode past me, peeling off his layered traveling clothes as he went. "Have you any other duties to tend before resting?"

"Nope. I took care of Arion, helped with a few things around camp, then got shooed in here the moment they were done setting it up," I grumbled. "They still don't want to let me do...*anything.*"

"You will get used to it, much as I have." Idris stretched his arms over his head, drawing my attention to the muscles in his back. "I am quite tired as well...perhaps tea, dinner, and a brief game before bed?"

"Sure." I nodded in agreement.

"Very well. Once I have bathed, I will fetch our dinner and return." Idris stopped in front of me long enough to run his fingers through my hair, giving me a brief kiss on the forehead. "Relax while you wait. If you *must* do something, there are some books on my side of the bed that might interest you."

I watched him leave, my gaze lingering briefly on his ass before I turned my attention to our bed. My curiosity piqued, I walked over to his side of the bed and rummaged through the nightstand. Sure enough, there were easily a dozen books crammed into it.

Strategy, war, and...fairy tales? I tilted my head, looking at the odd mixture of books. *Come to think of it, I don't think I've seen any fiction in this world. Well, not until now, at least.*

It was tempting, but I reluctantly chose to be responsible. I picked a book on strategy regarding mages and stretched out on the bed to read while waiting for Idris to come back.

Chapter Forty-Three
Testing the Waters

"So, where are we going?" I cut my eyes to the side at Idris. He had donned plated leather armor, a cloak, and had a sword sheathed at his side. Before leaving our tent, he had instructed me to wear armor as well.

"Hunting. We need more food for us and our men." He held a hand out to me, his gaze expectant. "Hand me your fan. You will never fasten your armguards correctly if you are holding that at the same time."

I obeyed, handing him the fan, then set about fastening the straps to hold my plated armguards still. The ridged metal was shaped and layered like large scales, giving me a solid, slightly pointed surface to strike foes with. Similar plate pieces ran down the front of my boots and encased my feet. The backs of my heels bore a dagger's edge protruding from one side.

When Idris offered me my fan, I grasped it, but he didn't let go.

"I would prefer you remain at range against our prey." He narrowed his eyes, his grip remaining firm.

"My martial arts skill is more for if something gets too close to me," I pointed out, frowning at him. "Most of the techniques I've learned from my other proficiencies are mid-ranged."

"Then why the fan?" Idris sighed.

"Because it means I have a slashy weapon on hand, I can still incorporate it into my other skills when controlling magic, and because it looks cool?" I held up three fingers, paused, then added a fourth. "Oh, and it has a magical focus in it as well. If I hold my fan, that frees all of my swords."

"Then there is one last matter I wish to address before we meet with our comrades." Idris slowed to a stop and pivoted to look at me, his expression troubled. "I have been acting far more reserved than I am accustomed to, in part because of your behavior prior to the gods severing your 'strings.' While I would prefer for you to see me in a favorable light, I do not wish to maintain this…persona any longer."

"Are you…asking for my permission, or something?" I tilted

my head, unsure of his meaning. I'd noticed the personality shift, sure. It was hard to miss. Why he'd brought it up in such a way was beyond me.

"Hardly." He shook his head. "Rather, a warning. You did not appear to approve of or like my behavior on Earth, which was admittedly..."

"Over the top?" I offered when he hesitated. "Not entirely unfaithful to your actual personality though, I'm guessing."

"You could say it was amplified, I suppose," he grimaced. "I—"

"Short and simple—you're concerned your real personality might piss me off, but you don't want to continue with a falsehood. Right?" I interjected. He gave me an agitated look and nodded. "You'd piss me off more by maintaining a fake personality."

"It is not fake." Idris pursed his lips. "Rather...an aspect. A more muted one."

"Tomayto, tomahto," I shrugged. "Castrating your personality would piss me off too. When I said I wanted to get to know you, I meant the real you. Not some small piece of you."

"I am not certain what I expected, but that was not it." He ran his fingers through his hair, a crooked smile spreading across his lips. "However, that is a relief. For what it's worth, I will endeavor to refrain from agitating you."

"Good luck with that." I raised an eyebrow at him, then shrugged. "So, what are we hunting? Anything I should know?"

"Only that your armor will do little if you sustain a direct hit." His smile faded to a subtle frown, his demeanor shifting to seriousness. "Emrys and Bruce will be capable of weathering the strikes, but the rest of us will not. We had best avoid sustaining damage."

"What is Drysi here for, then?" I asked. "Isn't she a healer?"

"She cannot mend a severed arm or torso," Idris snorted. "Were our healers so fantastic, I would not have scars. Drysi is here to heal…I believe Otherworlders call them 'status effects?' Poison, frostbite, burns, and the like. Afflictions."

"Got it. Damage over time and crowd control effects, most likely." I pursed my lips, considering it. If we were supposed to avoid taking damage entirely, then I had to think of Jeriskyr more like a hardcore action-based game. "I get the gist. If we take minor damage—"

"These creatures are large," Idris interjected, shaking his head. "Any physical hits will not be 'minor.' Their magic and the terrain would be the source of afflictions."

"Right. Caution, then." I made a sour face. At least *that* info made his reasoning clear enough. Sighing, I nodded to him. "Do these damned things taste good, at least?"

"Not as good as you." He slid his fingers under my chin and tilted my head back, smirking.

"Ah…is this what you meant by—"

"What good is growing closer to you if I am not permitted to flirt or tease?" He released me, chuckling. "I am growing more comfortable with what appears to be the 'real' Cerys. It is my hope that you will also become comfortable with who *I* am."

"Seems reasonable enough." I tapped my fan against my hip, thinking while I followed Idris once more. "Is my behavior really that different?"

"Like night and day." He shook his head slightly. "However, you do still appear to hesitate regarding personal affairs. I had thought you were opening up."

"I've been wondering what I will do if I find out that the Ebonwing members' fates are tied to whether I choose to remain in Jeriskyr or not," I informed him, causing him to frown deeply. "The gods don't seem...amiable. I'm inclined to think that they might make it so that the Ebonwing members can only return to Earth if I do as well."

"That..." Idris trailed off into a growl, scowling. "I will not allow such a thing."

"Oh yeah? And you're going to go against your gods *how*, exactly?" I snorted. "It's more that I've been trying to figure out which option would weigh on me worse. 'Dooming' them to remain in Jeriskyr, or leaving everything here behind. You and your world *are* growing on me. Rationally speaking, there aren't any *good* reasons for me to go back to Earth, either. My brother and Gwy—"

"Yes. Them. They would be all you have, yes?" Idris clamped

a hand over my mouth before I could utter his father's full name. *It would be best if our men did not learn that my father was 'relocated' as a human.*

"There you two are!" Seren chastised as we neared our waiting party.

Silas rubbed his chin, a shit-eating grin spread across his face the longer he looked at us. "Convince her to become queen yet?"

"Somehow, the idea really pisses me off when you say it." I squinted at him.

"In which case, I would ask that you keep your mouth shut, Silas." Idris promptly shot the green-haired demon a filthy glare.

"Oooh, scary," Silas laughed.

"Don't come running to me when he decides to shut you up himself." Seren gave Silas an exasperated look.

"Come on, let me have my fun." Silas flashed Seren a brilliant, playful smile.

"Your Majesty, we will need to hunt more than your initial estimate." Elidyr stepped forward, bowing slightly. When he straightened, he adjusted his glasses and continued, "The priests desire more food as well, and tasked us with acquiring it in return for allowing us to camp here."

"Very well. An additional one or two carcasses should be no issue." Idris shrugged, placing a hand on the hilt of his sword and closing his eyes for a moment. Several separate verses of song left him, followed by magic shimmering around our party. "We should find the echei near the northern rim of the crater."

With that, he began walking and our party quickly fell in around him. I grimaced to myself before following as well, playing with my fan while we walked. The crater appeared peaceful, so learning that our prey resided within its rim came as a mild surprise.

The temple complex at the crater's central, deepest point didn't appear to be well-defended. It rose out of the lake, a web of stone pathways floating just above the lake's surface. More buildings, statues, and shrines dotted the shore. I saw no walls or fortifications to speak of. No weaponry.

I shrugged and picked up my pace, soon catching up to Idris.

"If we're going to feed everyone at camp and the temple, we'll need, what, four or five echei?" Seren remarked as he floated alongside us. I glanced over at him questioningly, watching him spin his elemental cores above one hand. "*His Majesty* didn't tell you anything about what we're hunting?"

"She needs to be tested," Idris stated. "I told her they are large and that she is to stay at range. That is all."

"Large enough that four or so can feed this many people?" I raised an eyebrow.

"They're not *that* difficult to fight." Drysi blinked at us. "If Cerys has fought monsters in her world—"

"Our world does not have monsters," Bruce interjected, shaking his head. "At least, not in the way you might expect. On

Earth, the closest manner of being we have to monsters are...humans."

"Oh... Then you both need to be careful!" Drysi rounded on Bruce. "You especially! Is your armor on soundly enough? Would you like me to check the straps again for you?"

Careful? Bah. I refrained from rolling my eyes.

Half an hour later, I found myself hiding behind a rock with the rest of my party. 'Echei' were apparently creatures with a bull-like head, ape-like body, and werewolf-like forearms. Their talons reminded me of an eagle. Bony spikes protruded from their spines and down their thick tails. My companions assured me that they were 'normal' monsters and not some manner of chimera.

"You neglected to mention they're herd animals," I muttered, agitated. "They're the size of, what...elephants? *Now* I'm wondering why we need more than one or two."

"Not many edible parts," Emrys shrugged, grinning. "You've got gravity magic, right? How about you sink a bunch of 'em into the ground? That way we only need to fight one or two at a time."

"...what?" I stared at him, then back at the echei. "I'd have to drop the ground by at least fifteen feet, and I'm assuming they can climb with those arms!"

"As I said, a test," Idris stated, keeping his voice low—which only made him sound more mischievous. "If you fail, it is fine. These creatures aren't *too* dangerous for you and Bruce."

Meaning he and the others can wipe them out with ease. I pursed my lips, the corner of my eye twitching. First, I had to follow instead of lead. That was annoying enough. Now I had to deal with the fact that they could just carry us if they wanted? *Tch. Fine. They want me to try and wrangle all the echei into a hole with gravity magic? Whatever.*

I snapped my fan open in one sharp, downward motion. The soil below the echei dropped and the walls of the newly-made pit bowed outward, mud and stone pushing upward around the rim. The herd fell with the soil, making an indescribable noise. My assumption was that it was a mix of rage and panic, but it was unlike anything I'd ever heard on Earth. It made my skin prickle into goosebumps.

"You're up, Bruce." Emrys whacked the shield-bearing man on the back.

Bruce stepped around our hiding place with his weapon and shield ready. He made a motion with his sword, sending a shockwave of darkness toward the nearest remaining echei. The creature whirled around and charged him immediately.

Power expanded from the edges of Bruce's shield as he lifted it to block a broad swipe from the creature. In the next moment, he kicked the creature off, giving himself space to adjust his sword, then chased after it with his weapon held at the ready. Drysi lifted her ornate ebony staff and closed her eyes briefly, sending tendrils of darkness shooting after Bruce.

"You were not meant to interfere," Idris sighed at the woman, then shook his head. "Very well, a proper fight it is. Emrys, join Bruce in keeping the echei at bay. Silas, Seren, remain far from the creature. Elidyr, cripple it."

"And you still want me to be cautious?" I shot Idris a foul look.

"Within reason." He drew his sword, coating the blade in flames. "As a Shadowdancer, you are more flexible with your range. Elidyr, Bruce, Emrys, and I will *need* to be close."

"*Fine*," I sighed.

We all sprung from our hiding places, fanning out. Seren's ice cores exploded by the echei's feet, encasing them in thick ice. Only a second later, Silas exhaled smoke from his kiseru, creating a horned creature from it. The smoke-creature charged toward the echei and rammed its horns into its chest, drawing rivulets of blood. All the while, Elidyr flanked the creature and severed the tendons in one of its rear ankles.

Well, I suppose punching or kicking something like this wouldn't be very effective... I summoned my swords and concentrated briefly, encasing them in darkness. The swords flew toward the stumbling echei, piercing the creature's shoulder. A short motion from me sent the swords tearing upward, ripping its flesh fully open.

The sound of rumbling nearby caught my attention. I shifted to look toward the noise, discovering another echei charging at us. Grimacing, I darted out of its way and dragged the edge of my fan down its side. The lumbering creature attempted to turn, but I was quicker. I made an upward motion with my fan, sending the echei flying into the air.

With the creature suspended, Idris' form shifted. He took flight, landing on the creature's shoulders. His sword pierced the echei's neck with a loud *crunch* and the beast went limp. Flames spewed briefly from the other side of its throat, filling the air with the scent of charred flesh and fur.

"That was overkill, Your Majesty!" Seren called, his voice filled with laughter. The mage in question flew toward the first echei, slinging both of his elemental cores toward the creature. Each core split into six, creating an elemental whip of ice and light. When they collided with the echei, they exploded, taking a long strip of hide with them.

I grimaced. Whittling a living creature down like this was a little nauseating. With the other monsters we had encountered during our journey it hadn't bothered me, but these 'echei' creatures were a little too close to animals in appearance. The desire to provide them with a swift death gave me an idea.

An orb of abyssal darkness the size of a baseball appeared several feet above the echei's head. When it arched back with one arm to swipe at our tanks again, I took advantage of the sluggish motion and drove the gravity orb through the top of its skull. The orb plummeted as if it had fallen from a great height, cutting clean through the echei's skull and through the ground beneath it.

When the monster fell to the ground, lifeless, I let out a small sigh.

«Gravity Magic Proficiency has increased by 2 points»

«Gravity Magic Proficiency: 50/100 EXP to LV1»

«Congratulations, you are halfway to level 1 Gravity Magic»

"Well, that's two," Idris remarked, allowing his form to shift back to normal.

"I'd say three more." Emrys rubbed his chin. "They've got more priests and priestesses since last we were here."

Ugh, I feel sick, and I don't think it's the smell... I leaned against the base of a tree and grimaced, crossing my arms. *It was just a small gravity orb! For fuck's sake...*

"Cerys?" Idris questioned. When I shot him a sideways glance, he paused, frowning. "You...are not satisfied? You have used little magic—"

"Maybe too much gravity magic, too quickly." I shook my head, then winced. That made me *much* dizzier. "I haven't made a hole that big before, and that orb was new, too..."

"Perhaps I should have warned you to pace yourself, rather than to exercise caution," Idris stated dryly, closing the distance between us. "This will have to suffice for now."

"What will—" I started to ask. My question was answered before I could finish it. He pulled me into a deep, startlingly passionate kiss. A surge of fiery power rushed through me moments before he pulled away. For whatever reason, our companions looked more surprised than I felt.

"Your Majesty, sharing your power with someone—" Elidyr was the first to voice a complaint, but a motion and a sharp glare from his king silenced him.

"I take no issue with lending her a portion of my energy." Idris settled a dangerous gaze on our companions. "Now, we will dispatch the rest of the echei and deliver them to camp. Come."

Am I missing something significant? I inquired, hurrying after Idris. He rebuffed us before glancing toward me, his expression unreadable.

Sharing power in a world such as ours is dangerous at best. Idris returned his gaze toward the pit I had created and pursed his lips. *It is possible for the recipient to take more than they are offered. Had you been an assassin, turned against us, or similar, you could have killed me in seconds.*

"Seren, create a ramp with your ice," Idris instructed when I failed to think of any follow-up questions, let alone a response. "Elidyr, Silas, slaughter three more. I have seen enough—there is no more reason to play around."

"And what about me?" I tapped him with my closed fan.

"No more gravity magic for the day," he answered, his tone just as sharp as his gaze. "You should be able to use your Shadowdancer skills just fine, but I did not give you enough energy to support the use of gravity."

"Alright," I sighed, nodding. He was right and we both knew it, even if I didn't like it. It was obvious that I needed to determine why gravity magic had drained me so quickly, and how to build up my endurance. This wasn't the place to do either.

The echei barreled up Seren's icy ramp the moment it was completed, and Elidyr and Silas made quick work of their targets. With the massive creatures slain, Idris called a flute from his inventory and brought it to his lips. All around us, the remaining echei collapsed to the ground in a deep slumber.

"So, how are we getting all these back to camp?" I leaned toward Idris, keeping my voice low.

"I will put them in my inventory," Elidyr stated.

"...really?" I squinted at him, unable to ascertain if he was serious.

"Of course not," he snorted, before turning his attention toward camp, bringing his fingers to his mouth, and letting out a shrill whistle.

Some distance away, the air shimmered to reveal a few dozen soldiers and several makeshift sleds. I suppressed an agitated sigh. Again, there had been no real danger accompanying our hunt. Idris could have ordered the soldiers to join us at any time, meaning he had truly meant it when he'd said he wanted to test me and Bruce.

So, did we pass? I glanced sideways at Idris.

With flying colors. Idris put his flute away before sheathing his sword. *When we return to Cejari-ir, we will meet with the Grandmasters of Magic and determine what needs to be done regarding your gravity magic. It may simply be a matter of practice, but I wish to make certain that is* all *it is.*

I was thinking the same. I crossed my arms, grimacing when the direction of the wind shifted, carrying the scent of vacated bowels to me. *Now then, can we get going? Or at least get away from that stench?*

Certainly. Idris nodded, then shifted to give our party orders.

Some of the tension left me once we had moved away from the slain monsters. I sunk into thought as we walked, considering the approach I had taken with our fight. Even though I was meant to be a Shadowdancer, I kept relying on gravity magic instead of my primary three proficiencies. If I wanted to improve, that wasn't at all efficient.

Why not weave it into your style as a Shadowdancer? Idris suggested.

That's what I've been meaning *to do.* I made a sour face at him. *It's easy to fall into a trap of using only that magic, especially in a group. Dropping our enemies into a pit gives the rest of you free rein to massacre anything from safety.*

"Your Majesty!" A soldier rushed toward us the moment we entered camp. "We caught a prisoner whilst you were gone. She is demanding to speak with Lady Moonfire."

"And you did not kill her?" Idris raised a doubtful eyebrow.

"She says she belongs to Ebonwing, Your Majesty." The soldier bowed.

"Ebonwing? Very well," Idris sighed. "Emrys, Elidyr, Cerys,

with me. The rest of you, help butcher the echei."

I followed Idris through the maze of tents, my mind racing. An Ebonwing member, a female one, so far from Darmos? There were only a few people that could be, but I had no idea why any Ebonwing members would be in Rehlr-saffir.

"Cery!" Mirela exclaimed the moment we entered the tent. "Whoa, you're huge. Tall! I mean tall!"

"Right..." I tilted my head, examining her. She didn't appear to be injured, and her armor resembled traveling clothes. "What exactly are you doing here, Mirela?"

"She is truly a member of Ebonwing?" Idris inquired, glancing at me.

"Yep. This is Mirela, my spymaster." I paused, glancing at her. "Or should I say Alice and Ryan's spymaster, now? Speaking of...how is Alice?"

"I really don't get why she keeps asking me about you, and now you're doing it too?!" Mirela huffed, shaking her head. "Whatever. I'm here because Alice wants to meet with you."

"Darmos is a long way to travel—and far too dangerous for my future queen," Idris growled, stepping forward as if to shield me from the shackled woman. I raised an eyebrow at his back and then prodded him in the ribs until he moved out of my field of view.

"Not Darmos, silly!" Mirela looked Idris up and down, then grinned. "Or should I say sexy? I can see why you decided to roll a demon character, Cery. This guy is *way* hotter than I expected. You dating him IRL too, or can I have a go at him?"

"Mirela." I twitched, glaring at her. "If not Darmos, then where?"

"Oh, right. We made camp in the forest outside this crater," Mirela shrugged. "I had my men look for an entrance, but we couldn't find it, so I scaled the wall. Even if you kill me, we brought a timed bind-point with us, so I'll just respawn in our camp."

"You...convinced the humans to let you bring their champion so far from Darmos?" Idris frowned at Mirela. His low, suspicious growl made her perk up like an excited puppy. I rolled my eyes at her and began tapping my foot.

"Well, we had to bring an escort of Ebonwing adventurers along. Adric came too," Mirela replied. "I don't know what Alice wants to talk to Cery about, but she's pretty insistent."

"Well?" I gave Idris a pointed look, and he froze.

"You...wish to meet with her?" Idris paused, then let out a heavy sigh. "Of course you do. I will allow it, but only if you agree to meet away from your camp and allow us to come armed."

"Of course." Mirela blinked at him. "You can choose the place, Alice isn't picky. She told me that she will meet with you wherever and whenever you want, and with any restrictions you want to impose."

What does she even want to talk about? Why is she here? How is she here? I gnawed on one of my fingers. I was meant to be saving her, yet the Issradians had allowed her to venture so far from

Darmos. Something didn't add up.

Idris met my gaze and nodded subtly to indicate he agreed.

"I will scout for a suitable location, and you will come with me." Elidyr hauled the bound woman to her feet. "Your Majesty, I will return shortly to tell you what I have determined."

"Do not take long." Idris nodded to him. "We will meet with them after we have dined."

"See you soon, Cery!" Mirela called.

"You agreed to that too easily." I looked up at Idris.

"We have the advantage here," he pointed out. "Rehlr-saffir may be neutral, but it is still demon territory and humans are not welcome. Even if we do not attack their party, there are plenty of demons and monsters here who would. That woman, Mirela, she is far too weak to survive in this region for long. If the other Ebonwing members are of similar proficiency, we will be free of them soon."

"Which is why you're wondering why they let Alice come all the way here." I frowned, considering it. "Adric would be 'high level' since he's the emperor's guard captain—but that also begs the question of why he's here instead of protecting the emperor."

"And I want answers," Idris stated. He turned to look down at me, a smile slowly spreading across his face. "However, before any such meeting, it would be best if we were both at full strength."

"I'm hungry *and* I'm hungry," I whined, leaning against his side.

"Well, we can't have that, now can we?" he purred.

"Ahem," Emrys coughed, causing Idris to release an agitated sigh. "How about not eating, or 'eating,' in the prison tent? Hmmm? Don't you have your own tent to go to?"

"Increase our fortifications. After, assign soldiers to an escort." Idris gave Emrys a look which caused him to straighten. "Cerys is not setting foot outside of camp, let alone visiting the humans, without a full escort. A mere 'party' will not suffice. Even if the Ebonwing members are trustworthy, I do not trust their gods, or this 'Adric' man."

"Yes, Your Majesty." Emrys bowed, then took his leave.

"Perhaps dinner before dessert?" Idris teased, cupping my face.

"Oh, so you're calling yourself dessert now?" I scoffed.

"No, I am calling *you* dessert," he chuckled, shaking his head. "There is no sense in worrying about our meeting with Ebonwing right now, Cerys. Come, let us bathe before fetching dinner."

"Fine," I sighed, letting him lead me out of the tent. "Though I'm still gonna worry."

"Perhaps it was true when they said something about saving *both* of them from the Issradian Empire..." Idris murmured.

"I doubt they've had enough time to do a faction change quest." I shook my head. "Alice tends to act on a whim. It's entirely possible that she just wants to check in on me and there is no other motive to her visit. She tunnel-visions on things even worse than I do at times. Hell, it may not have even occurred to her that she could abandon the Issradian Empire since she's come all this way."

"We will know for certain soon enough." Idris made a vague motion. "For now, we should discuss your gravity magic while we bathe. We need to determine a way to manage its power drain until we have returned to Cejari-ir."

"Alright," I nodded.

I said that, but I was still consumed with worry. Darmos was a long way from Rehlr-saffir, and it struck me as suspicious that Alice had been permitted to leave the city at all. Even with an escort. Then there was the issue of why she'd wanted to contact me in person to begin with. Sure, we were close friends, but sending a messenger would have been safer.

I hope everything is okay... Well, as okay as it can be.

Chapter Forty-Four
Flies in the Ointment

"Do you really think they'll come?" Alice leaned toward Mirela, her hands clasped over her chest. "That Elidyr guy seemed really worried. *How* many times did he threaten you? Seems like he really cares about Cery and Idris!"

"I lost count!" Mirela snorted, crossing her arms. "Seriously. I had to point out *at least* six times how much lower-level than him I am—and that I can't fight!"

"How's Cery doing?" Ryan interrupted the commiserating women. "If their camp is mostly men, I'm sure she's enjoying herself, *but—*"

"Oh. Looks like she's getting along *real* well with Idris," Mirela smirked. "Got all twitchy when I mentioned wanting a go at him. I'd wager that's why we haven't heard anything out of her IRL for a while. With someone like that around, I know just how I'd be spending my free time too."

"Er...right," Alice muttered, her gaze downcast. Ryan watched her for a moment before shifting to look over at Adric, who was lounging nearby.

"Our other scouts aren't back yet?" he inquired, narrowing his eyes at the half-human man. Adric stiffened, placing a hand on the hilt of his sword as if for comfort.

"Not yet. Do you want me to go find them?" Adric grimaced at the nervousness in his own voice, then coughed to clear it. "The monsters in this region are far too much for them, and some can detect stealthed foes. If they wandered too close..."

"They would've respawned back at the camp already." Mirela shook her head. "Idiots probably just got lost. We've got the most important people with us, at least. I'm surprised the demons said we can keep our weapons, though."

"Well, if we died out here because we were unarmed, they'd be responsible in a sense. If they'd told us 'no weapons,' that is." Ryan shrugged, crossing his arms. He surveyed the clearing they'd gathered in. When he turned to look away from his companions, his eyes flicked to their true space-like state. *Nothing dangerous. Looks like the other kings have reached the entrance to Rehlr-saffir.*

Why are they not going through it?

"Ryan?" Alice nudged him in the back.

"Need to pee." He gave Alice a sheepish grin. "I'll be right back, gonna leave my character logged in."

To the Ebonwing members, it looked like Ryan's body went still, his expression blank and lifeless. After Meical finished bending time around himself, he roughed up his charcoal gray hair and let out an agitated sigh.

The kings *needed* to form an alliance. Without an alliance, there was no way Cerys could overtake the Issradian Empire. Whatever was holding up the kings and keeping them from entering Rehlr-saffir, Meical decided to take care of it himself.

Trivial monsters were the *last* thing he would allow to get in the way of his plans for Cerys, Idris, and demonkind. Defeating the Issradian Empire was merely a facet of what he hoped they could achieve. He sighed. *First things first—get the kings where they need to be.*

Meical dashed through the forest, soon exiting near the cliffs containing the entrance to Rehlr-saffir. He kept himself hidden, bending time and space around him as he strolled casually toward the grouped kings and their escorts.

Dozens of monster corpses littered the ground around the kings. Yet more lived, pressing the kings with their attack. Meical frowned, watching the unusual monster behavior. He saw no other deities nearby, yet the creatures attacking the demons were not known for such aggressive behavior—and certainly not against such an incredibly large company.

Corlyotir, you did not have anything to do with this, did you? Meical reached out to the goddess, irritated.

None of us did, Corlyotir answered, concern tingeing her voice. *I have almost finished with the matter you asked me to look into.*

Focus on that. Meical crossed his arms, watching the demons slay the monsters. A flash of amethyst and silver caught his attention, pulling his gaze over to the crevasse leading into Rehlr-saffir. *Huh. Cerys really looks like one of them now.*

The demoness wore dark leather armor with silver plates running down her shins and forearms. An amethyst cape hung halfway down her back. Several swords floated behind her, soon flying forward. Meical grinned crookedly when the weapons entered the portals created by Bruce. They reappeared soon after, piercing three separate monsters in their eye sockets.

Hah! They're making good use of the magic I gave them. Meical did a little dance before moving closer. *Now then, will you all behave? Am I going to have to slap anyone's wrists?*

"About time you showed up." Alwyn, a demon clad in full plate armor, turned to look at Idris. His attention soon shifted to Cerys, watching her with suspicion as she summoned her swords back to her. "This woman is your champion? A *Shadowdancer?* You made her take on such a difficult profession?"

"He didn't *make* me do anything," Cerys retorted, baring her fangs. "If he had tried to make me do something, I'd have kicked his ass! Well, tried to."

"So, the rumors regarding Lady Moonfire's vulgarity are true." Hywel sheathed his twin daggers and strode forward, rubbing his chin. "Your party appears to have left Rehlr-saffir for a purpose other than aiding us."

"You're one to talk!" Gar roared with laughter, balancing the shaft of his axe against one shoulder.

"Our companions know you, but Cerys and I do not. Identify yourselves." Bruce stepped forward, shielding Cerys from the various demons.

"Heh, fair enough." Hywel smirked, placing a hand on his hip. "I am Hywel Stormscythe, the King of Enth-tor. Neighbors with—"

"Oh, of course, *neighbors*." Eifion rolled his eyes. "With how many skirmishes we have had in the last month alone?"

"Hey, what can I say? You're good practice," Hywel grinned.

"My name is Alwyn Silverscale, my lady." Alwyn bowed his head briefly to Cerys. "I am the King of Siliarenth."

"Folont Pyretusk, King of Hecald-zahn," Folont offered simply.

"Gar Sablehusk—King of Verod-ust!" Gar grinned, examining the Nabyr-zahn party. "Brought Eifion with you, eh? I expected one of you to make a pelt out of him for that mouth of his."

"I'm hurt!" Eifion snorted.

"A pleasure to meet you all…I think." Cerys tilted her head, watching Eifion as he growled at Gar. "Am I going to have to put you on a leash, fluffy?"

"And your business outside of Rehlr-saffir, my lady?" Alwyn asked pointedly. "I doubt you would have stopped to aid us if your goal had been to return to Cejari-ir, and there is plenty of hunting within the safety of the crater."

"We are going to meet the Issradian champion," Cerys stated flatly, stunning the demons into silence. "Their champion and I are close in the world we come from. She likely came here to seek asylum. You've heard by now what the Issradians do to non-human women, especially champions, have you not?"

"Seek asylum?" Folont walked forward, his gaze focused on Cerys. "Even if that is true, you are meeting them with so few guards? No matter how talented, a mere Journeyman, especially a champion, should have a larger escort."

"Are you volunteering?" Cerys crossed her arms, her tone and expression challenging. "I'm not going back inside Rehlr-saffir until we've met with Alice, at minimum. If she, Adric, and the rest of the Ebonwing members truly seek asylum, that would be a boon for us. Without their champion, the empire will fall into disarray."

"And they could provide us with useful information," Silas added, motioning briefly with his kiseru. "We aren't changing Cerys' mind, anyway. She's more stubborn than King Bloodsong is."

"Take our men and make camp in Rehlr-saffir." Folont turned to give his men orders. "I will be accompanying Moonfire and Bloodsong to this meeting of theirs. If these Issradians will be of use, I would know of it."

"Well, are you going to let Pyretusk outdo you all?" Eifion teased the remaining three kings.

Kings Silverscale, Sablehusk, and Stormscythe released agitated sighs before turning to give their men similar orders. Before long, the six demon kings were sizing each other up in silence. Nearby, Emrys, Elidyr, Silas, Bruce, Drysi, Seren, and Cerys watched.

Well, it appears they are getting along for now. Meical rubbed his chin. *Good. It had better stay that way. An incubus, a draekin, a kitsune, an ifrit, a lamia, and a djinn...quite the motley bunch. Cerys will have her hands full with them.*

I suppose I should return to Alice and the others...

Meical time-warped back to where he'd started, feigning the action of returning from being 'away' from his character. As Ryan, he stretched his arms over his head and yawned.

"Welcome back!" Alice smiled at him. "I'm getting nervous. Do you think we should go make sure they're okay?"

"And do what, exactly?" Mirela snorted. "Provide moral support? I didn't bring my pompoms."

"I guess you're right." Alice puffed out her cheeks.

"You are lucky your chattering has yet to draw monsters here." Elidyr dropped out of stealth on a nearby log, his legs crossed. The hand resting in his lap held a slender, serrated dagger. "I recommend you be on your best behavior. Our party is larger than we had expected, and the other kings will be less likely to tolerate this folly."

"Other kings?" Alice gulped.

"Indeed. They insisted on joining us," Elidyr nodded, shifting to look toward the nearby tree line.

"This is all you've got as an escort, Alice?" Cerys questioned the moment she strode into the clearing. She put her hands on her hips and peered at Alice. "None of you are Journeymen yet, either? What, is Adric supposed to save you all?"

"Something along those lines, yes," Adric answered, resigned.

"Whoa, you're not a runt anymore!" Ryan exclaimed, turning his gaze to the demons behind Cerys. "Oh, nevermind. Guess you still are."

"Wha— You're one to talk!" Cerys stomped her foot, her tail flicking upward.

"Another friend of yours?" Idris inquired, shooting Cerys an amused glance before turning his attention to the Ebonwing party, and finally to Adric. "I am sure you are aware that we find this meeting rather...peculiar. At best. How did you convince the empire to permit Lady Alice out of the palace?"

"They claimed that it was alright, so long as she brought a proper escort along." Adric shook his head. "'Proper' meant a certain number of people, several of whom are not here right now.

They have yet to return from their scouting duties."

"Humph. I forgot how tiny humans are." Gar shoved a tree branch out of his way and peered at the Ebonwing players. Despite his lower half being that of a serpent, he towered over the humans and elves alike.

"Wow, Cery, you look awesome!" Alice exclaimed, darting forward. However, she skidded to a stop when Bruce stepped in front of Cerys, his shield up. "Wait... Aren't you... Bruce? What are you doing here?"

"Until we know what you want, I will not let anyone close to Cerys." Bruce narrowed his eyes at the elven woman. "Not even you, Miss Alice."

Cerys patted Bruce on the arm, causing him to step aside and take up his post slightly behind her again.

I knew the loyal AI dog would come in handy. Ryan tilted his head, examining the shield-toting demon. He broke into a cheerful smile, turning to Alice. "Well, that settles that, then. Introductions, then tell them your business here?"

"Right..." Alice sighed, her shoulders slumping, before dipping into a curtsy. "My name is Alice L'thilyia. I was chosen as the Issradian's champion because the human gods wanted Cerys to betray Nabyr-zahn."

"L'th...what?" Cerys tilted her head.

"I dunno. I was tired and it sounded elven enough," Alice shrugged.

"Right." Cerys pressed her fingers to her temples. "Because 'Alice' is *so* elven...'

"My companions are Adric Alfhard, the emperor's guard captain," Alice continued cheerfully, "and a contingent of Ebonwing members. The pink-haired one is Ryan, my co-leader within Ebonwing. You've already met Mirela."

"And your business?" Gar adjusted his grip on his greataxe in a threatening manner.

"We seek asylum!" Alice yelped, ducking behind Ryan. Of course, he was a human and she was an elf—he didn't make a good hiding place. "Adric, Ebonwing, and I want to join Nabyr-zahn. We have lots of information we can give you, and—"

"Like what?" Idris interjected, his gaze doubtful.

"Did you know the emperor is missing?" Adric questioned, causing the demons to grow still. "My younger half-brother is acting as emperor now. He is but a child and wields no power in the empire. In fact, he had ordered Eadgar to cease collecting taxes and to free the empire's slaves."

"He is telling the truth, Your Majesty." Elidyr turned to nod at Idris.

"Indeed he is..." Silas echoed, frowning.

"A champion seeking asylum in enemy lands... Now I've seen everything." Hywel placed his hands on his hips and examined Alice with a doubtful expression.

"Don't you have to do a quest if you want to change factions?"

Cerys coughed into her hand and gave Alice a pointed look.

"Oh—no, we're good on that front." Alice shook her head.

"A quest? More Otherworlder nonsense?" Alwyn questioned.

"Something like that." Cerys' cold glare and agitated tone silenced the man.

"Well, I am not opposed to taking in Ebonwing, Alice, and Adric," Idris stated, rubbing his chin. "However, you will need to make yourselves useful beyond offering information."

"Of course!" Alice exclaimed. "We—"

"Meical!" Corlyotir screamed, staggering from a portal nearby. Ryan's attention snapped to her. He inhaled sharply when he saw a bloody gouge through one of the goddess' shoulders. Caradoc appeared beside the women and caught her when she nearly toppled to the ground. "The human gods gave them the Eye of Epere, the Mirror of Yerm, and the Ewer of Yagea! *They brought them here! Stop them!*"

'The Eye—Damn it all!' Ryan clenched his fists.

"Meical? Who is she..." Alice followed Corlyotir's gaze and blinked at the scowling Ryan. "Ryan? What's going on?"

The prickling sensation of magic made Meical whirl around, his human disguise disappearing. A ripple was all he could make out, but Corlyotir was right.

A leather-clad human faded out of stealth and into the visible spectrum, one arm cocked back with a dagger held in his hand. In the next instant, the blade pierced through Cerys' stomach.

Cursing, Meical manipulated the gravity around Cerys, altering the blade's path.

"You...idiots..." Cerys gasped, her eyes wide as she stared at the Ebonwing member who had stabbed her. The demoness' knees buckled when the blade withdrew from her abdomen. "Id...ris..."

Several more Ebonwing members dropped out of stealth around her, their blades ready but unneeded. Confusion painted their faces as they looked down at the unconscious demoness and the blood pooling beneath her.

"Cerys? *Cerys? FUCKING HUMAN FILTH!*" Idris screamed with rage, power exploding outward from him as his full demonic form took over.

"Wait, she's supposed to have HP..." one of the Ebonwing members muttered, taking a step back. "Why'd she just drop—"

The human didn't get to finish her sentence before Idris' clawed hand tore through her, sending bits of blood, organ, and fragments of bone spraying against his companions.

«The *Eye of Epere* has broken»

«The *Mirror of Yerm* has broken»

«The *Ewer of Yagea* has broken»

"The Eye, Mirror, and Ewer..." Alwyn stared in shock. "How desperate are the human gods, that they would dedicate *three* relics to murdering one woman?"

"You...you fucking cretins!" Meical roared, grabbing one of the remaining Ebonwing assassins by the head. "What the fuck do you think you're doing? You were told to leave all the artifacts *in Darmos* and *alone!*"

The last few Ebonwing members who had appeared around Cerys died to the enraged King of Nabyr-zahn. Their corpses dropped to the ground in large chunks around the fuming demon, smoking.

"B-b-but we had a quest to kill—" The Ebonwing member clawed at the hand gripping his skull. "How could we pass up full legendary gear for the whole guild?!"

"C-Cery? S-she's not..." Alice whimpered, her eyes glistening with tears. "I told you all to abandon that quest! Cerys is my best friend! How could you?!"

Meical crushed the Ebonwing assassin's head with a snarl, his mind racing. He had kept the blade from puncturing any important organs, but Cerys would need immediate medical attention—and there weren't any healers skilled enough for that among either party. If Cerys was still going to end the damned game the gods were playing, she had to live.

Idris sprung toward Adric, Alice, and her escort next, consumed with bestial fury. Emrys and Elidyr chased after their king, managing to grab him and forcibly drag him away from the Ebonwing group—but not without sustaining injuries from their king themselves. He tore at them in his eagerness to kill the humans, but his aides refused to release him.

"Bruce, a portal to Cejari-ir. Now. I will aid you," Meical

instructed the bewildered AI. "You two, get him out of here!"

"I...yes. Of course." Bruce glanced briefly down at Cerys, gritting his teeth, before collecting the unconscious woman and constructing a portal.

"If Cerys dies," Idris snarled as his aides dragged him in the direction of the portal, "I will kill each and every remaining Ebonwing member before your eyes in this world *and* in yours. Jeriskyr and Earth will be burned to the ground!"

"Seren, Silas, the two of you will have to march your men back to Nabyr-zahn." Meical gave them a firm glare for good measure when they opened their mouths to protest, then turned his attention to Corlyotir and Caradoc. "Who wounded you?"

"The human gods attempted to capture me during my investigation..." Corlyotir glanced away, her expression pained. "Alas... I was too late. It seems that I cannot get even this right."

"W-why can't I log out?" Mirela asked, her voice choked. Slowly, her gaze drifted over to Cerys' limp body in Bruce's arms, her eyes widening in horror. In the next moment, she doubled over, retching.

"Cery. Cery. Cery!" Alice dropped to her knees, sobbing.

Meical reached out with his own power to stabilize the portal Bruce had made, then gently shoved Emrys, Elidyr, and their distraught king through it with gravity magic. Once Bruce and Cerys disappeared through the portal, it closed.

Meical turned to look at the stunned demon kings, and then

to Cerys' party.

"*This* is how far the human gods are willing to go," Meical stated, narrowing his eyes. "Three of their most precious artifacts, dedicated to slaying one champion."

"Their position must be weakening…" Hywel murmured, his gaze drifting to the bloodstained grass. "However, if the champion dies—"

"The blade missed her organs." Meical cut him off. "It is a matter of allowing the wound to heal, checking for poison—and thwarting further assassination attempts."

"I recommend resuming your soirée in Cejari-ir." Caradoc strode forward after resting Corlyotir on a log. "King Bloodsong will not stray far from Lady Moonfire's side. Should you still wish to discuss an alliance, you had best do so there."

"What is there to discuss?" Eifion piped up, a deadly gleam in his eyes. "The human gods entrusted powerful artifacts to Ebonwing and they still failed to kill the champion."

"What should we do about *them*?" Folont reached for the hilt of his sword, his tone murderous.

"Cerys would *want* Alice to be safe," Seren spoke up, gritting his teeth.

"And 'safe' as the last thing she would be if she came to Cejari-ir after her guild's actions." Adric sighed heavily, glancing toward the shocked, sobbing girl. He turned to bow deeply to the gods. "I will see to it that they all return to Darmos, my lords, my lady.

"…Lord Meical?"

"We are not walking," Meical snapped. He opened a large portal, reversed gravity around the Ebonwing members, and chucked them into it. Adric followed soon after, taking the hint. "Caradoc, take Corlyotir back and see to her wounds. I will be along when I can."

Meical left the confused and distraught demons behind, stepping through the portal. When he appeared in Darmos, he didn't even bother with his Ryan disguise and let out a heavy sigh, pressing his fingers to his temples. The damned Ebonwing members had nearly ruined all his carefully laid plans—and still could. If Cerys didn't recover, or if the damage was too grave…

Fuck. Her body on Earth. Meical ground his teeth. That would have to be investigated *immediately*. Otherwise, her body there would bleed out. He also wanted to check on Corlyotir and make certain her wound wasn't fatal.

"What…what…" One of the Ebonwing assassins rocked back and forth on his backside, his eyes wide in shock. "We all respawned, but… *Where is the logout command?!*"

"Do you *want* to turn Idris into a villain?!" Meical snapped, his anger rising again. "Because *that* is how you get a villain! What the fuck possessed you to attack a *demon king's* beloved?!"

"Meical, enough!" Caradoc and Corlyotir appeared beside Meical, grabbing each of his arms when he went to lunge toward the assassins. "We know this is how the human gods play their games! Manipulation, lies, deceit! It is not Ebonwing's fault."

"If I had been faster…" Corlyotir started, but cut herself off with a grimace and released Meical, gripping her wounded shoulder.

"My lord, I will handle matters here." Adric gave Meical a pointed look. "I will imprison the Ebonwing members in their guild hall and attempt to console Alice. You intend to look into matters before you return, do you not?"

"Wait! He owes me an explanation!" Alice demanded, looking up from her spot on the floor with watery eyes. "J-just who…"

"Adric can tell you all you want to know. I must go check on Cerys' body on Earth," Meical stated flatly, before disappearing through another portal, this one to the gods' domain.

Of all the artifacts, they had to go with the ones gods can't counteract? They are more desperate than I anticipated. Meical gritted his teeth, waiting for Corlyotir and Caradoc to appear. He watched the goddess plop heavily into a chair. "Your wound—"

"Check Cerys first. She is mortal, I am not." Corlyotir shook her head, wincing. "It hurts, but it is not lethal. Our champion is more important."

"I will send someone to Cejari-ir," Caradoc added. "Someone will have to talk Idris and his men down."

"Then we all have our tasks." Meical nodded, casting one last glance toward Corlyotir before opening a portal to Earth. *Good luck calming Idris down. If he didn't know how intimately he was connected to Cerys, he sure will now.*

One does not simply assassinate a demon king's soulmate.

Chapter Forty-Five
Soulbound

"Once Cerys' condition has stabilized, relocate her to my suite. Until then, I expect the infirmary to remain under heavy guard," I ordered, watching the healers and their aides cower. Next, I turned my attention to Emrys and Elidyr. "Collect the Ebonwing members we have been housing and throw them into the dungeons. If Cerys dies, so will they. They could have been planted in case this plan failed."

"Idris—" Emrys gripped me by the shoulder, steadying me when I staggered. "You're wounded?"

"In a manner of speaking." I shut my eyes in pain, forcing my breath to become steady.

"Your Majesty, please allow the healers to see to your wound." Elidyr frowned at me. "Cerys is safe, for now, and our men will capture the Ebonwing men within Cejari-ir with little issue. You needn't press yourself further."

I hesitated before pulling off my traveling coat and then my shirt. When the healers saw my back, they gasped. Concerned, Emrys and Elidyr moved to see what had stunned them. I glanced toward Cerys' unconscious form nearby, catching brief glimpses of her as yet more healers milled around her.

I had an inkling as to what the healers behind me had found.

"A Soulburn, in the shape of a butterfly..." Emrys exclaimed. "Idris, is she truly your—"

"Do not say it," I threatened, baring my fangs. Rage rose in my chest, threatening to spill over. Dark scales slowly spread from my fingertips and up my forearms while I wrestled with myself. *For my emotions to be confirmed by a threat to her life...*

"She will be fine." The man Corlyotir had called 'Meical' appeared in front of us, unfazed by the glare I settled on him. "I used gravity magic to alter the path of the blade that pierced her. None of her organs were damaged, but I believe the blade may have been poisoned. I have brought it for your subjects to inspect."

Meical placed the blood-soaked dagger flat on a nearby table. The sight of it made my stomach drop and my throat clench. If the man was telling the truth, then he had saved Cerys' life. He had proved his access to gravity and space magic, and Bruce appeared to trust the man—or at least know him.

I remained to be convinced.

"And just who the fuck are you?" Emrys snarled, hefting a greathammer.

"Meical—a rogue god, and the reason Cerys came to your world in the first place," Meical answered pointedly. He made a flicking motion toward Emrys' weapon, crumpling it into a useless ball of metal. "I will spare you the details. All you need to know is that I am a 'rogue' because I disagree with the game the other gods play, and I wish to see it ended.

"It is my belief that Cerys can achieve this."

"Take me to her," I demanded.

"What?" Meical sighed in exasperation.

"If you are the reason she is here, then you are capable of traveling to Earth." I yanked my shirt back on. "Her wellbeing is linked between worlds, is it not? At the very least, her mind must have retreated to Earth. Nothing our healers do will wake her."

"...she will not wake?" Meical frowned, glancing toward the nearby demoness.

"I believe I told you to take me to Earth," I snapped.

"Children." Meical sighed heavily, pressing his fingers to his temples. "Listen—"

"If she lives, you will use her to end the gods' game. If she dies, I will destroy this accursed world. You win either way." I stalked toward the abnormally short demon, losing control over my form along with my rage. "What do you lose by proving to me that her Earth body is safe?"

"Tch, I knew picking a stubborn one would come back to bite me," Meical muttered, crossing his arms. His bladed tail swished behind him while he thought. "Well, Caradoc favors you because of your caution. I suppose I can grant your request, if only to save myself from getting an earful from Corlyotir later."

Meical's tail slashed the air behind him, creating a rip-like portal. He gave me a pointed, impatient look when I hesitated.

"See to your orders." I glanced at Emrys and Elidyr, then finally in Cerys' direction. *I will see you again soon…*

I stepped through the portal and into Cerys' dark suite on Earth. Looking down at myself, I grimaced. This time, I was not in a temporary human body. My form was fully demonic. I shut my eyes and concentrated briefly, willing my appearance to return to normal. Unlike my first visit, there was no disembodied voice to capture, threaten, or greet me.

"She is being kept in her own suite?" I frowned at Meical when he appeared nearby.

"Take a look in her room." Meical jerked his head in the direction of her door.

Clenching my teeth, I did my best to steel myself against what I expected to be a horrifying sight. A deep frown overtook me the moment I opened her door. Within Cerys' bedroom, the bed was gone. The rest of her furniture had been moved to the corners.

In the center of the room, Cerys' nude form floated within a liquid-filled crystal. The magical power radiating from it was overpowering. Where her body touched the walls of her cage, the crystal had begun to turn the same shade of purple that tinged her spellcraft. A faint creaking sound made it seem as if the strange thing was *growing*.

"See? No wounds." Meical motioned toward Cerys' stomach. "The gods of Earth are a cautious bunch; everyone who has been sent to Jeriskyr is preserved in stasis like this. I checked. They don't want to 'risk' having to find and trade replacements."

"*Replacements?*" I snapped. "You speak of people as if they are things!"

"One of the many reasons I take issue with the gods' 'game.'" Meical shot me a look that indicated he felt as if he were speaking with a stupid child. "Did Cerys show you any TCGs while you were here? Trading card games. "

"No." I crossed my arms, my gaze flicking toward the crystal holding Cerys.

"Here," Meical paused to summon a deck of cards in one hand, using his other to pull a card off the top.

My stomach twisted when I saw the illustration on the card. Above it read: 'Cerys Moonfire, First Consort of Idris Bloodsong.' The painting beneath was clearly the woman in question, though I did not understand the remaining details on the card beyond

'Shadowdancer' and the numbers indicating her current proficiencies.

"And these," Meical added, pulling out three more cards. These belonged to the three Ebonwing members who had come to Cejari-ir. "Humans in this world have a game where they 'battle' with cards, and trade them for cards they want or are otherwise missing.

"That is how most of the gods see mortals. As resources, or game pieces to be traded. Jeriskyr's gods traded Gwythyr to Earth, and when it came time for them to collect, I convinced Corlyotir to choose Cerys as Nabyr-zahn's champion."

"Why?" I demanded, narrowing my eyes. "If you had your choice of anyone in this world, why her?"

"I have numerous reasons. Originally, I didn't think I would involve anyone from this world in Jeriskyr's affairs," Meical shrugged. "When I came here, I hated humans. Cerys, Alice, and their guild showed me that even humans have their merits. Furthermore, do you think Cerys belongs on Earth?"

"You know I cannot answer that without bias." I clenched a fist.

"The answer is that she's not suited to *being* human," Meical laughed. "I may be a rogue, but I'm still a god. Finding out who she was Soulbound to was a trivial matter. That she was Soulbound to the demonic gods' *favorite* king? Well, that was perfect!"

"You are just as manipulative as they are," I spat. Meical

instantly stopped laughing, his demeanor shifting to an oppressively dangerous aura.

"Says the one who ruined Alice's attempt to gain asylum, threatened to inflict psychological torture on her, and vowed to destroy two worlds should Cerys die." Meical narrowed his eyes at me. "I'll let Cerys take care of punishing you for the first offense. Rescuing Alice and Adric now will be difficult at best."

"You expect me to trust they had nothing to do with this assassination attempt?" I snapped.

"They did not. Ebonwing's members explored a dungeon several weeks ago," Meical began, shaking his head. "When they returned, it was with dozens of artifacts. I found it suspicious and ordered Corlyotir to investigate. Alice and I both ordered Ebonwing to leave the artifacts at our guild hall in Darmos, and for everyone to abandon the quest to assassinate Cerys.

"Alas, when a few hundred people all think it's a mere game…"

"Dozens of artifacts from one dungeon?" I echoed in disbelief.

"The human gods are desperate for a way to end her." Meical glanced toward the crystal at the center of the room. "You need to do some soul searching before she wakes up, *boy*. If you attempt to keep her from fighting, she will be too weak to protect herself—let alone overthrow the Issradian Empire, deal with the gods…"

Let her keep fighting? My heart ached at the thought. "If she is not here, and she will not wake up in the infirmary—where has her mind gone?"

"I will have to look into that," Meical sighed. "Being attacked by her own guildmates must have shocked her, but her soul isn't here. I checked. It is still tethered to her body here and in Cejari-ir. I will follow the trail. After returning you to your rightful place, anyway."

Meical released a burst of magic from his palm, shoving me back with just enough force to send me through another portal. My back hit a wall the moment I came out the other side.

"Your Majesty!" a healer exclaimed, rushing over to me. "You are unhurt? That strange man…"

"I am as well as I can be," I interrupted the man. "How is Cerys?"

"Meical spoke the truth—the blade missed her organs," the healer reported. "We have slowed the bleeding and are monitoring her for poisons or other toxins. It will be some time before our alchemists finish inspecting the blade she was attacked with.

"Caradoc and Gavan brought us herbs from other regions to use as medicine, but said they will not be able to help further than that."

Of course. The human gods give their pawns dozens *of artifacts, yet ours can only give us herbs.* I clenched my jaw. "See to it that the infirmary is warded against intruders, in addition to the increased guard."

"Your Majesty, you should let us treat your Soulburn!" The healer blocked me when I turned to leave. "It would not do for it to sap your strength fully!"

"You are right," I relented, my shoulders slumping. "Make haste. I am not finished giving out tasks."

I sat in utter silence while the healers worked to stem the leak of power from the Soulburn. I could barely feel it anymore, or anything else, for that matter. My awareness of my surroundings and even my own body were vague at best. It was as if I moved by muscle memory, nothing else.

The image of Cerys collapsing in a pool of her own blood flashed through my mind. In that moment, I had heard her attempt to call my name. Pain had seared through my back, likely the Soulburn, before I had lost myself to rage. After all my efforts to get to know her, to make her comfortable in her new world and get her to trust me, there was a very real chance that I would lose her before being afforded the opportunity to express myself to her.

Soulbound, love...who would have thought? I wondered if perhaps I was the only one who did not already know. Or if I simply had not wanted to accept the possibility.

Alas, the burn on my back was undeniable proof.

Soulburns only appeared under a select set of conditions, all of which were linked to one's soulmate—or Soulbound, as many in Jeriskyr called them. I did not know what to do with the information. Never had I thought that I would find mine, or that she would be a human from another world.

Or that her life would hang in the balance so soon.

"Your Majesty, we are done." A healer offered me a new shirt. "We will keep you appraised of Lady Moonfire's condition and relocate her, as per your orders, as soon as we are able."

I nodded to them in silence and left the infirmary in a daze, pulling my new shirt on as I went. Cejari-ir would require further fortifications, wards, weapons, and general security. With the coming flood of Otherworlders, there would be even more potential threats to Cerys' safety. It would be easier for our foes to slip into the city, and perhaps even the palace.

We would need strong wards, powerful enough to lock out anyone we did not want on palace grounds.

"The Ebonwing members have been taken care of, Your Majesty." Emrys strode toward me briskly, his mouth curving into a frown when he spotted me. "I recommend you return to your rooms for now."

"I will do no such thing. There is much work to do, and I will be sleeping in the infirmary until Cerys can be moved." I heard the hollowness in my voice, but it did not matter. Work. "Call the Grandmasters to the palace immediately. We will be increasing the security around the palace, and I will need their assistance in constructing the necessary wards."

"Very well." Emrys sighed heavily before glancing somewhere behind me. "Elidyr, keep an eye on him."

"Of course," Elidyr snorted.

"Did you question the Ebonwing dogs?" I shot Elidyr a

sideways glance.

"They were genuinely unaware of the assassination attempt and broke down when I informed them of what happened." Elidyr's expression twisted briefly with pain before resuming its usual cool composure. "I am not confident that someone will not attempt to turn them against us, but keeping them locked in the foul dungeons will not help prevent such a thing. In fact, it could make it easier."

"...make them comfortable, but do not free them." I crossed my arms over my chest, considering it. "Cerys will be angry enough when she wakes and discovers I had them put in the dungeons. Let's not give her more reason to be furious."

"Very well." Elidyr pursed his lips. "And the healers' reports?"

"They confirmed Meical's claims." I shook my head. *Dare I let myself hope?*

"After your duties, might you tend to Bruce?" Elidyr asked, his tone one of discomfort. "He is...struggling."

"Where is he now?" I questioned. The AI—of course. It had not occurred to me that the being might not be capable of processing, or might not know how to process, what had happened to his owner.

"Breaking all of the training dummies in the training yard, Your Majesty." Elidyr adjusted his glasses, grimacing.

Cerys... I took a steadying breath. The desire to protect her from further attacks was all that kept me going, from locking myself in my suite for the foreseeable future, or from beginning my campaign to raze Jeriskyr. *Perhaps I should destroy everyone on this rock aside from us? With no one else left, there would be no threats to her...*

I curled one hand into a fist. No, that was not the solution, no matter how tempting. Not yet, at least. She would not want me to do such a thing. But oh, how the notion made me shiver with anticipation. I could build her a palace of bones, a moat of blood...there were so many glorious possibilities.

Patience, I told myself. *Do not leap to such conclusions. Not yet.*

Chapter Forty-Six
Soulsnatched

I was floating. Slowly, I opened my eyes, only to find myself surrounded by darkness. Wherever I was, it was pleasantly cool. There was no pain. The realization made me stop for a moment, my heart sinking. After a wound like *that*, I knew damn well I should be in agony.

Okay, I can move. I'm breathing. I seem capable of feeling, I rattled off things to myself as I tried each. *Bit hungry, kinda thirsty. So, I'm still alive. I don't recognize any of these scents, though, and this darkness isn't simply nighttime.*

Clenching my fist, I attempted to concentrate my shadow

magic around it. Nothing.

"Oh goody, you're awake!" a feminine voice giggled. "Good, good! This is fantastic. Grabbing your soul while it was all busy floating around was such a pain, you know."

"...my soul?" I grimaced. "Who are you, and where the fuck am I?"

"This is my domain! Isn't it grand?" She laughed. "Maelona is the name, and I am here to help you in your war game!"

"Domain. One of the gods, then?" I sighed. "Where are Idris and the others? Do they know you've taken me here?"

"They haven't a clue! You needn't be so blue, because Maelona is here for you!" Maelona declared. "Your soul wanted to head back to Earth, but for now you must give that place a wide berth!"

"And why can't I see anything?" I sighed heavily. Attempting to kick the rhyming deity's ass in their own domain seemed like a bad idea. Furthermore, how was I to *not* worry? I had seen Idris lose control before I'd passed out. I was worried about him, and about my friends on both sides. *Mostly him...*

"Why, I am here to teach you telepathy!" Maelona declared. "Your mind will not return to your body for some time yet, so I am here to make certain you have something to ward off fret!"

"I think you reached a little too far with that one," I grumbled.

"If your mind is not your own, how do you expect to overthrow the Issradian throne?" Maelona scoffed. "Humans employ tricks and deceit. You cannot protect yourself merely with being quick on your feet. Hone your mind while you are confined, that you may fly blind."

"So, what, you're supposed to teach me to better use telepathy and the like?" I prompted her. "Why can't you do that in Nabyr-zahn? Why here?"

"Your mind fled your body from the shock of the attack," Maelona answered in a more serious tone. "It is unlikely you can handle the pain, so I brought you here to study the arcane. Once your body has further healed, I will return you to the playing field."

"And the darkness?" I questioned again.

"A matter of time and patience," Maelona laughed. "The more your mental capabilities grow, the more of my domain you can perceive. Alas, without casting off your humanity, this is something you will never achieve."

'Which definition of humanity are we talking about here?' I wondered, falling silent while I considered it. "It's an undeniable fact that I need to learn to use telepathy properly and learn how to shield my own mind. No matter how reliable Idris is, I don't want to have to lean on him in that way. Being protected like some fragile flower pisses me off."

"Excellent!" Maelona cheered. "Then we shall begin. Here, you will not grow tired and continue until the desired effect is acquired."

If I have to put up with all this rhyming... I let out a small sigh. "You promise to return me to my body in Nabyr-zahn after we're finished?"

"I want to see the Issradian Empire overthrown just as much as any other demon does," Maelona scoffed. "Corlyotir, Caradoc, and Gavan—you will meet him soon enough, I hope you like flowers—will see to it that your comrades are taken care of."

In the end, I decided to relent. There wasn't much else I could do in that situation and training my telepathy abilities was something I desperately needed to do. Learning from a deity sounded like an efficient way to go about it, though I wasn't at all happy about being 'pulled' into their domain in such a way. Especially not if Idris and the others hadn't been told.

"I assure you that bringing you here was far better than the alternative," Maelona stated. "Had your soul gone to limbo, the chances of anyone other than a god saving you would have been zero. We aren't meant to intervene, even if you are meant to become queen.

"Had your soul gone there, it wouldn't matter how well your body might fare."

"In other words, it would have left my body in a coma and my soul would've been trapped for eternity?" I rolled my eyes at the darkness. "We have tales of 'limbo' on Earth too. I get the idea."

"You understand—good. We can get on with it, then." Maelona's voice sounded closer now, but I couldn't feel her presence beyond that. "I will start by reading you the beginner books on the subject. Are you comfortable?"

"I'm fine," I stated.

"Excellent!" Maelona sat somewhere nearby, judging by the creak of leather. I heard the pages of a book rustle, and soon the deity began reading.

I just hoped I wouldn't be stuck in Maelona's domain for too long. Even if the deity had been 'normal,' it wouldn't have helped. I was already missing Idris, and I worried how he was handling what had happened to me.

Idris... I'll be back soon. Don't do anything crazy.

END OF DECK OF SOULS BOOK ONE, FATESEAL

Also: Please take a moment to leave a review!

Reviews are the lifeblood of any indie author and can make or break the success of a book. It doesn't need to be long, it could be a few words saying what you liked or five things you think could have been done better. Even a sentence or two would mean the world to me and would help me continue to write books in the future.

CONTINUE READING FOR CHARACTER PROFILES, HOW TO CONNECT WITH THE AUTHOR, UPCOMING RELEASES, AND MORE!

Cerys Moonfire

AGE: Mid-late 20's

GENDER: Female

RACE: Human (Earth) | Succubus (Jeriskyr)

PLACE OF ORIGIN: Earth

CLASS: Shadowdancer

AFFINITY: Darkness

SKILLS: Chrastr-gok, Shadow Magic, Spellsword, Gravity Magic

GOALS: Rescue the members of Ebonwing from the Issradian Empire and human gods' grasp.

PERSONALITY: Headstrong, stubborn, blunt, sassy, with moments of sultriness. Cerys is accustomed to holding herself back due to many humans on Earth thinking her behavior is inappropriate for a 'lady.'

Idris Bloodsong

AGE: Unknown, appears late 20s or lower 30s

GENDER: Male

RACE: Incubus

PLACE OF ORIGIN: Jeriskyr

CLASS: Dirgeweaver

AFFINITY: Darkness, Fire

SKILLS: Spellsinger, Spellsword, Musician

GOALS: Bring his kingdom, Nabyr-zahn, to a resounding victory against the Issradian Empire and rescue the slaves stolen from so many races. Make Cerys his queen.

PERSONALITY: Although Idris operates by a code of honor and is protective of his people, he is a brutal warrior. He is confident, toeing the line of arrogance. Idris believes demons are the rightful rulers of Jeriskyr.

About the Author

Bonnie L. Price was born in 1990 and has lived in four different states. At the age of twelve, while living in rural Upstate New York, she turned to writing as a way to entertain herself. Without internet or TV, there was little else to do during the long, cold winters.

What started as a way to amuse herself soon became a passion, and she's been writing ever since.

Want to connect with Bonnie?

FAN GROUP: FACEBOOK.COM/GROUPS/BLP.DEMONDEN

DISCORD: HTTPS://DISCORD.GG/GRUGC2R

AUTHOR PAGE: FACEBOOK.COM/BONNIELPRICEOFFICIAL

SERIES PAGE: FACEBOOK.COM/DECKOFSOULS

TWITTER: HTTPS://TWITTER.COM/BONNIE_L_PRICE

Other Works

Of Astral and Umbral

    #1 Beneath the Mists, available on Amazon.

    #2 Courting Balance, January 2019.

    #3 Coming later in 2019.

    #4 & 5: Pending editing and cover art.

    #6 In the process of writing, as of December 2018.

Deck of Souls

    #1 *Fateseal* Audiobook, 2019

    #2 Coming in 2019

Illustration

In love with the cover illustration? Want to see more from the artist? Check out the links below for how to follow her!

Want more female MCs?

Dawn Chapman
amazon.com/Dawn-Chapman/e/B014A0RUBC

KT Hanna
amazon.com/K.T.-Hanna/e/B00ZBPYU78/

Anthea Sharp
amazon.com/Anthea-Sharp/e/B006HQ2IFQ

Blaise Corvin
(*Nora Hazard* Series)
amazon.com/Blaise-Corvin/e/B01LYK8VG5

GameLit Society

If you're interested in more books like this one, then please do swing by the GameLit Society! It is a group on Facebook for everyone who loves the GameLit and LitRPG genres. There are plenty of awesome authors in the group that could use some love.

https://www.facebook.com/groups/LitRPGsociety/about/

LitRPG

To learn more about LitRPG, talk to authors including myself, and just have an awesome time, please join the LitRPG Group.

https://www.facebook.com/groups/LitRPGGroup/about/

www.ingramcontent.com/pod-product-compliance
Lightning Source LLC
Chambersburg PA
CBHW022142130726
47905CB00004BA/939